RIPPLES IN
OPPERMAN'S POND

RIPPLES IN
OPPERMAN'S POND

Doug Zipes

iUniverse, Inc.
Bloomington

RIPPLES IN OPPERMAN'S POND

iUniverse books may be ordered through booksellers or by contacting:

iUniverse
1663 Liberty Drive
Bloomington, IN 47403
www.iuniverse.com
1-800-Authors (1-800-288-4677)

Because of the dynamic nature of the Internet, any web addresses or links contained in this book may have changed since publication and may no longer be valid. The views expressed in this work are solely those of the author and do not necessarily reflect the views of the publisher, and the publisher hereby disclaims any responsibility for them.

Any people depicted in stock imagery provided by Thinkstock are models, and such images are being used for illustrative purposes only.

Certain stock imagery © Thinkstock.

ISBN: 978-1-4759-7535-2 (sc)
ISBN: 978-1-4759-7536-9 (hc)
ISBN: 978-1-4759-7537-6 (e)

Library of Congress Control Number: 2013902858

Printed in the United States of America

iUniverse rev. date: 04/29/2013

Also by Doug Zipes

Nonfiction
Into Africa
Taking Ban on Ephedra

Fiction
Stolen Hearts (with Joan Zipes)
The Black Widows (a novel)

Medical Textbooks
(Coedited/Coauthored)
Comprehensive Cardiac Care (seven editions)
The Slow Inward Current and Cardiac Arrhythmias
Cardiac Electrophysiology and Arrhythmias
Nonpharmacologic Therapy of Tachyarrhythmias
Cardiac Electrophysiology: From Cell to Bedside (six editions)
Treatment of Heart Diseases
Catheter Ablation of Cardiac Arrhythmias
Antiarrhythmic Therapy: A Pathophysiologic Approach
Arrhythmias and Sudden Death in Athletes
Heart Disease: A Textbook of Cardiovascular Medicine (five editions)
Electrophysiology of the Thoracic Veins
Sudden Death: A Handbook for Clinical Practice
Clinical Arrhythmology and Electrophysiology
Electrocardiography of Arrhythmias

Medical Articles
(Over 800 authored/coauthored)

RIPPLES IN
OPPERMAN'S POND

Doug Zipes

For my roommate and soul mate of over fifty years, my wife Joan, whose insight, not just into this book but into my life in general, has provided meaning and the foundation for happiness and success. Also, thanks to Michael R. Rosen, Patrick Perry, Peter Jacobus, Luisella Schwartz, Marilynn Wallace, and my children, Debra, Jeffrey, and David, for reading and critiquing an early draft. Finally, to Clair Lamb and Claire Matze, my gratitude for hugely insightful editorial comments.

I may be a twin, but I'm one of a kind.
—Author Unknown

PROLOGUE

Celtics basketball fans packed the Boston Garden, screaming and stomping for their home team. They thrashed the stale air with psychedelic posters: a big D alongside a white picket fence for *D-Fense!* And *Go Celtics!* The scoreboard shot off explosive candles, ending with *We Love Our Celtics!*

Boston led the Indiana Pacers by two points with three and a half seconds left in the season's final game. The Pacers needed the win to make the play-offs. After they grabbed a rebound, Dick Caruthers, the Pacers' coach, called a time-out.

"Listen, guys," Caruthers shouted over the pandemonium to the circling team, black giants dwarfing the white guy in the center. "Boston expects an inbound pass to Randy. But that won't work 'cause he'll be double- maybe triple-teamed, a setup for a steal. Instead, Randy, you set the pick for Lamont, who'll shake free in the far corner for the pass."

The coach shrugged off groans and grimaces.

"Yeah, I know it's a long pass. And risky. But Boston'll be looking for the inbound to the shooting guard, not a power forward deep on the other side of the court."

The grating blast of the buzzer signaled the sixty-second time-out was half-over. The coach quickened his tempo.

"Lamont," he said, nodding at the big black forward, "stay on the far side of the paint. The inbound goes to you, and you drive to the key. The Celtics'll think you're taking it inside for a slam dunk and we're settling for a tie to win in overtime. You'll pull at least one, maybe both guys off Randy after the pick. Instead of taking the shot, pass to him. Randy hits the three-pointer for the win. Clear?"

Lamont shook his head. "Too risky. Inbound to Randy, and him alley-oop to me. I guarantee that slam." One ham-sized fist smashed into the other open palm, sealing his promise.

The coach waved off the comment with his clipboard. "That still only gets us two, and I don't want to risk overtime in front of a hometown crowd in the Boston Garden. Indianapolis, it'd be different. Do like I said." A chorus of "hmms" ended the time-out. The huddle broke, and the team walked back on the hardwoods.

The Pacers executed the play exactly as planned: the pick, the long pass to Lamont, his drive to the basket, and a slick, behind-the-back shuffle to Randy Jackson. Both defenders peeled off to cover Lamont's charge, and Randy hit his patented fall-away jumper as the game-ending buzzer sounded. The three-pointer finished his sixth consecutive two-thousand-point season, guaranteeing the Pacers a play-off berth.

Not planned was Randy's midair collision with the Boston guard. Seeing through the ruse at the last minute, the guard raced back to block Randy's shot. His right elbow slammed above Randy's left eye. Unbalanced, Randy landed on a bowed-out ankle, fragile ligaments suddenly supporting 225 crashing pounds.

Randy's scream drowned the papery whisper of the ball's swish as he fell. The crowd, still as death, held a collective breath.

The trainer ran on court and stared at the badly turned left ankle, dark blood already ballooning the skin. "Oh, shit," he muttered, then turned crimson as ESPN amplified the expletive in the quiet of the great hall.

Assistants carried Randy off court, his six-foot-seven frame writhing on the stretcher. Once in the locker room, team physician Peter Fredericks, rimless glasses teetering on the tip of his nose, bent his lanky frame over the ankle and injected it with lidocaine to kill the pain. Then he iced and bandaged it tight to reduce internal bleeding. Fredericks stepped back, shook his bald head side to side, and muttered under his breath, "Doesn't look good—not good at all."

The red strobe from the ambulance outside washed the locker room in ruddy shadows as they loaded Randy for a CT and MRI of his ankle at the Mass General Hospital. On his way out, Randy flipped his teammates a thumbs-up. "Back in a few, guys," he said with a forced smile. Heavy lidded eyes spoke his real feelings.

The team moped around the locker room—no snapping towels or horseplay—and waited for the doctor's return. Lamont glad-handed here and shoulder-squeezed there, assuring teammates Randy would be fine. But the mood was somber.

Restless reporters milled in the hallway, predicting the Pacers' chances in the play-offs. "Done for," they concluded, already writing the next day's obit.

Two hours later, the doctor's expression said it all. "The orthopedic chief at MGH examined him. The anterior talofibular ligament has been stretched and probably completely torn," said Fredericks. "Possibly the calcaneofibular ligament as well. Lots of hemorrhage from ruptured blood vessels."

"Peter, English for Christ's sake!" Caruthers demanded.

"Randy has a sprained ankle."

"Why in hell didn't you say that in the beginning?" the coach barked. "Gotta make it seem complex."

"It *is* complex, Dick. Grade 3 sprain's the worst. I've hospitalized him a few days for intensive orthopedic therapy."

"It's not broken, so he can play, right?"

"No. His season's finished. Treatment's with RICE."

"Rice? What the fuck you talking about?" Caruthers asked.

Fredericks backed out of the coach's reach, palms up. "Sorry, only making a little medical joke. Or trying to. Acronym for rest, ice, compression, and elevation."

The coach stepped toward him. "No play-off games? Even with a steroid shot ... *or whatever else it takes?*"

"Absolutely not," Fredericks said, voice firm. "Ruin his ankle for keeps. Be happy if he's healed in time for next season."

"This is May, goddamnit. We're talking October."

"I know, Coach, but he'll be out at least three, four months."

"So, five months, he'll be okay?"

"Should be, if it heals properly."

"He'd better heal properly," said Caruthers. "There's millions riding on that ankle. Don't spare anything to make it totally normal again."

"I won't. He'll be on medication for quite a while, though."

"Double the doses. Triple them. Whatever's necessary, do it," the coach said through clenched teeth. "If he's not at opening game, you won't be either."

Without Randy Jackson, the Pacers lost their first round play-off in four straight games, and their championship season died. "Everybody better pray Randy's ankle heals by October," Caruthers said as the team split for the off-season.

CHAPTER ONE

We were identical, Dorian and I, but not at all alike. He was firstborn, seconds before midnight, December 31, and I followed on January 1, twelve minutes later. Those twelve minutes shaped my world, because Father loved his firstborn more than me.

Growing up, we were inseparable. We wore the same clothes, ate the same foods, and shared the same tubes of Brylcreme, Colgate, and Clearasil. But Dorian squeezed from the top and left the cap off. We even dated the same girls. No one could tell the Double Ds apart, so it was easy for Dorian to appear faithful to one while dating another, using me as his stand-in. We loved sports and played on the same football and basketball teams. We could read each other's minds, anticipating where the pass would be thrown or a block needed. Defenses thinking they saw double went crazy.

We both stood six feet two with light brown hair and an untamable cowlick, gray eyes, and the sure hands of a shooting guard, with long fingers that could palm a basketball when we were only twelve. We were football-big and looked a lot like our father, with a square chin, a slightly bent nose, full lips, and Clark Gable ears. At least, my right ear was big. My left ear started out smaller than my right because Dorian's head had pressed against it in the womb—so the doctor said. Dorian bragged he had impacted me even before we were born. By the time I was ten, both ears were the same size.

At our college graduation, Father said we could be whatever we wanted—after we graduated medical school. That presented a dilemma, because Dorian partied throughout our four years at Dartmouth College. Father blamed me for not making him study more in Baker Library instead of drinking beer at Sigma Chi.

But we did get into medical school and graduated—Harvard for me, and Syracuse for Dorian. I then trained at Duke to be a cardiologist and heart rhythm expert and, finally finished, joined the staff at the University of Indiana Medical Center (UIMC).

And now I was almost eight thousand miles from home—seven thousand, nine hundred and ninety-two miles from Indianapolis, to be exact. Although I had traveled to Europe twice, this was my first time to Africa, and I was excited about being in a place so different from anything I had known.

Physicians at UIMC staffed a hospital in Kenya that cared for Africans with HIV and AIDS, and they had been looking for volunteers. The plea resonated, so I'd signed on for six months at the Rift Valley University School of Medicine in Eldoret, Kenya. I didn't think there'd be much need for a heart rhythm specialist. Most likely I'd be practicing general medicine.

I landed in Nairobi, Kenya, and spent two days at the Hilton in the center of town. My room had a big window facing south, and I could see Mount Kilimanjaro when the clouds cleared.

The hotel was too Western, so I wandered to the markets where the smells of spices, sights of slaughtered game, and sounds of people speaking Swahili were more typical of Africa. At a woodcarving booth, I bargained for a scary witch-doctor mask and a family of elephants carved in ebony. I cabbed to the Karen Blixen house and sat at the desk where she wrote *Out of Africa*. On the way back, we stopped at the Giraffe Center where those long-necked creatures "squatted" to eat crackers from my hand.

On my third day, I traveled to Eldoret, got checked in, was assigned a room, and prepared to start my clinic.

I didn't have to wait long. That afternoon, four tall, muscular Maasai men wrapped in traditional red warrior robes with jangling, beaded, red-and-blue earrings walked into the outpatient building. They carried their chief in a chair secured to the middle of two long wooden poles. The skin of a lion draped the chair, its open mouth snarling over the chief's head. They were too tall to enter my office. So, with a grunt, each warrior removed the pole from his shoulder, placed it on the floor, and the chief stepped out of the chair. Dilated eyes shone in a dark, round face capped by thick, black hair as he spoke rapidly in Swahili, fingers stroking his left chest. I had no idea what he was saying but ushered him into my office and onto the examining table. The four pole bearers shot out the door.

I was about to call one of the nurses to interpret when the chief knotted a fist over his chest and keeled over. I checked for a pulse in his neck and found none.

"*Code red! Code red!*" I screamed into the hallway. "*Cardiac arrest!* I need a defibrillator *now!*"

"Where are you?" a disembodied voice responded from the end of the hallway.

"317A," I shouted. "Hurry!"

My tiny office was only big enough for a desk and an examining table. I half lifted and then dragged the man to the floor so I could kneel alongside to begin chest compressions.

He was tall, and his feet blocked the door. The nurse arriving with the external defibrillator couldn't get in. She finally wedged the door open a crack and handed me the defibrillator. I flipped open the case and stuck defibrillator pads on his chest. The machine analyzed the rhythm in seconds and instructed me to deliver a shock. I hit the red button. Nothing happened. I hit it again. Still nothing. His dark face was getting darker, lips turning purple.

I checked the pads: dried out and not conducting. Who knows when they used it last. "I need fresh pads!" I yelled.

Drawers opened and slammed closed in the hall. "No, that's it," the nurse said.

"Then get me ECG gel. Maybe it'll work." *Or he's a dead man*, I thought. We were now four minutes into the cardiac arrest. "Hurry or we're going to lose him! We've only got a minute or so left."

The nurse tossed the tube to me. I glommed conductive gel under each pad, mashed down, charged the defibrillator to max, and hit the red button again.

His jaw clenched, and his body arched as 750 volts walloped through it. A slow heartbeat, only about thirty per minute, started up—but it *was* a heartbeat, sending precious blood to his brain. I continued to massage his chest until his rate picked up to seventy and his pulse felt normal.

I took a deep breath and let it out slowly, puffing my cheeks in relief. I bent his no-longer-rigid knees, and the nurse came in. We lifted him back onto the examining table.

"Draw blood for a chem 7, lytes, and a CBC," I said to her. "Also, cardiac enzymes and repeat them in four hours."

"Yes, Doctor."

I wiped sweat off my forehead and read her nametag. "Good job, Chalondra. We saved a life today."

Her face was drained, eyes wide, but she managed a shaky smile. "Oh, my, Dr. Sloane. That was frightful, but you did it." She showed me her trembling hands as she prepared to draw the blood samples.

"Makes you feel good, doesn't it?" I said.

A full grin lit up her face, and her eyes sparkled.

"Oh, it does. I feel all warm inside of me." She pointed to her chest. "Almost like a whiskey," she said in a soft voice, glancing over her shoulder.

"And I know this patient. Mr. Abasi Sentwali. He has a wife and many young children. So it is a very good thing he will live. They all need him a lot. He is chief of a Maasai tribe about twenty kilometers away. The warriors who brought him told me the Maasai *laibon*—the tribe's doctor—treated him for chest pain with herbs and magic spells."

"He should have sent him sooner."

"Sometimes such spells can heal, Doctor. I have seen it."

"Maybe so, but not this time." I wasn't going to argue.

Chalondra finished drawing blood and started an IV. I hooked him up to a portable ECG machine. Sentwali remained unconscious despite a normal heart rhythm and blood pressure. We prepared to move him to the hospital, a few buildings away.

"Will he be okay?"

I nodded. "He's suffered mild brain damage from lack of oxygen. He'll recover over the next few days and be back with his wife and children in less than a week."

Then he stopped breathing.

I drove a fist into his sternum. The *whack* made Chalondra jump. Sentwali took a breath and then quit again. After several starts and stops, I decided to intubate him. I inserted a breathing tube into his trachea and connected it to a rubber Ambu bag that I squeezed to inflate his lungs as we rolled the gurney to the hospital. Once there, I connected the tube to a respirator that automatically breathed for him.

By afternoon, he was moving all four extremities and even squeezed my fingers. I debated taking the tube out, but I didn't trust him to breathe on his own. I thought he needed another day for his brain to heal.

The Umoja ward for male patients had thirty-six beds and a small intensive care unit. The well-trained staff was dedicated and the equipment as modern as Rift Valley could afford. But I hadn't planned on Mother Nature.

The violent storm erupted during dinner in the hospital dining room. The intensity of crashing thunder and jagged lightning stilled all conversation as thunderclouds settled in and enveloped us. A fierce salvo lit up the night and left the room in total darkness. The waiters searched for candles.

The head of hospital maintenance reassured us. "Do not be alarmed. The backup generator will kick on in exactly fifteen seconds."

We all waited—and waited. Nothing.

"What about the Umoja ward?" I remembered after several minutes. "Will it have power?"

"It should."

"Even though the backup generator hasn't started?"

"That could be a problem."

I jumped from the table. "Anyone have a flashlight?" I grabbed one and raced to Umoja. The buildings weren't connected, and I had to run about fifty yards outdoors. In moments, I was drenched. Lightning flashed around me, and I hoped the odds of being struck really were one in a million.

As I tore into the ICU, I heard Sentwali before I saw him, thrashing about in bed, fighting the tube in his throat. I knew that without electric power, the respirator no longer cycled. The endotracheal tube, once his lifeline, would suffocate him.

I held the flashlight in my teeth and tried to deflate the tiny balloon holding the tube in his trachea. Yanking it out would damage delicate tissues. Rainwater from my wet hair dripped into my eyes, and I couldn't find the release valve. Finally, I disconnected the end of the tube from the respirator. Sentwali gasped harshly once, twice, and stopped breathing. I hit his chest but got no response. I breathed into the end of the tube. He might have AIDS, but he was going to die without air.

After several moments, I heard a grinding sound like grating gears that overpowered the noise of the storm. Lights flickered twice and flashed on, lighting up the room. The respirator began cycling, whooshing air into the room.

It was too late. Sentwali's pupils were fixed and dilated. He was dead from asphyxiation.

Chalondra was the first to come running in from dinner. I told her what had happened.

"Oh my God, that poor man. What a horrible way to die," she said.

Devastated, I stood at his side, holding his pulseless wrist in my hands. "I should have taken the damn tube out," I muttered.

"You can't blame yourself. It was the storm and the electricity." She looked at me, pain in her eyes. "Maybe you should get some rest, Dr. Sloane. I can manage here." She patted my shoulder and headed me toward the door.

The thunderstorm had blown over, and I walked outside. The sweet smell of its aftermath, a combination of ozone and fragrant soil spores dispersed by the rain, could not relieve my gloom. I went to my room and cracked open the bottle of Jack Daniel's I'd brought along for an emergency.

CHAPTER TWO

"Does his wife know?" I asked the following morning. We met on the Umoja ward and were standing in front of the nurses' station. I stared at the empty bed that had been Sentwali's.

Chalondra nodded. "We sent word to her village last night to come to the hospital as soon as she could. The laibon said she collapsed on hearing the news and will not come in."

"Can we change her mind? I want to explain what happened in person."

Before Chalondra answered, the phone rang. The secretary to the hospital director was "inviting" me to explain to the director, Jesse Gaudet, what had happened.

A lovely woman met my knock at the director's office. "I'm here to see Dr. Gaudet," I said.

She smiled and beckoned me to follow her into the office, a small room with white walls dominated by a dark wooden desk in the center. Two brown rattan chairs with blue cushions decorated by embroidered animal shapes and a three-drawer, black, metal file filled the remaining space. A small-screened window was open, and a ceiling fan lazily stirred the hot air.

She came up to my chin, maybe five foot five or six. A tortoiseshell comb swept auburn hair off her neck, but a few strands escaped and teased her shoulders as she moved her head. I wanted to tuck them behind an ear. Her high cheekbones and slender, straight nose reminded me of the exotic women on the Copacabana Beach in Rio de Janeiro, the perfect blend of African American, Spanish, and Indian in exquisite combinations. I pictured her in a bikini. She'd hold her own on Copa, or any other beach.

She pulled up a chair and motioned me to sit down. "I'm supposed to see Dr. Jesse Gaudet."

"I know," she said, extending her hand. "Jessica Gaudet." Her radiant smile lit up the office, and her deep hazel eyes crinkled in the corners from laugh lines that made her look amused—from my discomfiture no doubt. "I guess the nurses didn't tell you."

I laughed. "No, Dr. Gaudet, I expected a guy."

"Please call me Jessie, with an *ie*." The light had shifted, and her eyes seemed to shimmer.

"And I'm Daniel."

"Daniel or Danny?"

"Mostly Daniel. Only my family called me Danny, when I was a kid."

She smiled and fingered a tortoiseshell necklace that matched the comb. "Thank you for coming to see me, Daniel. The nurses told me Mr. Sentwali died. I'm so sorry for him and his family, and for you too. Your face tells me how much this hurt you."

She put her hand gently on my arm. Her voice had a lilt to it, American but something softly southern, refined. And I liked the physical contact. She wasn't shy. I was expecting some sort of a lecture, particularly from a heart surgeon—a notoriously arrogant lot, even the women. She took me off guard.

"Tell me from the beginning what happened."

I recounted the entire episode. "So, between the laibon and me, and I guess Mother Nature, we set him up for a perfect storm. Literally."

"Don't be too hard on yourself or the laibon. Belief in the supernatural is deeply rooted in African society and actually may have prevented his cardiac arrest until he got here."

"C'mon, Dr. Gaudet—I mean, Jessie. You really believe that?"

She shrugged. "I grew up in New Orleans, where it was part of our culture, and I've lived here for two years."

I sat back in my chair and shook my head. "I can't believe what I'm hearing—and from a cardiac surgeon, no less!"

Her laugh was musical. Then she looked pensive. "Are you religious?"

"Not really. My father emigrated from Russia when he was a little boy of three or four. Our family name was Slovinsky, and I guess it was Jewish. At some point, he changed the name to Sloane and married my mom. She was Catholic, and my father didn't care, so I was raised a Catholic. But I'm not sure what I believe anymore. You?"

"Jewish. My ancestors were thrown out of Spain in 1492, same year Columbus set sail. They wandered Western Europe a couple of hundred years and eventually made it to America. They settled in New Orleans in the late 1700s."

"You can trace your family back that far?"

"To about 1850. Before that is Internet guessing. I do have a claim to fame, though. A distant relative, Lewis Solomon, was the first king of Mardi Gras in 1872."

"Impressive."

"But I was going to ask whether you thought believing in the miracles of Christianity, such as the resurrection of Christ or the virgin birth, is any different than believing in voodoo?"

"I'm not a believer, but how can you compare the two?"

"Actually, the Creoles in New Orleans syncretized both."

"I don't know what that means—syncretized."

"They reconciled differences between Christianity and their beliefs and melded them into an all-inclusive, functioning religion."

"How could they believe in supernatural voodoo stuff *and* Jesus? That's comic books and the Bible."

"Right. Like believing wine is Christ's blood and wafers his body? Or a statue of Jesus cries tears, or Moses parted the Red Sea? Western religions have as much mysticism as African."

"This is totally bonkers."

"Not really. Different people have different belief systems that can be surprisingly similar."

"Maybe."

"You don't sound convinced."

I shook my head. "I believe in science—cold, hard facts. If it can't be proven scientifically, then it's all … I don't know … garbage. Theirs, ours, or anybody's. No concrete proof, it doesn't exist."

"It's that simple?" She held her hands out, palms up. I saw no rings, but that could be because she was a surgeon. They scrub and glove so often, jewelry's a nuisance.

"It's black or white, fact or fiction."

Jessie brushed away a lock of hair that had fallen over one eye. "Okay, we've both made our points. We'll agree to disagree. What do you want to do about Mr. Sentwali?"

"I need to explain to his wife what happened."

"*We* need to, since the hospital is partly to blame."

"Can we visit her village?"

"Are you up for a Land Rover ride in the African bush tomorrow morning?"

"Perfect. She should hear firsthand what happened to her husband."

"We'll leave right after breakfast." Jessie stood. "One last question."

I looked at her quizzically.

"What're you doing for dinner?"

CHAPTER THREE

The African bush chills your bones at five a.m., barely warms by six, and fries your brains at noon. Experienced travelers wear layers to peel as the day progresses. I wore so many I looked like the Michelin tire man.

"Other side," Jessie reminded me, tilting her head to the passenger's side as we left breakfast. "We drive on the left here." That felt weird, sitting on the left without a steering wheel.

The Land Rover was a roofless four-wheel drive utility vehicle. Jessie handed me a blanket. "You'll need this until it warms up," she said, revving the motor. Even at 15 mph, the wind cut through, and I cocooned deep inside the blanket, only my nose and eyes exposed.

My stomach growled. "Hungry?" Jessie asked.

"We should've brought some of those eggs or made sandwiches for lunch," I mumbled.

She flicked an exasperated look. "Energy bars are in the glove box, but anything smelly would attract visitors happy to make *us* lunch."

We drove in silence as the rising sun woke the bush. I shed the blanket and peeled off my outer clothes. Herds of impalas leapt through the air, short black tails swishing back and forth like windshield wipers in the rain, heels high to show vitality and strength. They scattered teardrops of dew that sparkled in the early morning sun. As we turned a corner, a family of warthogs led by a burly male with fearsome, curved tusks yellowed with age exploded across the road. Only another warthog could love faces that ugly.

Jessie pulled to a stop.

"What's the matter?"

"Shush," she whispered, a finger on her lips. "Just listen. The bush is talking."

Soon I heard low rumbling and clicking sounds. "Elephants chatting over breakfast," she explained.

"And the clicking?"

"Sparring adolescents, tusk on tusk."

A huge gray apparition appeared directly in front of us. The three-and-one-half-ton matriarch paused, looked up and down the trail like a pedestrian crossing the street, and spied our car. In an instant, her trunk rose, ears flapped, and she shrieked, trumpeting the sound of a hundred New Year's noisemakers. Her attack was so swift I only had time to put my fist in my mouth and mutter, "My God, we're dead."

The beast slammed her brakes inches from the car, backed up fifteen feet, and repeated her murderous assault. Again she came up short, retreated, and then charged a third time. Stopping once more, she laid her trunk on the front hood, nostrils dancing along the windshield. They quivered as she tasted the air, *our* air. She towered over us, the top of her huge head one and a half stories high, surprisingly tiny eyes staring into ours.

Finally, satisfied we posed no threat, the huge beast backed off and ambled into the bush, padded feet like giant shock absorbers silent as a prowling tomcat. I caught my breath when tons of gray beasts followed her wake, each appraising us but posing no threat. It was ten minutes before I could breathe again and stop shaking. Jessie sat behind the wheel, smiling.

"Incredible, aren't they?"

"I've never been more scared. I thought for sure she'd trample us." I put my hand on my chest. "My heart's racing two hundred a minute!"

"A mock charge, to test your mettle."

"Thanks. *Now* you tell me."

"What's the song from *West Side Story*? 'Keep cool, boy, keep really cool!' Remember, guys are from Mars."

I noted her calm demeanor. "Maybe you are too."

"Nope. Venus, like the book says. But I've spent a lot of time in the bush."

She started the motor and slowly pulled forward after the last elephant glided by and melted into the bush. We hit a washed-out section of the road. My teeth rattled together, and my head bashed the side of the car. "Got to hold on."

"Thanks. Your warnings seem to come after the fact."

She laughed and stopped near a cluster of trees.

"What now?"

"Snack time. Still hungry?"

"Of course."

Jessie opened the car door and stepped out. "Wait a second until I check for snakes and stuff." She pulled out a long wooden rod from the back of the car and walked around, prodding the base of the trees.

A minute later, she called, "All clear. You can come out."

I stepped gingerly into the grass, visions of tripping over a black mamba or a puff adder flitting through my head.

We sat on a large rock in the acacia-tree cluster, chewing nutrition bars and drinking cold tea. In the distance, we could see herds of wildebeests and zebras grazing together.

"They're buddies," Jessie said, pointing the stick at them. "Zebras hear and see better than wildebeests, so they spot predators earlier. But the carnivores like wildebeest meat more than zebra, and they're easier to take down. So each side wins something."

"That philosophy would settle the Middle East."

"Or a dozen other places in the world." We sat back and gazed at the blue sky. I felt tranquil watching the grazing animals. The pain of Sentwali's death faded a little.

Jessie nudged me from my reverie. "African e-mails are about to begin."

My eyebrows rose in amazement. "Your cell phone works out here?"

She shook her head and pointed to a lone vulture circling overhead. "He's on reconnaissance, searching for a fresh kill. Watch."

We were reasonably cool in the acacia shade, and the vulture riding air currents overhead was mesmerizing. After ten minutes, it swooped down onto the plain.

"Now, that's the 'send' message. *'Fresh meat, y'all invited to dinner.'*"

"Sent where?"

She pointed at a group of six vultures roosting together in the same treetop. A moment later, they flew to where the single bird landed. *"Message received."*

"That's it?"

"No, those birds just hit the *'reply to all'* response. Wait."

Several minutes later, we heard them in the distance, their high-pitched, crescendoing "woo-*up*, woo-*up*" carrying far in the stillness. "Hyenas."

"They got the last message?"

She nodded. "They're on their way to steal the kill—probably a wildebeest—from whatever animal made it, maybe a couple of lions. The hyenas wouldn't be able to take it from a whole pride, but will easily chase off one or two, or a cheetah."

"What about a leopard?"

"Chase him too, but a leopard would've carried the kill high into a tree safe from theft."

"Doesn't seem fair to the animal that made the kill."

We heard sounds of a squabble in the bush, the hyenas' laughs drowning out the lions' growls.

Jessie brushed a ribbon of hair from her face and sipped her tea. "There's no right or wrong—or guilt—in the bush. It is what it is; the only concern's survival. The big take from the small, the strong from the weak, and the fast from the slow. Mother Nature has no conscience. Nor should it."

"Sounds like Wall Street."

Jessie smiled. "Or Washington."

An hour later, we saw the outline of bramble fences made from acacia trees that formed the corrals for the animals kept by the Maasai. Houses like oversized muddy igloos ringed the corrals. Two women were busy building a new one. I stared at their shaved heads and pierced earlobes hanging halfway to their shoulders. Colorful, beaded jewelry dangled from their necks, ears, and wrists.

A cluster of small children in various types of dress and undress formed a circle around us and then started shouting and jumping. Mothers followed and had to separate two of the older boys fighting to get close, no different from kids in Indianapolis shoving at a Pacers game.

A man approached, my height, maybe taller. Countless suns had baked his wrinkled black face. A florid red-checked cloth, a *shuka*, draped his broad, muscular shoulders, and a bone gourd hung from a rawhide rope across his chest. He held a long wooden staff with a ball carved on one end. The circle surrounding us parted silently, and all the jostling stopped. Clouds of flies settled on faces, eyes, and clothes of the stilled youngsters.

"The laibon," Jessie said.

"Yes, I am the laibon. Thank you for coming," he said in English mixed with a Swahili accent. Carved, wooden lion head earrings jangled from stretched holes in his ear lobes as he spoke.

Jessie introduced us in Swahili and explained what had happened at the hospital.

The laibon nodded and responded in English. "I have sedated Sentwali's wife with herbs. She is quite upset, as we all are to have lost our chief in such a way."

"How did he become ill?" Jessie asked.

"Four days ago, he and his brother-in-law fought over who owned which calves because their herds had interbred."

The laibon turned to me. "Our cattle are a gift from our god, *Enkai*, and fighting over them is an insult to him." He glanced at Jessie and stared at me, unblinking.

"The next day, he began to have chest pains. I treated him with *buchu* and devil's claw, which helped for a while, and sent him to see you. My magic kept him alive, and your magic should have cured him. Instead, you let him die."

"I'm so sorry. It was unfortunate."

"At birth, Enkai grants each man a guardian spirit to protect him during life and carry him off at death. The guardian spirit transports evil men to a desert and the good to a land of rich pastures and many cattle."

He shook the staff in my face. "Which place will you go, Doctor?" His lips parted in a sneer, showing yellowed teeth.

Jessie shoved between us. "He will travel to the place of rich pastures and cattle because he is a good man."

"Maybe that is so. Let us find out." He clapped his hands twice.

A twin, almost, standing at the outskirts of our circle, pushed his way in. He held a hollow cow's horn that rattled as he handed it to the laibon in exchange for the gourd. The laibon pointed his staff at the circle, and it widened.

He moved to the middle, looked skyward, and chanted an invocation. Then he placed a hand over the horn's opening and shook it. The clatter sounded like dice rattling in a gambler's cup at the craps table. He bent his knees and jumped straight up three times. The third time, he fell to the earth and emptied the horn. A dozen or so angular colored stones, a little bigger than marbles, rolled in the dust. Both men stared at them and gasped, speaking rapidly in Swahili.

Jessie cried, "No!" and staggered against me. She yelled something at the laibon.

He nodded, and the other man collected the stones, placed them back in the horn, and handed it to the laibon. He repeated the ritual but this time flung the contents to the edge of the circle of people. Both men walked over and stared down at the stones. They shook their heads as before, muttered something, and collected the stones. Jessie inhaled sharply and put her hand over her mouth.

"What the hell's going on here, Jessie? What's all this mumbo jumbo?"

"Wait a minute," she said and ran to the men. They talked in Swahili for a moment, and then the men shoved past her and out through the circle. I put my hand on the laibon's arm as he hurried by.

"Hold it!" I yelled at him. "What're you trying to do?"

He shook off my hand and brushed his arm where I had held it. He looked from there to my face.

"Enkai has forever cursed you for the death of our chief. I have nothing more to say." He glowered a moment, pressed his lips together, and strode away.

We were silent as we drove back to the Rift Valley Hospital. The bush had lost its allure. Jessie drove with a determination and concentration that left no room for small talk.

Finally, I broke the silence.

"Jessie, you don't really believe that stuff, do you? I mean, their god, Enkai, cursing me? For Christ's sake, I barely met the people and don't know anything about their religion. Even if I believed in jumping men throwing stones, why should their god affect me? And who or what is their god, anyway?"

She drove on silently, but her look seemed to lighten.

I tried again. "Jessie, it's all nonsense. A curse only works if you believe it. So now, every bad thing's due to the curse? We get a flat tire, it's the curse? I slip on a banana peel, the curse? And if nothing bad happens, it's a day stolen from the curse?" I shook my head. "No, Jessie, that's just a bunch of weird superstition."

"Any different from religion? Don't Catholics think nonbelievers will go to hell? Muslims do too, if you don't believe their way. Mormons even baptize dead Jewish holocaust victims by proxy so they can enter heaven. Isn't that like the laibon's curse? Whether you believe or not, you can be damned or saved. It's not all black and white, Daniel. Even medicine has its gray areas."

"Maybe so, but this stuff's *all* craziness."

She slowed and glanced at me. "Could be, but I can't stop thinking I'm responsible."

"Nonsense. I chose to come. Thanks for butting between us. I thought the guy was going to bash me with that big stick."

"He was wrong. You *are* a good person, Daniel. I feel I know who you are and that I've known you a long time."

No one I cared about had ever told me that. Certainly not my father, and my mother was too timid to say anything he didn't approve of. I didn't know what to say.

Jessie pulled the car to the side of the road, stopped, and turned to me. I tucked a strand of hair behind her ear—finally. Then I leaned over, cradled her head with one hand, and gently brushed my finger across the perfect M of her top lip.

She stared into my eyes with a teasing smile. "And?" she said when I hesitated. "That's it?"

I kissed her, tenderly at first, but more urgently when she put her arms around my neck and pulled me toward her.

She withdrew.

"What's the matter?"

"I have a question," she said, an innocent look on her face.

I searched for clues but found none. "Okay, what?"

"Does the curse carry over to family members?"

I was stunned but saw she was grinning.

"Only if they misbehave."

Sunrise and sunset are incredibly beautiful times in Africa, with tangerine skies as the animals began their day or prepared to end it. We'd sit on the veranda that overlooked an expansive plain with a large water hole and watch the giraffes and elephants and other grazers amble by, and I learned to listen to the bush. Soon, we were having dinner together every night and, when I was very lucky, breakfast as well.

My father's sudden death ended my Rift Valley stay a month shy of the six for which I had volunteered. I knew my mother would be devastated, and I had to get home.

"Will you come with me?"

"I promised to serve as director another full year."

"Cancel it. Jessie, I want you to come with me. Now."

"And?" she prompted.

I smiled. "And marry me?"

"Deal."

CHAPTER FOUR

We were sitting in my brother's new office in New York City. I had missed my father's funeral by two days because of flight delays out of Nairobi. My mother was angry, certain I was late on purpose.

"She'll get over your being late, Daniel—not to worry. She's lost her anchor is all. Jesus, she's never gotten a driver's license or even balanced a checkbook, and now she's all alone."

I looked around his office. "Looks like *you* own the checkbook." The view from the fortieth floor of the Time Warner Center on Columbus Circle was spectacular. I could see Central Park through the picture window behind Dorian's desk, with the trees boasting pink, yellow, and white blossoms, and fresh green grass carpeting the ground.

Dorian smiled and swept his arm around the large corner office, eyes lingering on the big chandelier in the center, a replica of the Metropolitan Opera's starburst lights. Our father, a big donor to the Met, used to drag us kicking and screaming to opera performances.

"I may own the checkbook now, but I put in plenty of dungeon years under him."

"Yeah, right. Poor guy. Weren't you driving a Mercedes last time I checked?"

"Relatively speaking, they were dungeon years." Dorian looked pensive. "You know, the old man died last week, sitting at this very desk, opening his fourth pack of cigarettes at five o'clock in the afternoon. He was only sixty-six. Hard to believe. No way in hell I'd be the CEO at age forty if he hadn't." Dorian shook his head and leaned back, putting his feet on a corner of the huge cherry-wood desk, avoiding the inlaid mother-of-pearl trim. "I figured I had at least ten more years of slavery before he freed me."

Father's full-length oil portrait hung on the opposite wall. "He seems to radiate disapproval, staring down at us mere mortals." I shuddered. "Give you a hundred bucks to trash it." I paused. "Make that a thousand."

Dorian shook his head. "The board authorized that painting for thirty-five grand. And besides, he wasn't that bad. He built this business, didn't he? And the employees loved him for his fairness and loyalty to them."

"They should. He spent more time with them than he did with us," I said.

"Well, he was building the business. For us, remember? He told us that lots of times."

"Yeah, each time he missed my birthday. I don't know about you, bro, but I only remember the shitty things that happened growing up, not the good ones. Remember the apple fight you started in old Smiley's orchard?"

Dorian chuckled that familiar, high-pitched sound. "Yeah, slinging those green apples at each other."

"And when Smiley complained we ruined his trees, Father got pissed at me."

"Served you right."

"Bull crap! If it wasn't for little Janie Ann snitching you threw the first one, I'd still be grounded."

"Nah, I'd have told him."

I smiled at Dorian. "Yeah, right, confess your own sins? Like telling him it was you who flipped the coin at Opperman's Pond that almost got me killed? Not during this lifetime, you won't."

Dorian frowned when I said that, stood, and went to the window.

"You okay?" I asked. He didn't answer, just shrugged and stared out at Central Park.

I sat back and remembered. Opperman's Pond was a fishpond the size of a football field, three blocks from our house. Tall, dense pines isolated the water and rolling hills and served as sentinels guarding our kingdom from adults. In our sanctuary, we slayed dragons, swam the moat to save fair maidens, and rode white horses into battle against evil knights.

After the weather turned cold, we couldn't wait to start ice-skating and playing hockey. One December when we were eight or nine, we decided to flip a coin to choose who would test the ice. Dorian fished a quarter from his pants pocket and tossed it high in the air. I called heads as he speared the coin in flight. "Sorry, little brother," he said, "it's tails."

Halfway across the pond, the ice gave way, and I crashed through. In a minute, I was frozen and sinking. Each time I tried to climb out, the ice broke, and my waterlogged clothes dragged me under. I fought, coughing and screaming, but the snow-covered pines muffled all cries for help. As I went under the water for the third time, I saw Dorian belly-inching toward me along the ice. With my last bit of strength, I kicked to the surface and grabbed the dead tree branch Dorian thrust at me. The ice held as he backed up and dragged me out. We crawled to the bank and sat shivering, me from the icy water, and Dorian from the scare, I guess. Then we ran home. Father dubbed him a hero and me a dumb shit. Father did visit me in the hospital for my pneumonia, though, and even snuck in a pizza when the nurses weren't looking.

But Dorian had saved my life and made sure I never forgot it. He framed the newspaper picture of the Pleasantville mayor presenting him a medal for bravery and hung it over his bed in our room.

He rode that icy save forever. Whenever I raised an eyebrow, his response was that high-pitched chuckle and, "Opperman's Pond, bro, don't forget." I grew to hate that chuckle.

"I do confess my sins," Dorian said, brushing away my rejoinder with the back of his hand. He returned to his desk and put his feet back up. "I've turned over a new leaf. Sheila's made me into a new man."

"How's number-two wife doing? Or are you planning for number three?"

"Just two. All I can afford."

"Come to Kenya with me. You could become a Maasai warrior and buy wives for fifteen cows each. Twenty for top-of-the-line virgins."

"Cheaper than New York. Dorothy took me big time. Fucking lawyers complained my little head controlled the big one. But I didn't make that mistake a second time. I made Sheila sign a prenup so I could live by my new credo."

"Which is?"

"If it flies, floats, or fucks, lease it!"

I laughed. Dorian could turn tragedy into humor, step back and laugh at it. "The prenup's a lease?"

"Closest thing my lawyers could come up with," Dorian said.

"Is there another after Sheila?"

"Who knows? Life plays all kinds of tricks." He grinned at me. "And you, little brother? What's with your life?"

"Did you like Jessie?"

Dorian pulled back in mock surprise. "What kind of a stupid question is that out of the blue? 'Did you like the woman I'm going to marry?' What the fuck do you expect me to say? 'No, she slurped her soup'?"

I shrugged. "You could've."

Dorian took his feet off the desk, stood, and stretched his back. "She's lovely. Perfect for you. So when's the wedding?"

"Invitations go out this week. In exactly one month. June in Indianapolis is gorgeous. Too early for mosquitoes and late enough for roses."

"Am I best man?"

My turn. "What the fuck do you expect me to say? 'No, you slurp your soup'?"

This time, he shrugged. "You could've."

We both burst out laughing. I saw him wince. "Your back?"

Dorian nodded. "I got an ergonomic chair in my dungeon office, but the guys haven't moved it up here yet."

"You exercising?"

"Daily, but my back still talks to me every day."

"Even after the disk surgery?"

He put his hands on the small of his back and massaged. "Some days it shouts, and other days it whispers, but it never misses a day communicating. Today's a shouting day."

"Take something for it?"

Dorian gave me the biggest smile. "Aha, my dear younger brother, that's the million—or probably multibillion—dollar question, about which you will hear at our board meeting tomorrow morning. Our father would've wanted the board meeting to go on as scheduled. In the meantime, how about a Scotch, neat? A sip or two of my twenty-five-year-old Macallan fortifies me against all the ills in this world, including my wife and my back. It is the golden nectar of the gods."

"Which gods?"

"Why, the Greek God of Medicine, to start with. Asclepius."

"You better hope your fate's better than his. Asclepius pissed off Zeus, who toasted him with a thunderbolt."

"Wall Street's not happy," said John Anderson, the company's chief financial officer.

We were having coffee the next morning at Starbucks in the lobby of the Time Warner Center, an hour before the board meeting. "Why not, John?" I asked.

"Because Sloane Pharmaceuticals only has one new drug in the discovery pipeline, and four multibillion-dollar-a-year medicines with patents expiring in the next eighteen months," Dorian answered for him.

"The stock price has fallen by 18 percent in the last six months. I warned Dorian the board meeting's going to be tense," John added, pointing a finger at my brother.

"I might have to cancel my order for the yacht."

John didn't smile. "Dorian, cut the bullshit and focus on what I'm telling you. Company's stock's heading straight for the toilet. And once the cheaper generics hit the stores, patients will switch because they'll think the new meds are biologically comparable. We'll have to cut our retail price 50 percent or more to stay competitive," John said. "You don't need a PhD in finance to—"

Dorian waved him off. "I told Father to fight the fucking Food and Drug Administration, Daniel. I wanted to keep the generic drugs off the shelves for one more year. We needed breathing space. I wooed those FDA guys every which way I could legally, and some not so legally, but no dice."

"Maybe somebody paid them off," John said.

"Had to. They knew the copycats were inferior. That's why we sued the bastards for nonequivalency. But even the judge was against us. You were there, John. You heard that high-pitched, squeaky voice." Dorian squeezed his nose and raised his voice an octave. "'No, the generics will work as well as your drugs, Dr. Sloane. Your patents will expire on schedule, so get your act together and move on.'"

We all burst out laughing.

"Motherfucker," said Dorian. "If he thinks I'll support his reelection campaign, he's blowing smoke up his ass."

"Okay, but think about what I told you, Dorian, about making future layoffs," John said. "We've got to prepare for the financial meltdown coming at us like a freight train. Downsize the work force 10 or 12 percent."

"No layoffs. Father never did, and I won't either. We protect our workers. They're loyal to us, and I'll be loyal to them. We'll make it through. We've got the winner in the bag, though I may need your help to convince the board, Daniel."

John wrinkled his brow and rubbed his chest.

"Anything wrong, John?" I asked, alert to the gesture.

"Your brother gives me heartburn."

CHAPTER FIVE

I watched Dorian walk to the lectern, almost a swagger. For a guy who'd become CEO less than a week ago, he radiated confidence. He wore a blue blazer and white turtleneck shirt with a white handkerchief in the front pocket. A jeweled American flag gleamed over his breast pocket like a medal. The flag and the shiny brass buttons made the jacket look like a uniform.

I smiled as Dorian scanned the board members sitting around the long Honduran mahogany table. He squinted his eyes like someone planning strategic moves. The tabletop flickered in the overhead light, and I remembered my father bragging that the Lalique glass engraved with the Sloane company logo was a steal at three hundred K.

Our family controlled 51 percent of the stock, but only my father, Dorian, and I attended the board meetings. The other six board members were business types who successfully ran their own companies and sat on other boards to advise other people how to run theirs.

There were no smiles as the board concentrated on the financial flow sheet John provided. He droned on about how bad the numbers added up and what dire straits the company was in. But frankly, I got lost in the business minutiae. Finances never interested me. I couldn't even remember how much stock I owned or what it was worth—or had been worth—before it took a dive. But not the board members. They sat riveted on what John was saying and were intently studying the flow sheet. I sensed an ugly undertone building.

Dorian silenced the murmurings with outstretched hands. "I know you're all concerned about the finances of Sloane Pharmaceuticals," he said, looking at John and fingering the diamond stud in his left ear. "So am I. But the pages of this notebook contain salvation."

He picked up a four-inch-thick, white, spiral-ringed notebook and held it high for all to see. He looked like a priest holding the Holy Bible, or a rabbi, the Torah. I wondered if he was going to say a prayer over it.

His fingers trembled as they traced the red label on the white spine, *Redex*, touching each letter almost reverently. I guess it *was* holy, and I couldn't really blame him. At breakfast, he'd said those pages held the key to the rest of our lives.

The board looked from one to the other, eyebrows raised, and then at the CFO for reassurance. John shrugged.

Dorian continued. "Redex will save the company, will save us all, and make billions doing it. I give you my word."

"Damn well better," a board member muttered in a gruff stage whisper. "This," he said, shaking the financial sheet, "sure as hell isn't." A thick, black mustache turned his face into a fierce scowl.

"Redex," Dorian said again, ignoring him and stretching out the word. He rolled the R, I think to let the sound sink in and echo in the room. "The research data contained between the covers of this book hold the fate of Sloane Pharmaceuticals and its twelve thousand employees worldwide, as well as this board," Dorian said.

He stared into the face of each board member, reminding me of a general sizing up his troops. He needed to do something because, to me, these troops weren't buying what their general was selling. They looked pretty angry. "Close your eyes and imagine the name Redex in your mind's eye. Think about the word and visualize what it might represent."

We just sat, looking at him.

"No, I'm serious. Humor me." He paused as we shut our eyes. "Okay, open. Marketing thought a name containing 'red' projected inflammation, and 'ex,' its elimination. Did any of you think of that?" A couple of hands rose tentatively.

Dorian nodded at one of his assistants, who wheeled in a small cart holding copies identical to the one he was waving but a quarter as thick. He'd told me he didn't want to burden the board with too much detailed technical information, and this summarized the research results. The assistant set one copy in front of each member. Some picked it up and riffled the pages. Others let it lie and stared at Dorian. I couldn't tell whether they were angry or just not believing what Dorian was saying.

"You might say I intend to bet the farm, or in this case, the firm, on Redex, and you'd be right," he said. "But I'm convinced a pain pill without stomach upset will distinguish Redex from all other nonsteroidal anti-inflammatory drugs, the NSAIDs like ibuprofen and naproxen. This will be a blockbuster. My outside analysts predict a billion dollars in sales the first year, incrementing at a billion a year over the next two years, and maxing out at $5.4 to $5.8 billion annually."

Nods and budding smiles replaced frowns and downturned lips as the members of the board looked from the report to each other and back to Dorian. They sat up straighter in their chairs. He paced back and forth, shoulders square, head high.

"How do you know how effective Redex will be?" asked the mustached board member. "And why has the stock price continued to fall if this is so good?" He waved the report at Dorian. "This is a lot of pie in the sky for a company on the verge of bankruptcy."

"Excellent points," Dorian said. "Drug development has been totally secret to reduce chances of piracy, so Wall Street knows nothing about this, only that we're studying a new drug. Been in development over a year. Father fought my doing it and barely allowed me enough capital to keep the project going. He didn't think it'd work, but he was wrong. I know it will work. Stock price'll rise soon enough. As to effectiveness, concrete answers will have to wait for the clinical studies. Right now, we have every indication from preclinical work—"

"What's that?" interrupted another board member.

"Animal studies done prior to human studies," Dorian answered. "Initial information indicates the mechanism of action of the drug—how it works," he parroted his chemists, "makes it a superb anti-inflammatory compound without side effects. Eliminating inflammation also eliminates pain and promotes healing. So joints get better without stomach upset or risk of bleeding. Nothing on the market comes close."

"Dorian, sounds great," I said, standing and looking around at the others. "Congratulations to you and your team. We need a drug like this." I was the only practicing physician on the board, and Dorian figured what I said would have great weight. They all looked at me. "But what's the mechanism of action? *How* does it stop pain and inflammation?" A planted question.

"The drug blocks a complicated set of enzymes in the body called benzodiabenases or BDs, Daniel. The chemist who discovered it is waiting outside the boardroom. Sit down, and he'll tell you," Dorian said, motioning for his assistant to get him.

"Daniel, and members of the board," Dorian said when the chemist entered, "this is Mikhail Borovsky, lead chemist on the Redex discovery team. Mikhail graduated number one of the 215 in his class at the Lomonosov Chemistry Department of the Moscow State University. He got his PhD in chemistry and chemical biology at Harvard and a second one in marine biology at Cal Tech."

Mikhail had small brown eyes too close together, capped by a single bushy eyebrow that needed trimming. He wore thick glasses and long hair in a ponytail. A pointy nose and skinny arms made him look like a ferret wearing glasses. Despite the glasses, something about his eyes was chilling, like looking into a very deep, dark well and barely seeing a reflection of light off the water's surface. The top of his head just reached Dorian's chin. He wore jeans and a T-shirt that said "Nerds Will Inherit the Earth." Dorian had copied his one-earring look, although Dorian's was left and Mikhail's right.

Dorian had told me that because Mikhail was "only" a PhD, the company MDs teased that he wasn't a real doc. The first time they said that, Mikhail had flown into a rage and actually came out swinging at a guy almost twice his size. Since then, he'd seemed to take it in stride. His smarts made up for any deficiencies.

Dorian draped his arm over Mikhail's shoulder and faced him toward the board. Mikhail looked around the room, blinking his eyes as if he were just seeing light. He had beads of sweat on his forehead and moved his tongue over dry lips.

"Mikhail is brilliant," Dorian said to the board, and Mikhail bobbed his head in tacit agreement. "He might even win a Nobel Prize for this discovery. Father let me recruit him from Valley Pharmaceuticals in Indianapolis. We had to fight off their company lawyers, who claimed industrial espionage." He puffed his chest a bit. "I told them what they could do with that claim." Dorian turned to Mikhail. "Mikhail, tell the board how Redex works."

Mikhail stood next to the wall at the head of the long board table, not moving. I thought he was frozen with stage fright. Dorian hit a wall switch, and a blackboard descended from a slit in the ceiling. He handed Mikhail a piece of chalk and rotated him to face the blackboard.

The chemist's hand was shaking. The guy who might be a future Nobel Laureate appeared terrified of public speaking. He began with a wobble in his voice that matched his trembling hand, looking over his shoulder as he wrote.

"There's these enzymes called benzodiabenases that—"

"What's an enzyme?" asked the same banker who had queried about preclinicals.

Mikhail turned to face him, eyebrows creased together. "A protein that

catalyzes—speeds up or makes happen—a chemical reaction in the body."
I thought his tone was patronizing, not a good approach to the group that
controlled the money. There were lots of blank faces, and Dorian butted
in.

"Let me explain," Dorian said. "So one chemical—the enzyme—acts
on another chemical and converts it into a specific product necessary
for the body. Without enzymes, we would die," he said, triggering my
memory of college chemistry. "The enzyme BD, the key player here,
changes a chemical normally found in the body into one that triggers
inflammation and pain. We figured if we could block BD, we could stop
the inflammation and pain."

"Where did this BD enzyme come from?" the banker asked.

"Good question. BD is in the body all the time, but in very low
amounts. Any type of injury—arthritis, for example—makes the body
synthesize more BD as a signal something's wrong. That's where the pain
comes from." Dorian paused, appeared to collect his thoughts.

"So," Mikhail continued, finding his vocal cords, "I also have a degree
in marine biology and have always been interested in the octopus. There's
this fascinating creature, *Wunderpus photogenicus*, found only in the Indo-
Malayan Archipelago. He's a long-armed animal and, like other octopuses,
regenerates a new limb if one is amputated."

I watched the chairman of the biggest construction firm in Washington,
DC, known for his political prowess, fidget in his seat and check his gold
Rolex several times. Finally he sipped from his glass of water, cleared his
throat, and spoke. "All this science is great, and I love the octopus also,
especially fried, but I've an appointment back home tonight, and my plane
is waiting. So please, cut to the chase. What has any of this got to do with
Redex and Sloane Pharmaceuticals?"

Mikhail looked at him with the expression of a teacher confronting
a slow student. "I'm coming to that, if you give me half a chance without
interrupting."

The man, red-faced, snapped his mouth shut and seemed to bite his
tongue.

Mikhail continued. "The unique thing about *Wunderpus* is that it
apparently experiences no pain if it loses an arm. When an octopus gets
upset, its skin becomes red, just like our faces. It's an alarm display triggered
by activating pigment-containing cells called chromatophores." He looked
at the businessman's red face, now turning magenta. "What intrigued
me was that *Wunderpus* remained placid when he lost an arm. No alarm,

so probably no pain. To summarize almost six years of research, I found that *Wunderpus* secreted a substance that blocked BD, and that chemical prevented inflammation and pain."

A few nods of understanding brought a smile to his face. He seemed to relax a bit.

I knew Dorian couldn't afford to lose momentum. He needed the board for a critical vote. He looked at Mikhail. "Come right to the point."

Mikhail's eyes flared, but he complied. "Here's the thing to remember: aspirin and other NSAIDs like ibuprofen or naproxen partially block BD but do it in a way that can cause stomach ulcers and bleeding."

"That must be where Redex comes in?" the banker piped up with a "see-how-smart-I-am" look on his face.

"Yes, exactly, a pure BD inhibitor without that side effect," Mikhail said, his face relaxing. He continued. "I spent much of my career, first in Indianapolis and then the past year at SP, isolating the BD inhibitor from *Wunderpus* to specifically and totally block only that enzyme, eliminate inflammation and pain without upsetting the stomach."

"Aspirin without heartburn," said the banker.

"Or bleeding. Exactly." Mikhail stopped, basking in the shine reflected off their faces. "Dorian's been a believer I could do this, but his father was not."

I stood. "First, Mikhail, let me congratulate you on an incredible body of work. Brilliant, really brilliant." I waved the binder with one hand and pointed at it with the other. "I know you must have spent many late hours creating this drug. You told us there are no stomach side effects, but are there any others?"

Mikhail looked from me to Dorian and back again, perhaps first realizing we were identical twins. Then he smiled. "Good thing you two wear different clothes. What was your question again?"

"Any side effects?"

Mikhail gave me a "do-you-think-I'm-mentally-challenged-or-what" look. "Of course, we considered that. None. No side effects at all. Further, the dose we need to eliminate inflammation and pain is far less than the dose that would create any problems, so complications won't happen—can't happen. We're free at home."

"More than home free," Dorian said, smoothly correcting the slang, taking control of the conversation, and gently pushing Mikhail to the side. "We have, or Mikhail has, hit the proverbial grand-slam homerun."

He stood before the board and raised the white binder before him, like Charlton Heston in *The Ten Commandments.*

"Redex, with this unique mechanism of action, is SP's savior. In addition," he smiled, "my chemists say they can tweak the molecular formula just enough to change Redex without losing effectiveness. We'll claim it's a new drug, get a new patent, a new name, and a different indication. Presto." He snapped his fingers, and the click reverberated in the quiet room. "Redex gives birth to *Painex*—Redex for arthritis and Painex for headaches. And grandsons or granddaughters can extend patent control indefinitely. No look-alike broadsides like we've just lived through."

The rest of the SP board meeting was a bit contentious, but, with my father dead, I watched Dorian take over and sell them his dream, just like my father could. They opened the purse strings on the remaining money in the bank. They also secured a $500 million line of credit from several banks, the lion's share from one in Indianapolis whose chairman was a family friend. The board approved funding for two pivotal clinical trials required by the FDA to validate the Redex concepts. "Once those studies are completed, six months from now," Dorian promised, "FDA'll fast track its approval, and the money will pour in like monsoon rains ending the dry season. By first quarter next year, we'll be back in the black, pay off the loans, and be well positioned for the next ten years at least."

"Back in the black," parroted the banker. "I like that. Ought to make it the Redex slogan."

When the meeting was over, Dorian looked drained. He closed the door to his office, heaved a big sigh, and poured us both a generous Macallan.

He raised his glass at Father's portrait. "Redex will more than double, even triple the sales of any single drug he ever developed. And then will come its offspring, maybe even several generations. He wouldn't even recognize the company he started. Too bad he's not here to see it."

"Yes, he'd like to see his favorite son do well."

"And so would his favorite son." Dorian stood and stretched next to the window, massaging his lower back.

"Stress of the board meeting?"

"Actually, it's a little better. I might have to quit the over-forty basketball league, though, 'cause it's so hard on my back. But I do like keeping in shape and kicking ass. Once Redex is ready, my back pain will be history, and so will some of the ex-NBAers I play with."

A siren from the street below captured our attention. Evening traffic was picking up in midtown Manhattan. Dorian pressed his forehead against the cool pane, looking down at the gathering cars rounding Columbus Circle and cramming into Central Park South. He glanced at his Patek. "Time to drive you to the airport, my dear brother. Don't want you to miss your flight back home to Indy."

CHAPTER SIX

On the flight home to Indianapolis, I reflected on how different our lives had become from those early days of apple fights and Opperman's Pond. I silently wished Dorian well and hoped Redex was the success he thought it would be. We really *were* not at all alike.

We both liked chemistry, Dorian because he saw his future in the family drug company, and me because the effects of drugs on the body fascinated me.

In our senior year at Dartmouth College, professor Fletcher High taught analytical chemistry. He looked like Einstein, with big, clear brown eyes and unkempt, bushy gray hair and eyebrows. He only came up to my shoulders and walked kind of stooped over, I guessed because of arthritis. He'd been at Dartmouth forever and was a good guy, especially with the jocks. He'd give us extra days during basketball season if we were late with an assignment.

But he drew a line in the sand with the last exam dubbed "Name That Drug." We passed it or flunked the course. An F in chemistry killed any chance for medical school.

Fletch handed out glass vials containing an unknown chemical, and we had two hours to identify it. Five students at a time took the exam, sitting widely spaced in front of a bank of instruments. No talking. Dorian's exam was the day after mine.

I studied until three in the morning and drank gallons of coffee, so I was shaky at seven. I had had nightmares about dropping the vial, an automatic failure. My hands shook so badly, I cut myself shaving and showed up at the lab with Kleenex stuck to my neck.

I cradled the flask Fletch gave me with both hands and set it in a test tube rack like a Fabergé egg. In the first hour, I categorized the compound as a poison and spent the second doing tandem chemical analysis to narrow it down. I was pushing the two hours, but Fletch gave me an extra fifteen minutes.

I wrote "strychnine" on a piece of paper, signed and dated it, went to the professor's office, and handed him my paper. I should have figured it might be a poison. Fletch had critiqued police TV episodes often enough, grousing, "That's bullshit. If they only knew what *real* field work was like." He checked the answer against the flow sheet on his desk and gave me a short nod. "Correct. Good job."

I had my final A and celebrated with a few beers. When I returned to the dorm, Dorian was freaking out, pacing up and down in our room, eyes red and pupils dilated.

"I can't do this!" he screamed. "I have no idea how to analyze any of this shit." He grabbed the chemistry book written by Fletch himself, tore it in half at the binding, and tossed the pieces out our second-floor window. "I don't want to work in the family business anyway. Fucking chemistry is bullshit." He collapsed in a chair, head in his hands.

I knew he'd cut a few classes, but I didn't think it was this bad. "Calm down," I said. "I'll help you." I put my hand on his arm, but he shrugged me off.

"I can't," he cried. "Don't you understand? I don't know any of this crap. I've been cheating off your papers all term. I couldn't care less about analyzing chemicals." He jumped up from the chair, his eyes pleading.

"You've been *what?*" I shoved him back down. "What're you talking about?"

"I've been copying your papers, whatever was due. But I can't fudge the final, so there goes medical school. Father'll make me the lowest lackey in the company," he said, heaving himself up and pacing again.

I didn't know what to say. I looked at my brother, his tears welling up.

"You got to help me. Please, Daniel. I saved your ass once."

I put a palm up, fending off Opperman's Pond.

"There's only one way I can pass that final."

"And that is?"

He grabbed me by the shoulders and stared into my eyes. "*Not take it.*"

"You son of a bitch," I said, slapping his hands away. "You absolute son of a bitch! Do you know what you're asking me do? If I'm caught, we'll both be bounced out of Dartmouth so fast—"

He nodded. "Will you? It's the only way I can pass. I promise I'll work hard after this. Only get me through analytical. I'll bust my ass after that."

I stared out the window. I could see the Baker Library tower and guys walking across the quadrangle. I loved this place. How could I cheat like that? It was against everything I held important. But how could I not? I pictured my father ripping into me if Dorian flunked chemistry and didn't get into medical school.

If I was nervous the first time, the second was ten times worse. I had visions of Fletch seeing right through me, of dropping the vial, or tipping over my Bunsen burner and setting the place on fire. When my alarm rang at seven the next morning, I woke up exhausted. I showered and dressed, picked out one of Dorian's shirts, and skipped shaving. I briefly flipped through my chemistry book one more time. Finally I practiced Dorian's signature. He was still asleep when I left.

Fletch passed out vials to five of us scattered throughout the lab. When he came to me, sitting at Dorian's workbench, he stared hard and hesitated. But he said nothing, handed me the vial, and moved on to the next student.

After two and a half hours of testing, I thought I had the solution: arsenic. I carefully checked my results, wrote down the answer, dated it, and signed my brother's name. I went to Fletch's office and stood in front of his desk.

"What do you think, Daniel?" he asked, looking from my paper to me.

"It's Dorian, sir, not Daniel. My brother took the exam yesterday."

"Hmm, interesting," he said, staring at my neck. "Daniel cut himself exactly where you did, on the Adam's apple. Yesterday, a piece of tissue stuck to it, while your cut's already healing."

Legs weak, I started to sweat. "Yes, sir, we used the same razor blade, and both of us got cut." I bit my tongue. *How stupid was that?* I'd never make it as a trial lawyer.

"Maybe you should invest in a new blade," he said, eyes focused on my throat.

"Yes, sir, thank you, I will."

"You know, Daniel—sorry, Dorian—people do strange things under pressure."

He pushed back from his desk and put his feet on a corner, his eyes never leaving my face. He laced his fingers behind his head and tipped back. "As a premed, I'm sure you're aware that a treadmill test exercises the heart to show how it reacts to stress. Exposes underlying weaknesses that can cause a heart attack but don't show up during normal activities."

"Yes, sir, I've read that." I started to shake. I hoped he couldn't spot my throbbing pulse.

"I think emotional pressure, particularly when it's adverse, is a kind of stress test of one's character. Some people fold and expose underlying weaknesses, like the heart does on a treadmill, and some become heroes. Which person are you?"

"I guess I don't know, sir. I haven't had that kind of test yet."

"Haven't you, now?" Fletch said. Our eyes locked, and my throat tightened. "Whatever, I would hope that—Daniel, and you, Dorian, would be the kind of brothers not to cave under that kind of pressure. To do the right thing, whatever the cost."

"Yes, sir. I hope so too." My skin was clammy. I wiped my hands on the sides of my pants.

He took his feet off the desk and sat up straight.

"Life's a long race, Dorian. An expedient decision to solve today's problem may not be the best one for tomorrow. In the final analysis, it's how you finish that counts. The sin's not so much losing the race as not entering at all because you fear you *might* lose."

"Yes, sir."

He returned his attention to my answer sheet and studied it a long time. "Wasn't it arsenic?" I asked, breaking the silence with a quivering voice.

Fletch crossed his legs and looked off into the window before turning back to me. "It was, but that's not the issue, now is it?"

I was so scared I could barely answer. I shook my head the slightest bit. "No, sir."

Fletch pursed his lips over my paper. "Yes, arsenic is the *correct* answer," he murmured almost to himself, tapping my signature with his finger. "But is it the *right* answer?"

Then he watched me for several moments, studying my face. I knew he was deciding what to do.

Fletch had the power to ruin my life—*our* lives. I looked at his fingers, gnarled with arthritis, and thought of the song, "He's Got the Whole World in His Hands." Those hands held our world, with the absolute power of an emperor. Thumbs up or down, gladiator lived or died. All the hours I spent studying would go up in smoke.

He pointed a crooked index finger at me. "I think under the circumstances, even though you turned in the correct answer, *Dorian*, giving you a C would not be too unkind. What do you think?"

My heart, pounding in my chest, slowed, and I exhaled the breath I didn't even know I was holding. "Yes, sir, I think it would be quite acceptable."

"Good. I'm glad you agree with me." He sat back in his chair and intertwined his fingers across his lap. His face was stern, with hints of softness around the eyes, maybe compassion. "Be sure these circumstances don't ever happen again. Hear me?"

"Yes, sir, I do. They won't. I give you my word."

"Remember what I said about how you act under pressure. I think you have what it takes. I'm not certain about your twin. Life's full of stress tests, physical and mental. All kinds, every day. You spend a lifetime building a reputation and in a second can lose it. Don't cave, ever. Don't disappoint me, or most of all, yourself, and make me regret my decision."

"No, sir. I promise I won't."

It was all I could do not to bolt from that office. Dorian and I faced exposure as cheats and certain expulsion, our whole lives branded forever.

I ran back to the room ready to tear my brother apart. But the door to our room was locked, and a plaid tie hung on the doorknob, code for, "I got a girl in bed. Come back in an hour." When I heard that high-pitched chuckle, for the first time I *really* hated my brother.

CHAPTER SEVEN

Jessie and I had an Indianapolis garden wedding with only family invited. We discussed Jewish or Catholic ceremonies and eventually agreed to both: a priest and a rabbi, actually two, since the temple Jessie belonged to had a husband and wife who were both rabbis.

We settled down to jobs at the medical center, she in the operating room, and I in the electrophysiology lab, and bought a house in Carmel, Indiana, just north of Indianapolis. The company's CFO, John Anderson, turned out to be one of my first patients.

A week after the board meeting, John had cardiac arrest while watching his thirteen-year-old reach third base on an infield single but get tagged out stealing home. John had screamed at the umpire and collapsed. The father of the catcher, an off-duty cop, ran for the defibrillator in the trunk of his squad car. He shocked John's heart back to normal so quickly, John told them he wanted to stay and watch his son pitch the next inning. But the EMTs carted him off to the hospital, and Dorian flew him to Indianapolis on the company jet.

"John, I'm ready to trigger sudden death. Any last-minute questions?"

John squirmed on the operating table, frowning with his eyes half-closed. The OR cap sat on his head with a slight tilt, giving him a jaunty look that belied his anxiety. As I spoke, he scrunched his eyes totally shut.

"Like a death row inmate before the lethal injection?" He clenched his fists and licked his lips. "No, nothing, Daniel. But remember, screw up, and I'll kick your ass good." He tried to smile, but he was too scared. Only the corners of his eyes wrinkled.

He squinted at me. "Wait, one last thing. Is this stuff," he nodded at the IV, "truth serum?"

"No, that's pentothal. You're getting propofol."

"The drug that killed Michael Jackson?"

"Yes, but I know how to use it."

"Will I babble?"

"I hope so. Got a honey your wife doesn't know about?"

"Ha, I wish. Just curious."

"Whatever you say is confidential," I said, patting his arm. "And don't worry about kicking my ass. You won't be dead long."

John mumbled something indecipherable through the green plastic oxygen mask my assistant nurse Ginger placed over his nose and mouth.

I knew patients often savored the drama. They forgot the actual procedure with wires in their groin threaded into their heart, but they remembered dying—or thought they did.

"The doc warned me I was going to die ... and then he did it. He actually killed me and brought me back. Just call me Lazarus!"

John would be asleep, but that wouldn't spoil a good family story. *"Yeah, I saw the white light and felt really peaceful. I floated out of my body and met my dead mother-in-law. Finally got to tell her to fuck off! Worth the whole trip. Glad I had a round-trip ticket, though."*

I slowly pushed the propofol into his vein and checked the flashing green lights of both defibrillators. I'd once had a defibrillator fail when I attempted to stop the cardiac arrest I had induced in a young biochemist. I had sent the nurse running into the adjoining cath lab to borrow theirs. The Navy SEALs' warning, "Two is one; one is none," describing the two combat helicopters on the Pakistan mission to kill bin Laden, resonated with me. Always have a backup, whether it was a device or a plan.

"Count to ten, John." He got to five when the milky liquid, often dubbed "milk of amnesia," reached his brain and knocked him out. His face relaxed, and he slept as I set about "killing" him.

I nodded to Ginger. She hit the switch, triggering a tiny amount of electricity through the wire sitting in his heart. The metal electrode delivered the current precisely during a thirty-millisecond window. I always marveled that this insignificant amount of electricity given to the heart did nothing 97 percent of the time but could kill during this ultra-short interval.

Each season, newspaper headlines stunned readers with *commotio cordis*, the tragedy of a healthy young athlete who died when struck in the chest with a baseball or hockey puck during that miniscule 3 percent interval. Almost always, the kid walked off the field rubbing the sore spot on his chest, dying the furthest thing from his mind. Yet, he might have come within a thousandth of a second of doing just that.

This time, John's heart skipped a few beats, shrugged off the electricity, and returned to a regular rhythm.

"Ginger, again. Increase the current a smidge." Not a very precise order, but we'd been doing this dance for a while, and I could count on her to know exactly what I wanted.

Ginger tweaked the output and hit the switch. John's heartbeat bolted from seventy-five to two hundred, then three hundred, and settled in at 550 beats per minute. The ECG on the monitor screen traced the jagged peaks and valleys of a heart beating chaotically like a bag of squiggly worms.

Technically, he was dead.

I had murdered him.

Ventricular fibrillation killed a thousand people every day in the United States. During VF, no blood flowed because the heart, with a belly dancer's undulations, beat too fast to pump. The brain died in three to five minutes, six to eight max.

VF killed the person who collapsed shoveling snow midwinter, erroneously reported by the TV news anchor to have "died of a massive heart attack." Or the traveler who crumpled unconscious in Chicago's O'Hare Airport and was saved by a shock from the wall-mounted automated external defibrillator manned by a complete stranger.

Or that kid hit in the chest with a baseball.

Or John Anderson, angry at the umpire.

But John didn't need the AED this time. The implantable cardioverter defibrillator I had just secured in his chest was his watchdog. I had told him, "The ICD's an emergency room in your chest. It monitors every heartbeat, so if your heart goes too fast or too slow, it will treat it."

Whoom! John's body bucked as fifteen joules of electricity jolted it.

Success. A normal rhythm restored in 7.9 seconds. Some patients wouldn't even get dizzy and might not know their ICD had fired. Others, more tuned to their body's sensations, described a "mule kick in my chest."

Whatever, this was lifesaving therapy at its best. John Anderson, with a 30 percent chance of dying, now had a 99 percent chance of living.

The ICD turned sudden death into sudden life.

Not bad for a device half the size of a cell phone implanted under local anesthesia. I had invented the "C" part of the ICD, the implantable cardioverter, during my first years at UIMC before I went to Africa. I had done it while consulting for a device company, so they got all the money, and I got my name on the patent. That and a signed picture from Vice President Cheney before his heart transplant, thanking me for inventing half of the device in his chest. "You may be a great doctor," Jessie had said when she read Cheney's letter, "but you're sure a shitty businessman!"

"Anything more, Dr. Sloane?" Ginger's voice brought me back to the present.

"Almost finished."

"Want me to talk to his wife? She was chewing her fingernails to the bone before we started."

"Thanks, I will." I tied the last stitch and bandaged the incision. "Done."

I peeled off my gloves and shrugged off the gown. "John can go home in three or four hours. I'll leave a script for pain meds."

She turned from the table where she was busy collecting the instruments I had used. "Have a good weekend. Say hi to Jessie."

Ginger's whole life revolved about this room, I thought as I left the electrophysiology lab. Divorced, she had only a cat named Sheba. She took call 24/7. This morning, I had come in on the tail end of a conversation she was having with a young doctor who was late.

"Patients should never have to wait, unless we're tied up in an emergency," she said. "How would you like it if you knew somebody was going to be sticking a wire in your heart, and the doctor kept you waiting an hour to do it?"

"I overslept," he said. "I was up most of the night." The arrogance in his voice came through. *Who the hell is this nurse lecturing me?* it said.

"Not good enough. Next time, I'll tell Dr. Sloane," she chided. "And that'll be your last time." She was right. A top-notch nurse beat a junior doctor any day. Her dedication was irreplaceable.

CHAPTER EIGHT

A month after we were married, on an afternoon like any other, my office phone rang.

"Sounds like someone important," my secretary said. "He wouldn't leave his name, only that he was a doctor and wanted to talk with you about a patient."

I got calls or e-mails like that from all over the world, someone asking my opinion about how to handle a VIP.

"Put him through."

"Dr. Sloane, I'm Peter Fredericks, the Indiana Pacers' team doctor. I've got a problem, and I need your help."

"Okay, go ahead."

"Maybe you're aware that Randy Jackson, the Pacers' star, sprained his ankle at the end of last season."

"I think the world knows that. Maybe not the whole world, but certainly the basketball world."

"Aha! You're a fan. That's great. But confidentially, the ankle's not healing well. He's been in a cast for months, and it's still swollen and painful. The nonsteroidals kill his stomach and caused some bleeding, so he won't take any. The season's going to start in a couple of months, and we need Randy 100 percent healthy."

"Did you try the NSAIDs with antacids?"

"Yes, ibuprofen and antacids, but that didn't work. I tried others too."

"How about steroids?"

"I did, two five-day courses. His ankle improved but then swelled again as soon as the Medrol stopped. I'm concerned about repeating a second trial of steroids, and he certainly can't take them long-term."

"So, let me guess. You read about Redex and you want me to talk to my brother and get it for your superstar."

"The preliminary results are very impressive. I realize the FDA hasn't approved it yet, but I wondered if we could we get Randy into one of the Redex clinical studies."

"Recruitment's been closed for several months now. They've already got the full quota of patients."

"I was afraid of that."

"How badly do you need the drug?"

"We're desperate. It could determine our entire season. Without Randy, we folded in the play-offs like a bad poker hand, and that's the way the season will be."

"It's possible the FDA would let you use Redex under what's called a 'compassionate use clause,' which permits patients not part of an approved study to receive investigational drugs in exceptional circumstances."

"Could you get Randy the drug? It'd be worth a couple of seats behind the Pacers' bench."

"I'll do what I can. Let me call my brother and get back to you."

Two days later, Randy Jackson started on double doses of Redex, and I had season tickets so close to the Pacers' bench, Jessie and I could overhear the coach and watch him diagram Randy's next moves. It brought back memories of playing basketball at Dartmouth.

Nine months later, Randy was leading the Pacers down the April homestretch to a record-setting league championship. He had totally healed taking Redex. His TV ad-libs about his miracle drug beat any commercials my brother could buy. These sold more pills than the clinical study results, even though a study of three thousand rheumatoid arthritis patients showed Redex beat ibuprofen in relieving joint pain without stomach upset. The second trial in patients with osteoarthritis also labeled Redex the unquestioned winner. Mikhail had been correct; no side effects reported.

And with Redex approved in January by the FDA, Dorian was salivating over early sales, already doubling preliminary estimates.

Jessie's poke in my ribs jarred me back to the game. Randy had scored forty-two points, thirty of them in the first half, and the Pacers were on cruise control with less than two minutes left. The Detroit Pistons, down by eighteen points, weren't trying too hard.

"Did you see that?" she asked.

"See what?"

"Randy stumbled."

"Oh, shit, is it his ankle?"

"His ankle seems fine," Jessie said. She pointed at Randy. "He looked kind of spacey, only for a second, and sort of missed his footing—hard to describe. Maybe I was seeing things."

The Pacers went on to win, and we thought no more about it until the next home game against the Lakers a week later. Randy's play was lackluster, and Kobe Bryant was unstoppable. But late in the fourth quarter, after a steal and full-court driving layup, Randy grabbed onto Lamont for several seconds. I saw his knees buckle and his eyes roll back into his head. The Pacers called a time-out, and the team doctor, Peter Fredericks, ran onto the court.

Jessie and I looked at each other. "What do you think?" I asked.

"I don't know. Temporal lobe seizure?"

Fredericks and Lamont helped Randy to the bench and sat him down in front of us. Randy was drenched in sweat, hanging his head between his legs. The trainer threw a towel over his head and shoulders and got him to take sips of water. After a while, Randy lifted his head and looked around bewildered, blinking and squeezing his eyes open and shut.

"What the hell happened?"

Fredericks answered, "I think you got dizzy for a moment or two. Okay now?" Randy nodded yes. "You want to go back in the game?" Randy said no and sat there, head in his hands, rocking back and forth.

An elegant woman, at least six feet tall, wearing a skintight emerald-green knit dress, strode to the bench. A large silver disk hung from a chain around her neck, bouncing on her ample chest. She moved quickly but gracefully, a model on a runway. Her knee-high, tawny leather boots clacked like castanets on the hardwood floor.

"Wow! Look at those boots! Manolo Blahnik. Over $1,600," Jessie said, pointing. She waggled her finger at her own feet. "Knockoff Uggs. Wal-Mart. Ninety-nine dollars on sale."

She was ebony black with a high forehead, big almond eyes, a generous mouth painted crimson, and a single braid of black hair trailing almost to her waist. I thought of a regal Aida at the Metropolitan Opera. She leaned over Randy, and he gave her a tight smile.

"Are you okay?" the woman asked. I heard Randy mumble something.

The woman stood and turned to the team doctor. "Peter, what's going on? What happened to my husband?"

"I don't know, Crystal. He just stumbled."

Her angry eyes flashed. "It was more than a stumble. I saw that much. You're the doctor. You should know what's wrong with him. That's what you're paid to do." Her harsh tone belied the elegant appearance. She tossed her head, setting emerald teardrop earrings in motion.

"Calm down, Crystal. Calm down. Randy's fine now. We'll figure this out later. Meantime, you have to get off the court."

One of the referees walked over, pointed at her, and jerked his thumb toward the exit. "Please go back to your suite."

She studied Randy's face for an instant, pecked him on the cheek, and clattered off.

"What do you make of all that?" Jessie asked.

"The woman or the episode?"

"The woman's obviously his wife. I meant the episode," Jessie said.

"I don't know, but he didn't look good."

"I agree. Vasovagal?" Jessie asked.

"A faint in the middle of a ball game, after a full-court run? Possible but unlikely," I said.

"But it *is* possible."

"More likely an arrhythmia or an epileptic seizure," I said.

The *Indianapolis Star's* headline the next morning questioned, "Pacers shooting star up in flames?" The article quoted Fredericks strongly denying any health problems. Interest in a famous Hollywood couple's breakup reclaimed the headlines until two weeks later after a game against San Antonio.

Randy was standing alone midcourt. Even from where I sat, I could see he looked glassy-eyed, dazed. He took a few faltering steps to his left and stared at the ceiling. Then he flailed his arms and collapsed to his knees, falling face forward. His head hit the hardwood floor with a sickening thud. The trainer and Fredericks ran to him, and he struggled to sit, both hands pushing up from the floor. Randy shook his head like a boxer nailed by a vicious right hook. But he went down again, on his back, his arms and legs twitching in a sort of seizure.

Jessie and I were about to run on court when he sat up, combed both hands through his hair, and spoke to the doctor. Blood welled from a bruise on his forehead. The incident passed as abruptly as it had started. He was fine again but went straight to the lockers.

The next day, papers reported that Randy had a seizure and Fredericks was sending him to the famed Rochester Clinic in Minnesota for a complete evaluation.

Four days later, just before Jessie and I turned out the lights to go to sleep, the phone rang.

"Dr. Sloane?"

"Yes."

"This is Crystal Jackson, Randy Jackson's wife."

I sat up straight, fully awake in an instant. "Wife of *the* Randy Jackson?" That woke Jessie, and she sat up staring at me, wide-eyed, mouth open.

I heard Crystal Jackson laugh into the phone and say something to someone else nearby. "The very same. I got your phone number from Peter Fredericks. I'm sorry to be calling so late at night."

"That's okay. How can I help you?" I held the receiver out so Jessie could listen.

"You know Randy's been at the Rochester Clinic?"

"So I read in the papers."

"Dr. Sloane, tomorrow morning's paper will have an article about my husband. He's been evaluated by an onslaught of Rochester Clinic doctors, from neurologists to surgeons to electrophysiologists, to—well, you name the specialty, and they've seen him. He's had every test known to science and is absolutely worn out. He's been stuck so many times—"

"That he's a pincushion," I finished for her. "I can imagine. Sorry about that."

"Of course it's not your fault. But this Dream Team, that's what the press is calling them, has decided Randy is seriously ill and needs some sort of a fancy pacemaker, the kind Cheney got years ago."

"An implantable cardioverter defibrillator?" I asked.

"Yes, that's it. They called it an ICD and said he was through playing basketball."

"What did they say was wrong?"

"A fast heartbeat causing the spells."

"Did they explain what it is?" Knowing the doctors at the Rochester

Clinic, I was certain they had. But patients sometimes don't absorb the information.

"They said it was first cousin to cardiac arrest, but slower, about two hundred a minute."

"Ventricular tachycardia?"

"Yes, that's it."

"Did they record the ventricular tachycardia?"

"He's been on a heart monitor since we arrived, and he's had a few beats of this ventricular thing, maybe three or four. But each time he's felt fine. Nothing like during the game. And then he had one brief dizzy spell, said he was about to black out, but his ECG was fine with no ventricular beats."

"So it's hard to blame the spells on the ventricular tachycardia."

"Exactly what I was thinking. Now, I went on the Internet—that's where I found your name, right in our hometown—and read that some athletes can have a few ventricular beats normally and it's no big deal. In fact, you wrote that in one of your articles."

"Correct. It can happen."

"Well, the Rochester Clinic docs didn't think it was normal, so they did a study running wires up his leg and into his heart and tried to start up the fast heartbeat."

"What happened?"

"They couldn't start anything."

"That makes ventricular tachycardia less likely."

"Then they attached him to some sort of a table, almost like an ironing board, and kept him upright for half an hour."

"That's called a tilt table test, to diagnose ordinary fainting spells. What happened?"

"He started to black out like he did on court. So they called it a positive test, but then they said they still wanted to implant this ICD thing to be on the safe side. They said he could be having the fast heartbeats that could kill him even if they couldn't start it with that wire."

"Despite the positive tilt test?"

"Yes, they said those results could be misleading, especially in well-conditioned athletes."

She paused and said, "Just a minute," to someone. "Sorry, I'm talking to Randy. He wants to check out of the hospital now."

"Have you discussed leaving with any of the doctors there?"

"No, they're hell-bent on putting in this ICD. If we let them, Randy's basketball days are probably over. I won't permit that, not in my man."

"Are any of the doctors there now?"

"They just called a press conference and gave their diagnosis to the reporters without even telling us. You'll see that on CNN tonight at eleven and in the morning papers tomorrow."

"What do you want me to do?"

"I want to fly Randy back to Indy immediately and have you examine him. I didn't realize you're as world-famous as these guys at Rochester—maybe even more. We should've stayed right in town. If you agree he needs an ICD, so be it. But if you don't, the hell with this Dream Team, and let's keep playing basketball."

"Immediately, as in right now?" I looked at the clock. It was ten minutes to eleven.

"Our plane's ready, and the car's parked outside, motor running."

"You didn't give me much warning."

"Same as the Rochester Clinic doctors gave us."

Their plane arrived close to 2:00 a.m. It was after 3:00 before I had Randy admitted to the hospital and on a monitor in the CCU. It was too late for any kind of workup, so I tucked him into bed. Crystal stayed, and I went home.

CHAPTER NINE

I dialed my brother's private line. We hadn't talked in almost a month. He picked up on the first ring. At home, Jessie and I fought over who would *not* answer the phone because the ring usually meant we had to stop whatever we were doing and get to the hospital.

"Hey, Daniel. What's going on, little bro?"

"I need a favor," I said.

"Name it."

"In a minute. First, you doing okay?" I asked. "How's Sheila?"

"In transition. Both of us are talking to lawyers. But now's not a good time to split. It's too fucking expensive, despite the prenup. I'm worth too much, thanks to Redex.

"So the stock's doing well?"

"Through the roof. Up ten points this week. We've made back what the generics cost us and are repaying the loans."

"Did you buy that new yacht yet?"

"It's on order, delivery after the divorce. You can afford one too. You're worth 20 percent more than a month ago."

"Nice. I'll sell some stock and go sailing."

"How's the Pacers' star doing? The *Times* this morning quotes the Rochester Clinic Dream Team saying he's retiring from basketball. True?"

"That's one of the reasons I called. Confidentially, he's my patient."

"No kidding! He's my idol. A real basketball legend. If only Father hadn't convinced me to be a doctor—"

"You would've become a basketball great. I've heard that as often as you saving my life at Opperman's Pond. Come for a visit, and I'll introduce you."

"Been real busy with Redex. I'm taking it myself when the guys beat me up at basketball. I feel so good we could market it to replace Viagra."

"Careful. Nonspousal sex is stressful. Remember Nelson Rockefeller and Happy?"

"Ah, yes, but he was at least seventy by then. When you're young, it's *good* stress, the best kind, especially with a mistress. So tell me about Randy Jackson. What's happening?"

I told him what I knew, totally violating patient confidentiality.

"No coke or stuff like that? Some of the energy drinks cause arrhythmias."

"We're only starting the workup, and I don't have all the answers yet. Recreational drugs are always a possibility. I'm sure he's had plenty of opportunity, but frankly, he's not the type. There was a rumor his mother was a cocaine addict, but not him."

"So what's next? You going with the ICD like the Rochester guys recommended?"

"Not yet. My Rochester counterpart, a guy I trust, said this whole thing's been blown out of proportion. They were only discussing the ICD, not recommending it, and one of the Dream Team renegades looking for his fifteen minutes of fame called the press conference. My friend tried to stop the Jacksons from leaving, but they were so pissed, nothing was going to keep them at Rochester."

"Let that be a lesson," Dorian said, "and stay away from the press. Nothing but trouble. You can't hide when you're taking care of VIPs because their spotlight catches everybody. So, if you're boffing some young chick when Jessie's in the OR, the press'll find her and name you father of her brat."

"Thanks for the counsel. I knew I could count on your sage advice. But I don't need to worry."

"Never can tell. And watch out for Randy's wife. I heard that after a sponsor reneged on a multimillion-dollar endorsement two years ago, Crystal hexed him, stuck pins in a look-alike doll, and chanted voodoo spells on YouTube. A week later, the CEO died in a head-on car crash when a drunk ran a red light. The press jumped all over that, and websites popped up offering Wanga doll look-alikes of your favorite enemy for a hundred bucks. Pins were extra."

"You're real helpful." But the thought triggered a flash of the Maasai curse. I shivered. "That's not why I called." I paused. "How good's your basketball?"

"What do you mean?"

"Are you as good as you keep telling me?"

"Better. I whip those over-forty guys routinely. Even the two ex-pros. Why?"

"How would you like to play a real professional, one-on-one?"

"What are you getting at?" A hint of excitement crept into his voice. "Hey, wait. You're thinking ... no, you can't mean Randy Jackson? Holy shit!"

"Think you could do it?"

"You gotta be kidding."

"I'm deadly serious."

"When?"

"Tomorrow, if you're not too busy."

"I'll drop everything and fly in tonight on the company plane."

"What about Redex?"

"It'll survive a day without me."

I laughed. "I thought you might feel that way. We'll prepare the guest bedroom."

CHAPTER TEN

The next morning in the UIMC hospital, I sat on the edge of the bed as Randy moved his long legs over to make room. Crystal curled in an armchair, legs tucked beneath her. The silver disk hung from her neck. I could see engravings, but they made no sense to me. Her long braid was coiled around her head like a crown. The fringe of dark eyelashes and black eyeliner enhanced a feline appearance, and I sensed the feral cunning of an alley cat beneath the elegant exterior.

"So what've you learned?" Randy asked in a soft voice. His gentle, almost humble demeanor was not what I expected from a guy whose last season set a Pacers' scoring record and rewrote the NBA record book with the most assists, rebounds, and steals.

But if Randy was the lamb, Crystal was the tigress, ready to protect her mate. The press had dubbed her "Crystal the Pistol." People knew not to mess with *him* if you didn't want *her* in your face.

I rested a hand lightly on his knee. I like to be physically close to my patients when I discuss their problems. Ten years ago, as I lay on a CT table with a hot appendix, I only wished for someone—*anyone*, tech, nurse, doctor—to rest a hand on me and say, "You're going to be fine. We'll have that appendix out in a jiffy." The physical comfort of a light touch and pleasant words, even to a physician knowing what was going to happen, still mattered.

Randy shifted his feet and jolted me back to the present. "Randy, I've read through the Rochester records twice and reanalyzed their test results. As expected, they did a very thorough job."

"They sure ran a lot of tests."

I nodded. "But we still don't have a diagnosis. Your heart echo was normal, and the calcium score was low, so coronary disease is unlikely."

"What's that?"

"Obstructions in the arteries to the heart. Atherosclerosis stuff. And I

51

wouldn't expect any in an active twenty-seven-year-old whose cholesterol's perfectly normal. Anyone in your family with heart attacks?"

He shook his head no. "Our two kids are healthy, and I have no brothers. My father's alive at seventy and still plays some basketball, pickup games and stuff. He acts like he's fifty. Got a new girlfriend every week."

"That's for sure." Crystal frowned. "Sleeps with anybody in a skirt," she muttered. Randy frowned at her.

"Any family history of heart trouble?"

Another negative.

"What did the Rochester people say about epilepsy causing seizures?" Crystal asked.

"Randy's brainwaves and MRI were totally normal."

"So that leaves the ventricular stuff?" she asked, unwrapping her legs and pulling her chair closer.

"Rochester's records show four bursts of three or four heartbeats, each at the rate of about two hundred per minute. That's too short to produce symptoms. Also, as you told me, Randy had a dizzy spell like he did on court, but his heart rhythm was perfectly normal. And the positive tilt test fits with an ordinary faint. All that's against ventricular tachycardia."

"So no ICD, and I keep playing ball?" Randy asked, smiling. He put his hands behind his head. Sharply defined biceps and triceps rippled. He was one of the few NBA players with no tattoos.

"Probably, but VT can come and go. It's still a possibility."

"You're supposed to be the pro here." Crystal pointed a manicured finger in my face. The facets of her large white diamond reflected rainbow colors in the overhead light. Her long nails, painted black, glittered with sparklers. "What's going on then?"

"Crystal, take it easy," Randy said, patting her shoulder. "Dr. Sloane's doing the best he can. We only got here last night."

"Sorry," she said with a phony look of contrition.

"I understand your concern. We're trying to balance the career of maybe the greatest basketball player ever against the possibility of an arrhythmia that could kill him. Not a fair deal."

"So what's next?" Randy asked.

"The treadmill stress test at Rochester was normal. But playing basketball is different, with sudden starts and stops, not like on a treadmill. If we have you play basketball while recording your ECG, we might be able to provoke a spell and diagnose VT they might've missed."

"And how're you going to do that?" Crystal asked. "The press'll be crawling all over us. As it is, I had to leave the phone off the hook last night, and the hospital room has an unlisted number."

She stood and paced in front of Randy's bed, hands on hips, face defiant, protecting her mate.

I followed her with my eyes. "Exactly what I've been concerned about."

"More importantly," Randy said, "it wouldn't be fair to my teammates for me to play rigged with some sort of an ECG machine, worried I might have a cardiac arrest or something. I can't give it 100 percent."

"We can't do this during a regular game. It has to be something private," I said. "Only us."

"Like how?" Crystal asked in an accusing voice, stopping her pacing long enough to again point her finger at me.

"Hear me out," I said. "This just might work."

"I'm thrilled, but why me and not a Pacers' teammate?" my brother asked after I picked him up at the Indianapolis airport.

"Because with another pro, even a Pacer, word would leak out, and the press would be all over us. I want no spotlights until I have a solid diagnosis and treatment plan. I can rent a local basketball court. We slip in unnoticed, and Randy and you go one-on-one until one of you quits."

"And guess who that'll be?"

CHAPTER ELEVEN

The next day, TV cameras blanketed the hospital. I asked a tall African American physician friend, hat pulled low, to wear Randy's Pacers warm-up jacket. Hospital staff in white coats surrounded him, and I directed the entire entourage to walk slowly out the main hospital entrance. Press, TV, and fans were there, drawn like iron filings to a magnet.

We waited a moment and then slipped out the Emergency Department exit into a waiting black Cadillac Escalade.

"Introductions later," I said, sliding into the front seat, and they into the back. "Dorian, just drive away."

I turned around. "Randy, you and Crystal duck your heads for a few minutes. We'll be out of here in a jiffy."

I gave my brother directions to the gym a mile from my home in Carmel. I had reserved it for three hours.

Twenty minutes later, we parked the SUV in the lot around the back and spilled out. "Randy and Crystal, this is my twin, Dorian. He's CEO of Sloane Pharmaceuticals, which supplied the Redex."

"A pleasure to meet you, Dr. Sloane," said Randy, shaking hands. "And thanks for the miracle cure."

"No titles," I said. "Only Dorian and Daniel."

"How do we tell you apart?" Crystal asked, looking from Dorian to me.

"I'm the good-looking one," we said simultaneously. Everybody laughed. We'd been there before.

I shepherded everyone inside the empty gym. "The scam got us out, but reporters are sure to be looking for us by now."

We entered a dim hallway with a small refreshment stand on the left, a half-spilled popcorn bag and empty Coke bottle still on the counter. Popcorn mashed into the floor looked like dirty snow on a dark rug. The hall smelled of old sweat and new air freshener. Double doors on the right opened into a well-lit, full-sized basketball court.

Randy pushed through and looked around, eyebrows raised. After a slow three-sixty, he walked to the basket and jumped to touch the rim. "Close enough to ten feet," he said. "Should work okay."

"Remember, Randy, this isn't the Conseco Fieldhouse. We're here—"

"I know, I know," he said with the first show of impatience. "Let's get on with it, man."

He had to be stressed, poor guy, about to play a forty-year-old amateur in a pickup game that might decide his professional career.

Crystal put a finger on his lips, kissed his cheek.

"We *will* get on with it, baby, we will. Last test, I promise, and then you'll be back playing like before. We're almost there."

He blinked back tears, and she stroked his face with both hands. His smile seemed forced as he bent to kiss her lips.

Both Randy and Dorian wore sneakers and peeled off warm-up pants to basketball shorts underneath. When they took off their sweatshirts, we all burst out laughing. They both wore Randy's blue-and-gold jersey, with number 31 and his name across the back.

"We won't be able to tell who's scoring," I said.

"Ha," snorted my brother.

Ginger, my nurse, had arrived earlier. She brought over the portable electrocardiogram transmitter, about the size of a cell phone. Tiny wires ran from it to white adhesive patches, to be stuck on Randy's chest.

"Randy, Ginger's my assistant. She's going to hook you to this ECG transmitter. It'll fit in the small of your back and be held in place with this belt." I held it up for him to see. "You won't even know it's there. The transmitter sends your ECG to that computer," I said, pointing to a table Ginger had set up halfway down the court on the sidelines, "where I'll be monitoring each heartbeat. If I see anything dangerous, I'll blow the whistle. No whistle, just keep playing and, I assume, whipping my brother's butt."

Randy draped his arm over Dorian's shoulders and looked him in the eye. His expression was kind. "Thanks for doing this. I appreciate it."

Dorian's face beamed. "My pleasure to play ball with you," he said in a small voice.

After they stretched and warmed up for fifteen minutes, I said, "Okay, guys, let's get going. Remember, this is a hard workout, so pull out all the stops. I'm not interested in the score"—their eyebrows rose—"even though you two might be. I only want Randy's adrenaline flowing to see what happens. Try for as little body contact as possible. We don't want anyone hurt."

They both smiled and shook hands center court like a couple of prizefighters starting fifteen rounds. Randy tossed the ball to Dorian. "Take it inbounds. I'll defend that basket," he said, pointing down court.

And so they went at it, up and down the court, driving for the basket, pulling up short for a jumper, faking moves, behind-the-back dribbles, fighting for a rebound, whatever it took. My brother was in good shape and kept up, although Randy outscored him at least two to one.

I sat glued to the computer screen, Ginger on one side, and Crystal on the other. The only heart rhythm Randy developed was a sinus tachycardia, a normal increase, to the 130s, with no symptoms.

After fifteen minutes, I called a break. They came to the sidelines, panting for breath and chugging Gatorade.

Randy stared at my computer, watching his heartbeat dance across the screen.

"That me?"

"Yes, completely normal," I said.

"Good on one hand, bad on the other."

"True, but better to have a normal heart rhythm. We'll find out what's going on. Just give it time."

They sat in the stands and chatted as their breathing returned to normal. "You guys ready for another go?"

Both came onto the court again. Dorian grabbed the basketball out of my hands before Randy was ready and tore down the court for an easy layup.

"Did you see that, folks?" he shouted into his fist, an imaginary microphone. "An old Ivy Leaguer scores an easy two points on the Great One."

"Yeah, and it'll be his last two in this lifetime," Randy said, snatching the basketball.

They started once more, this time with easy bantering, teasing each other, each goading the other into a higher level of play.

"C'mon, kid," Dorian said. "Where's this super athlete of the year I keep reading about? Has to play an old man to run up the score?" Dorian stripped the ball from Randy's hands again and ran to the basket for another layup.

"Sonofabitch!" Randy yelled, tearing after him and racing half-court to block his shot. With each stride, Randy closed the gap, reaching my brother a step before he released the ball. They leaped for the basket together, Randy stretching a long arm over Dorian's shoulder, and came down in a tangle of bodies. Dorian jumped up and bent to give Randy a hand. But Randy didn't move. I looked at the screen. Nothing but static. The ECG recording was lost. I heard Crystal scream.

I grabbed the defibrillator and yelled at Ginger, "Bring the crash cart!" We ran to the end of the court. Dorian was standing over Randy, whose arms and legs were twitching as we had seen before. But he wasn't getting up.

I reached him as his eyes came back into his head. He began purposeful movements, shaking his head to clear cobwebs. I attached defibrillator pads, but by that time, the recording was normal. Any VT, if it had been there, was gone.

"Shit," was all I could say.

Dorian helped Randy stand. "You okay?"

Crystal put her arms around him for support.

"I am now. I wasn't a minute ago. Same feeling as before."

"I know, and we missed it because one of the wires came loose."

Before I could suggest a second try, we heard pounding on the door to the gym. I could make out a crowd of people through the opaque glass on the top half of the door.

We all stared at each other, frozen in place. "What the hell are we going to do?" Dorian asked.

"Damn! I should've thought of this earlier." I scanned the gym. There was no place to hide. Then I spotted restroom signs. "Ginger, into the ladies' room with the monitoring gear and defibrillator. Put everything on the crash cart and go. Now! Before they tear the door down!" The pounding was getting louder, but the lock held.

She ran off, pushing the cart. "Okay, we let them in, and the story is, Randy needed a little workout. Dorian, you were visiting me, you supplied the drug that cured him, and because you were a basketball buff, Randy thought it would be fun to give you a chance to shoot some hoops as a thank-you. Crystal came along to watch." I looked at their faces. "Plausible? Will it work?" I asked.

They all nodded. I opened the door to the press mob.

CHAPTER TWELVE

Long faces filled Randy's hospital room.

"Dr. Sloane—Daniel, I can't take any more of this," Randy said, lying back on his bed. "I was all keyed up for an answer today, one way or the other, and now we still don't know."

I sat on one side of the bed. Crystal crowded in on the other, nestling against her husband, her head on the pillow alongside his. Her body offered him comfort, but her eyes were on fire, blazing at me.

"I'm sorry, Randy, we were very close. But without recording your heartbeat during a spell, I can't make a diagnosis. You could still be having the VT, which, as the Rochester guys explained, can kill you."

"Suppose I play all my games with a defibrillator and a doctor courtside?"

I stood and looked at both of them.

"Randy, let's be clear about this. While the VT is more likely to occur while you're playing ball, it could happen anytime. You could be at home watching TV, at a movie, making love. It's not only during basketball. Yes, I want you to be able to play basketball, but more importantly, I want to keep you alive. Of course, if it's not VT and only a faint, then I don't want you a cardiac invalid, worrying all the time whether you're going to die. And we certainly don't want to implant an ICD if you don't need one."

"Why not? What's the problem with that?"

"It's not that simple. ICDs can have complications."

"Such as?"

"Such as giving you a shock when you don't need one, and *causing* a heart rhythm problem. And we don't know how well they work for an athlete during competition."

Randy leaned his head back on the pillow and shut his eyes. His arms were rigid at his sides, fists balled. His mouth creased into a straight line, and his lips, clenched tight together, blanched. He shook his head and mouthed, "Fuck."

Crystal sat up and challenged me. "You're the hotshot doc with the big-city reputation, supposed to have the answers. What's next? We'll never get away with another basketball game."

"Well, there's one more test we should do. They didn't do it at Rochester, and we haven't done it here because of Randy's young age and negative family history, the calcium score, and normal echo. That's a heart catheterization."

"What's that?" Randy and Crystal asked simultaneously.

"We run a tube up your leg artery, sort of like the study you had at Rochester, put it in your heart, and inject dye to take a picture of how well your heart contracts—"

"Wait a minute," Crystal interrupted, the accusatory finger waggling. "I thought that's what the echo did, showed his heart contracted normally."

"You're right, it—"

"Then why repeat the test? I get the feeling you're groping, Doctor."

"Not really. We'd also take pictures of the coronary arteries to be sure there are no obstructions."

Crystal jumped off the bed. "You already told us blockages were highly unlikely because there was no calcium and no family history. You using my husband for a guinea pig, Doctor? Maybe run up your charges? Ride the back of this basketball star?"

I bit my tongue, seeing how upset she was. "Crystal, you should know better than that. I'm only trying to be sure we've studied all possibilities. There could be obstructions even with no calcium."

Randy opened his eyes, sat up in bed, looked first at Crystal and then me. "We're finished here, Dr. Sloane. I'm leaving. Now."

"Randy, wait—"

He swung his feet off the side of the bed and stood. "I appreciate all you've done, and the guys at Rochester too. I really do. But I've had it. At least for now. Maybe I'll come back in a few days, or a few weeks, and let you do that catheterization or whatever else, but I've got to get out of here today. I'm going stir crazy."

"I understand, Randy. It's your decision. I can only advise you. And I'm telling you that you shouldn't leave yet. Not until we've finished and have a diagnosis."

Randy already had his back to me, emptying out the few things in the closet and laying them on the bed.

"Crystal, maybe you can reason with him."

She gave me her best tigress look, eyes squinting and fists tight. "He's made his mind up, but you better be right on this."

"Me? Hold on, Crystal. First, don't threaten me. Second, I'm giving you my best advice. He's the one who's decided—"

"Based on the information you've given him."

"You check out AMA and—"

"What's that?"

"Against medical advice."

"And what happens?"

"Your insurance won't cover hospital expenses."

"Big deal. And?"

"And I'll resign as your physician."

Randy jumped in. "Doc, I want you to continue. Just give me a few days home, and I'll come back. I promise."

This was a losing battle. "Promise me one thing. *Under no circumstances are you to play basketball until we've made a diagnosis.* Until we do the heart catheterization and decide what to do. Are we clear on that?"

"I hear you."

"I also think you should be taking a medication that—"

"No drugs," Crystal said, putting up a hand to stop traffic. "Uh, uh. No. You don't know what in hell's going on, and you want to treat him with drugs?"

"It's called a beta-blocker, blocks the effect of adrenaline. It's very safe and could be useful for the fainting as well as the VT."

"And if it blocks adrenaline, what effect will it have on his performance?"

"I don't know."

"Is it approved by the NBA?"

"I don't know that either."

"You don't know the answer to two critical questions, but you want my husband to take this beta-blocker. You do remember he's a *professional* athlete? Like, he gets paid real money, real *big* money, for his performance? And that performance has to be good. Not only good, but great."

Randy walked over and put his hands on her shoulders. "It's okay, Crystal. Let him write the prescription."

"Look, Crystal," I said, my patience wearing thin. "I know you only want what's best for your husband. So do I. But remember, we're dealing with blackouts that could be life threatening. I understand Randy doesn't want to complete the workup now, but he should be taking a medicine that might prevent future episodes."

"Please write it, Doc," Randy said.

I wrote the prescription and handed it to him. He promptly passed it to Crystal. She crammed it into her purse.

"One last thing, Randy, before you go. We've got to tell the press something," I said to his back as he finished packing.

Crystal stood in front of me, hands waving for me to focus on her. She pointed her forefinger at me with thumb up, a pistol. "Here's what you tell them, so listen carefully, Doctor. You tell them in no uncertain terms Randy Jackson's fine, he's healthy, and he's coming back to play basketball soon. You tell them anything else, and I'll sue your ass from here to Timbuktu. You got that?"

"Easy, Crystal," Randy said. "He's only doing his job."

That afternoon it seemed like the entire sports world of reporters and TV stations crowded into the hospital auditorium. Randy and I sat on stage with the dean of the medical school, Jim Hazelton, who introduced me to the media and sat down. The dean was a tall, skinny guy with an ill-fitting brown toupee, brown eyes, and a brown suit. I took the microphone and faced the crowd. This was not my usual venue for giving scientific lectures, and my heart raced a bit as I addressed the press.

"Randy Jackson's had a thorough workup at two outstanding medical institutions by the best doctors available. He has what's called an athlete's heart, a slight enlargement—"

Crystal was staring at me, shaking her head.

"From all the physical conditioning that commonly occurs in world-class athletes. It's nothing to worry about and can be normal in such situations.

"He's had a few irregular heartbeats that also can be normal in athletes. The most likely explanation for his spells is what's called neurocardiogenic syncope—in laymen's terms, a common faint. That's the only diagnosis we can make with certainty at the present time."

"So can he return to basketball?" asked the *Sports Illustrated* reporter.

"Not immediately, but very soon."

"No restrictions?" from the *Washington Post*.

I caught Crystal's eye. She was squinting, eyes half-closed, and giving me a look I could only call evil. She fingered the silver disk around her neck. I pictured her sticking pins into my look-alike doll and my body recoiling in pain.

"Too early to tell for sure, but probably none."

"If I understand you correctly, Doctor," a tall man, well dressed in suit and tie, stood and spoke with some assurance, "this event you labeled neurocardiogenic syncope happened in a twenty-seven-year-old top athlete in the peak of physical condition running full court for a layup. Correct?" The reporter didn't wait for me to answer and continued. "This is the very same event that happens to the little, old lady in a hot and crowded church who stands up too suddenly after a long and boring Sunday sermon. Do I have that right?"

The dean whispered behind me, "Medical reporter for the *New York Times*, but also a doctor. Name's David Armstrong."

I shrugged. "It may sound farfetched, but yes, that's the best explanation we can come up with. The same disease process can affect diverse individuals. You wouldn't question the diagnosis of cancer or pneumonia in a child and an octogenarian. Fainting can occur in people of different backgrounds." I paused. "Does that answer your question?"

He shook his head. "No, but thanks for trying," he said and sat down.

The dean took the mike and motioned me to take my seat. "Thank you all for coming. This concludes the press conference. If we have statements in the future, we'll let you know."

"Does Randy Jackson have anything to say?" someone shouted. All heads turned to him.

Randy looked at Crystal offstage. She nodded slightly, and he shuffled to the center of the stage. He may have been a superstar on the hardwoods, but he seemed uncomfortable here. The dean handed him the microphone. Randy's face was grim.

"First, I want to thank all the doctors at Rochester and Dr. Sloane here," he turned and tipped his head in my direction, "for all they did for me. I think I'm fine now and am ready to get back to playing basketball with the Pacers."

"When will that be?"

"As soon as I can. That's all I have to say. Thanks." He waved to the audience, turned, and walked off the stage. Crystal was waiting for him. They left hand-in-hand.

CHAPTER THIRTEEN

"He died! He's dead!" Jessie screamed as she ran in, grabbing the remote. She switched from ESPN to CNN. "I just heard it when I was on the treadmill."

I struggled to sit up on the couch, where I had dozed off after somebody scored against the Indianapolis Colts. "Who died?" I asked, still groggy from sleep.

"Randy Jackson!"

In the space of a few minutes, all hell broke loose. The phone rang, the computer dinged with e-mails and Facebook notices, and my cell buzzed with text messages. Somebody rang the doorbell and pounded when I didn't answer.

The announcer went on, "... interrupt with this story just hitting the wires. Randy Jackson, Pacers legendary star, died an hour ago at age twenty-seven in Carmel, Indiana. Apparently, he and a group of friends played an unscheduled pickup basketball game in a rented gym north of Indianapolis. Competing full court for about twenty minutes, Jackson stopped, clutched his chest, groaned, and fell to the floor, unconscious. A teammate dialed 911 while the others administered mouth-to-mouth breathing and chest compressions. An emergency crew arrived nine minutes later and found him in cardiac arrest from an ultra-rapid heart rhythm called ventricular fibrillation. They shocked his heart several times but could not bring him back. Resuscitation attempts continued on the way to Northern Hospital, where he was pronounced dead at 4:22 this afternoon. We have no news yet of funeral arrangements.

"Jackson had just received a full workup and, in a widely viewed press conference, was pronounced fit to return to basketball, according to his doctor, Daniel Sloane, a cardiologist at the University of Indiana Medical Center in Indianapolis. Preliminary interviews with his friends at the scene indicate Jackson told them Sloane had given him a clean bill of health to play basketball. More later as additional information rolls in."

The buzz of a helicopter overhead drew me to the window. A line of cars snaked into our small street and parked at the curb. Three news vans, coiled antennas searching skyward, drove as close as they could.

The shrill clang from my beeper jolted me. It was Dean Jim Hazelton. *Call immediately*. I dialed that number first.

"Jim, Daniel here."

He started yelling in my ear.

"Whoa, slow down. I don't have the foggiest idea what happened. I just saw the news on CNN … No, I expressly told him *not* to play basketball until I had completed the workup. He knew that. So did his wife. I wanted to cath him. Crystal was standing there when I told him."

The dean went on about the press interview.

"I thought I was very careful. You heard it all, for Christ's sake. If you had a problem, you could've said something. You heard me say he *probably* could return to basketball, but not immediately. The workup was incomplete. The only definite diagnosis was neurocardiogenic syncope, but that didn't exclude VT. Randy and Crystal both knew that. I can't help it if the press got different ideas."

Shit, I thought. This was exactly what Dorian had warned about.

Jessie tugged my arm. "Crystal's on the other line," she mouthed.

"Jim, I've got to go. His wife's on the other line."

I hung up and switched over. "Crystal, I'm so sorry—"

"You fucking son of a bitch!" she screamed so loud Jessie heard her. "You killed my husband! You killed Randy!" She was sobbing uncontrollably. "I'll get you for this, I promise you that. You'll pay for killing my Randy, I swear to Christ. *You fucking bastard, you will die for this.*"

"Wait, Crystal, listen to me."

"He trusted you!" she shouted. "*I* trusted you. You told him he'd be okay, it was only a faint, and he could still play. I heard you say that in his hospital room, you lying bastard. I heard you say that—I heard you—" Her voice trailed off into sobs, and someone hung up the phone.

The hammering on the front door had stopped and then started again. I opened the door to a Channel 8 TV reporter and cameraman. Before either of us said anything, a guy jumped from his car, ran to the house, and heaved a rock through the picture window. The cameraman swung to catch the action, and I pushed the reporter away. I slammed the door and bolted it.

In the living room, a cantaloupe-sized boulder wrapped in a sheet of white paper lay on the rug in a pile of shattered glass. I grabbed it and ducked away from the windows.

You murdered randy, you bastard. We will murder you.

A shotgun blast, like a giant firecracker followed by breaking glass, blew out the rest of the picture window. Shotgun pellets peppered a mosaic into the ceiling. A blue Waterford crystal vase—a wedding present from Jessie's parents—lay in pieces on the coffee table.

Jessie took one look and shrieked. I had seen her face down a charging elephant unfazed, but gunfire in her home was something else again.

"Calm down. Back into the kitchen and call 911." I opened the door to the hall closet.

"What're you doing?"

I unlocked the box that held my .45 revolver. "We can't just sit on our butts until the cops get here. This is our home. Anyone tries to break in, they're going to get shot." I spun the chamber, making sure the gun was loaded.

"You're not going outside, are you? Please, don't." She tugged on my arm. "It's too dangerous."

I peeked out the fractured living room window and saw what looked like a lynch mob moving toward the house. I couldn't fight them all. We'd be better off barricaded in a room. But where? Upstairs? In the basement?

Sirens in the distance settled the question. The crowd looked toward the cresting sound and stopped advancing. A patrol car came into view and sped into the driveway. Two Carmel cops scrambled out. One look at the crowd, and the officers quickly approached the front door. Jessie let them in.

"Your neighbor called 911. What's going on?"

I handed over the note and explained.

"Look, tempers are high, and Jackson's fans are furious. Most likely this is an empty threat and will blow over in a few days. But to be safe, we need to get you out of here. We'll watch your house until you get back."

Shouts from the crowd grew louder. We heard automatic gunfire and instinctively ducked. Bullets sprayed the front of the house, and tires squealed from the drive-by.

The cops called for backup. They drew their weapons, and one of them opened the front door a crack.

The crowd chanted in unison, "You killed Randy. You killed Randy.

We'll kill you. We'll kill you." Three big guys waving baseball bats talked in a huddle, looking at the house and pointing at the front door.

After an eternity, a black SWAT van, red light flashing and siren wailing, jolted across the curb up onto my lawn. The van forced the crowd to back off. Six cops in black uniforms, helmets, and Kevlar vests jumped out. Five of them lined up facing the crowd, and one ran in through the front door.

"What's going on?" asked the SWAT commander. The officers explained, and the commander went into the living room and surveyed the damage.

"Stay in the kitchen," he ordered, going out the front door. Jessie and I crowded around one of the small windows as he took a bullhorn from the van, stood in front of his SWAT team, and addressed the crowd.

"All of you, move off this lawn and go home," he told the crowd. "Any wrongdoing will be addressed according to legal procedures, not by a mob. Now, back off and go about your business. There'll be no more violence in this neighborhood." His voice was calm, commanding.

A skinny African American kid in a Randy Jackson sweatshirt stepped from the crowd, waving a baseball bat.

"Not scared of you, copper. That doctor in there"—he pointed the bat at the house—"he killed Randy, and he's going to pay for it." The kid turned to the crowd and pumped the bat and his other fist over his head, chanting, "Randy Jackson, Randy Jackson." The crowd responded. The fever pitch, quieted a moment ago, rose to another crescendo.

The SWAT commander shouted into his bullhorn. "Kid, go home or you'll be arrested. All of you, go home or you'll be arrested."

He handed his bullhorn to a team member and grabbed for the youngster. The kid danced out of reach, picked up a rock, and threw it. The stone bounced off the commander's plastic visor.

"Kid, get out of here. I'm warning you for the last time. Go home."

"Or what?" He strutted in front of the SWAT team, waving the bat, daring them to do something, egging the crowd on. "What you going to do about it, shoot me?"

The commander drew his Taser. "Stop it now, or I *will* tase you."

"Oh, no, anything but that," the kid mocked, boogying in front of the squad. "Anything but that," he said in his best Br'er Rabbit imitation, pointing to the bouncing laser spot the commander targeted on his chest.

"You asked for it!"

"Go for it. I always wondered what it felt like."

The Taser gun pinged. Barbed probes shot out, pierced the sweatshirt over his heart, and stuck in his chest like darts in a board. The boy collapsed as thousands of volts crashed through his body. He lay facedown on the ground, arms and legs twitching in response to the shock.

"Hands behind your back."

The kid didn't move.

"He's faking!" yelled one of the SWAT officers. "Shock him again."

The commander pulled the Taser X26 trigger again, this time for a longer interval. Again, four-ampere pulses at 1,140 times a minute coursed over wires attached to the probes in his chest.

"Had enough?" the commander asked. The boy didn't respond. "You want another tase or you going to be a good boy now?"

The kid was motionless. The commander crouched over the boy.

"He's not breathing," the officer said. He felt his neck. "No pulse either. Call the EMTs. Quick." The crowd, murmuring, edged closer, moving nearer the house.

I had my front door open a crack and heard the cop say "no pulse." I laid my .45 on the floor and ran out, past the line of SWAT officers, to the boy. I heard someone in the crowd shout, "There he is," but I ignored him.

"Let me," I said, shouldering the officer aside. I confirmed the pulseless carotid and began chest compressions. "Jessie!" I shouted. "The defibrillator's on the floor of the master bedroom closet!"

Thirty seconds later, she ran from the house carrying the external defibrillator. I pushed up the boy's sweatshirt and ripped off his shirt. The Taser barbs were fish-hooked through the skin just above and below his heart. I pried them out and secured defibrillator patches to the boy's chest. The defibrillator registered ventricular fibrillation, and a computer voice from the machine said, "Shock indicated." I pushed the discharge button, and two hundred joules jolted his heart.

I checked the ECG. Still VF. I ignored the next "Shock indicated" and instead massaged the kid's chest one hundred times a minute for two minutes. I thought my arms were going to fall off. I checked the ECG. Still VF, but his lips were pretty pink. The crowd had circled us, and their murmurings increased in the background. Someone's hand gripped my shoulder, but I shrugged it off.

I hit the discharge button, and the VF stopped. Normal sinus rhythm returned. The boy stirred. A siren announced the emergency squad's arrival, and EMTs barreled out. I let them take over. They inserted an IV in each arm, breathed for the boy, and gave some fluids. The kid sat up and looked around, dazed and bewildered.

The crowd applauded and yelled, "Way to go, Doc!" I couldn't help but smile. I had saved the youngster's life, and the hostile crowd was now on my side.

I watched the EMTs load the boy onto a stretcher and race off to the hospital. The crowd lingered a bit before finally dispersing, followed by the SWAT team. I made sure there were no stragglers before I went inside the house. Jessie was waiting for me. I hugged her tight.

"You two okay now before we leave?" asked one of the Carmel cops.

"Thanks. I think so," I said. "Helluva way to spend a quiet Sunday afternoon at home, isn't it?"

They grinned. "Go on the Internet, and I'm sure you can find someone to repair your window, even on a Sunday." We shook hands, and they left.

I found a locksmith open and had him add deadbolts to the doors. The hardware store sent over a guy to replace the picture window. The phone company gave me an unlisted number, and the damn thing finally stopped ringing.

Later that evening after the repairs, we talked about leaving town. It didn't feel right to do that before the funeral, but staying might be dangerous. I decided to check into a downtown hotel.

As we drove off, I looked at the replaced picture window. I still had trouble believing what had happened. Running from my own house in my own town was inconceivable.

CHAPTER FOURTEEN

Crystal refused all requests for an autopsy. "Nobody's touching my Randy!" she screamed. Then her father-in-law convinced her it was necessary and they owed it to Randy to find out what killed him.

The autopsy room was crowded with Peter Fredericks—the Indiana Pacers' team doctor, the arrhythmia expert from Rochester Clinic, the Indiana State Health Commissioner, Dean Hazelton, the *New York Times* reporter representing the entire press corps, and me.

I had no idea what to expect. If Randy had neurocardiogenic syncope, the autopsy would show nothing. If he died from ventricular tachycardia, his heart might have an old scar from an infection, maybe a congenital problem, but should show *something*. I hoped the heart would be normal.

The chief of pathology at the UIMC wielded the knife. He opened the skull first, checked the brain, and pronounced it normal. Next, he opened the chest cavity, sliced through the pericardium, unfurled its edges, and exposed the heart. We hung over the table, staring at that critical organ.

"Normal external appearance." He severed the heart from its connections, placed it on a nearby table, and cut open the chambers. "The atria and ventricles are normal, as are the heart valves. Let's check the coronary arteries." He took a small pair of curved scissors and dissected the left anterior descending, like cutting open a strand of spaghetti lengthwise. This artery supplied the front of the heart with blood and was dubbed "the widow-maker" because, when obstructed, it could cause sudden death.

"Oh my God," was his only comment. We all strained to look. "Totally occluded along almost its entire length."

"Impossible," said the cardiologist from Rochester. "The calcium score was zero."

"Two possible reasons," the pathologist said, looking up from the heart. "First, the obstruction may not have been there long enough for calcium to deposit. Second, and most likely, African Americans have less calcium buildup than Caucasians, so the obstruction could've been there a long time without calcium forming." He gently teased out the yellow fatty atheroma plugging the lumen. It slid out, looking like a long, cheesy worm.

"This obstruction would've been obvious if a heart cath had been done." His eyes held mine for a long moment, drawing everyone else's to me as well.

"This clot here," he said, pointing to a tiny mound that looked like a small clump of purple Jell-O clinging to one end of the worm, "finished him off. Before this coup d'état, he had blood flow around the atheroma and could run on a treadmill or play basketball without chest pain. But this little guy"—he lifted the clot with forceps—"plugged the artery like a stopper in a narrowed hose, causing sudden death from ventricular fibrillation."

"So much for your diagnosis of neurocardiogenic syncope," the reporter from the *New York Times* mumbled, shaking his head and giving me a squinty-eyed look. He wrote that and more in the lead article in the *Times* later that day, using more than a thousand words to tell the world I had misdiagnosed Randy's heart condition, and that bypass surgery and an ICD would have saved him.

I left the morgue devastated. How had I missed a diagnosis so egregiously, causing a patient to die?

I kept replaying the events that led to Randy's cardiac arrest. Had I committed "reverse prejudice," cutting corners because my patient was a celebrity? Had I spared him inconvenient or painful tests I would have insisted on for the usual patient and ended up hurting him? The only thing was the cardiac cath, and Randy had refused it. Would I have been more insistent with another patient? Frankly, I didn't know.

I had no time to ruminate. Reporters with microphones surrounded me as I descended the steps from the autopsy to my car. They already knew the results.

"Hey, Dr. Sloane, how'd you blow it?" one yelled at me. "Another team pay you to gut the diagnosis?"

I was about to take off his head when Jessie came running up. She'd been waiting outside the medical center. She threw all 110 pounds at the circle of reporters, broke through their ranks, and stood on her toes in front of me.

"Don't you dare say another word like that to my husband, you horse's ass!" she yelled. "He's done more good for more people than you can possibly imagine."

"Not for Randy Jackson, he didn't."

"Look—"

I didn't see the egg coming. It exploded on my forehead. Sticky yolk dripped into my eyes, and I reached for my handkerchief. I did see the tomato, and ducked. It splattered the white shirt and tie of the *Times* reporter standing alongside. CNN cut to my grin when they ran the video later that day.

While food fights beat baseball bats, this time the cops were prepared. They dispersed the mob before they had a chance to run through any more of their menu.

Jessie and I went to the funeral the next day at the Tabernacle Presbyterian Church in Indianapolis. We arrived early to beat the lines. Randy's fans were sure to overflow the place later in the day.

I signed the visitors' book, and we got in line. Crystal and her family stood next to Randy's casket in a large reception room, greeting well-wishers. I needed to extend condolences to her and Randy's family—for me, for them. The same feelings I had had after the death of the Maasai chief, Sentwali.

Crystal was striking in a black skirt, black jacket, and white blouse. A broad-brimmed black hat with a veil covered her face. The silver disk hung from her neck.

She saw us from a distance and turned to whisper in the ear of a man with rust-colored hair who stood behind her. His thick neck and chest told me what he did for a living. I wondered why she had a bodyguard.

The man walked over to me. Taking my elbow in a crushing grip, he drew me out of the line and spoke in a low voice.

"She doesn't want you here. Please leave quietly right now."

"Now just wait—"

"Jessie, no." I put my finger to her lips. "Not now. It's her right." I nodded at the bodyguard and steered Jessie to the exit of the church with one hand in the small of her back and the other on her shoulder. Two cops—looking around, it seemed like the entire Indy police force was there—escorted us to our car. We left without another word.

We were lost in our own thoughts riding home. The few days in the hotel had been a reprieve of sorts, but we were looking forward to our own bed.

A winter snowstorm blanketed the road, but when we got home, the driveway was plowed and the walk shoveled, thanks to our outdoor service guy. I panicked for a moment when I couldn't unlock the front door, forgetting I had changed the locks. After fumbling in my carry-on, I dug out the new key and opened the door.

The house was totally trashed.

So much for new locks and deadbolts. The back door swung loose on its hinges.

Graffiti on the walls accused me of murdering Randy, of sabotaging the Pacers, of not believing in God, and of having a few choice sexual aberrations, mostly with animals. Slashed furniture exposed down stuffing that flew about like snow with the draft from the open front door. Shattered mirrors, gouged wood, ripped wallpaper, and broken glass surrounded us.

A rage boiled inside me. I thought I would explode. The ignorant bastards knew nothing of the facts and yet violated my home, my space, my *being*. I wanted to strike out at someone, anyone.

Jessie was a statue in the entryway, her fist in her mouth. "I thought the police were watching the house."

"So they said."

"What happened to the alarm?"

"Good question." I checked the alarm panel and found dangling wires.

"Could they still be in the house?"

Another good question. I went for my revolver in the hall closet. Gone. "I guess I'd better call 911."

The police were prompt and apologetic. They searched the house and suggested we change locks again. They figured that whoever had done this had gotten enough anger out of their system and all would revert to normal. I wasn't so sure. We headed back to the hotel we had just left.

This time the cops were right. The finality of a funeral and burial helped bring closure, and they abandoned their investigation. Over the next several weeks, no more articles appeared in the paper, I had no death threats, and the city returned to normal. In six weeks, the house was repaired, redecorated, and refurnished. I began to see patients again, and Jessie was back in the OR.

Toward the end of May, on a beautiful spring morning, with flowers bursting, a clear blue sky, and the sun shining, I received a registered, special-delivery letter.

The big brown envelope was hand-delivered to me at the medical center from a large law firm in town, Geraldo, Thornton, and Hashbrough. It alleged, in thirty-three single-spaced pages, that my medical treatment of Randy Jackson fell below acceptable standards of medical care for the community and charged me with malpractice for allowing him to play basketball prior to finishing a full evaluation, including a cardiac catheterization. That wrong decision was the proximate cause of his death, the suit claimed. Had I not breached my duty as a health care provider, Randy Jackson would still be alive today. And not only alive, but also earning money, either playing basketball, announcing the game, or advertising products.

The suit was for $350 million, his estimated earning potential over the remaining ten to twelve years of his basketball career. The initiator of the lawsuit—no surprise—was the surviving widow, Crystal Jackson.

Now I understood her decision to allow the autopsy. The newspapers said she had collected on a $15 million life insurance policy the Pacers had, but that obviously wasn't enough for her.

I felt devastated, violated. I knew one in two cardiologists got sued during a lifetime of practice, but I never expected to be one of them. I had always practiced careful, conservative, evidence-based medicine focused on the patient—and now this. I stared at the paper in my hand, furious at Crystal and wondering when all the madness was going to stop.

CHAPTER FIFTEEN

Port-au-Prince, Haiti

Crystal Jackson stepped from the American Airlines 777 and descended the steps onto the steaming tarmac, her Gucci carry-on clutched to her chest. The hot, humid air settled about her like a wet towel. She inhaled deeply and tasted the familiar tang of salt from the ocean. But the dissonant decay from the city made her stop breathing. When she could no longer hold her breath and her lungs demanded she breathe again, she did so tentatively, taking in little puffs of air as tasters, appetizers before the main course.

She squinted through tinted Versace sunglasses at the fiery orb that turned the airport into an oven so hot her spiky heels sank nearly a half-inch into the blacktop. She was exhausted and longed for a leisurely, bubbly soak in a cool tub. Her own tub in her own bathroom, home at last.

Long after the earthquake that devastated the island nation, the Toussaint L'Ouverture International Airport still showed signs of destruction. Crystal walked to the baggage area, passing two men plastering a jagged four-foot hole in a wall. Her luggage appeared last, despite the priority VIP tags from traveling first class. She hailed a porter and exited the airport, trailed by the sweating baggage handler pushing the luggage-laden dolly.

A *tap-tap* stopped alongside as she stood on the sidewalk. "Looking for a ride?" the driver of the brightly painted minivan asked in English, heavily accented by Creole French.

"Yes, but no other passengers. I don't want to wait." She knew how the *tap-tap* operated.

"Sorry, I need to fill the cab with at least ten people to make any money."

"Fine, I'll pay ten times what you charge one person. How much?"

"Where do you want to go?"

"Pétionville. Are the roads passable?"

"For you, I will make all roads passable. We will take Route 1, but then

74

we have to detour past the Presidential Palais International because it was destroyed. We will continue on the Route de Delmas."

"Oh, no, not our beautiful Palais," she said, her voice choked with sadness.

"Yes, and the cathedral and Palais of Justice, all ruined by the earthquake."

She kissed the silver disk and gave silent thanks to Bondyè that Maman was not hurt. "So how much? I want a price before we start."

The driver thought a moment, and Crystal knew he was figuring how much he could rip her off. "Six hundred gourdes—no, better make it eight hundred because of the detour. You see, the roads are lined with people living in tents, so I have to go slowly not to hit anyone. My brother drives a *tap-tap* and sent an old lady to the hospital last week with a broken leg."

Crystal figured twenty dollars was a bargain. She got in the backseat.

The driver practiced his English as he drove.

"Where do you live in Pétionville?"

"Avenue Morne Calvaire."

"Ah," he sighed, looking at her in the rearview mirror. "In one of the mansions?"

"Yes, it's a big house."

"So, you are very rich?"

"Not always, but now I'm comfortable."

"Is your house okay?"

"We were very lucky, so not much damage."

"Do you remember the Muncheez pizza restaurant?"

"Yes, we used to ride our bikes there for lunch." She leaned forward, smiling as she remembered.

"Well, before the earthquake, only you rich people could eat at Muncheez. The owners turned it into a community soup kitchen, and they give about a thousand free meals a day."

"That's nice of them. Are many without food? I read that crowds have crossed the eastern border to Dominican Republic or tried to escape in boats to the States."

He shook his finger in emphasis. "It is true. Some say fifty thousand a year. Many climb into boats and don't even know where they are going. They just go and disappear. My cousin Emmanuel, his best friend, and ten others left last week. He called to say good-bye, and then he was gone. I will never see him again."

Crystal was tired of talking and sat back, crossing her arms over her chest. The driver got the message, and they rode in silence. She watched the tent cities fly by, hundreds set up since the earthquake.

They drove slowly past Champ de Mars, where hordes of people walked vacant-eyed around piles of garbage and puddles of foul, standing water-breeding legions of mosquitoes and flies. The stench was overwhelming. She saw people strip and bathe out in the open, standing over small plastic tubs to recapture the water. She shuddered, thinking of the sanitary conditions—cholera now, and who knew what next.

An hour later, they approached her neighborhood, and she gazed out at the green rolling landscape where she grew up. Her peasant parents had given her to the Grégoire family as a live-in domestic when she was only eight. The Grégoires became her foster parents and raised her in return for working in their house. They gave her a First Communion, made certain she spoke flawless English without an accent, and then sent her to Indiana University in an exchange program, where she met Randy.

Randy. How could she go on without him? Her eyes welled.

Crystal clutched her silver disk and *tap-tapped* the tin door. The cab halted in front of a three-story gingerbread Victorian brick and timber mansion painted in bright blue, yellow, and red and set back in a lush garden. An intricately carved wooden veranda wrapped around the second story. Tall double doors flew open as Maman heard the *tap-tap's* noisy motor. Crystal paid the driver and ran to her.

"My poor baby, my poor Christelle," Maman cooed, holding her close. "I'm so sorry for you." Maman was shorter than Crystal, slim with gray hair and eyes. In her seventies, she had developed the early signs of Parkinson's disease, and her hands tremored in perpetual motion.

Stoic until now, Crystal burst into tears, her head on Maman's chest, as she had done so often growing up. "Mamie, I feel so alone now. I loved Randy so much," she sobbed, arms around her for support. Maman had always been her pillar of strength.

"I know, my child, I know," Maman said, stroking her hair. "How are my grandbabies? Why didn't you bring them?"

"They're okay, with my housekeeper. I've told them Daddy's away for a while. I can't deal with the truth just now. I can barely make it myself."

"You just have to go on. When Papa died, I felt like you do now. Life's often not fair. But there's nothing you can do about it. Come," she led her to the doors, her arm draped over her back, "let's go inside and have some tea."

No, Mamie, you're wrong. There is something I can do about it.

They sat in the kitchen where Crystal remembered Guerda cooking her favorite meals. "Where are Dadou and Guerda?"

"I gave Dadou the weekend off. She worked so hard all week preparing the house for you. Even though she and I are alone, the house still gets messed up, and it's so big for her to clean without help. I let Guerda go because we eat so simply since Papa died. I don't need a cook anymore."

"Have you thought about moving to something smaller, maybe in Port-au-Prince?"

"I have, many times, and even when Papa was still alive, we talked about it. It's a good thing we didn't. The earthquake would've killed us there. As long as you send me money to keep this house, I'll stay here."

"I will, Mamie, I promise. When will Dadou return? The last time I saw her was five years ago at our wedding."

"On Monday. After Papa died, she stays with me all week and goes home to Nicolas on weekends."

"Maybe I'll visit her before then. Does she have a phone yet?"

"No, but she's moved, you know."

"Yes, you told me. Remind me where she went."

"To Carrefour, after the quake destroyed her home in Port-au-Prince."

"How are they doing?"

"They blame themselves for Laurette's death, of course, even though Nicolas was working in the fields and Dadou was here, so there was nothing they could do when the hurricane hit. Poor Laurette. She was the only one home. They found her body under the ruins of the house that evening."

"It's so sad." Crystal covered her face with her hands. "She and I practically grew up together as sisters."

"I know. Dadou and Nicolas were devastated. Children should bury parents, not the reverse. Anyway, they built a single-story pine house with two rooms and two windows. Dadou says they planned the house to last only a few years, but when I visited, I saw it had a concrete foundation and a slanted metal roof hooked to hurricane straps, so it should last longer. She painted it all blue to ward off any more evil spirits."

"Is she still religious?"

Maman eyed Crystal for a moment before speaking. "I don't know.

Laurette's death changed her, made her more secretive, and religion is something we don't talk about. Ours has always been a good Catholic home," she said, waving her arm to take in the house, "and if she serves the *Loa*, I don't want to know about it."

But I do, thought Crystal. *I definitely do.*

CHAPTER SIXTEEN

On Sunday morning, the *tap-tap* dropped Crystal off in front of the blue house with the angled roof, and she hurried to the door. A dried chicken skull and bones were arranged in a pan on a table to the side of the door, and a *paquet's congo*—a small, sacred leather package to ward off evil—hung from the doorjamb. Before Crystal could knock, Dadou opened the door. Ample arms enveloped her.

"Let me look at you," Dadou said after squeezing the air out of her. She held Crystal at arm's length. "The tragedy has given your face some lines, but you are still as beautiful."

"And you, Dadou? You've had your own tragedy. I am so, so sorry about Laurette. She was like my sister." She put a comforting hand on Dadou's arm.

Dadou was short, barely reaching Crystal's shoulder, with a thick waist and arms, and thighs to match. Her black, wiry hair was twisted into cornrows with braids capped by red beads. Despite her age, close to that of Maman, no gray showed.

Dadou crossed herself. "I know. It was the will of the Loa. Taking my daughter was the spirits' way of telling me I didn't pay them enough attention. Before the earthquake, the Loa warned us something bad was going to happen, but we didn't listen, and many died." She reached up to touch the *paquet's congo* and dry-kissed the end of her finger. Crystal brought her silver disk to her lips. Dadou noticed. "You still carry that for your Loa?" she asked.

Crystal nodded. "My spirit protects me always."

"Come in so we can talk." Dadou took Crystal's hand and led her inside.

They walked into a living room–kitchen combination with a wooden table in the middle, surrounded by four chairs. A small sink, stove, and refrigerator lined two walls.

The door to the bedroom was closed. In a corner stood a low table holding a *govi*, a small earthen urn, highlighted by reflected light from a flickering candle. Dadou nodded at it.

"I am trying to capture Laurette's spirit in that urn. We used to talk to each other a lot, and I miss her. I want her to come back so we can talk again."

Crystal raised an eyebrow but said nothing. She looked around. "Where's Nicolas?"

"Usually he goes to church with me, but this morning he is working the fields, so I will go alone. I am bringing this urn. Would you like to come? I know Laurette would like that."

The Christian Conservative Church of Haiti was a single-room wooden building painted blue with bright red doors. The tin roof was flat, covered by a black tarp. Inside, whitewashed wooden walls contrasted with the packed dirt floor.

A large red sequined *Drapeau Vaudou*, or voodoo flag, hung on the back wall over three wooden tables serving as an altar. On each table sat a large white candle, six glasses of water, and multiple dishes filled with meats, vegetables, and fruits, giving off delicious aromas. Along with the drapeau depicting a *veve*, or symbol, these served as beacons for the Loa, or voodoo spirits, to find the building and enter. The veve on the flag was reproduced on the dark dirt floor of the church with sprinkled golden cornmeal.

"This diagram is Laurette's veve," Dadou said. Every Loa had its own. "So we will use this to call her. I am sure she will come."

A *houngan*, voodoo priest, and a *mambo*, priestess, both dressed in white robes with gold collars and trim, led the service, beginning with a song to Bondyè, the supreme god. Because Bondyè was unreachable, they directed the worship to the Loa, spirits of lesser entities, and sang songs to please them.

Papa Legba, as the Loa guardian of the crossroads between the present and spirit worlds, was the first to be recognized, followed by four other Loas. Each had his own special song.

When the songs finished, the houngan led in a young, brown-and-white goat bleating with terror. The goat's eyes were wild. Saliva dripped from its mouth as it tugged and jumped at the end of the cord the houngan held tight around its neck.

The houngan handed a long knife to the mambo. The mambo recited an incantation and danced three times around the goat, shaking the knife in the air. Then she turned and, with a quick slash, cut its neck and collected the dripping blood in an earthen plate. When the goat stopped moving, she nodded at Dadou.

Dadou left her seat, holding rosary beads in one hand and the urn in the other. She knelt before one of the three tables. Hands shaking, she set down the urn and crossed herself twice. She lit a candle, recited two Hail Marys and Our Fathers, and kissed the feet of Jesus, crucified on a cross that hung alongside the Drapeau Vaudou. She dipped her right forefinger in the goat's blood and drew a cross on Laurette's drapeau. Then she greeted Papa Legba and asked permission to speak directly to Laurette. Papa Legba granted her wish, and she began to talk to Laurette. The congregation watched silently.

Dadou fell to the ground. Her eyes rolled back, and she began to rock from side to side, twisting and thrashing her arms and legs as if she were running. She mumbled phrases and shouted incoherently. Six male members of the congregation formed a protective circle around her so she would not bump her head on any furniture. After three minutes, the fit stopped as suddenly as it started. Dadou sat up, rubbed her eyes, and asked what had happened.

"Laurette mounted you. She became you. You were possessed. And now she has left you to wait in that urn," said the houngan, pointing. "All is well. The Loas are pleased once again."

Dadou stood on shaky legs, crossed herself again, touched Jesus's feet, and mouthed a thank-you. The houngan helped her back to her seat and walked to the front of the congregation. He led them in their final songs, thanked Papa Legba for allowing Laurette to come, and ended the service. The congregants rose, each making the sign of the cross, and walked to the tables to eat and drink.

Dadou clutched the urn to her chest, whispering to it and stroking its sides as she and Crystal prepared to leave.

Crystal put her hand on Dadou's shoulder, halting her walk as they exited the church. She gripped the silver disk tightly with her other hand. "Dadou, I hope you won't think evil of me, but I need to find a *bokor*."

At the word, Dadou turned her shoulder away from Crystal and shielded the urn under her sweater. "We only do good things in this church, healing and such. There are no bokors here."

"I know that. But tell me where to find one. I need a voodoo sorcerer."

She turned to face Crystal. "Why?"

"Personal business."

Dadou stared at her friend. "Then you need to find a *bizango* society."

"What's that?"

Her smile was brief. "Don't you remember your country's history?"

"I was too young."

"When Papa Doc Duvalier ran Haiti, he used the black magic of secret societies to make the *Tonton Macoutes*, his secret police, feared more than anything in the world. They formed these societies that drugged people and cast spells on those who resisted Papa Doc. They butchered some and turned others into zombies with *coup poudre*, voodoo dust. These were called bizango societies run by the bokor. Is that what you want?"

Crystal looked into her eyes. Her nod was almost imperceptible. "Tell me where I can find one."

"You need to be very careful. The authorities are lynching bokors, claiming they were the cause of the cholera."

"Tell me where I can find one," Crystal repeated. "My Loa will protect me." She squeezed the silver disk with both hands, shut her eyes tight, and held it to her lips. "I have her veve inscribed here." She held out the disk.

Dadou lowered her voice and clutched the urn to her chest. "The closest bokor is the *Cochons Gris*, the gray pigs."

"How do I get there?"

CHAPTER SEVENTEEN

We were in the final days of my malpractice trial. My life had turned upside down in the eighteen months since I had been served on that pretty day in May. Motions, counter-motions, depositions, and fact-finding had been exhausting. Randy's less than twenty-four-hour hospitalization had been examined under a high-power microscope.

The trial was being held in a small town outside Indianapolis called Noblesville, a few miles north of where Randy had played his last game. My lawyer obtained a change in venue on the grounds that he could not seat a fair and impartial jury in Indianapolis. Plaintiff's lawyers had argued for live CNN coverage, but Judge Henry A. Dotter would not allow that.

Jesus Geraldo, principal partner of Geraldo, Thornton, and Hashbrough, waved a white handkerchief in his left hand—like Pavarotti in concert—and mopped his face and head. He stalked the courtroom, a three-hundred-pound bully in red suspenders, a blue striped dress shirt, and shiny green tie. My lawyer told me Geraldo was colorblind. Wet, eyebrow-shaped shadows were already darkening under his arms, and beads of sweat glistened on his forehead beneath a thick head of stringy, black hair.

Dwight Walker, of Caleb, Harris, and Walker, had warned me not to be fooled by appearances. "He's got a razor-sharp mind, Daniel. Be careful, especially of his last questions at the end of the day when you're tired and perhaps not thinking too clearly. Those will be bunker busters."

In the last six months, I had spent so much time with Dwight, I had no time to see patients or do any research. We spent hours in mock trial rehearsals, Dwight hammering hard with questions Geraldo was likely to ask. He even convinced me to wear a dark pinstripe suit, white shirt, and burgundy tie. A simple, silver Seiko watch with a black leather strap replaced the gold Baume and Mercier Jessie gave me when we got married. Dwight didn't want flashing yellow distracting jurors. I drew the line at a shorter haircut, though. My hair was longish and full in the back, and I wasn't about to get it cut short.

Fortunately, Redex sales continued to do well, as did SP stock. I sold shares to cover legal expenses.

"Plaintiff calls Dr. Daniel Sloane to the witness stand," said the GTH lawyer. Geraldo's appearance contrasted sharply with Dwight's gray, balding hairline, trim frame, charcoal-gray three-piece suit, and polka-dot bow tie. The two of them reminded me of the old Laurel and Hardy comedy team, but I didn't expect to be laughing. I tried to get comfortable on the witness stand, but the chair was hard metal. Whenever I changed positions, it sounded like a nail scraping a blackboard. One of the jurors in the panel seated to my left winced at the grating noise.

Judge Dotter sat on a raised platform in front of a huge desk to my right and stared down at the entire assembly. He was a tall man, appearing even larger in his black robe. Dwight told me he had played college basketball for Notre Dame, probably not good for my case. He looked like a frown in a dark overcoat.

My mouth was dry, and I took a sip from a plastic bottle of water I carried to the stand. The bailiff came running over and set a paper cup on the side arm of my chair. "Only drink from the cup," he whispered. "Judge Dotter hates it when a witness drinks from the bottle." I nodded my thanks.

Directly in front and below the judge's desk sat the court stenographer, recording every word. The lawyers sat in the middle of the room: Caleb, Harris, and Walker on one side of the aisle, and Geraldo, Thornton, and Hashbrough on the other. I had chosen Dwight as my lawyer because he had been a good friend of my father. I knew there was some risk because as a senior lawyer in the firm, he had not personally tried a case for many years.

Crystal Jackson, as plaintiff sitting at the counsel table, faced me, her eyes boring holes into my head the entire time I was on the stand. Though her stare was disconcerting, her appearance was even more alarming. Crystal, the fashion model, had been transformed into a Haitian high priestess. A red, gold, and white turban covered her black braids, coordinating with a flowing red-and-gold robe and red six-inch heels. No designer clothes for this Haitian mambo. The familiar silver disk hung from her neck. I figured it had some religious significance. I couldn't see the objects she held in her lap or the contents of the large black cloth bag at her feet, but somewhere I imagined a doll with pins stuck in it. Dwight told me he had objected to her bringing all her paraphernalia into the courtroom, but Dotter had overruled, supporting Crystal's claim they were religious articles for her mental and emotional support.

Jessie and Dorian sat in the first row of the spectators' gallery.

After the clerk swore me in, Geraldo fired his first question. "So, Doctor, you want the jury to believe you performed all the necessary tests in the workup of Randy Jackson?"

"No, the workup wasn't finished. I wanted to perform a heart catheterization before Randy left the hospital, but he refused."

"I see," said Geraldo. "And where is that piece of information detailed, pray tell?" He mopped his forehead with the white handkerchief, pushing it inside his collar to wipe his neck.

"In the discharge summary."

"Ah, yes, the famous dictation that cannot be found, correct? Kind of like the seventeen minutes erased from the President Nixon tapes?"

"I object, Your Honor. The Nixon tapes have nothing to do with this trial," Dwight interrupted.

"It's only a reference to them, Counselor. Overruled. The witness may answer."

"I don't know about the Nixon tapes, but I summarized what happened to Randy Jackson in my discharge dictation."

"What about the heart catheterization that was never done?"

"I explained about the heart catheterization to Randy and Crystal the afternoon before he checked out."

"And of course you wrote down that important fact somewhere in the patient's chart, correct? After all, you wanted to document what you said to him, yes?"

"No, we were busy at the time he was checking out, getting ready for a press conference. So I didn't do it then, and I forgot to do it later."

"You forgot to do it later. You *forgot*. Do you often forget to write down important pieces of information, Doctor?"

"Not usually."

"Not usually. But of course you mentioned such an important fact to other medical personnel. You conferred with a nurse or a doctor, maybe? Someone we haven't deposed yet, perhaps?" As Geraldo walked around, his thick thighs rubbed together, swishing in the still courtroom.

"I don't remember. I did tell my wife."

"Oh, now I'm sure *that's* helpful. A pity she won't be testifying." He smiled at the jury. "Doctor, do you know a Dr. James Harrington?"

"Yes, he trained with me many years ago."

"He went on to become a pretty good researcher, did he not?"

"Yes, he did."

"Are you proud of what he has accomplished?"

"Yes, I am."

"So you would have no reason to question his honesty, would you?"

"No."

"Doctor, I spoke with him about his training with you, and he said one of the dictums you used to motivate young doctors to publish their research results was, 'If it's not written, it doesn't exist.' Do you remember ever saying something like that?"

"Objection, Your Honor. Hearsay."

"I'll allow it, Mr. Walker. Please answer the question, Doctor."

"Uh-huh."

"Doctor, you'll have to respond with yes or no for the court stenographer. She can't record uh-huh."

"Yes, I do."

"And you have used that admonition to spur on many other young trainees also, have you not?" Geraldo asked.

"Yes, I have."

"Well, Doctor, don't you think that statement would apply here as well? *If it's not written, it does not exist?*"

Bastard, I thought. I didn't answer.

"Doctor, perhaps you didn't hear my question. Would you like the court stenographer to read it back for you?"

"No, I heard it."

"Well, then, please answer it, Doctor. Certainly something as important as recommending a heart cath should be documented in a written form. True, Doctor?"

"I told you, I said it but I didn't write it down in the chart. But both Randy and Crystal heard it, and it was in the discharge dictation."

"Well, Doctor, Randy Jackson can't testify, can he? The discharge dictation is somewhere in cyberspace. And his wife, Crystal Jackson, in her deposition given under oath, swore you never said that to them. She said you told them the workup was completed and it was likely that Randy could return to playing basketball."

"That's not true. In fact, I told them they would have to find another doctor if Randy didn't agree to a cath."

"Another doctor, you say. You would dismiss the world's greatest basketball player as a patient? Is that what you'd have this jury believe?"

"Absolutely, if he didn't take my advice."

"And you have a long list of such patients, Doctor?"

"No, but I don't seek them or the publicity that goes with it."

Geraldo fluttered his handkerchief in my direction in a dismissive gesture, I think because he didn't like my answers. Sure enough, he switched to where he had been going.

"So, back to the heart cath you say you recommended to Randy. Are you accusing the deceased's wife of lying, Doctor?"

"I am here under oath to tell you what I did. I cannot be responsible for what Crystal said. Maybe she just forgot."

"Like you forgot to write it down, Doctor? Forget something that would affect her husband's entire life, their entire livelihood? I think not. I think it far more likely you never said it."

The courtroom was quiet. I felt the eyes of the jury on me like a lead weight pulling me down, and I started to sweat like Geraldo. I tried to remember to keep my arms at my sides.

"Doctor? An answer, please, sir. We are all waiting." His *swish, swish* echoed as he prowled in front of the jury.

Dwight jumped to his feet. "Objection, Your Honor. There's no question before my client."

"Overruled."

Geraldo paused in front of the jury and swept his handkerchief hand in their general direction. "So, tell us, Doctor, tell the jury. Did you in truth plan to order a heart cath?"

"I did, damn it. I told them both it needed to be done." I shook my finger at Crystal. "She knows I did."

"Doctor, no profanity in the court, please."

"Sorry." My lawyers had drilled me: "Don't lose your cool." This was as much a show for the jury as it was a trial based on the evidence. Each juror would observe how I handled myself. Let him or her see a careful, composed physician, a balanced thinking man. And here I was blowing it by getting angry.

Geraldo mopped his face with the handkerchief and turned his back on me. He knew he had scored.

"I think the jury has heard enough on this topic," he said, looking at them with a smirk. "Let's move to another one. Like—whether—or—not—Randy—Jackson—could—play—basketball." He spaced the words distinctly to let the enormity of that statement sink in. "Did you tell Randy Jackson he could do that, Doctor? Play basketball?"

"No, I told him under no circumstances could he play until the workup was finished."

"And of course you documented that by writing it in the patient's chart? Or did you forget that important item also?"

"Your Honor, there's no call for counsel's sarcasm," Dwight Walker said.

"Your Honor, I am only trying to get the facts from the witness. If the learned defense counsel thinks this is unacceptable sarcasm, perhaps he should get out of his office and try more cases."

"Enough bickering, both of you. Get on with your questions, Mr. Geraldo."

"Yes, Your Honor. Doctor, please answer the question."

"No, I didn't write it down. I told that to Randy before he left the hospital. Crystal was in the room and heard me say it."

"Doctor, once again your testimony is at variance with Crystal Jackson's testimony at her deposition. Let me read what she said. Joe," he turned to an assistant at the table, "please project Bates number 5679."

Page 79 from Crystal's deposition flashed on separate video screens in front of me, the judge, the lawyers, and the jury.

Question: What did Dr. Sloane tell you and your husband about Randy returning to play basketball?

Answer: That he could do that—play basketball again.

Question: When?

Answer: Most any time. He even said it at the press conference.

The lawyer again turned to his assistant. "Joe, now please project Bates number 4971."

"Doctor, I represent to you that this is an exact transcription of what was said at the press conference when you discharged Randy Jackson after completing your examination."

Dwight stood, hand waving. "Objection, Your Honor. Dr. Sloane has testified he had *not* completed his examination yet and that Mr. Jackson checked out AMA, against medical advice. Counsel is misrepresenting Dr. Sloane's testimony."

"Sustained."

"Thank you, Your Honor."

"My apologies to the court, Your Honor," Geraldo said, fanning himself with his notes. "Doctor, I will read into the record this transcript of what you said at the press conference. The *Sports Illustrated* reporter asked this first question:

"'So, can he return to basketball?'

"'Yes, I believe so. Not immediately, but very soon,' you answered.

"'No restrictions?' That was a question from the *Washington Post* reporter.

"'Too early to tell for sure, but probably none.'

"Did I read that correctly, Doctor?"

"Yes."

"Do you deny saying that, Doctor?"

"No, but—"

"Good, because you indeed said that. So then, you did give him permission to play, did you not?"

Goddamn lawyers twist things around. "No, I definitely did not."

"Hmm. It seems to me that a 'Yes, he can return to basketball ... with probably no restrictions' is permission to play."

"Objection, Your Honor. Counsel is trying to put words in the doctor's mouth."

Before the judge ruled, Geraldo said, "Withdrawn. We'll let the jury decide that one."

He walked to the plaintiff's table and picked up a piece of paper.

"Doctor, you made a diagnosis of neurocardiogenic syncope. Is that correct?" he said, waving the paper at me.

"Yes."

"Would you explain to the jury what that is?"

"A faint."

"That's a big word for a fainting spell."

I shrugged. "It is what it is."

"Thank you, Doctor, that's a very helpful explanation," he said, turning to the jury with a sneer. "But a faint wouldn't kill him, would it?" He had his back to me again, facing the jury but talking to me. It was rude and very effective.

"No, not likely."

"So he had an abnormal heart rhythm problem, did he not? A rapid abnormal heart rhythm?"

"Yes."

"And that's what killed him, yes? A ventricular tachycardia?"

I nodded.

He whirled to face me, seeing me nod out of the corner of his eye.

Again, very effective. "You have to say the words, Doctor. The stenographer cannot record a head nod."

"Yes."

"So, yes, he had a ventricular tachycardia that killed him, correct?" he repeated.

"Yes, most likely."

"What do you mean, 'most likely'?"

"Well, it was never documented. Ventricular fibrillation was found by the EMTs during the cardiac arrest."

"EMTs are the emergency medical technicians, correct?" Geraldo asked.

"Yes."

"Ventricular tachycardia can transform into ventricular fibrillation, correct, Doctor?"

"Yes."

"And ventricular tachycardia was found in the ECG tracings at Rochester Clinic, correct?"

"Yes."

"And would be treated with an implantable cardioverter defibrillator, correct?"

"It could be, yes."

"Which could terminate the life-threatening heart rhythm, correct?"

"Yes."

"And which the so-called Dream Team at Rochester Clinic recommended, yes?"

"Well, one member—"

"Just yes or no, Doctor."

"I can't just answer yes or no."

"Your Honor, please."

"Dr. Sloane, you have to comply with counsel's request. Your lawyer will have his turn to supplement your answers if he so chooses. Please answer."

"Yes."

"But yet you didn't order one to be implanted in Randy and save his life, did you, Doctor? You had ample evidence he was having the arrhythmia. You could have saved the life of the greatest basketball player this world has ever seen, who had years of playing time left. There's no law that says he could not play after an ICD was implanted, is there?"

"No, but it's not likely he could have continued."

Geraldo ignored my response. "Instead, you allowed him to commit suicide by playing the sport he loved."

Dwight started to stand, but Dotter cut him off. "The jury is instructed to disregard the last sentence. Mr. Geraldo, focus your questions without the hyperbole."

"Yes, Your Honor. Dr. Sloane, please answer."

"It's not that simple."

"Pray, tell us why."

This was Geraldo's first screw-up. When we rehearsed, Dwight told me good attorneys didn't ask a witness "why." It gave too much latitude for the answer. I took advantage of his mistake.

"First, at Rochester he had only short bouts of VT and no symptoms from it. The only time he was symptomatic, he had a normal heart rhythm. So it was impossible to diagnose VT as a cause of his spells."

"Why is that, Doctor?" Geraldo asked, snapping his handkerchief at me.

"Because he had VT without symptoms, and symptoms without VT. So how could I blame the symptoms on the VT?"

"Thank you, Doctor, but I'll ask the questions. Couldn't he have had longer runs of VT at other times that produced symptoms?"

"Of course, but that was never documented."

"But you were suspicious that was a possibility, weren't you? That's why you tried to precipitate a spell while monitoring Randy Jackson during a basketball game with your brother, Dorian, correct?"

"Yes."

"Is your brother Dorian in the courtroom today?"

"Yes."

"Would you point him out to the jury?"

I did. Dorian flushed.

"You didn't have Randy play against one of his teammates, did you?"

"No, I wanted to avoid any publicity."

"And maybe give your brother a thrill?"

"Objection, Your Honor!" Dwight shouted.

"I withdraw the question, Your Honor."

Son of a bitch. Three of the jurors were nodding with slight smiles on their faces, looking at Dorian. Two others were jotting notes in a small ringed notebook, and a third was typing into an iPad.

"Dr. Sloane, the hour is late, and I'm sure you're tired after this long trial. Let's put aside your not documenting what you allege you said and finish by talking about your total failure to diagnose coronary atherosclerosis in my client. Would you explain to the jury what coronary atherosclerosis is?"

I turned to the jury. "That's when the arteries supplying the heart with blood get plugged up with cholesterol plaques." My lawyers had schooled me on that. Answer questions looking at the jury, not at the lawyer. *Be the learned professor and teach them.* After all, they were the people I had to convince, not Geraldo.

"It's a pretty common disease, is it not, particularly in men?"

"Yes."

"Usually after age thirty-five?"

"Yes."

"But it can occur in younger people. True, Doctor?"

"Yes."

"So it's a diagnosis you consider early in the workup of a symptomatic person like Randy Jackson, correct?"

"Yes, I did consider—"

"Thank you, Doctor. Just a yes or no answer will do."

"But I—"

"Yes or no, Doctor!"

"Yes."

"Thank you. Does heredity play a role? So, if your father had the disease, would you be at increased risk of getting it?"

"Yes."

"That means Randy Jackson was at increased risk since his father died at age thirty-seven of a heart attack, correct, Doctor? Only ten years older than Randy."

"No." *Now I had the bastard. Time for him to squirm.*

"Why not, Doctor?"

"Randy had no males in his family with coronary disease at an early age. In fact, he told me his father was seventy and still played some basketball. And I did document that in his chart on admission." I said that in a commanding voice, looking directly at the jury.

"Yes, so you did," Geraldo said, waving a page from the chart. "You wrote that down right here." He pointed to my signature on the admission page while walking in front of the jury.

"Doctor, do you see Randy's father in the courtroom?"

"I do."

"Would you point him out, please, for the jury?"

"He's sitting in the first row of spectators in the gallery." I pointed to the man I recognized as Randy's father from his picture in the newspapers. "That's his *adoptive* father."

CHAPTER EIGHTEEN

Geraldo stepped aside so the jurors could see my face. "You heard right—his *adoptive* father. Do you see his *biological* father in the courtroom?"

I heard Jessie and Dorian gasp, and I felt the blood drain from my face. "He was adopted?" was all I could stammer. I shifted in the chair. The screech was riveting.

I had committed a cardinal sin. Being surprised by a lawyer's question was unavoidable, but *showing* surprise was a serious error. Somehow I was expected to bluff it through. I failed.

I looked at Dwight. His eyes were as big as mine. Jessie was slowly shaking her head in disbelief. The Rochester docs had missed it as well. Everyone had.

Geraldo hid a smirk behind the paper in his hands. He waited until the shock settled in. "Your Honor, may I approach the bench?"

"Yes."

Swish, swish.

Geraldo stopped at the lawyers' table, picked up a few papers, and walked to the judge's desk. Dwight trailed behind him. Geraldo handed several papers to the bailiff, who passed them to the judge. He gave copies to my lawyer and me.

"Your Honor, I offer as exhibit 41 a notarized affidavit from Randy's *adoptive* father, Herman Jackson, the older brother of Randy's *biological* father, William, identified by the witness a moment ago. In it, Herman Jackson details how Randy's real father, William, was an alcoholic who died of a myocardial infarction at age thirty-seven. Randy was always ashamed of his biological father and never acknowledged him."

"Objection, Your Honor. No foundation, hearsay evidence. This document is not admissible." I knew Dwight was doing his best, but I didn't think he was being very effective. Geraldo was too street-savvy tough for him.

Dotter squinted for a long moment before deciding. "Counsel," he said to Geraldo, "do you intend to call Mr. Herman Jackson as a witness?"

"No, Your Honor, in the interest of time. But I'm quite happy to if you wish me to establish proper foundation."

"Then, I'll allow the affidavit, Counsel, to speed the trial along. Continue."

Dwight sat down in a huff, banging his open hand on the desk. I didn't know much about courtroom decorum, but I guessed that was not a good thing to do. Dotter looked at him, opened his mouth as if to say something, but was silent as Dwight turned his back on the judge to confer with another lawyer at his table.

Geraldo addressed me. "So, Doctor, Randy Jackson could have inherited a predisposition for early coronary disease, could he not?"

I stared at him, debating how to respond. Another rule Dwight drummed into my head was never to lie. I was caught and tried to wriggle a little. "Yes, I guess so, *if what you say is accurate.*"

Another trap. "Oh, it's accurate, all right, Doctor. Make no mistake about that. I have checked the court records, and William is indeed the biological father, Herman the adoptive one."

Geraldo walked to his desk with an outstretched hand. Joe handed him more papers as he walked by without even slowing. This was a well-rehearsed drama.

"Your Honor, here are Randy Jackson's adoption papers properly certified, which I offer as exhibit 42, and William Jackson's death certificate, likewise certified, as exhibit 43." He gave copies to Dwight and me.

Geraldo looked at his notes. "Your Honor, permission to approach the defendant."

"Granted."

"Doctor." Geraldo handed me another piece of paper. "This is the notarized autopsy report of Randy's biological father, William. Please read this document and tell the court what it says."

Dwight tried once more. "Objection. Again, counsel has laid no foundation for this document."

Dotter didn't wait a second for this one. You don't slam your fist and turn your back in his courtroom at a ruling you don't like. "Overruled," he almost snarled. "Proceed."

I scanned the autopsy results. The man had died of an acute coronary occlusion of the very same artery that killed Randy. He also had alcoholic cirrhosis.

"So, Doctor Sloane, please tell the court what William Jackson, Randy's biological father, died from."

"An acute myocardial infarction."

"So, for the jury, Doctor, that's a heart attack due to an obstruction of the very same artery Randy had, true?"

"Yes."

"Now, Doctor, had you taken an accurate history from Randy, and found that his father died of a heart attack due to blockage of the very same left anterior descending artery blocked in Randy, wouldn't a prudent cardiologist practicing an acceptable standard of care have ordered a heart catheterization?"

"Yes," I mumbled in a voice the jurors barely heard. My heart pounded in my chest, and I shifted in my seat. *Screech.*

"So we have a classic example of *fate loading the gun*—the genes Randy inherited from his father—and *the environment pulling the trigger*—Randy playing basketball. You failed to ask the right questions to establish *the gun was loaded* and restrict the appropriate behavior to prevent him from *pulling the trigger.*"

I didn't know if he was waiting for an answer, but I wasn't going to give him any.

"No more questions, Your Honor."

Judge Dotter checked the clock at the back of the courtroom. "It is now 11:47. We'll break for lunch and resume promptly at two."

At two o'clock, Geraldo stood before the judge. "Your Honor, I was going to call Crystal Jackson as a witness, but we have her sworn deposition, and she would be saying the same things in a court testimony. Since the hour is late, and this trial has gone on for over a week, the plaintiff rests."

Dwight took over. He grilled Herman Jackson on the stand, but Herman only affirmed what Geraldo had established in the affidavit. Dwight examined the pathologist who had performed the autopsy on William Jackson but got the same information noted in the autopsy report.

Finally, he called Crystal to the stand. I had told him that was a mistake, but he overruled me.

A fashion model had replaced the Haitian priestess. Her brown tweed Armani suit was striking, enhanced by a paisley scarf in sunset colors of gold and bronze. Large gold hoops dangled from her ears, and stiletto boots, the color of honey, reached to her knees, clicking with confidence as she strutted the runway to the witness stand. No claws showed, but I didn't doubt for a minute they were there.

"Mrs. Jackson, Dr. Sloane has testified he told you and your husband he wanted Randy to have a heart catheterization."

Almost before Dwight finished the sentence, she said in a calm, authoritative voice, smiling at the jury, "That's an outright lie. He never said any such thing. He said the workup was over."

"Dr. Sloane has also testified he told your husband not to play basketball until the workup was completed and he had a diagnosis explaining your husband's spells on court."

"Another bald-faced lie, sir." Her headshake sent her earrings bobbing, circles of gold in the reflected light. "You saw the transcript from the press conference. He told Randy and me the same thing in private, that Randy could return to playing basketball almost immediately without restrictions."

"What do you mean, 'almost immediately'?"

Crystal recovered from her stumble like a pro. "Well, Randy had been stressed by the long workup at Rochester and UIMC and needed a few days off to rest. After that, he could return to basketball."

"So he played a pickup game with his friends three days after he left UIMC Medical Center?"

"It was only a casual thing, kind of stretching his legs, that's all, before he returned full-time to the Pacers."

Dwight probed but got nowhere. Crystal was very good and very damaging.

He should have listened to me.

CHAPTER NINETEEN

The jury returned three hours later. I could predict their decision as they entered because every juror stared straight ahead or looked at Dotter. When the jurors' eyes avoided mine, I knew the verdict would be "guilty as charged."

"Have you reached a verdict, ladies and gentlemen of the jury?"

"We have, Your Honor," the jury foreman said, passing a slip of paper to the judge. Dotter read the note and instructed the foreman to deliver the verdict.

"We, the jury, unanimously find that the conduct of the defendant, Dr. Daniel Sloane, fell below an acceptable minimum standard of care and that this behavior was the proximate cause of the sudden death of Randy Jackson. We award his widow, Crystal Jackson, the full amount requested."

Bedlam erupted despite Dotter pounding his gavel and yelling, "Order! Order in the courtroom!" Finally, Dotter appeared to give up restoring order and called a thirty-minute recess.

Apparently he had expected the decision. When he returned, he was prepared with his own set of rulings.

"I find the monetary award excessive and hereby reduce it by half to $175 million." He looked directly at me. "But I also order, because of the extreme nature of your failure to diagnose coronary atherosclerosis in Randy Jackson, that you be placed on supervised probation for a period of not less than one year. During that time, a court-appointed cardiologist will review every diagnosis and treatment recommendation you make on each patient within three days of your evaluation. After one year, I will review whether you are performing to the standards expected of a cardiologist in the State of Indiana and consider ending the probation period."

I was devastated. My malpractice insurance totaled a million dollars, a laughable amount under the circumstances. My total worth, including my house, all my stock, and our two cars was less than 10 percent of what

I now owed Crystal Jackson. How the hell I would get the money was beyond me. But more important was the humiliating probation the judge imposed. In ten seconds, the judge had transformed me from a paragon among cardiologists to a pariah, from an internationally respected leader to someone with a scarlet letter seared into his forehead.

Crystal approached, smiling and holding out her hand. Now that she had won, I figured she had sheathed her claws to greet the loser. In fact, she was wearing tawny leather gloves. We shook hands—she didn't bother taking off her gloves—and pulled me toward her. She slipped her other hand behind my neck, drew my face close to hers, and whispered in my ear, "You deserved that and more for killing Randy. I hope to God you die."

Then she mumbled something else that sounded like "baker," and I tried to pull away. But her hand around my neck held me tight, and she continued.

"I'll follow you wherever you go, *Doctor* Sloane, all over the world if I have to, so you'd better always watch your back. You won't know when it's coming, but I won't ever give up till I've gotten even." She spun on her heels and left me standing there, feeling stupid.

The international press was waiting for me as we descended the courthouse steps. Following the wake Dorian plowed, I pushed my way through with no comments. I left it up to Dwight to talk to the press, and I was sure he would give them the usual spiel of a wrong decision, grounds for appeal, and so on.

Dean Jim Hazelton didn't wait until I got home. My cell phone rang as we all got into the car. "We need to talk. I just heard the jury's verdict and the court's order."

"That didn't take long. Bad news travels fast, I guess." I tried to keep the bitterness out of my voice.

"Daniel, I'm sorry."

"Thanks. I plan to appeal, Jim," I said. "My lawyers said the judge had no right to allow Geraldo to admit those documents."

There was a moment of silence before Dean Hazelton responded. "You realize, don't you, that this changes everything. Even if you manage to have the verdict overturned—which I doubt—you're branded. I actually agree with the decision."

"You do? Knowing that I carefully—"

"No!" Hazelton almost shouted as he interrupted me. "No, Daniel, you did not. You of all people, a prominent cardiologist, know to document everything. But even more important, to miss early coronary disease when the guy's father died from it—Christ, we drum the importance of family history into the head of every medical student from day one. You know that better than anyone."

"I do, Jim. Crystal lied, totally. She—"

"Enough, Daniel. The facts speak otherwise."

I was too emotionally drained to argue, especially with the dean. Universities have short memories. All the good things I had done had been forgotten in an instant.

"You win, Jim. I guess I just blew it."

"I'm putting you on administrative leave, at least until this cools off. I don't want patients seeing you and then giving a sound bite to the press about how you did or didn't examine them. And I certainly don't want whoever the court appoints as your supervisor to be hanging around right now."

"Who's that going to be? Do you know?"

"I don't know, except the court ruled it couldn't be someone from UIMC. So, it's likely to be from one of the competing cardiology practices in town, and we need that like a hole in the head. Someone in private practice supervising a tenured full professor at UIMC? You got to be kidding. Not while I'm dean."

"Doesn't sound like much of a future for me, does it?"

His silence answered my question. Finally he said, "Get some rest. We'll talk again next week. I have someone covering your patients."

Dorian, Jessie, and I sat around the kitchen table, most of the Chinese takeout still in little white cardboard boxes, gradually leaking onto the tile counter.

"You ought to sponge that up before it stains," Dorian said to no one in particular, but none of us moved. My head was still in the courtroom. I guess we all were.

After a few minutes, I stood and started pacing. I was seething at the injustice of it all. "I can't believe it, the power of a judge. One minute I'm a hero to thousands of patients and doctors, and the next minute I'm a bum." I shook my head in disbelief.

"That's an exaggeration," said Jessie, flipping her hand to erase the idea. "You're not a bum, and you know it. You're the same honest, caring, and brilliant doctor you always were. Your patients will still love you, and doctors around the world will still respect you for the insightful research you've published over the years."

"You made a mistake, that's all," Dorian said.

"Not you too!" I stood in front of my brother, fists clenched. "I made no mistake, Dorian. Crystal lied through her teeth. I *did* tell him not to play basketball until he was cathed."

"Calm down. You should've written all that stuff in his chart, like that fat lawyer said."

"It was in the discharge summary."

Dorian poked a chopstick into the chicken chow mein, sitting in a mass of congealed brown jelly. "So what will you do?"

I sat down again. "About which? I merely have to come up with $175 million, plus find a new job."

"You don't think you can stay at the medical center?"

"Not from what the dean said. I can't take care of patients without supervision, and he won't permit the outside supervision required by the court. I suppose I could only do research, but that's not enough for me. I need to take care of patients."

"Insurance physicals?" Dorian asked.

"The bottom rung in medicine? I'd quit first."

"Industry? Come and work in the family business."

"Doing what?"

"Storeroom apprentice?"

"What?" I said, rising for the bait.

"Only joking. Cool it. Man, are you hyper," Dorian said, pushing me back into my chair. "Seriously, you could work in new drug development. We always need top-notch scientists there."

"What about clinical studies? I could monitor some of the Redex trials still being done, or design some new ones."

"No, I've got enough docs working that area already. Don't need to waste your talents there."

"I don't want to be a bench scientist full-time. I could stay at UIMC if I wanted to do that. I *need* to see patients. That's why I went into medicine in the first place." I was silent for a moment, remembering something that resonated while I was a med student at Harvard. "A guy named Peabody years ago said the secret of patient care is caring for the patient. That's who I am—what I am."

"Then what other options do you have?" Dorian asked.

"Want to see some lions?"

"Lions?" My expression must have been quite blank because Jessie burst out laughing.

"Yes, lions and elephants as in—"

"Kenya?" It finally dawned on me. "Jessie, you can't be serious. Back to Kenya?"

"Why not? We had fun there. I'm sure they still need volunteers."

"That was two and a half years ago. Seems like another lifetime."

She wore a wistful look, and I saw the glimmer of tears. "It does."

"What about income?" Dorian asked. "How're you going to pay the millions the court awarded Crystal? And besides, the court might not let you leave the country owing all that money."

"What's my stock worth? Ten, twelve million total?"

"More since we launched Redex."

"Okay. At best, Jessie's and my combined annual income is maybe six or seven hundred thousand. So, even if the court garnished our entire annual wages—Dwight said they could only take half of mine, and not touch Jessie's—and grabbed every penny we have in savings, Crystal would have to wait more than a hundred years to get fully paid."

"They couldn't touch the company, could they?" Dorian asked, concern in his voice.

Jessie jumped up and stared at Dorian. "You're more worried about the damn company than your own brother."

"Jessie, you're misinterpreting—" Dorian started to say.

"The hell I am," she interrupted.

"Stop it, both of you. Jessie, sit back down. Dorian, I checked with Dwight. I have stock, which they'll take, but that's all."

"I'll buy your stock to keep control in the family. Market value. I sure as hell don't want Crystal involved. But you'll still be more than $150 million short. What can you do? I'll lend you some money, but—"

"Dwight suggested a reasonable strategy. I threaten Crystal with an appeal. A new jury might reverse this verdict, a risk she may not want to take. So I offer her half the stock and 20 percent of my salary in return for total settlement. No appeal, but no more money. Everything's finished. If she balks, I'll raise it to all the stock and half my salary. Same deal. We walk, and everything's done. That'd wipe out all our savings, but we'd keep the house and still have a reasonable income together with no more debt."

"And if she doesn't accept?"

"Then I'll either go through with the appeal—and probably lose another year in the process—or I'll have to declare bankruptcy, and she'll end up with a lot less."

We were all quiet as the reality of those words sunk in.

Jessie broke the silence. "It's obvious you want to stay a clinician," she said. "Why not do that full-time and give up the research?"

I thought about that while sipping black tea that had grown cold. It wasn't very good hot, a lot worse cold. I dribbled it back into my cup. "Yes, I could do that. I *need* to see patients. I could live without teaching and research if I had to."

"How about this," Jessie went on, standing and pacing the kitchen as I had done. "Why not join a private practice cardiology group here in town, like Cardiology Doctors of Indiana? The judge said your supervisor could come from CDI. That way, you could see patients and be supervised so subtly no one would even notice, and after the year's probation, rejoin UIMC."

"Brilliant," said Dorian. "Now I know why you married her. Smarts," he said, pointing to her head.

"No, it was for those surgeon hands." I took them in mine and kissed both palms.

CHAPTER TWENTY

An hour later, I drove my brother to the airport. I pulled curbside at the US Airways sign. "I appreciate the moral support."

"Opperman's Pond all over again. You got to stay off the thin ice though. I can't keep saving your freezing ass forever."

"You and Jessie are both great with advice *after* the fact," I said.

"Kind of like explaining why the stock market went up or down the morning after." He chuckled. "If private practice doesn't work out, let me know."

"You'll be the second one to find out."

"Bye, bro, and good luck." Dorian leaned over and kissed my cheek. He came away wiping his face with the back of his hand. "You're all wet."

"I know." I was starting to sweat profusely. "I don't feel too good."

"Can't blame you. Lots of shit in your life right now. Go home and get some rest."

"I plan on doing just that. Thanks again. I'll be in touch." He waved as he entered the terminal. I drove off as an airport cop approached on his Segway, probably to tell me to move my car.

It was late afternoon. Traffic had been building. Part of Interstate 465N was under repair. Lanes had been narrowed, and it was slow going at 45 mph. Despite that, I found it hard to focus on the road, maybe because of the tight, curvy lanes. So many thoughts about what lay ahead swirled around in my head that my hands felt clumsy on the wheel. Twice I triggered irate honks from drivers when I veered into the wrong twisting lane.

I passed through the repair zone, and traffic sped up. Without warning, the sweat began to pour off me. My shirt became drenched. The road ahead transformed into a dancing ribbon swaying side-to-side in the flickering sun, and I struggled to keep my car in lane. I felt lightheaded. Horns blared all around me. My face turned numb, and then my hands, and then

I couldn't feel the accelerator under my foot. I tried to hit the brake, but my foot couldn't find it.

And then I felt—nothing.

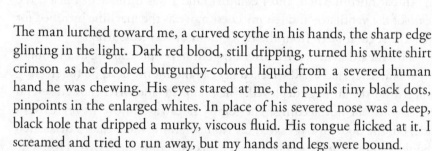

The man lurched toward me, a curved scythe in his hands, the sharp edge glinting in the light. Dark red blood, still dripping, turned his white shirt crimson as he drooled burgundy-colored liquid from a severed human hand he was chewing. His eyes stared at me, the pupils tiny black dots, pinpoints in the enlarged whites. In place of his severed nose was a deep, black hole that dripped a murky, viscous fluid. His tongue flicked at it. I screamed and tried to run away, but my hands and legs were bound.

"Help me! Help me!" I shouted.

"It's okay, Doctor, it's okay. You're hallucinating. No one's going to hurt you. Calm down," a woman said.

Bewildered, I looked around the room and saw more bloody people. "They're all over the place. They eat human flesh. My God, don't you see them? The guy behind you is sucking brains from a severed head!" I strained at the leather straps. "They're going to kill us and eat us! Don't you see that?"

She pushed my head back on the pillow. "Easy, Doctor, easy. In six days, no one has killed or eaten you yet. I'm going to give you some Valium for your delirium tremens. You'll be asleep in a jiffy."

"No! Don't! That's when they'll attack, they'll—"

I woke what felt like hours later. Jessie was sitting on the bed alongside me. I tried to sit up but fell back exhausted.

"Jessie, please make them untie me. Please, Jessie. We've got to get out of here, now, before they come back." I looked around the room. "They're not here, but they'll come back, Jessie. I know they will. Jessie, we've got to get out. They'll kill us!"

She bent over me and held my head. I felt her lips on my ear, and I pulled away. "Not you too, Jessie! Help, she wants to eat me! Somebody, help!"

I heard footsteps enter the room and saw a woman move close. She held a knife in her hand and was going to stab me. I tugged and tugged …

I slowly regained consciousness. I recognized the Intensive Care Unit. I was on my back looking up at the ceiling, a new vantage point for me. I heard voices all around, but I couldn't turn my head. The damn tube in my throat hurt like hell, and I couldn't talk; I was intubated. I heard the *swish* of the ventilator and felt my chest move as the machine breathed for me. The regular *bleep* from the ECG monitor was reassuring.

I overheard snatches of conversation from people coming in and out of my room. They said I had wrecked my car and hit my head on the steering wheel after the air bags deployed. The brain CT and MRI showed several contusions but no bleeding. The semi I sideswiped stove in my driver's side, but the door air bags saved me from anything more than a dislocated shoulder and gashed leg. I had been helicoptered to the UIMC Hospital.

I heard them say I was out of my head the first ten days, raving about people wanting to kill me. The doctors thought it was DTs from alcohol withdrawal, but my blood tested negative, and Jessie assured them I had drunk only one glass of red wine at dinner.

Then they blamed it on the head trauma and were worried about permanent brain damage. They said I was not responsive, and my blood pressure was low. Intravenous dopamine maintained a systolic pressure of eighty to eighty-five, barely enough to keep me alive.

I tried to speak around the tube, but no sound came out. I tried to move my arms and legs, but my limbs felt like lead. I couldn't even blink. What was happening to me? Was I was totally paralyzed?

Jessie entered the room, and I felt her hands on my arm. At least I did have feeling. She bent over to kiss me, and I saw her face when she came into my visual field.

She looked terrible, with dark bags under both eyes, all veiny and reddened. Her face was drawn, the beautiful prominent cheekbones skeletonized. She'd lost weight. I'd bet she hadn't eaten a full meal in ten days.

"How's he doing?" I heard her ask the nurse. "Any change?"

No verbal response, so I figured the nurse gave a negative headshake.

"When will Ed Grogan be around?" I heard Jessie ask.

"He's due to make rounds any minute. Would you like me to page him?"

"No, I'll wait. I canceled my surgery, so I have time."

A chair scraped, and Jessie flitted back into my field of vision. I felt her sit down next to my bed. Then she leaned over and held my left hand. The IV tethered my right. She stroked my forehead and laid her head alongside mine on the pillow. I felt her lips against my ear. "I love you, Daniel," she whispered, her warm breath soothing. "I love you with my whole life. Please get better, please. Please." She started to cry, little quiet sobs. I felt her tears slide down my cheek.

"I need you, my love. You make me whole. You must get better. You just have to. I have no life without you." Her sobbing increased. I thought my heart would burst. I tried to answer, to tell her I loved her too, but I couldn't move a muscle, nothing.

Heavy footsteps approached my bed. "Hi, Jessie." I recognized the voice of Ed Grogan, one of the staff cardiologists. He was a good guy and an expert diagnostician. I liked him because he lived Peabody's axiom: he wasn't scared to take an unpopular view if it benefited the patient.

Jessie lifted her head from my pillow. "Hi, Ed. Glad you're here. Anything new?"

"Give me a moment to catch up," he said. I heard pages turning as he scanned my chart. "Not really."

There was something about his *not really* that I guess Jessie must've picked up on, perhaps his inflection. "What is it?"

"Jessie, I don't like the way things are going. It seems we're fighting a losing battle. First, Daniel started out raving like a lunatic from the head trauma. Now he's totally paralyzed, even though the EEG shows brain function and no serious bleeding. His blood pressure keeps falling, and his kidneys are about to fail. We'll have to start dialysis in the next day or two, and we'll need to use bigger guns to maintain his blood pressure. I've had endocrine, neurology, surgery, pulmonary, renal, and even general internal medicine evaluate him, and they all struck out. The only thing keeping him alive is the respirator and his IV meds. We're feeding him by tube, and we've reached the point of no return."

I wondered whether some comatose victims experienced this same thing, doctors talking about them as if they weren't there. I used every muscle in my chest to shout, but I couldn't move.

"What do you mean?" Her voice shook.

"I reviewed the advanced life directive Daniel has on file. It explicitly states he wants no life-sustaining measures if his future holds no hope. Now, I realize it's only been ten days and there *is* brain function, but we're at the point when we have to decide whether to escalate therapy even though he's shown no signs of improvement."

Jessie sat up on the side of my bed. I felt her tense and squeeze my hand hard.

"As a surgeon yourself, you know we can't keep the endotracheal tube in much longer, so we'll have to trach him. We can't keep the feeding tube in his throat, so we'll have to put a gastrostomy tube in his stomach. We're running out of usable veins, so he'll need a permanent IV port." He stopped for a moment, maybe to catch his breath, and Jessie groaned. "His kidneys are shutting down, and he'll need peritoneal or even hemodialysis. And finally, his heart is starting to fail because of the persistent hypotension, so he'll need a left ventricular assist device or a heart transplant. That's a lot of surgery in someone not improving neurologically. Do you really want us to do all of this? More importantly, do you think Daniel would want all of this? He could end up in a nonresponsive vegetative state for a long time."

"Oh my God," Jessie said with a sharp intake of breath. "I don't know, Ed. I don't know. I don't want him to suffer needlessly." She brought my hand to her lips, and I felt her tears on my fingers.

"Nor do I, that's just my point," Ed said. "Think it over while I examine him."

Jessie stood, and Ed came to the bedside, slipped off my hospital gown, and listened to my lungs and heart. His fingers probed under my arms and into my abdomen. I knew he was testing for corneal and pupillary reflexes, and judging by his grunt, there weren't any. He pushed a knuckle into my sternum. It hurt like hell, but I couldn't move an inch. He ran a key along the sole of my foot, but my Babinski reflex was dead. He tapped his rubber hammer, but nothing moved.

"Jessie, I'm sorry. No improvement whatsoever. Neurologically, he's dead, and the rest of his organs are trying to follow. I can find no reason to expect this to reverse. Basically, he's a vegetable, and there's every indication he'll remain so."

"No, no!" Jessie cried, falling on the bed alongside me. "Daniel, help me," she said. "What should I do?" Her face was almost on top of mine, our lips touching. Her sadness overwhelmed me. I wanted to cry. I couldn't believe my life would end like this: a prisoner in my own body, exactly like the stroke patients I'd cared for. If they pulled the plug, they'd be killing me and not even know it!

The image of Sentwali dying and the Maasai laibon rattling stones in a cow horn burst in front of my eyes like a surreal dream. The words spoken by the laibon came alive: "Enkai has forever cursed you for the death of our chief." Panic built, but there was nothing I could do. I couldn't believe what was happening. Was my paralysis really from the curse?

CHAPTER TWENTY-ONE

Jessie's face hovered right over mine. I desperately wished to take her in my arms and hold her, love her. I didn't want to die. But how could I express emotions if I couldn't even move?

Jessie jumped up. "Ed! Ed!" she yelled. "Look!" She was pointing at my face. "He's got tears in his eyes. *Daniel's crying!* He's alive, Ed, he's alive!"

Ed's face came into my field of vision. "Holy Christ, you're right. He *is* crying. Oh my God. He is alive! I don't have a clue what in hell's going on, but he's definitely feeling emotions, and he's alive. He probably understands everything we're saying."

I wanted to scream, "Yes! Yes!" but all I could do was let the tears flow.

Jessie pushed Ed out of the way and found my eyes with hers. She grabbed my hand. "I'm here, my darling, and I'm not going to let anything happen to you. We're going to make you well, whatever it takes, I promise." She gave me one of her special light-up-the-room smiles. My heart did a little dance as she wiped away my tears.

Over the next few hours, a whirlwind of activity took over as medical teams pulled out all the stops and raced to outpace whatever was killing me. Finally, late in the day, Ed Grogan collapsed into a chair at my bedside. "We've got him in a good place, Jessie. He's stable. Now all we need to do is find out what the hell's happened, what's caused all this," Grogan said.

"What did neurology say after they reexamined him?"

"They're completely baffled. This neurological state's impossible to explain by any known diseases. Whatever he's got has affected every nerve in his body, so most likely it's some form of toxin, maybe a bug he picked up from the car accident. Somebody was saying he was almost acting like a zombie."

"A what?" Jessie's voice was high-pitched in excitement. "Say that again," she demanded.

"Which part?" asked Grogan.

"The part about the zombie."

"One of the neurologists-in-training is a young doctor from a small island in the Caribbean called Anguilla, near St. Maarten. He was talking about witchcraft and said some places still practice sorcery brought from Africa hundreds of years ago and that some poisons could create a zombielike state."

"Crystal Jackson! That's it! She's the one! At the trial, she dressed like a witch, and Daniel told me she probably was sticking pins into a doll meant to be him." She clasped a hand to her mouth and was still. "Oh my God."

"What?"

I could almost feel her reading my mind.

"The curse."

"The what?"

I heard her explain about the Maasai god, Enkai.

"Hold on, Jessie. Giving Daniel a poison's something I can believe, but you don't become paralyzed from a curse or sticking pins in a doll. Sorry, I don't buy that. And if it's a poison, how did he get it? And how has it lasted almost two weeks?"

I remembered all the stuff Crystal carried into the courtroom. Could she have had a poison in that black bag?

Both fell silent. Then Jessie said, "It must be in his bloodstream, or the paralysis would've worn off."

"Sounds reasonable."

"So, did any of his lab tests show *anything* unusual?"

I heard the rustle of pages. "No. His serum sodium's a bit low, but everything else is totally normal. The lab did a tox screen and came up empty."

"Yes, but that only screens known poisons and drugs. What about something totally unknown in the United States?"

"If you don't know what it is, how the hell do you screen for it?"

"Precisely my point," Jessie said.

Silence again.

"I know someone who could do exactly that," Jessie said.

"Do what?"

"Screen for an unknown chemical, a totally weird drug."

Good for you, my love, I thought. *You know where to go.*

"Who?"

"A professor at Dartmouth named Fletcher High." She took my hand, leaned into my vision, and smiled. "He taught Daniel analytical chemistry, and Daniel revered him because of something that happened while he was a student. Daniel used to say that the guy was so brilliant he would take apart TV police episodes and teach the class how the analysis should have been done. Maybe he can help."

"That was a long time ago. Is he still alive?"

"I don't know, but we're going to find out."

"I found him!" I heard Jessie shout. "He's retired and living in the Hanover Hills outside Dartmouth. He agreed to help!"

Fletcher High used his old lab at Dartmouth—maybe even the one I had studied in—to analyze my blood and urine. He called two days later. Jessie put him on the speakerphone.

"There are multiple chemicals in Daniel's system. The first and most important is tetrodotoxin, or TTX, a poison from the liver and skin of the puffer fish that blocks the body's sodium channels. That inhibits all peripheral nerve activity, causing total body paralysis. But the mind still functions."

Jessie asked, "Don't the Japanese eat raw puffer fish?"

"Yes, a delicacy called *fugu*, only served in special restaurants where the chef has been specially trained and licensed to prepare the fish safely. The Japanese get a tingling sensation on their tongue from very mild TTX exposure that enhances the taste of the fish. Several Japanese die each year from eating improperly prepared fugu. The liver and skin of the fish can be dried and ground into powder as a poison. If you Google *witchcraft in Haiti*, that's what you come up with."

"Any other toxins?"

"The second ingredient, also part of the witchcraft cocktail called a zombie cucumber, is *Datura stramonium*, sometimes known as jimson weed. The seeds and leaves contain a hallucinogenic compound. That, plus a third chemical from the skin of the cane toad, *Bufo marinus*, explains the hallucinations. *Bufo's* a big guy, can weigh two pounds with lots of hide, and the chemical is highly irritating to human skin. When the three are combined, the toad skin inflames and fissures the skin to permit absorption of the chemicals. Usually the jimson weed works first. Then its effects disappear when the TTX kicks in."

"My God, what a list. What do we do about it?" Jessie asked.

"First, a careful physical examination. Look for exposed skin where the powder could have been deposited and traces still remain. Assuming Daniel was dressed when he was poisoned, check his face, hands, or neck. Use gloves and wash that area thoroughly. I would have thought the hospital staff would've found something when they bathed him, but maybe they weren't that observant. Once the reservoir of toxins is removed, treat the TTX and *Datura* poisons. The skin will heal itself from the toad irritant."

"Paralysis is the most important thing now."

"Yes, Jessie, I agree. Lots of sodium IV and salt in his feeding tube will overwhelm the paralysis. Salt will also improve his blood pressure. Treat *Datura* with physostigmine."

"Professor High, I don't know how to thank you. You saved Daniel's life. God bless you."

"My pleasure, Jessie. Daniel was one of my favorite students. I'm glad to help. He's a good guy with the right instincts. It was also an excellent excuse to get me out of the house and test my analytical skills again."

"How quickly will we see results?" Ed asked.

"Almost immediately. The poisons are fully reversible once you get rid of the primary source and give the antidotes. There's a case report of a zombie in Haiti eating salt and waking up to attack its keeper."

As soon as Jessie hung up, Ed began a thorough examination. The surface of my hands and face might have been poisoned, but any powder there had long since worn off. He studied my neck carefully and found nothing—until he had an attendant roll me over.

On the back of my neck, he found a matted clump of gunk hidden in the thick hair. I should have gotten the haircut my lawyer suggested.

"Get me a small scissors and forceps, like in a suture removal kit," he told the nurse. His voice rose with excitement.

She returned in a moment with the kit, opened it, and handed Ed the instruments. I heard snipping and then, "Here it is, all tangled in this clump of hair. Send it to the lab for analysis. Tell them to look for TTX and *Datura stramonium*. Now please get me a scrub brush and some bactericidal soap. I'm going to give Dr. Sloane a VIP haircut and shampoo."

An hour later, after two IV liters of 0.9% sodium chloride, two IV doses of 1 ml physostigmine and salt in my feeding tube, I began to make noises around the endotracheal tube and to breathe on my own. My fingers twitched. I could follow Jessie's roaming with my eyes. I could also return her delicate kiss on my lips, the most delicious kiss I had ever gotten—or given.

The zombie had survived.

The following morning, I was transferred from the ICU to a private room. My tubes were out and my legs wobbly, but I was walking, holding on to Jessie for support. Damn, did that feel good! My blood pressure returned to normal, as did everything else.

"Crystal poisoned me! She turned me into a goddamn zombie!"

"And how're you going to prove that? It's her word against yours—'she said, he said.' Not even worth the trouble," my lawyer, Dwight Walker, said the next day when he came to visit me.

"Worth the trouble? She almost killed me, and it's not worth the trouble? I don't get it."

"C'mon, Daniel. Who'd believe she'd try to kill the person who has to pay her millions? Slay the golden goose?"

"That's garbage, and you know it. She'll have enough money from my stock even if she never got another dollar from me. She said she was going to kill me—and damn near did."

"But how will you prove it?"

The cops agreed with Dwight. They reminded me that, in the late seventies, Scotland Yard never solved the murder of a Bulgarian dissident writer named Georgi Markov, stabbed in the leg with the tip of an umbrella coated with the poison, ricin. Or the case of the Ukrainian Viktor Yushchenko in the midnineties, poisoned with dioxin. "Hard to prove things like that. No witnesses, no evidence, or circumstantial at best. Time to get on with your life," they said.

Would Crystal get on with her life? Would she be happy with a close decision, not a knockout? Or did I need to watch my back, as she threatened?

CHAPTER TWENTY-TWO

"So you want to join CDI?"

I was having an interview of sorts with the CEO of Cardiology Doctors of Indiana, a clinical cardiologist named Horace Lindorf, whom I had trained during his cardiology fellowship at UIMC ten or twelve years before. The interview was not going well.

The problem was simple: he hated my guts.

"Why should I give you a job here? You're damaged goods, a malpractice risk. Even if UIMC waives the one-year noncompete clause, you're a liability. And in today's climate, I don't need any more liabilities."

Lindorf sat tall behind an L-shaped mahogany desk in the paneled boardroom of CDI. He wore his white jacket with the obligatory stethoscope draped around his neck and glowered at me. He had Hollywood looks, with dark wavy hair, square jaw, and gray-green eyes. Lindorf was a better businessman than cardiologist. I had given him plenty of grief about his borderline cardiology skills during his fellowship training. He passed his cardiology boards by a hair on his third try. One more wrong answer, and he would have flunked and have to repeat a year of training before retesting. I knew his exact score because I was chair of the committee that wrote the certifying examination.

But the hard time I gave him clinically wasn't what made him dislike me.

I remembered the exact moment the rift began. I was in Nice, France, at a biannual cardiology symposium. I was walking to my hotel along the Promenade des Anglais, gazing out over the rocky beach crammed with seminude bodies and enjoying the blue Mediterranean Sea when my cell phone rang.

When I clicked it open, a woman who wouldn't give her name asked what I would do if some guy in my division was sexually harassing an employee. I probed, but she would offer no details. In the end, I told her I

115

would report the incident to the university's Ethics and Personal Relations Committee. She hung up.

After I returned home, she called again. This time she told me her name and explained the situation in detail. She was one of our techs, a beautiful single mom, and Lindorf was putting the make on her to the point of inappropriate physical contact—late-night groping—and repeated invitations to a local Hilton, which she refused.

I reported the conversation to the EPR Committee and called Lindorf into my office. I told him about the accusations, that I was obligated to report it to the university, and that they would want to talk with him.

He threw a fit, categorically denying the charges and claiming *she* was harassing *him*. She finally got a court order for him to leave her alone, one that matched with his own. She left the university after that. Six months later, Lindorf divorced his wife of twelve years and married a pretty ICU nurse in her midtwenties, just out of nursing school. Fortunately, he had no children.

I thought the entire episode remained a well-handled, confidential event, but Lindorf blamed me for not supporting him and squashing the incident after the first phone call. UIMC dropped the case when the tech moved away.

"Why should you hire me? Because you're short-staffed and because cardiologists with my capabilities and experience are hard to find, and because you just opened a new hospital extension and need to admit more patients or you'll soon close these doors. You know better than I that your overhead will bury you if you don't increase your patient load. And this elegant wood paneling," I looked around the room and ran my hand over the wall, "will fall to the auctioneer."

"I don't much like you, Daniel," he said. "You don't mind if I call you Daniel, do you, *Professor* Sloane?" His look was one of derision. "Our relationship's a bit different than twelve years ago."

"Whatever suits you, Horace. I'm here for a job as a clinical cardiologist and need someone to supervise me, per the court's orders. I'll do my work, you do yours, and we'll stay out of each other's hair."

Lindorf sat in silence, looking at me, rolling around a couple of pencils on his desk. They clicked in the stillness of the room, and I pictured the cogs in his head doing the same, aligning in some sort of geometric pattern, maybe like Rubik's Cube. It was clear we saw the world differently, but I thought we could get along.

Finally, he spoke. "Tell you what, Daniel. I'll hire you under the following conditions: I'll be your supervisor. You'll start at the pay scale of doctors just out of training. You'll have the on-call schedule of a junior physician and do whatever coverage and scut work the senior guys need done. Take it or leave it."

I stood. "Thanks for seeing me. I'll think about it and let you know." I turned my back on him and walked out.

I returned a week later. No other cardiology practice in Indianapolis was hiring. The job at CDI was the only one available unless I wanted to pick up and start over in another state. I didn't. UIMC let me out of its noncompete clause, and I signed a year's contract at a salary of $180,000 for a sixty-hour workweek, renewable by the consent of both parties, and began practicing cardiology like a youngster all over again.

The salary sounded impressive. But once I had done the math, it came out to maybe $60 an hour, which—after four years of college, four in medical school, seven in postgraduate medical training, and many years of experience as a practicing clinical cardiologist—might be considered a tad light.

I worked the shifts as I had during my internship, thirty-six hours on and twelve off. Lindorf reviewed my charts and cosigned my diagnoses and treatments.

We had no trouble until the fifth week, when a young man about thirty came in with atrial fibrillation, a fast heartbeat in the heart's top chambers.

"What are your symptoms?" I asked.

"A little shortness of breath, some fatigue, and palpitations. They get worse when I jog, but usually I feel fine."

"Why don't we try medications first? If you respond, great. If not, we can consider a more aggressive treatment. Sound okay?"

"Fine, Doc. I don't want any surgery if I can help it."

I started him on some drugs, to return for a follow-up evaluation in a few weeks.

The next day, Lindorf stormed into the closet that passed for my office, waving the patient's chart in my face before throwing it down on my desk. It slid to a corner, knocking over a coffee cup, fortunately empty.

"Why didn't you send him to the electrophysiology lab for a catheter ablation? We could've cured him of the atrial fibrillation."

A catheter ablation was like a major heart catheterization during which areas in the heart causing the abnormal impulses were located and burned electrically.

"The patient wanted to avoid surgery, and I thought it was in his best interest to try medical treatment first. If that doesn't work, he'll consider an ablation."

"So, you sent him home with some prescriptions instead of ordering a procedure we could've billed for eighty-five grand. More, if there were complications."

"You have a problem with that? Besides, the ablation cure rate here is only about 30 percent, and your complication rate almost half that. I'm not sending a patient to an EP lab with those results." The EP cure for AF was a difficult procedure, but at UIMC, it was 71 percent, with 3 percent complications.

"Do it again and you won't be here long."

"Go to hell. When the patient comes back, and only if he's still symptomatic, I'll consider an ablation."

Lindorf stood there glaring at me, hands on hips. "You really don't get it, do you? Or don't you give a shit? Which?" he said, his face crinkling into a scowl.

"I do get it, and I do give a shit. But patients come first. Maybe *you* don't get it."

Lindorf stomped out of my office, slamming the door so hard the pictures on my wall shifted.

I had just finished my thirty-six-hour shift and went home. I was dog-tired and steaming mad and slammed the door even harder when I left. Hell, it was *their* door.

Since I had started working at CDI, Jessie and I rarely saw each other because of conflicting schedules. Tonight, our times off coincided, and we went for dinner at our favorite Italian restaurant, Capri.

The first glass of a Farina Amarone calmed me down. I told Jessie what happened. "That son of a bitch," she said. "He should be the one supervised."

"Tell it to the judge."

"Maybe I will. Or to the medical society. What are you going to do?"

"Not much I can do. Stay out of his way as much as possible. I certainly don't intend to change how I practice medicine."

"What will he do?"

"Unpredictable. He can't fire me, at least not according to my contract, so I guess I'll just have to put up with his bullshit and dodge his bullets best I can. Try not to argue with the guy who's got the car keys."

Three weeks later, Lindorf was in my office again. "In my face" is more accurate.

"Why didn't you order a defibrillator implant for Mr. Eccles?"

"Because he's eighty-four, has less than three months to live, and wants to die peacefully at home."

"And how do you know that? Or am I missing some godlike prophesying qualities you've been hiding?"

"If you read my carefully documented comments in that chart you're waving around, you'd realize he has severe heart failure with an ejection fraction of about 10 percent and an adenocarcinoma of his lungs that's already metastasized to his spine despite chemo and radiation. Either will kill him in weeks or, at most, a few months. He and I had a long discussion about implanting an ICD, and he decided he did not want one. He wanted to go home and actually hoped he'd have VF because it's a quick and easy way to die, not messy like cancer. His wife agreed, and they left quite comfortable with that plan. And they signed a note in the chart indicating that was what they wanted."

"So we don't get to implant a device."

"Correct, at least not this time."

He slammed a fist on my desk. "Second time you've cheated the CDI practice out of a procedure. There won't be a third."

"Cheated the practice! Are you crazy?" I jumped up and walked around my desk to face him. "We're talking about a human being here, not a goddamned bottom line. The last time I checked, we do what's best for the patient, not for the practice. Remember the Hippocratic Oath and all that stuff you promised when you graduated medical school? Let an old man die in peace. What in hell's the matter with you?"

His face was red with rage. "With me? With you! I warned you once. I have no intention of warning you again. You're done here. Get your stuff and clear out." He pushed his finger in my chest. It took all my restraint not to take a swing at him. I was six inches taller, fifty pounds heavier, and I wanted to mess up those Hollywood looks in the worst way, flatten that Roman nose across his smug face.

I stepped back. "Sorry, Horace, you can't fire me like that. I checked my contract in case something like this arose again. You have to bring the incident before the hospital credentialing committee—which, I might add, is made up of representatives from all specialties, not stacked with your buddies. You might end up getting fired yourself."

"Don't count on it, Doctor. When I say you're done, you'd better believe it." His mouth curved down into a snarl. "You screwed me a dozen years ago, and now it's payback time, Danny boy. You'll learn not to fuck with me again!" He turned and stomped out.

Three mornings later, my second special-delivery registered letter arrived from the court. In it, Judge Dotter detailed how I continued to make inappropriate decisions that denied patients their right to have the best and most modern treatments available, thereby jeopardizing their health. I had made these wrong decisions despite close supervision from Dr. Lindorf. Therefore I was henceforth prevented from taking care of *all* patients until I completed remedial training under the tutelage of board-certified cardiologist Horace Lindorf, MD. Upon satisfactory completion of a three-month clerkship without salary, and a letter attesting to that fact from Dr. Lindorf, the court would consider lifting the ban. If I failed to comply after that, I would lose my license to practice medicine for a minimum of one year.

I sat in my cubicle, stunned. My initial impulse was to charge into Lindorf's office and tear him apart. But he'd expect that, maybe even wanted it so he could report me to the court. He'd probably have security guards waiting to throw me out. Provoking this judge even a tiny bit further might cost me my medical license. This round went to Lindorf.

CHAPTER TWENTY-THREE

"You should've flunked him from his cardiology fellowship when you had the chance."

Jessie and I were eating Chinese takeout—again. She'd been in the OR all day, and I couldn't cook worth a damn. The hot and sour soup wasn't bad, but the vegetable fried rice was soggy, and the garlic shrimp tasted funny. Freezer burn, Jessie diagnosed. Fresh, the Peking Duck Restaurant said. We needed to branch out. Maybe Thai next time.

"I'll do insurance physicals before I work with Lindorf."

"Fine with me."

I shook my head. "It may come to that, but not yet."

"Back to research at UIMC?"

"Too late. Hazelton called this morning and 'suggested' I might be happier elsewhere in view of the court's recent decision."

"Times like this, you really learn who your friends are. What'd you tell him?"

"That I had tenure, and he couldn't fire me without real cause. He said he was only making a suggestion, that he had to worry about UIMC's reputation."

"Baloney. He's covering his own butt, and you know it."

"Doesn't matter. If the university doesn't want me to stay, I won't, even if I have the legal right to protest."

"So what's next?" Jessie asked.

"Dorian's got an opening in new drug development."

"In New York?"

"Temporarily."

"How long is 'temporarily'?"

"Six months, tops. Dwight's working on an appeal, getting depositions from my patients and colleagues to try and change Dotter's mind."

"Six months is a long time."

"Honey, I don't know what else to do," I said.

"You really want to work for your brother?"

"No. You have a better suggestion?"

"This would be Opperman's Pond, big time."

"Tell me. Plus, he's all about money now. Whenever we talk, it's how much the stock's worth, what new toy he's bought or new girlfriend he took to bed."

We were both silent, thinking. "Move to another state and start over?" Jessie asked.

"I checked on that. The court has me listed in some sort of a national database, so Dotter's restrictions would apply anywhere."

"Where would you live in New York?"

"Dorian's got a friend who'll sublet his apartment on East Eighty-Sixth Street. Nice neighborhood, Upper East Side near Central Park, so I can jog mornings and even walk to Columbus Circle in nice weather."

"You're sure about this? New drug development with your brother's company? No patient contact, only bench research, working for your brother?"

I nodded. "He can't be that bad to work for. John gets along with him okay. At least his defibrillator hasn't gone off, so I guess he can't be under that much stress."

"You aren't John. He's a lot easier going and not apt to disagree with Dorian. You, on the other hand—"

"You have other suggestions?" I asked.

Jessie put her hand on my cheek and leaned forward for a kiss. "When will we see each other?" Her eyes were wet.

"Weekends. We'll alternate. You fly to New York one weekend, and I'll fly to Indy the next. It's only two hours. We've always wanted more time in the city for Broadway shows and restaurants, the opera and stuff. Now's our chance to do those things."

I landed at LaGuardia Airport at noon a week later. Dorian met me at the baggage claim. My Samsonite roller was one of the first bags off. I had packed only basic stuff; I'd be going home weekends, or Jessie would be coming in, and I planned to send out anything I needed to be cleaned.

Dorian called a porter to wrestle the bag off the conveyer belt.

I looked closely at Dorian. "You got rid of the earring."

"I did. Didn't fit the CEO image."

The porter led the way curbside where Dorian phoned his driver. A few minutes later, we were sitting in the back of his robin's-egg-blue Bentley convertible on Grand Central Parkway heading to the city. The air was cool with heavy clouds overhead, so the top was up.

"Nice," I said, running my hand over the soft tan leather. It seemed to caress my hand. "Cost a few shares of SP stock?"

"A cool quarter of a mil, but beats spending it on alimony."

"Fortunately, not my problem." I took in the plush interior. "Stock's not high enough for a Rolls?"

"Actually, I did check out the Rolls-Royce Phantom, but the sticker price's double this. My ex used to say, 'You drive a Bentley but are driven in a Rolls,' so she nagged for an upgrade. I compromised. I got a chauffeur for the Bentley and a divorce for her. Besides, driving a Rolls in city traffic is an accident waiting to happen. Other drivers stare at it and forget to drive."

"Sheila's gone?"

"With the wind, but I have live-ins. I rotate them periodically. Fewer complications. A pretty bauble, a night on the town, and I'm a hero. Hugh Hefner's my role model. I even bought a ruby-red silk dressing robe like his. No pipe, though."

"Where do you keep the ladies?"

"One lives in my house in the Hamptons, and the other in the house in Old Naples on the beach. Works out fine for everyone. I go south when it's cold and north when it's warm. Story of my life."

"I can't believe that. You just shuttle between them?"

Dorian smiled. "Too bad you're so happily married. At least, I assume you are."

I patted his knee. "Good assumption. Don't go fixing me up with any of your friends."

"Not even a few innocent drinks one night after a hard day in the salt mines? I can't party with my brother?"

"You can, but not with your lifestyle. I really am here to work."

"I resent that. I work damn hard. I didn't get all of this," he patted the plush leather seat, "from sitting on my ass, you know."

"I know, but Crystal took all my stock and gets a third of what you pay me."

Dorian frowned. "But at least it's over, right?"

"It is, but it's been a helluva nightmare." I told him about Lindorf.

"That son of a bitch!" Dorian slapped an open hand on the seat. "He's not good enough to wash your shirts. He barely passed the goddamn certifying exam you wrote, and now you have to take a clerkship with him? That's absolute bullshit! Dotter has his head up his ass."

Before I could respond, the chauffeur glanced over his shoulder. "Dr. Sloane, was it 17 or 27 East Eighty-Sixth Street?"

"Twenty-seven."

"Thank you, sir. Then we're here." The car stopped in front of a six-story gray building on the corner of Eighty-Sixth Street and Madison Avenue, and the doorman rushed out to help. He was a tall, broad-shouldered man wearing a full-length black coat with gold trim and brass buttons down the front, and a matching top hat.

"You are Dr. Sloane, I assume, moving into Dr. Bevier's old apartment," the doorman said, taking the luggage from the trunk.

"That's correct. What's your name?"

"Casey, sir. I'm the senior doorman, here most days. Anything I can do to help, let me know. I shopped for some essentials and can go again if you give me a list of what you want."

"Very thoughtful, Casey. Thanks."

"No problem, sir. I also took the liberty of having the maid clean thoroughly again this morning. She'll come back twice a week, more often if you want. I figured with only one person, that'd be enough."

"That should be fine." I turned to Dorian, and we stood there, kind of awkward, facing each other.

"Okay, bro. I'm going to leave you here. Sounds like Casey's got everything under control. Any problems, give me a call. When do you want to start work?" Dorian asked.

"Tomorrow, of course."

"I figured that. I get in around nine thirty. How about we meet for coffee and eggs? There's a nice café right around the corner from the Time Warner Center, on the west side of Columbus Circle. Bohème at the Circle. My treat for your first meal as a SP employee."

"Deal. Thanks, Dorian, I—" I put a hand on his shoulder. Dorian shifted his feet and looked away, past me.

"This isn't a handout," he said after a moment. "You'll bring expertise to our new drug development program and will earn your way. I plan to bust your ass, and you'd better deliver. I don't much like hiring family."

CHAPTER TWENTY-FOUR

After breakfast, we walked to the Time Warner office building and took the elevator to the fortieth floor. A stunning buxom blonde sat at a big desk in a large reception area decorated to look like an elegant living room. The walls were polished dark wood with a half-dozen overstuffed leather lounge chairs and two large couches. Side tables with lamps held current magazines and newspapers. Behind her desk was a closed door labeled Office of the CEO.

She greeted Dorian. He flashed her a smile. "Tonight, Tiffany?" he asked.

She shook her head. "I'm sorry, sir, but I'm busy tonight."

We walked another fifteen feet to his office door. "I'm wearing her down," Dorian whispered. "Probably'll take another week or so, but flowers will do the trick. Bunnies are all the same. Give them a carrot, and they're yours."

"Depends how you spell carrot," I said.

With a hand resting on the door to his office, Dorian smiled, paused a moment and glanced into a camera mounted over the doorjamb. "This is my brand-new 3D facial recognition security system. It takes a one-second snapshot and in less than a second compares my face to its entire database of thousands of stored visuals. A dozen sensors on a CMOS chip—"

"What's that?" I asked.

"I don't know what the initials stand for, but it's some sort of sophisticated memory chip that remembers what I look like from facial structure, skin texture, and other stuff, even smiles or frowns, and does it from multiple angles. When it makes a match, it unlocks my door."

Click.

"See?" We entered his office. "Wait here a minute and let me get my office pass card, and I'll let you into your new office. We're running late, and you've got a meeting with Mikhail shortly."

He hurried to his desk, opened the center drawer, and took out a white plastic card. "Come with me."

We left the office, and the door closed behind us. I followed Dorian down the hall to a similar but smaller reception lounge in front of two offices labeled with John's and Mikhail's names.

Dorian checked his watch. "I'm going to change plans. I'll have Mikhail take you to your office after your meeting, okay? I don't want to keep him waiting, and I've got another appointment." He introduced me to the receptionist, who dialed Mikhail, and strode off, back to his office.

"So, what's your experience in new drug development?"

Mikhail Borovsky, lead chemist of the Redex discovery team, had a new office. Egyptian blue stuffed chairs on a cream-colored carpet still had a new store smell. Framed diplomas were propped against his desk, not yet hung on the powder-blue-and-white striped wallpaper.

Dorian had just promoted Mikhail to senior vice president, director of research. Success seemed to have bred self-confidence. This wasn't the same guy who had been tense and stumbling in front of the board so many months ago. The ponytail was gone. A brown Zegna suit, white shirt, and maroon tie had replaced the T-shirt and jeans. The earring remained, but the glasses were gone, replaced by contacts, I figured.

"No experience, really, in new drug development. I'm not a chemist or pharmacologist, though I've studied investigational drugs in various animal experiments. But I've never created a drug from scratch."

Mikhail pushed back from his desk and scratched his head, bushy eyebrows arched. "Then why did your brother assign you to my team?"

I shrugged. "I guess he had to put me somewhere."

"Family," he harrumphed. "You're a clinician, right? A cardiologist?"

"Yes, although I also do research and teach."

"But you're primarily involved with patients, only an MD, right? Not a PhD?"

"Yes."

"Then you should be doing something like that here, also. True?"

"I suggested that to Dorian, but he was pretty adamant SP had enough people working in clinical areas."

Mikhail propped his chin on intertwined his fingers, leaning his elbows on his desk. "That's what happens when the CEO's too busy bunny baiting—that's what your brother calls it. Look here," he said, reaching behind his desk to open a file and extract a thick manila folder. "We've been doing a major clinical trial of Redex against Calcaine, the most potent of the other nonsteroidals, and I need someone to supervise it. I've named it the Redex Beats Calcaine trial. We're into RBC for a hundred million." He flipped me a summary sheet.

I frowned, hearing the title of the study that already assumed a favorable outcome for Redex. But I scanned the sheet and whistled. "Wow. That's huge. Ten thousand patients?"

He nodded. "The largest of its kind, ever. Five thousand randomized to Redex and the same to Calcaine, costing $10,000 a patient. So, the company has made an investment of $100 million. But the trial has slowed. We had a good guy in charge, Igor Platzov, but he was killed in a car accident several months ago, and his replacement needs to have a good kicking in his ass."

"An ass kicking. Yes, I can see what you mean. From this," I pointed at the summary sheet, "recruitment's dropped almost to zero."

He nodded. "RBC is what the FDA calls a pivotal trial. If we can show Redex beats the nonsteroidal drug king, Calcaine, with no stomach problems, we'll displace Calcaine and rule the anti-inflammatory market, not only in the US, but all over the world. We'll have tens of billions in annual sales. Does that interest you?"

"Could be. Where's it headquartered?"

"How good is your Russian?"

My eyebrows shot up, and I shifted in my seat. "You're kidding."

"I do not kid. Moscow and St. Petersburg mainly, but three other large Russian cities as well—Novosibirsk in Siberia, Yekaterinburg in Central Russia, and Samara on the Volga near Europe."

"Why Russia?"

"We've used up all our US and European test sites and had to get creative. Also, the cold winters make a lot of people have arthritis and need such medicines."

"The Russian docs cooperative?"

He nodded. "They're excellent scientists, and Western research gets them dollars and a chance to travel west for meetings. Also, I still have a lot of friends in Moscow who want to help."

"How long would I be away?"

"The trial has been going on for a year and has a year to go, so probably six months to get it back on track and another three to guide it toward a successful conclusion. The last three months, it should be automatic. But we would fly you back and forth, so you would spend one week each month working here. And you would get additional hardship pay."

"How much is that?"

"Fifty percent of your base pay."

"Hmm, now *that* interests me. Can those monies be paid separate from my regular salary?" I explained about Crystal.

"I'll have the lawyers research that. We'll do the best we can, but I cannot guarantee it."

"During my stateside week, I'd want Jessie flown in to spend it with me."

He waved his hand. "Not a problem. Anything else?"

"And SP continues to pay the lease on the sublet?"

"Of course."

"I assume all transatlantic travel is business class and first in the US?"

A nod.

Under the circumstances, I couldn't pass up an opportunity for patient contact and a good salary. "Mikhail, I want to talk with Jessie first, but I think you've got a deal. When would I leave?"

"You have a passport?"

"Sure."

"Then, probably a couple of weeks to complete the rest of the paperwork, find you a place in Moscow, a car, and stuff like that. And I'll give you a week in Indy before you leave, so let's plan for a month from today to be on the safe side."

We left his office and walked to mine, which seemed miles away from this high-rent district of senior executives. He let me in with a white pass card similar to Dorian's. The office was small with beige walls, a brown rug, a desk, and several wooden chairs. It would do.

I called Jessie as soon as Dorian left. She wouldn't be happy, but we could use the money. More importantly, I would be doing clinical research with patients.

"Daniel, you promised only six months, and that was going to be in New York."

"I know, Jessie, but this is too good to pass up. And we'll have a week together each month in New York. Maybe you could meet me in Russia when I finish, and we'll sightsee Moscow and St. Petersburg."

I went back to Dorian's office. I had to ask directions twice and figured I might need a GPS working there. His secretary was out. Loud voices stopped me in front of his door. It sounded like Dorian was very upset with Mikhail.

I knocked. "Dorian, Daniel here."

After a moment, "Come in."

They stood toe-to-toe, ready to square off. Mikhail held his ground though Dorian towered over him. I probably chose a good time to enter, or Dorian might've killed him. "Am I interrupting?"

Dorian's face, flushed with anger, relaxed at the sight of me. "Come in, bro. No, it's not a big deal." He pointed at Mikhail. "He's just—committed us to a large cash outlay to test a new drug without consulting me, and I'm giving him the what-for."

"If you didn't want me to make decisions, you shouldn't have made me VP for research."

"Still, you should've run it past me first." He glared at Mikhail, his mouth rigid and eyes narrowed. "We'll have to monitor this situation carefully, very carefully," he said, emphasizing each word. "You *hear* me?"

Mikhail stared right back, caterpillar eyebrows hoisted high. "I *said* I would take care of it," he said. "Don't worry."

After a moment, Dorian conceded. His smile was forced, but he draped a big arm around Mikhail's shoulders and led him toward the door. Mikhail gave me a brief nod, frowned at Dorian, and left.

"So, what was that all about?" I asked. "You two were ready to kill each other."

"Like I said, Mikhail made a big decision without checking with me first. I probably built it into a bigger deal than it was worth. Let's change the subject. Mikhail tells me we're sending you to Siberia." Dorian chuckled, closing the office door. I laughed too. "Bring long johns and a warm coat."

He steered me to a chair and sat down alongside. The austere portrait of my father stared down at us.

"Think about him a lot?" I asked.

"Every day I pass that picture, which is most days."

"What do you think about? Did you love him?"

"Feared more than loved." Dorian wrinkled his mouth. "You?"

"Not often, but then I'm not reminded of him every day. I used to think about how he loved you more, and that motivated me. So maybe it was positive."

"That's crap, and you know it. He treated me like shit at work. I'm sitting at his desk running this company because he was a heavy smoker, no other reason. If he hadn't keeled over, I'd still be in a tiny, windowless office on the ground floor sharing a secretary with two other VPs. That's one of many reasons I'm so glad about Redex. He never would've developed it. I often dream he's gagging on my success."

"Maybe he didn't love either of us. Who knows? He was never home. But what matters is what we think he felt, not what actually happened."

Dorian waved his hand, dismissing the topic. "Enough of this psychobabble bullshit. Only keeps my shrink in Italian suits. So, you excited about going to Russia?"

"Yes, that's what I came in to tell you. I know you had me slated for bench work, but Mikhail figured I could be of more use helping with the RBC trial. I assume you're okay with that."

"That's fine. I didn't think we needed clinical support for Redex, but he's convinced me otherwise. Told me to stop chasing bunnies and get back to running the company. For a little guy, he grew steel balls pretty fast, and big ones at that."

"You helped."

"I did, but he deserved the promotion because of Redex. In fact, most of the company's resources are now tied up in that drug, one way or another. It was his idea to go to Russia. Until recently, we had a good guy running the study."

"He told me. That must've been terrible. What happened?"

"I don't have all the facts, only that he'd been drinking and was found at two a.m. in a car half-submerged in some lake near his home. The Russians didn't do an autopsy, but the coroner ruled drowning as the cause of death. They did get a toxicology screen, and the blood-alcohol level was point two five or something like that, about three times the upper limit."

"Did he have a family?"

"I don't know. Mikhail's handling it. But you need to be forewarned. The Russians drink like fish. Vodka with lunch and dinner, poured like water at room temperature into juice glasses from a bottle in the middle of the table. So take care."

"That's not an exaggeration?"

Dorian leaned toward me, serious. "Hell, no. First time I went a couple of years ago to set up the RBC study, my host Sergei Lopakhin took me to the Café Pushkin. Lopakhin is Putin's physician and scientific advisor. The café's like going back in time, with waiters outfitted as nineteenth-century servants working in Pushkin's house."

"Impressive company. The café is in Moscow?"

"Yes. The building's three stories high, and the prices increase with each floor. One of the floors—I forget which one—is like an old library with shelves of Pushkin's books, and you eat among them. You need to try it for dinner. Fantastic, except for the goddamn cigarette smoke. Russians smoke as much as they drink, and they do it everywhere. Even the physicians during conferences. Anyway, at dinner, my host handed me the vodka bottle and said, 'Tonight, you drink as much as *you* want. Tomorrow night, you drink as much as *I* want.' And did we ever! I think I was drunk every night I was in Moscow. And nobody's worried about a DUI. They drive in any condition."

"I'm safe. I don't even like vodka."

"Doesn't matter. You can't refuse. I tried. The *tamada*—he's the toastmaster at a dinner—looked me straight in the eye and said, 'I toast you and your family. *Up your bottom!*' He meant 'bottoms up,' but I got the picture when he chugalugged the vodka and turned the glass upside down on the tablecloth to show it was empty. Trust me. It's hard to say no."

CHAPTER TWENTY-FIVE

The Boeing 767 left New York's Kennedy airport on time at 5:00 p.m. with a scheduled 10:25 a.m. arrival at Sheremetyevo International Airport, about twenty miles northwest of Moscow. Moscow's busiest airport, Domodedovo, was still being repaired after the Chechnya Black Widows triggered an explosion that ripped through a terminal, killing thirty-seven travelers.

I could've flown Aeroflot, the Russian airline, for half the price of the Delta ticket, but I wondered what the airlines had skimped on to get the airfare so low. That made me nervous.

After we hit cruising altitude, I relaxed and began to replay in my head the events since that phone call from Crystal. My God, how that had changed my life.

The flight attendants came by wheeling a cart with the usual array of before-dinner treats and interrupted my thoughts.

"What reds do you have?"

She held a wine bottle in each hand. "A Hess cabernet from the Napa Valley or a Domaine Drouhin pinot noir from Willamette in Oregon."

"I'll have that one," I said, pointing to the pinot.

After two glasses, the baked chicken dinner and risotto weren't half-bad. I finished with coffee and a rather large Rémy Martin. At least Delta splurged for the VSOP cognac rather than the cheaper VS.

I was outlining in my laptop how I was going to restart the RBC trial when I heard the overhead page. "If there's a physician on board, please push the flight attendant call button."

I didn't know what to do. The restrictions from Judge Dotter flashed through my mind. Did they apply at thirty-five thousand feet in an airplane on the way to Russia? Also, I had downed all that booze. Was a physician with an alcoholic buzz better than no physician at all? If there was a complication, was I still covered under the Good Samaritan laws that protected volunteers? I was about to find out.

I pushed the call button.

A flight attendant rushed to my seat. "You're a doctor?"

I unbuckled my seatbelt and stood. "Yes, I'm a cardiologist. What's the problem?"

"Thank God!" she said. "A passenger in coach just had a seizure and is making funny noises. She doesn't answer to her name. Please come quickly."

I followed her down the aisle to a passenger in a middle seat about halfway to the back. She was staring straight ahead with a glassy, fixed gaze despite an attendant shaking her shoulder and calling her name. Red-tinged drool dripped from her lips, perhaps from biting her tongue during the seizure. I heard her gasping respirations over the noise of the plane. Two other people, a middle-aged man and an elderly woman, stood in the aisle looking helpless.

"He's a cardiologist," the attendant announced to the group, pushing me to the center.

"Thank God," muttered the man. He shook my hand. "I'm a dermatologist and don't have any idea what's wrong with her."

"And I'm a psychiatrist," chimed in the elderly woman. She shrugged, helpless. "They said she had a seizure."

The two passengers on either side vacated their seats. I pushed up the armrests and stretched her out, head toward the window. I slid a small pillow under her head, squeezed down alongside, and felt her pulse. It was rapid—I guessed 110 or 120 per minute—and thready. Her face was pale, glistening with a fine patina of sweat. She was breathing at least twenty times a minute, slipping into shock.

"Do you have an emergency kit with a blood pressure cuff and stethoscope?" I asked the flight attendant.

"Yes, Doctor, right away," she said and hurried off.

I did a quick physical exam. She was white, around fifty, dark hair with gray roots. Her limbs were flaccid, but she squeezed her eyes in pain when I pinched her arm. Her eyes were brown, pupils equal-sized, small, and round. I didn't have a flashlight but guessed the light reflex would be normal. Still, a stroke was a possibility.

"Does anybody know this woman?" I shouted over the noise of the plane and her gasping. A lot of headshaking: no. I asked the people who had been sitting on either side of her, "Did she say anything about herself before she got sick?" Again headshaking. "Did she seem normal until the seizure?" *Yes.* "Did she have a lot to drink?" *No.* "Did she eat dinner?" *No.*

This was going to be like veterinary medicine. No help from the patient.

But she was going into shock and in danger of suffering irreversible brain and kidney damage. I had to do something—now.

The attendant handed me the emergency kit, a small orange knapsack with the zipper sealed by a plastic clip. I found the blood pressure cuff and stethoscope. Seventy over forty, which might explain her mental state.

I finished examining her through her clothes. Not ideal, but I didn't want to undress her in front of the entire coach cabin. Her lungs were clear, no heart murmurs, and her belly felt soft. Her legs seemed normal, but phlebitis and a blood clot to her lungs were possibilities. I still didn't have a diagnosis. Regardless, I had to get her blood pressure up.

"Elevate her legs," I told the flight attendant. "Build a mound with some pillows and blankets for her feet to rest on." While she did that, I emptied part of the survival kit in the aisle and found a bag of sterile saline, an IV needle, and tubing. There was also a pair of scissors. An onlooker gasped as I cut the sleeve to her shoulder, probably shredding an expensive blouse.

As I was about to stick her with the needle, the plane lurched in turbulent air. I waited a moment for calm and plunged in the needle. I hadn't started an IV in quite a while, but I hit the vein on the first stab, secured the needle in place, and let the saline run in wide open. Her blood pressure didn't budge. Her vacant eyes stared straight at me, not registering or moving. I needed a diagnosis or she was going to die.

"What's her name?" I asked the flight attendant.

"Sandra Halsted," she said. "I checked the passenger list."

An idea flashed. "Open the overhead luggage rack and see if she has a carry-on."

The attendant lifted out a blue roller bag. "Set it down in the aisle and open it." Inside were clothes and a cellophane bag that she must have shown to get through security. "Give me the bag."

Bingo! A syringe, needles in a case, and three bottles of medicine, one of which was insulin.

She hadn't eaten dinner. Insulin without food had driven her blood sugar so low it had caused a seizure and now was going to kill her. I figured she had to be a diabetic in an insulin coma.

I tore into the survival kit, praying some thoughtful person had anticipated my need.

I found it. A 50-milliliter syringe labeled D50W, doctor's lingo for concentrated sugar water.

"Thank goodness," I said.

Before I finished injecting half, she started "m and m," moving and moaning. After a bit more glucose, she focused on me and whispered, "Thank you. You saved my life."

Three minutes later, she was sucking an orange and explaining. She had taken her full evening insulin dose but had gotten airsick and skipped dinner. Before she could tell anyone, she had a hypoglycemic seizure and became semicomatose. She felt quite well now, thank you very much, and could she please have some dinner? And by the way, I owed her a new Escada blouse, but she was going to keep this ruined one anyway and frame it. Would I please autograph the slit sleeve?

When I got back to my seat, the captain broadcast over the loudspeaker what had happened. The passengers cheered and clapped. Several came up to shake my hand. The captain announced free drinks for all, "courtesy of the doc who saved a passenger's life."

Lindorf and Dotter could both go to hell. I was a doctor again, saving lives, doing what I did best.

CHAPTER TWENTY-SIX

Hours later, the gentle shake of the flight attendant woke me out of my Ambien sleep to a snowy, dark January morning. I had slept through the landing. My US passport and visa got me through the checkpoints easily. I exited to the lobby, where a long line of men stood holding signs scrawled with the names of passengers. I walked the gauntlet pulling my suitcase until I found the man with my name on a sign.

"*Dobra yeootra,*" I said, trying out my Rosetta Stone purchase. "Good morning, I'm Daniel Sloane." I held out my hand.

Evgeni Kiselenko spoke passable English, though with a strong Russian accent. He introduced himself as we shook hands. He was a stocky guy, with broad shoulders, a round face, and a flat nose that had been broken more than once. A fur Cossack hat, pulled to his eyebrows, made him look like the archetypal James Bond villain. When he took off the hat to say hello, I saw a knobby, shaved head, a dead ringer for the character Odd Job in *Goldfinger*.

"Dr. Sloane, it is pleasure to welcome you to my country. Dr. Borovsky has told me much about you, and of course I have read many of your articles on arrhythmias. I am Dr. Evgeni Alexandrovich Kiselenko, but everybody calls me Sasha. I will be very happy to work with you on this important project."

He handed me his card with Russian on one side and English on the other. He grabbed the Samsonite and said, "If you don't mind, please to follow me. I have driver outside to take us to your new apartment. The Leningradskoe Highway is now very crowded with many cars and trucks entering Moscow for work this morning, and it will take us more than an hour to get there."

We walked past a line of Russian taxis, mostly ancient Ladas belching blue-white steam from their exhausts as drivers kept motors running to stay warm. I hugged the blue North Face fleece jacket tight around me.

This last-minute splurge turned out to be a lifesaver as the frigid winds whipped around the corner.

The driver of a black Mercedes four-door stretch sedan idling at the end of the line jumped out and ran to take the suitcase from Sasha. He popped the trunk, hoisted my bag inside, and dashed curbside to open the door for me, all the while talking in Russian. Sasha grunted a reply, and I climbed into the backseat.

Inside, fresh white lace doilies lined the back of the seat and armrests. A wide leather organizer divided the backseat in half and held bottled water, an unopened bottle of Stolichnaya vodka, and glasses, no ice. I remembered what my brother told me and hoped it was too early for the driver to be drinking.

Sasha got in on the other side. "I have told the driver to take his time so you can enjoy our beautiful countryside as we drive toward Moscow. Also, parts of the road become very icy, and accidents are common."

"Like the doctor who ran the RBC study. That was so tragic."

Sasha gave me a funny look.

"The one who drowned," I said.

"Ah, yes," he nodded. "He was careless driver. Often, we have black ice you don't see until too late, and you skid off into a lake and drown, like Igor Platzov."

We pulled away from the curb and passed the line of taxis. From the corner of my eye, I saw a tall African American woman pause with her hand on the door handle of the first cab in line. In that moment, Crystal's eyes locked onto mine. She ducked her head and disappeared inside the cab. I swiveled around, but we had already entered the long line of cars leaving the airport. She vanished from view.

My God. Crystal! Sasha's chatter was lost on me as I mentally replayed the scene. Could it really be her? I looked out the rear window, but she was gone. She must've been on the same flight, probably in first class, and I hadn't seen her from my seat in business class. But how did she know I was coming? And what was she planning?

"Are you all right?" Sasha asked.

"Yeah, thanks, I'm fine. Trying to adjust to land again and the time change after that long flight."

"Today is Friday, so you will have all of today and the weekend to have nice rest in the apartment I rented for you."

"Where is it?"

"Leningradsky Prospekt, on Alexandra Nevskogo Ulitsa, just southwest of the center of Moscow. You will like it a lot, I am sure. You will live on the ninth floor of a new brick building. Your apartment has two bedrooms, a built-in kitchen, a small living room, and new furnishings. You can take the Kaluzhsko subway line, transfer to the Koltsevaya that goes directly to the Chaznikov Institute of Cardiology. That's where the RBC headquarters is located. Or if you rent a car, there is parking in the basement of the apartment building and in the institute."

"When did you rent the apartment?"

"About a month ago, when Dr. Borovsky e-mailed you were coming."

"Did you sign a lease?"

Sasha gave me a quizzical look. "Yes, of course, for six months."

"Can you break the lease if I wanted to move into a different place?"

He shook his head and gave me a strange look. "I have paid almost four hundred thousand rubles—about $12,000 for the first two months' rent, which I would lose. It is very expensive, but I was told to rent the best available space. You do not like this apartment, and you have not even seen it yet?"

"No, it's not that. It's only—oh, never mind. I'm sure it'll be fine." I sat back and watched the countryside stream by. Whoever told Crystal I was going to Moscow probably knew about the apartment and would learn the address of a new one if I switched. And she certainly knew the Chaznikov Institute where I'd be working. I'd have to watch my back. Speaking of which—I turned and stared at the taxi following close on our heels. I couldn't make out who was in it, but I could guess.

Sasha looked at me, a question on his face as we passed through a forest of white birches. "You are worried about this car behind us?"

"No, only looking at the scenery." I pointed. "The trees are beautiful, all covered in a layer of white snow."

"Yes, they are. The white birch is the national tree of Russia. Several times each year, the trees are—how do you say it, knocked?"

I smiled. "Almost. Tapped."

"Yes, tapped, and we drink the sap for good health. The white birch trees are all over Russia." The car came to an abrupt halt behind a long line of traffic sitting still as a parking lot. Sasha had an angry exchange with the driver, who only shrugged and drummed his fingers on the steering wheel.

"What's the matter?" I looked behind us, but the taxi was gone.

"We are too close to Rublyovka. The traffic has stopped."

"What's Rublyovka?"

He looked at me like I was from outer space. "You do not know this name from your newspapers or TV?"

I shook my head.

"This is area where all Russia's new millionaires live—or most of them. It is the most expensive land in Moscow, maybe four million US dollars for half an acre and twenty-five million for a house. They build houses four stories high because of little land. When you buy a new house in Rublyovka, you get a helicopter as part of the price, like an ordinary person in your country might get better rugs or wallpapers. The landing pad is on top of the house. Moscow now has more billionaires than any other city in the world."

"But why did the traffic stop?"

"The area has so many new houses from the new millionaires that traffic has spilled over from the Uspenskiiy and Rublyovka Highways to the Leningradskoe Highway, where we are. Also, Putin lives in Rublyovka. Twice a day—he takes a different route each time back and forth to the Kremlin—the roads around close down so he can race in and out in his S600 Pullman Guard."

"I never heard of that car."

"It is a Mercedes, like a tank but with luxury." He asked the driver a question. "Sergei just told me it weighs twelve thousand pounds, is bulletproof, including the tires—the Germans test it with five hand grenades exploding at once underneath the body of the car—and costs a million and a half dollars. Putin's chauffeur spent two weeks in Stuttgart, Germany, to learn how to drive it."

"But they still stop traffic for his safety?"

"No, not for safety, for speed. Putin is not afraid of anything or anybody, especially driving in that tank. He likes to race at 160 km per hour—one hundred miles per hour US—for the fun. So all other cars have to get out of his way."

After we sat another five minutes or so, cars started inching forward until we hit our normal speed. Forty minutes later, I was shown my second new apartment in a month.

CHAPTER TWENTY-SEVEN

I unpacked after Sasha dropped me off. It's harder for me to fly east than west, and a wave of fatigue bowled me over. I could barely keep my eyes open. After texting Jessie from my iPhone that I had arrived safely, I crashed fully clothed. I woke three hours later, wondering where the hell I was.

I was hungry and checked out the tiny kitchen. A red cloth embroidered with yellow and pink flowers covered a white plate on the kitchen table. On the plate sat a saltshaker and a fresh loaf of Russian black bread that smelled delicious. A note pinned to the cloth read, "The traditional Russian welcoming for important guests is bread and salt, the essentials of life. They go best with a glass of vodka. I hope your visit with us will be successful." It was signed by Sasha.

Nice.

I continued my forage and found the kitchen stocked with milk, coffee, cans of soup, a six-pack of Evian water, and a package of sausages. And, of course, a bottle of Stolichnaya Cristall vodka. I ate a sausage sandwich with a bowl of soup and sipped a small glass of vodka. I had barely finished when the phone rang.

A strange voice asked, "Dr. Sloane?"

"Who is this?"

"You do not know me, but I must talk with you."

Not good. I knew the sleeping pill Ambien could produce a post-sleep hypnotic state. I once had a patient who woke, drove his car straight into a ditch, and never remembered a bit of it. This phone call was real, but who would be calling me?

"I have informations for you," the caller said. "We need to meet."

"Tell Crystal to try some other time."

"Crystal? I don't know what is crystal."

"Yeah, right. Tell her no more zombie spells."

"I still do not know what you mean. Or what means zombie spells. Do you want my informations or not?" the caller said.

Maybe I was wrong. "What kind of information? Who are you?"

"My brother did not drown. He was killed."

"Who was your—?" It hit me. My heart rate sped. Alarm bells chimed. "Who *are* you?"

"Igor Platzov worked for your drug company. I am Leonid, his older brother. Igor was murdered."

"Let me make this clear. Igor worked for my brother's company, not mine. I'm here to replace him as head of the RBC trial, and I don't know what you're talking about. And I still think Crystal put you up to this."

The phone line went dead. I put the receiver down with a shaking hand. I stood and looked out the window, but the street was deserted. Maybe the guy was telling the truth, and he had nothing to do with Crystal. But it was something for the police, not me. I was about to call Sasha when the phone rang again.

"I think you must talk with me."

"Why?"

"Because maybe you will be next found in a lake."

That stopped me cold, and my heart started to pound. "Why should I trust you?"

"You have no one else to trust, and your life could be dangerous."

"I'll call the police."

"Ha, good luck with *our* police."

"Okay, I'll meet you but not alone. I want to bring Sasha Kiselenko." I figured Odd Job earned his busted nose honestly and would be a good guy in a jam. "Where and when?"

"No. You must be alone."

Yeah, and maybe end up in the lake. But why would anyone want to hurt me? I wasn't a threat. It didn't compute. "Okay, I'll meet you here."

"Not in your apartment. A more public place. Do you know how to get to Red Square?"

"Tell me."

"You are near the Kaluzhsko subway line. Get off at Ploshchad Revolyutsii station, right next to Red Square. In English it means Revolution Square. The station is famous with many sculptures and archways."

On the flight over, I had read that Moscow subway stations were decorated like palaces with mosaics, frescoes, and crystal chandeliers. Go try that in New York.

"That's the one with the dog sculpture?"

"Yes. Walk a few hundred meters to Red Square. You will see Lenin's Mausoleum on your right. It's a reddish granite tomb along the Kremlin Wall. In front will be a long line of people waiting to get in. Get in line and go through the tour of the tomb. I will stand outside to see if anyone is following you."

"Why would anyone be following me?" I thought of Crystal, but there was no reason she'd have anything to do with the RBC study. Or was I missing some connection?

"Only do as I ask, please. Look for me when you come out of the tomb."

"How will I recognize you?"

"I will be wearing a black ski parka, the kind you have in the US, with the hood over my head. Also, I will hold a book under my left arm, Tolstoy's *War and Peace*. It is a very fat book with a brown cover. That will be enough to find me, yes?"

A crowded Red Square was good for anonymity, but I thought of the Bulgarian dissident writer Markov stabbed in the leg with the ricin-tipped umbrella. I was getting sucked in way over my head. My heart, already pounding, skipped a few beats. Should I really be doing this?

But could it be crucial to the success of the RBC trial? "Okay, when?"

"One hour will give you plenty of time. Come up to me and say, 'I read that book you are holding.'"

The Moscow subway system is a man-made marvel with no graffiti and LOLs—little old ladies—all over the place, sweeping and polishing. Escalator cops called *dezhurnayas* patrol the hundreds of moving stairs to be sure nothing slows the three-minute vertical ride of over two hundred feet. I figured the Moscow unemployment rate must be pretty low.

I got off at Revolution Square. In the station, the bronze statue of a border guard down on his left knee, right hand gripping a rifle, and left hugging his dog sitting next to him, occupied a prominent section. Millions of fingers had rubbed the dog's long snout for luck, buffing the dark bronze muzzle into a shiny yellow veneer. I added my pat as I walked past.

Red Square looked exactly as I had seen so many times on TV during the Soviet years of military parades. Gray granite paving blocks covered almost four football fields long and more than two wide. I walked up a sloping entrance past the ornate State Historical Museum to Lenin's tomb, his body preserved there since his death in 1924. On the opposite side of the square stood the gigantic GUM department store, newly remodeled for the modern, boutique shopping demanded by Russia's new millionaire class. Directly south was St. Basil's Cathedral, the colorful, multi-domed church highlighted in every travel brochure about Russia.

The line to the tomb was long. I didn't spot anyone who fit Leonid's description. An hour later, I finally got inside. Lenin was stretched out on his back in a specially constructed crypt, looking peacefully asleep. The guidebooks said his body was chemically preserved, while rumor had it as a wax replica from Madame Tussaud's Wax Museum. We circled at a shuffling pace and were outside again in ten minutes.

I saw a man in a black parka standing behind a group of tourists. I approached and asked, "Are you Leonid?"

He stared straight ahead.

I pointed to the book under his left arm. "I read that book you are holding."

He nodded. "Please, do not talk and only follow me to the subway. We will go to my house where we can be safe. I have papers to show you."

"Why all this cloak-and-dagger stuff?" I asked, and then thought maybe he didn't understand that phrase. But he was already walking off, toward St. Basil's. I had no choice but to follow and pulled up my North Face hood against the bitter cold wind blowing through the open square.

I could only glimpse St. Basil's Cathedral as we hurried past, one of the most unique and picturesque churches in the world. Nine onion domes in blues and greens, yellows, whites, and golds sat like swirling frozen custards topping a sugar cone. Tsar Ivan the Terrible had commissioned the cathedral in the mid-1550s and blinded the architect after completion so he could never build another as beautiful. Four hundred years later, Stalin threatened to demolish St. Basil's because it slowed his soldiers marching en masse from Red Square. An architect named Baranovsky stood on its steps with a knife to his own throat, promising public suicide if Stalin damaged a single brick. Stalin had spared the church and imprisoned Baranovsky.

Leonid walked quickly. When I tried to catch up, he quickened his pace. I think he did not want to be seen walking with me.

We entered a subway station, boarded the Arbatsko line going northeast, and sat on opposite sides of the car. Three stops later, Leonid got out, and I followed at a distance. I trailed behind, down a long hill to a complex of deteriorating gray cement buildings that looked pre-WWII. Laundry flapped from gray ropes strung between windows. A dirt path snaked in and around the buildings, which all looked the same.

I shadowed Leonid as he entered the furthest building. A bare, flickering overhead bulb vainly tried to light a narrow lobby devoid of furniture. The rank odor of garbage, stale food, and dirty laundry clogged the air. A tiny elevator stood to one side, but Leonid motioned me to the stairs. "Does not work for a year," he whispered.

We climbed three flights, exited a rusted door into a dark hallway, and stopped in front of apartment 3C. Leonid unlocked the door, and we stepped into a postage-stamp-sized living room. An even smaller kitchen and a door that opened to a bedroom comprised the entire living area. I saw no bathroom and remembered the smell of urine from one we passed in the hallway.

Leonid took a deep breath, exhaled, and smiled for the first time. His face relaxed.

"Welcome," he said, extending nicotine-stained fingers. "Let me take your coat." He shook out of his parka, and I could see the man for the first time: slight, balding gray hair, and a face that was a roadmap of wrinkles. Thin, gray eyebrows roofed brown eyes that hid behind rimless spectacles.

"Please to sit down." He motioned to a worn couch covered by a stained blanket. His hand swept the room. "I am sorry for this, but my retirement pension as a senior scientist at the Chaznikov does not pay very much. My wife is also retired. She is medical doctor—maybe you know 90 percent of practicing doctors in Russia are women—and earns a little bit extra reading electrocardiograms at the Chaznikov Hospital. She is there now. My son and his wife are both doctors and also working. They live with us too."

I looked around and raised my eyebrows.

"Yes," he said, "it is very crowded." He shrugged. "But it is a home, which many people in Russia do not have even though we have many millionaires. But that is not what I wanted to discuss with you. First though, I forgot my manners. Maybe you would like some tea?"

"No thanks. Let's come right to the point. Why am I here?"

"I told you. Because my brother was murdered."

"And how do you know that?"

"He never drank and was an expert driver. For him to drive into the middle of a lake and drown, it is impossible to happen. He drove the institute car for many years—it was his job as leader of many drug studies since he had to travel to different Russian cities—and he was always very careful."

"Why would someone want to kill him?"

"I thought you would know that." He walked to the kitchen, filled a teapot, turned on a gas jet, and struck a match.

"I came to Russia to replace him as head of the RBC trial. I have no idea who would want to kill him or why."

"Maybe some peoples at another drug company who manufactures the other drug? Maybe this Redex was turning out to be too much better, and they did not like it?"

"That drug is Calcaine, manufactured in the United States by Goodal Nearing Drugs, in California. GND's a multibillion-dollar giant compared to Sloane Pharmaceuticals. I suppose they could be worried, but the results are blinded." I paused to see if he understood.

He nodded. "Yes, I know the word, blinded. It means no one knows who got sugar pill and who got real drug, so no one knows what is outcome. But there are always ways to find out such informations."

"Even so, why would they kill your brother?"

"Maybe to stop the study if your drug was better."

"SP would only replace him, as they have. The outcome of this study is pretty important, not to mention the millions of dollars it's costing."

"I agree with you. I do not think those are the reasons, either, but I wanted to know what you thought. I have the real reasons in papers—"

Pounding on the apartment door cut him off midsentence. He put a finger to his lips and motioned me to hide in the bedroom. Before I could move, I heard a loud crack, and the door gave way.

Two big guys crashed into the room, yelled something in Russian, and flashed badges. Leonid's face paled. He raised shaking hands over his head.

The taller one approached him, giving me a "keep-out-of-this" look. I saw something dark and thick in his hand, maybe a blackjack. It flashed as his fist slammed the side of Leonid's head. He collapsed like a felled tree, blood spewing from his scalp as his head thudded on the floor. One guy moved to each side, lifted him effortlessly, and carried him past me. I grabbed at the guy's arm, but he slammed me in the chest with the blackjack. I fell back onto the couch, gasping, the breath knocked out of me.

The entire event must've lasted less than thirty seconds. The room emptied as quickly as it had filled. Leonid's feet dragged on the floor as they carried him out.

I had no idea what was going on or what to do next. Should I call the cops? Or were these guys the cops? Stupidly, I had left Sasha's card with his phone number at my apartment. The best thing was probably to get out of the apartment and find my way back to mine.

I was halfway out the door when the teapot whistled. I dashed back in to turn off the gas. On the kitchen table, I spotted a sealed envelope labeled *Chaznikov* lying next to the book Leonid had carried. When I heard voices in the hall, I froze for a moment, as the conversation got louder.

I stuffed the envelope underneath my shirt and ran toward the door. The jamb had been splintered, and the door hung loose on its hinges. I peeked into the hallway and saw an elderly man and woman. They stopped talking when they spotted me and stood there, openmouthed.

I raced around them to the stairwell and bolted down two and three steps at a time, barely breathing until I hit the ground floor. I searched for a rear entrance but couldn't find one. The old couple most likely had called the police about a robbery. I opened the front door cautiously. No one was there. Across the street, a big black car raced off.

I got lost on the winding dirt path until I recognized the street leading to the subway station. I walked back up the hill as fast as I could without drawing attention. We had ridden the Arbatsko line, and I needed to take it back to Ploshchad Revolyutsii and transfer to the Kaluzhko line. I exited after two stops instead of three, realized my mistake, and had to change trains two more times, but an hour later I found my apartment.

I couldn't remember whether I had locked my door when I left, so I was not alarmed to find it unlocked.

That is, until I saw the voodoo doll sitting on the kitchen table, its dismembered head stuck on a spike next to the body. Crystal had even dabbed catsup on the severed neck, an unnecessary touch of realism.

CHAPTER TWENTY-EIGHT

I tried to piece together what was happening. Why was Crystal here? How did she get into my apartment? Did she have an accomplice? Did she have anything to do with the RBC trial? I called Sasha and told him about Leonid. He said he'd drop everything and drive right over. Then I called Dorian. As I dialed the United States, I looked out the apartment window. A few people were walking on the street below.

"Holy shit, bro. Get your ass home immediately. The RBC study isn't important enough to jeopardize your life."

"I'm okay, Dorian—at least I think I am. They didn't come for me. I just happened to be in the wrong place at the wrong time." Without realizing it, I started pacing up and down. I guess I was pretty keyed up. "Do you know this guy, Leonid Platzov, a senior scientist at the Chaznikov?"

"No, but then I wouldn't know the people working there except for Sasha and one or two others. But it's you I'm worried about."

"I'll be fine. My only issue is Crystal. I think I underestimated her."

"The kidnapping sounded pretty dangerous."

"Yes, but like I said, not for me. Do you want this study done or not? You told me the company's neck was on the line for big bucks. Snake eyes now and it all goes down the drain. Besides, I need the combat pay."

Dorian laughed. "Okay, but stay away from any rough stuff. Let Sasha handle it. Promise?"

"Will do. Say hello to all your bunnies, and if you talk with Jessie, don't mention anything about this. I texted her, and I'm going to call her later."

After we hung up, I remembered the papers in my shirt and took them out to read at the table. Before I could open the envelope, I heard a knock on the door, probably Sasha.

With the security chain on, I peered through the peephole. Sasha wore a worried look. I unbolted the door and let him in. "I am so sorry for you. It must have been very frightening."

"It was, but even more for Leonid."

"That is something I have to tell you. There is no Leonid Platzov at the Chaznikov Institute. I did not recognize the name, so I called the head of administration, thinking maybe he was just hired. But, no, he does not exist."

"Impossible! He called me. I met with him and went to his apartment." I thought a moment. "Perhaps because he's retired?"

"No, I checked that list also. Could you find the apartment again?"

I stopped to think. "Maybe. I know we got on the Arbatsko subway line at Red Square and got off in three stops. I followed him to his apartment but wasn't paying much attention. It was on the third or fourth floor." I shrugged. "I couldn't find the same dirt path when I left."

Sasha pursed his lips and tried to hide a disappointed look. He rubbed a hand over his bald head. "What do you want me to do? I already called the police and told them I would give to them more informations after I spoke with you."

Why would Leonid lie about being a retired Chaznikov scientist? If he had lied about that, what else had he made up? If the badges were real, he was probably in a gulag cell somewhere for something related to his brother's death. Maybe he'd killed him? If the badges were phony, maybe this was some sort of industrial espionage. Or maybe he was already dead. Too many maybes.

Damn, this was Saturday. I'd only been in Russia little more than twenty-four hours. I ran a hand through my hair. "What do you suggest?"

"The police investigated Igor's death and were satisfied he drowned in a car accident. I do not know if he has this brother, Leonid, and why the brother is now saying Igor was murdered. From my position as director of the Chaznikov Institute, none of this really matters. What is most important now is to restart the RBC trial as quickly as possible and make it finish on time. There is much money at stake, as well as our reputation, and we need the outcome to show Redex beats Calcaine. That is what we must do—get back to focusing on the study."

"We *hope* Redex beats Calcaine."

Sasha rolled his eyes, paced in front of me, looked around the room, and spied the voodoo doll. He walked over and picked up the two pieces, looking from them to me. "You?"

I nodded.

He frowned. "Why?"

"It's a long story and not related to anything here. Somebody back home doesn't like me."

"He's here in Moscow?"

"She. And yes, I saw her at the airport when we drove off."

"So she followed you to Moscow to do something bad? She was in the cab behind us?"

I nodded again. "She says I was responsible for the death of her husband. He was a basketball player and—it's too involved to try to explain. She's very angry."

Sasha looked at his watch and then at me. "You have had a very full day today. Are you hungry?"

I nodded.

He took me by the arm. "Come, the hour is getting late. Let me bring you to dinner. I am not married, so we will go find a very nice restaurant and have some very nice vodka and caviar with some very nice Russian black bread and talk about pleasant things with pleasant people."

I couldn't argue that logic. "Give me a few minutes to wash up and change my clothes. There's a bottle of vodka, if you want a drink." I pointed to the Stolichnaya. "I'll be right back."

The Night Flight restaurant-nightclub was in northwest Moscow.

"This is one of the best restaurants in Moscow," Sasha said. A valet took the Mercedes's keys, and we walked toward the glittering entrance. Tiny blinking, white lights covered the evergreens surrounding the restaurant. Set in the snowy background, the scene looked like a Hallmark Christmas card. "It is also a nightclub, and it is said that only to have dinner here is like only to read an article in your *Playboy* magazine without looking at the pictures." He smiled, probably with insider's knowledge.

Two well-muscled guys guarding the door admitted us. I thought about Leonid, but this was a different pair.

"The chef is from Sweden," Sasha explained as we entered, "and prepares every different cuisine you can imagine, from Old Mother Russia to the best of Paris. The elk and reindeer steaks with morels are fantastic."

I looked around. Oil paintings and a series of Andy Warhol's prints of Marilyn Monroe covered walls of dark paneled wood, probably mahogany. Long, horizontal picture windows overlooked Tverskaya Street below. The maître d' greeted Sasha by name and led us to a table in a quiet corner of the nightclub. We sat in red velvet chairs that matched the rug. Reflected light from crystal wall sconces illuminated the artwork and bathed the room in a warm, soft amber glow.

I nodded at our table for four. "Are you expecting guests?"

"You never can tell," he said, smiling. "I like this corner without tables nearby. Sometimes spies from other countries sit at a close table to listen."

I gulped. "Here?"

He nodded. "This is a very popular restaurant for important peoples. And after vodka, who knows what falls off a loose tongue? You do not have such things in your country?"

I shrugged. "I have no idea."

He gave me a knowing look. "I am sure you do. But let us order some food. If it is fine with you, I will do that. I come here often and know what is best on the menu. And this is a business dinner, so the institute will pay for it. But don't tell your brother." We both laughed.

A head gesture, and a waiter materialized. Sasha spoke to him in Russian, and a moment later, he set down a bottle of Grey Goose vodka in the middle of the table.

"No Stolichnaya?" I asked.

Sasha shook his head. "Russian vodka is for tourists. This is better." He poured half a glass for us both. "In Russia, we have many toasts with dinner. So pace yourself and start with little drinks. As the tamada, I will make this first toast to your President Obama. May he lead the world in peaceful pursuits."

A first for me, toasting our own president.

"Now it is your turn," Sasha said after a few minutes of silence.

"Okay, I will toast—well, I don't know. Putin or Medvedev?"

"Putin, but is safer to do both."

I held up my glass, now refilled by Sasha. "May President Putin and past-President Medvedev join with President Obama to make a peaceful world for us all."

By the time the caviar arrived with an assortment of blini, minced onions, chopped egg, and crème fraîche, I was feeling the vodka.

"Beluga," Sasha pronounced, waving his hand over the array of plates. "Only the best." It was delicious, better by far than any I had tasted in the States.

By this time, we had toasted German, English, Italian, French, and Chinese world leaders and ran out of names. Sasha started on my family.

"What is your wife's name?"

I told him.

"A man's name?"

I explained.

"So, here is to Jessie, may she enjoy good health and happiness." He paused, grinned, and raised his glass again. "And maybe have a little Jessie sometime soon in the future?" Sasha drained his glass and turned it upside down. My brother had warned me. I felt pressured to do the same.

The vodka bottle was half-empty. We had eaten nothing more than the appetizer. "Sasha, maybe no toasts for a while until we get some more food. My head is starting to spin."

"Nonsense. *Za vash*," he said, "to you." We drank again. I caught his barest headshake, and two women, a brunette and a blonde, walked to our table.

"Ah, yes, here come my two good friends, Alena and Katerina. Please, lovely ladies, join us for a bit of food and some drink." He got up and hugged them both, holding Alena a bit longer. He gestured at me while looking at them.

"Alena and Katerina, this is my good friend, Doctor Daniel Sloane. Daniel, they do not speak too much English, so we will only enjoy their beautiful looks, yes? Maybe like scenery."

I stood, and Alena sat down next to Sasha and Katerina next to me. They were gorgeous. Katerina typified Swedish beauty with shoulder-length, soft blonde hair, blue eyes, and high cheekbones. I could picture her in a Vidal Sassoon shampoo commercial, swishing her hair in rippling, golden waves while showing lots of cleavage in a half-opened black lace negligée.

A waiter approached with four tureens of a purplish-colored soup, each garnished with a dollop of floating cream. The aroma of simmering meat and cooked beets made me realize how hungry I was.

"Borscht, a typical Russian red cabbage and beet soup with chunks of lamb, just like my mother made," Sasha explained. "This restaurant cooks it better than any other in Russia." He looked at me and smiled. "Try it. You'll like it."

"You sound like my mother," I said. "That was her stock phrase to get us to try any new food."

"I wasn't thinking of the food," Sasha said, grinning at the ladies, "but it does apply to the borscht also. Let us drink to the ladies," he said, raising his vodka glass. "To two creatures as lovely as God ever made."

I hesitated.

"Come along, Daniel. You do not like the company? Bottoms up!" He chugalugged his vodka and turned the glass upside down again. Shamed into it, I did the same. By this time, we had finished almost three-quarters of the bottle, and my head was really swimming, bringing back memories of Dartmouth fraternity parties.

In the distance—it seemed distant but was really only ten or fifteen feet away—a band started playing an American song, something slow and romantic. I recognized a Sinatra tune but couldn't think of the name—maybe "I'm in the Mood for Love." Katerina took my hand and stood, looking at the dance floor. She didn't say anything, and I hesitated. She tugged.

"Go ahead, my friend," Sasha said. "A little dance cannot hurt, and I will not tell a soul, I promise."

Katerina tugged again, more insistently, and I yielded. I stood but had to grab the back of the chair as a wave of dizziness hit me. I followed and started dancing, holding her at arm's length.

In a millisecond, she stepped inside my arms, into me, molding her body against mine. She was taller than Jessie and rested her cheek against mine, her breasts pressed against my chest. They were soft, no implants. Despite my not wanting to let it happen, I got an erection. Katerina felt it, lifted her head briefly to smile at me, and pressed her hips even closer. She nibbled at my earlobe. We danced slowly, she holding tight, and me trying to resist—sort of. Finally the song ended, and we walked back to the table.

Sasha and Alena had gone, and the waiter had cleared the table. Katerina did not seem surprised. She took me by the hand and led me out of the restaurant.

In the lobby, Katerina walked toward a red velvet staircase with a shimmering gold banister. She stopped at the foot of the stairs, looked at me and then to the top of the stairs. Finally, she beckoned.

My mind raced. How could I betray Jessie? But, my God, I was so aroused, and Katerina was so beautiful. And I was in Moscow, and Jessie would never find out. And it was only sex, pure passion, and I would still love Jessie as much as before. And I would never see Katerina again, and I was drunker than shit, and—

I left Katerina standing there, a bewildered expression on her face as I stumbled out of the Night Flight. Outside, the muscle guys looked at me with surprise.

"Please get me a taxi." When it came, I spilled into the backseat, gave the driver my address, and went back to my apartment and a cold shower.

CHAPTER TWENTY-NINE

Excruciating abdominal cramps woke me about three in the morning. I tore to the bathroom. So much for the best restaurant in Moscow.

After my stomach settled a bit, I went back to bed. An hour later, I had a repeat performance, this time with vomiting. And then an hour after that. It kept up until daybreak when I staggered into the kitchen, weak, and tried to make coffee. My hands shook so much I spilled grounds on the floor. Finally, I emptied an Evian bottle into the pot. The coffee maker hummed, but the smell made me nauseated—unusual. I loved the aroma and taste of a fresh perk.

Another bout hit me. I raced to the john again. I thought of Leonid having to use the communal bathroom in his building. Very shaky, I staggered from the bathroom to the bedroom. This was not just an upset stomach from spoiled caviar or too much vodka. I was really sick. I collapsed on the bed, dazed and fragile.

What had I eaten? After leaving Leonid's apartment, I returned to my apartment, didn't eat anything, but had a shot of vodka. Then I called Sasha. We went to dinner where I drank more vodka, ate some caviar and a little borscht. I returned to my apartment, made coffee. *Wait a minute. No, I didn't.* I was too tired and drunk for that. I was thirsty, though, from all the liquor, and tossed off a bottle of Evian.

The thought triggered my thirst again. I stumbled into the kitchen, barely able to stand upright. I almost didn't have the strength to unscrew the Evian cap, but it came off so easily, I spilled some on the floor. I tipped the bottle to my lips, drank it down, and almost immediately raced back to the john. What the hell was going on?

By Sunday morning, I was so dehydrated I called Sasha. I must've passed out because I woke to him shaking me.

"Dr. Sloane—Daniel, are you okay? Talk to me, please. Can you sit up?" Sasha gripped my shoulders and pulled.

"I'm sick, Sasha, really sick. I've never felt so bad."

"What happened last night?"

"I came home after dancing with—what's her name. We came back to the table, and you were gone, so I took a cab here and went to sleep. Then I woke up sick." I paused for a moment, fighting another bout of nausea.

"You did not like Katerina?"

"I did. She was lovely. Gorgeous, actually. But I just couldn't."

"That is okay. I understand."

"You haven't been sick like this, have you?" I asked.

"Not at all, and I ate and drank as you did, even more."

Another bout of cramps hit me, but I had no strength to move. "Sasha, I'm embarrassed to ask, but can you help me to the bathroom? I've got to go again and don't think I'll make it."

Sasha half carried me to the toilet and set me down on the rim, closing the door behind him. I exploded again, nearly passing out. The cramps doubled me over. I heard him talking to someone on his cell phone.

He said through the closed door, "I have called an ambulance for you. They will be here in a moment. I am taking you to the Chaznikov Hospital. You are too sick to stay here, especially alone."

"No argument from me. Can you help me on my feet?" I remember him opening the bathroom door, and that was it, until I woke up in the hospital hours later.

Disoriented, I looked around to get my bearings. A plump brunette with a peaked nurse's cap stood alongside my bed, adjusting an IV dripping a pale yellow fluid into my arm.

"What's that?" I asked, pointing to the IV bottle.

"Ya ne ponimayu," she said, shaking her head, brows drawn.

"I know you don't understand, but maybe you can call Sasha—that is, Dr. Kiselenko?" I spoke louder and more distinctly, as if that would facilitate the translation. To my surprise, it did.

She smiled and nodded vigorously, pointing to the door. *"Da, da, Doctor Kiselenko."* She left the room and came back with Sasha in tow.

"Hello, my friend. You have decided to stay among the living?"

"My God, Sasha, what happened to me?"

"You blacked out from dehydration, all that diarrhea and vomiting.

You lost more than half your body fluids and were going into shock." He checked my chart. "Blood pressure sixty-five over thirty on admission. You probably would have died in another hour." He nodded at the yellow bottle. "That is the seventh liter of saline and plasma in the last eight hours, and you will probably need one or two more after that. Your body has been dry like a desert, drinking up the rainfall."

"I don't remember much after you came to the apartment."

"Yes, you have been, how do you say, quite out of it."

"Thanks for saving my life." My eye caught the IV. "What's in it?"

"Tetracycline. The only clinical situation I have seen with so much fluid loss has been cholera, so I picked an antibiotic to kill that bacteria. You improved 100 percent in the last four hours. For some time, I was not certain you would do it okay."

"I didn't know cholera was endemic to Moscow."

"It is not, at least not in the places you have been. It is usually from contaminated food or water, but the water samples from your apartment building tested without disease. I checked with the restaurant. Night Flight said they have had no reported illnesses."

"You're sure it was cholera?"

"The lab test was positive."

I was silent, thinking. *Cholera.* Where the hell could I have contracted cholera? I only knew it had surfaced in Haiti after the earthquake. How did it get to Moscow? *Crystal!* But how did she—?

"Sasha, did you examine the bottled water I had in my apartment? The Evian bottles?"

"No, why should we?" He stopped and scratched his chin. Then he waggled a finger at me and nodded his head. "The lady who left that little doll without the head. She is doing bad things to you?"

"Sometime during the night or this morning when I was so weak, I was afraid I couldn't unscrew the cap on the bottled water. It can be hard to break the seal."

Sasha nodded, understanding.

"But the bottle opened easily. Too easily."

There was a moment of silence as he processed. "Because it had already been opened?"

"That's what I'm thinking."

"Maybe when the lady left the doll?"

I nodded.

Sasha pulled out his cell phone and spat a series of commands. "We will bring the water here for testing immediately. In the meantime, do you want to call your wife or brother?"

I thought about it. But there was nothing either could do. "No, as long as I'm not about to die. No sense in worrying them. Let's just get on with the reason for my visit."

"Are you strong enough to get dressed and go home after several more liters of saline, or do you want to stay here longer, maybe overnight or an extra day?"

I sat up in the bed and swung my feet over the side. A momentary wave of dizziness swept over me. Then I felt almost normal again, the nausea and diarrhea thankfully gone.

"Amazing how a simple antibiotic more than fifty years old brought me back from the brink," I said.

"That, and add to it the IV fluids. Cholera can be deadly without treatment, but fluids and antibiotics cure it easily."

So Crystal was still attacking. She was relentless. Apparently, getting my money had made no difference to her. Sasha's phone rang. He listened for a moment, scowled, and turned to me. "They cannot find the bottled water. Where did you leave it?"

"Sitting on the counter in the kitchen, next to the refrigerator, still in its plastic container."

He relayed the information, listened, scowled even more, barked an order, and hung up. "Gone. Cleaned out. No trace of bottled water in your entire apartment. She is a clever lady."

"Tell me something I don't know. Sasha, can we change the locks on that apartment?"

He nodded. "That was the last instruction I gave over the phone. Maybe you should spend the night here until that is done."

"No, I'll be fine once the IV fluids are in. I'd like to go back to get ready for work tomorrow. We still have a study to run."

"I will have one of my people wait for you in the apartment to be sure you have no more uninvited visitors. We will change locks tomorrow in the morning. I will send a car for you at around 8:30 or 9:00."

"Sounds like a good plan. Thanks."

"You will need five more days of tetracycline to be sure we killed all the bacteria. Drink plenty of fluids. A relapse would not be a good thing."

I stayed in the hospital and ate dinner as the last two liters dripped into my vein. Someone drove me back to my apartment. I propped a chair against the door and collapsed on the bed. I thought a moment about

Leonid and wondered where he was now and what was so important about the papers.

The papers! I had totally forgotten.

I forced myself up and tried to remember where I put them. I searched the apartment, but they were gone. The door had been unlocked, so anyone could have walked in. Could it have been Crystal? Why would she want those papers? And what had Leonid found that he wanted to share?

CHAPTER THIRTY

I slept straight through the night, a good seven hours. Refreshed, I made coffee with water I boiled for ten minutes. The bouquet smelled like perfume. I found no pinholes in the eggshells, and the seal on the package of bacon was intact. To be safe, I fried them both long enough to kill any cholera bacteria—and the taste as well.

After breakfast, I went downstairs to a waiting car. The Chaznikov Institute comprised three impressive, large brick buildings built around a frozen central lake. Snow blanketed most of the spacious grounds, but I could envision well-manicured lawns and flowered walking paths in the summer.

My driver flashed a badge, and the wrought-iron fence swung open. He headed for the middle building, the administrative home of the RBC study. The building on the left was research, and on the right, the hospital where I had spent the previous day.

Sasha stood just inside the marble entrance waiting for me.

"How was your night? No more dolls without heads or poisoned water?"

"Quite boring, actually. I fell asleep and woke up like an ordinary person, had breakfast, and here I am, ready for work."

"Sometimes it is good to be ordinary. Come," he said. "We will take the elevator to the fourth floor where your office is waiting."

Sasha slid a security card in an elevator slot and hit four. We rode in silence. We exited into a small lobby where a slim woman sat behind a desk, typing into a computer. She was attractive, in her midthirties with wavy, ginger-colored hair and soft brown eyes, but a dour look. She stared at me, probably appraising the new arrival and perhaps not liking what she saw.

Sasha gestured to her. "Natalia Smirnova, this is Dr. Daniel Sloane that we waited for a long time to come." Sasha turned to me. "Natalia is the administrative secretary who runs the study. She enters the information from the patient forms into a central database from all the investigators in the four cities plus Moscow. She is the only one who knows the code, which participants received Calcaine and who got Redex."

"*Ochin preeyatna*, Natalia."

"Ms. Smirnova will do, *spasiba*."

She spat out the thank-you. Her response froze my extended hand. I let it drift down to my side.

Sasha came to my rescue. "Come." His hand nudged the small of my back. "Let me show you your office."

To the right of Natalia's desk was a door labeled Principal Investigator, Redex Beats Calcaine Study. He took a key from his pocket, unlocked the door, and we entered.

The small room had a black wooden desk in the middle, two matching chairs in front, a coat stand in one corner, and a four-drawer, ugly green filing cabinet in the other. The walls were bare. A computer screen and keyboard took up the left half of the desk's surface, and a telephone sat on the right. A copy of the *New York Times* lay in the middle.

"It is okay?" asked Sasha, handing me the office key. He picked up the *Times* and apologized. "It will always be a day late, but better than nothing, yes? On-time news you must get from the computer."

I nodded. The office was dingy but well lit, had heat, and would suffice. "It will be fine, thanks."

He glanced at his watch. "It is now 9:30, so I will give you an hour to get comfortable with everything." He looked at Natalia through the open door as he said that, but I expected no comfort there. "At eleven o'clock, I will make a lecture on Redex. I have invited the RBC investigators from each of the thirty-one hospitals that are part of the study to meet you and to hear my update. We have an auditorium on the first floor, and I will see you there. Will that be satisfactory?"

"Sounds fine, Sasha."

"Okay, I go now to prepare my talk. Natalia knows everything about the Chaznikov Institute, so ask her for anything you need. I am sure she will be very helpful to you." He practically shouted the last sentence, but Natalia kept typing.

My office computer was ready to use. I logged onto the UIMC server to answer my e-mails. The first message informed me that I had won twelve million euros in the European lottery: "Please send your social security number to verify." I hit delete. The second e-mail was from the widow of the president of the Central Bank of Nigeria, wanting to wire forty million

US dollars into my private account for safekeeping. "Please send your Bank Name and Account Number." *Delete.*

I almost deleted the next e-mail from MickeyMouse@gmail.com without even reading it, but I caught Leonid's name in the message.

> Did you read the informations from Leonid
> yet?

I inhaled sharply and stared at Natasha's back through the open door. I got up and closed the door softly.

> Someone took them from my apartment. Is
> Leonid all right?

The response was immediate.

> Dead. Swimming in the same lake like
> his brother. Whoever did it gave a clear
> message for us to stop making troubles
> or this will happen to you too.

The buzz from the computer alarm shook me. A flashing message reminded me to go to the auditorium. Natalia must've entered my appointments.

> What trouble?

I waited a few moments, but no answer came. I had to leave. I deleted the messages, logged out, and locked the door.

A spreadsheet was open on Natasha's computer as I passed. I got a brief glance before she covered it with a notepad, giving me an icy stare. "I will be in the auditorium, Ms. Smirnova." She didn't respond.

The auditorium was an oversized office with five rows of collapsible wooden chairs, eight to a row, mostly all occupied. In the last row, a man in a blue, open-neck shirt sat alone. He had a large, smooth forehead and a closely cropped, uneven haircut that suggested his barber had a tremor. He was fairly young—late thirties, I thought—dark-complexioned with thick, black hair and eyebrows. The shiny forehead beckoned ever so slightly to the chair alongside him. He moved books from the chair seat to the floor, and I walked over and sat down. A woman, probably in her late forties, with dark brown hair, a coat draped on her arm, sat to his left and repositioned the coat across her knees. Neither said a word. From the folds of her coat, she removed a book and passed it to the man.

Without really thinking, I glanced at the book, now in his lap. *Jesus!* I thought, seeing the brown cover of *War and Peace* I'd last seen on Leonid's kitchen table, or a duplicate. I looked at the man, but he ignored me, staring instead at the empty podium in the front of the room where Sasha would lecture.

Before I could say anything, Sasha reached the podium and addressed the crowd. He greeted everyone in Russian and then switched to English, probably for me.

"Good morning to all of you, and thank you for taking time from your busy schedules to visit Moscow for this Redex Beats Calcaine investigators' meeting. I am sure you are all anxious to meet our new principal investigator, Dr. Daniel Sloane. Daniel, where are you sitting?" He scanned the group and then spotted me. "Ah, there you are, in the last row. Please to stand up so everyone can see who you are."

I stood and gave the crowd a short wave.

"Daniel has moved to Moscow from Indianapolis, a Midwest city near Chicago, and you will all have a chance to meet him. He is an outstanding researcher, clinician, and teacher, and I am sure will lead the RBC study to its successful conclusion. He will be visiting each of you in your own hospitals in the future. Thank you, Daniel."

I smiled and sat back down.

"The reason for us to have this meeting," Sasha continued, "is to review the two published Redex studies, in case some of you did not read them, update you on our own RBC trial results, and solve any troubles you may have in recruiting new patients. Any questions before I begin?"

There were none, so Sasha started his presentation, reviewing the two published papers. Since I knew them, I let my eyes wander.

The group was well-dressed, mostly middle to older age. At least a third of them smoked, something unheard of in a stateside lecture, or even one in Europe. An acrid smell filled the room. Although most Russian physicians were women, this crowd was almost all men, typical of those in charge of research and the medical establishment itself.

When the room lights dimmed for Sasha's slides, I felt a pressure against my knee. I moved my leg, but the pressure followed. I looked down, and there was the book in the guy's hand, pressing against my leg. The man was trying to pass me the novel!

CHAPTER THIRTY-ONE

I struggled to focus on Sasha as my mind raced. Had Leonid intended to give me the book rather than the papers I took? If so, why? I ran a hand over the newspaper, feeling the outline of the thick book beneath.

Finally, Sasha wound down. "This last slide is the update on the RBC trial. As you know, we are recruiting ten thousand patients and almost half have already been randomized between Redex and Calcaine. Now you can see from this slide," he said, pointing to a column of figures on the screen, "that drug A appears to be superior to drug B. Pain is relieved better, and side effects are less, almost totally absent. We suspect A is Redex but will not know for sure until completion of the trial and the code is broken. Only Natalia knows, and she is sworn to secrecy. I will stop my lecture here and answer the questions from you."

The applause was courteous, brief, followed by silence so quiet I could hear people breathing on either side of me. I thought about the sharp give-and-take after Dorian's presentation to the board. Not here. For some reason, the audience was subdued.

Finally, a hand popped up toward the front of the room. Sasha pointed at the person.

"Director Kiselenko, there were a number of patients on your list from my hospital that I didn't recognize their names. I thought I knew all the peoples I recruited into the study."

"I'll check with Natasha on that, but maybe someone else in your hospital recruited some. Perhaps one of your junior peoples when you were out of town? She is very careful to enter what you send. But we will check since it is very important to be sure the list is accurate."

Another hand rose. "Director, I have had the same experience with three patients on the list I didn't recognize."

"I would give you the same answer."

I heard a lot of mumbling in the audience and could see nodding heads.

Sasha patted the air with both hands, quieting the crowd. "I am sorry you do not recognize all of the patients from your own hospitals, but I would not expect you to remember all of them, especially when we are talking about many thousands. Regardless, to prove the superiority of Redex once and for all, you need to continue recruiting until we have reached the ten thousand necessary numbers. We are halfway there. When the study finishes, I promise all of you a free week at the Sochi Spa Resort on the Black Sea. You know Sochi will host the Winter Olympics next year, and they are preparing it now to be quite beautiful. We will pay all expenses, and you can bring your families. We will pay for them, also. Only finish the study promptly."

There was silence. Sasha waited and then asked me to say a few words.

I carefully laid the newspaper down on my chair before I walked to the front of the room.

"On behalf of my brother, Dorian, CEO of Sloane Pharmaceuticals, and Dr. Kiselenko, director of the Chaznikov Institute," I smiled at Sasha, "I am pleased to have been given the responsibility of running this trial. You are all experienced doctors and will need very little guidance from me, I am sure. I plan to learn from you rather than the reverse." This drew a lot of murmurs and smiles.

"In the coming weeks, I will visit each of you at your hospitals to see if you are having any problems and discuss how to solve them together. The biggest issue will be to restore recruitment to the previous rates. That is often the hardest part of a clinical study, and you must maintain your commitment. It is especially important to convey enthusiasm to the people with whom you work so they continue to do their part. I want this study to succeed as much as any of you, particularly since I've never been to Sochi. I hear it is lovely, as the director said."

This got vigorous applause, and Sasha ended the conference. I tried to return to my seat, but all my new friends wanted to shake my hand and say a few welcoming words. When I finally broke free and got to my chair, the newspaper and book were gone!

The room was emptying, with the last few stragglers just leaving. The man and woman sitting next to me were also gone. Had they taken the book back, or had someone else? I searched under my seat and the neighboring ones. Nothing.

Methodically cleaning the room were a team of three elderly women, hair bound in gray kerchiefs, gathering up litter and dumping it into a large yellow round plastic pail on wheels. They pushed it from one row to another, emptying ashtrays, filling it with debris. I went over to the pail and started sifting through papers, coffee cups, and other junk.

"*Nyet, nyet, no, no!*" One of the ladies tried to push me aside.

I tried to explain. "I lost something, and you may have put it in here." All I got was *nyet*.

Sasha appeared at my side. "Is there a problem?"

"No problem, Sasha. I had the *Times* with me and laid it on my seat when I talked to the group. I think one of these nice ladies may have thrown it away by mistake."

Sasha rattled off an order, and they backed away from the pail to let me look. I shoveled through the trash, trying to keep my back to him as much as I could. I spied a corner of the newspaper and reached for it. The bundle was thick, so the book was likely still in its folds. I plucked it from the pail and tucked it deep under my arm before I turned around.

"Thanks, Sasha. I've got it. I'm going to go back to my office to get caught up with the news."

He gave me a funny look. "Fine. We have a luncheon for all the investigators at 1:30. I hope you will be there."

"For sure. See you then."

I hurried to the elevator and back to my office. Natalia was not at her desk, probably at lunch. I closed the door and took out *War and Peace*, flipping pages for any notes or papers tucked inside. The print was in Russian, so I was clueless. The front cover had the title, author, and a picture of a Russian Orthodox Church in a small town. The back cover appeared to give a synopsis of the story with a picture of Tolstoy. I saw no clues as to what was going on here.

I opened my computer. An e-mail message from Mickey Mouse waited.

    Did you read the book?

I e-mailed back.

    I scanned the pages but didn't find
    anything.

He was online.

Carefully to look at pages 165 to 167.

I reopened the book and saw that those pages had been skillfully cut out, with new ones substituted. Each of the pages contained lists of names with one of two Russian words after each name.

DS: So?

MM: Do you understand the Russian?

DS: I am trying to learn, but it is a difficult language.

MM: The word ЖИВОЙ, the phonetic would be zhivie, means to be alive, and the word МЕРТВЫЙ, or miortvie, means to be dead.

DS: So?

MM: Many names have МЕРТВЫЙ after them.

DS: I still don't see the connection. Are you saying many people died taking Redex?

MM: No. This is a list of peoples recruited into the RBC trial from one hospital in Yekaterinburg. Over two-thirds were dead when they were recruited.

DS: Oh, oh. Names from a national death registry?

MM: Yes, maybe someone is falsifying data?

DS: How do I know these lists are correct?

MM: Have a look at Natalia's computer.

DS: And how do you propose I do that?

MM: Not a problem. Her login ID is nsmirnova. Her password is ilovesasha, not too original, but I am sure she didn't expect hackers.

DS: Why did you do that?

MM: The study numbers did not add up correctly. Sasha hid that for quite a while because the study was spread out among many investigators in different cities. Each one thought the other was recruiting patients into the study. Natalia was the only one who knew what all peoples were doing. Four thousand missing patients at $10,000 for each one is $40 million. Where did it go, I wonder? Certainly not to the dead peoples.

DS: That's why Igor was killed?

MM: He first noticed the discrepancy.

DS: What do you want me to do?

MM: Tell your brother. He must notify the authorities to arrest Sasha and then pick someone else to be in charge of the Chaznikov. If we go to the police, we will end up swimming like Igor and Leonid.

DS: So, Leonid did work at the Chaznikov?

MM: Of course. Who said no?

DS: Sasha.

MM: Igor suspected Sasha and Natalia were running a—how do you say it in English?

DS: A scam?

MM: A scam. So he hacked into Natalia's computer and found out for sure. He told Leonid and gave him the proof—a printout from her computer. They hid the informations in the pages of the book. Different pages have the same kind of informations from other hospitals about the dead peoples in the study. After Igor and Leonid did that, they both went swimming. I hope you know how to swim.

DS: I doubt Sasha would physically harm me, because of my brother.

MM: Still, it is better to watch out for your back and not to be sorry.

My computer buzzed, warning that lunch was in fifteen minutes. I asked a question.

DS: Will you be at the lunch?

MM: Yes, but it is better you do not know who I am.

I heard voices in the hall. Natalia and Sasha were returning.

DS: Have to go.

Natalia sat at her desk, and Sasha came into my office without knocking. "So you are ready to go to lunch now?" he asked.

"In a moment," I said, deleting all my e-mails and shutting down my computer. "Okay, now, let's go."

As I walked out of the office and locked the door, I saw *War and Peace* lying in plain view on my desk. But if Sasha saw it, he didn't say anything, and we entered the elevator.

We reached the ground floor, and his cell phone rang as the elevator door swung open. "It is Natalia," he said, patting my shoulder. "Maybe you go ahead to the dining room. This call will not take long, and I will join you in a moment."

The lunch was pleasant. I sat with Sasha. We had no speeches and ate a delicious borscht, followed by lamb stew. A bottle of Stolichnaya stood in the middle of each table, and a few doctors poured glasses. Others finished with tea and a cigarette.

After lunch and a few good-byes, we returned to the fourth floor and walked toward my office. On the way, Natalia handed Sasha a thick manila envelope. He followed me into my office, closed the door behind us, and sat down in one of the chairs in front of my desk. *War and Peace* was gone, and my computer was on.

To my horror, the entire string of e-mails I had exchanged with Mickey Mouse before lunch was on the screen! My mouth dropped open, and my heart started to pound.

Sasha smiled at me. "You see, Daniel, your computer is synchronized to Natalia's, so your Mickey Mouse correspondence was revealed and preserved on her computer." He opened the manila envelope and took out *War and Peace*. "The book has been, maybe we can say, revised, or perhaps sanitized?" He placed it on a corner of the desk. "Many pages have been safely shredded."

I tried to show confidence I didn't feel. "That doesn't matter. I plan to call my brother and tell him what you've been doing, you and Natalia. Phonying up patients, stealing his money."

"No, I do not think you will."

"Don't threaten me with drowning."

"I will not. You were quite right to tell Mickey Mouse I would not do anything to harm you physically." He reached into the manila envelope and pulled out a thick set of glossy prints. "But what about these?" He tossed them on my desk.

I picked them up. "You son of a bitch!"

The prints showed Katerina and me totally nude in various stages of very explicit lovemaking. First, I was taking off her clothes, and she mine. Then we were in bed in an array of positions: she on top with her breasts in my face, me on top, and me taking her from behind.

"These can't be real! How did you—" My mind groped for an explanation. "You Photoshopped these prints!"

"Me? *I* didn't do anything. *You* are the one in the pictures."

"You bastard! You had a photographer take pictures at the Night Flight, didn't you? Then you superimposed the heads onto the bodies." I gripped the pictures in my hand and shook them in his face, barely containing my rage. "This never happened, and you know it!" I ripped them in half and then ripped them again and again until they were tiny fragments. I threw the pieces in Sasha's face and stood over him, my fists clenching and unclenching, almost feeling them encircle his thick neck.

"Now, calm down, Daniel, calm down. I do not want to call security. They are on standby in case I need help, though I do not think I will." He rubbed his broken nose with an index finger.

He stood and put gentle, restraining palms against my chest. "It does not matter what I did or did not do. What does matter is what your wife, Jessie, knows or thinks she knows. What is she to believe when you have not even called her since you have been here?"

"How do you know?" It dawned on me. "You bugged my apartment, didn't you?"

I pushed him into the chair. He sat back, totally relaxed, with a brief, apologetic smile. "Yes, unfortunately, I had to do that," he said in a bored voice. "It was very risky for us to have the brother of the CEO to be here working. Not a good idea. I needed to watch you quite closely and be prepared with the pictures. Your voodoo friend, Crystal, helped us out as much as she could. She did a good job, I suppose, for one not too skilled in these kinds of works. Actually, cholera was a clever idea."

"But you saved my life."

"What else was I to do? You knew nothing yet, perhaps might not ever know something, and your brother would surely find out if I let you die from the cholera. No," he shook his head, "I could not let that happen. Besides, it is really your fault. If you had not been snooping around, nothing like this would have happened."

"It was *my* fault Crystal tried to kill me?"

"But she didn't succeed. Her timing was wrong, that was all. Maybe we can give her another chance to try later on."

"Yeah, right. That makes me feel a lot better."

"But we have to work with the present."

"And how do we do that?"

"That is easy. You do what you came to do, run the RBC trial—but run it my way, of course. That guarantees the outcome and a little profit. I suggest that, after you think it over very carefully, Daniel, you will agree with me, and we will all have a very nice time together. From the studies that were already published, we know Redex will be superior to Calcaine, so why waste a lot of money on a trial? We simply make up a few facts, and quickly as a wink, the study will be done. SP makes a lot of money, and so will we for our troubles. I am happy to share some of the profits with you. How about maybe 10 percent?"

I grabbed my coat off the coat stand. "I'm going back to my apartment. I can't stay here anymore."

"That is probably a good idea. Go back and rest up. You must still be weak from the cholera and maybe not thinking too clearly. I will come by in a few hours, and we can talk some more and plan the future together." He paused. "Oh, and by the way, there will be another set of these pictures waiting for you on your kitchen table. I have an unlimited supply. More than enough to send to Indiana and New York and maybe other places also." He kicked at the pieces on the floor. "You have made a pretty mess with this bunch."

I glowered at him.

"Go to the apartment and relax, Daniel. You are too tense. Drink some vodka, have a nap." He dismissed me with a wave of his hand. "You do not need to let me in. I have my own key."

CHAPTER THIRTY-TWO

I took a taxi back to my apartment. The manila envelope was lying on my kitchen table. I took out the photos of my invented infidelity, poured a bit of vodka, sat down, and studied them, now with a much cooler head. I couldn't tell whether the female body was Katerina's. Only someone who knew me intimately would recognize the male body was a bit too sculpted to be me—Jessie, I hoped, after I explained what had happened. But suppose Sasha had a broader audience in mind, such as a mass e-mailing to my friends and patients? What if the pictures went to Judge Dotter? He'd probably make sure I lost my license to practice medicine forever.

A feeling of homesickness overwhelmed me. I missed Jessie. I missed the life I had had before that phone call from Crystal and all that had happened since. I knew I had taken care of Randy appropriately. If only he hadn't played that damn pickup basketball game—if only he had returned for the cardiac catheterization—if—if. Life was full of ifs.

Dorian had warned me about getting involved with a celebrity. He was right. It had ended in nothing but trouble.

I sat with the pictures in my hands, slowly flipping through the prints, studying the bodies. The woman was quite beautiful. I assumed it was Katerina: lovely breasts, a tapered waist, and shapely legs. And a real blonde. The guy's body was also nice. I didn't spend a lot of time looking at myself nude, but I thought this guy could easily pass for me, though a little more muscular.

Then it hit me. I gaped at the picture in my hand and saw what I had been groping for. How dumb not to have spotted it earlier.

An hour later, I heard my apartment door open as Sasha let himself in.

"Hello, Daniel." He saw me studying the glossies. "I hope I am not disturbing you." He took off his coat, made himself comfortable in a chair, and pointed at the pictures. "I have been thinking. Since you have had already photo sex with Katerina, maybe you would enjoy the real thing? I can arrange that, if you like. I guarantee no photos. Only you and Katerina in a room at the Night Flight, or even here, if you would like. I promise to turn off the hidden microphones."

I felt total contempt for him and didn't bother to hide my feelings.

"Do not look that way at me, Daniel. I am about to become your best friend and benefactor. I know you need the money. We will work together to finish this study, at least on paper, get Redex positioned as the greatest NSAID in the world, and make a lot of money doing it. What do you say about that?"

"McBurney."

"I beg your pardon."

"You heard me. McBurney, or more accurately, McBurney's Point."

"Excuse me for not knowing this point, Daniel, but I do not have an idea what you are saying."

"Don't they teach you that in medical school in Moscow?"

"Not in Moscow or in Stanford. I suppose you noticed I have dropped the tortured syntax of uneducated Russians attempting to speak English. I spent four years in Palo Alto. So maybe you would be kind enough to explain McBurney's Point to me?"

"Stanford's a great school. But you must've cut a class or two." I gave him a tight smile. "McBurney's Point is one-third the distance between the right anterior iliac crest and the umbilicus." I paused to be sure he understood.

"The right hip and belly button. What about them?" He fidgeted in his chair.

I sat, waiting for the light bulb to click on like it does in cartoons. *Pow!* But it didn't. He shifted again. I let him squirm, savoring his disquiet.

The room was still, a Hollywood movie scene before all hell broke loose. I let the tension build. The movie would have music playing in the background, like the *1812 Overture*, ready to climax with roaring cannons.

I rose and walked over to him. I stood in front of his chair, captured his eyes with mine. I played with my belt, undid it and then the top button on my pants, and let my slacks drop to the floor.

Sasha sat motionless, an astonished look on his face. "What are you doing, Daniel? Are you mad? Have you completely lost your mind? I like girls, not boys."

He moved to push me away, but I put my left hand on top of his bald head and held it stationary. With my right thumb, I dragged my boxer shorts down an inch or so and pointed my index finger at a spot just inside my right hip.

"This is McBurney's Point, Sasha, known to every surgeon as the skin site directly over the base of the appendix where they make the incision for an appendectomy. What do you see?"

The light bulb went off. I pictured nerve endings in his brain sizzling and popping. "A scar," he said in a small voice.

"Yes, Sasha, a scar. From my appendectomy, years ago. Would you care to show me that scar on the body of the man in the glossies?"

He was silent.

"No. There's no scar on the guy in those pictures because there's no Daniel in those pictures. And my brother and, most importantly, my wife, will know immediately the body's not mine, and the pictures are a fraud. Good try, my friend, but you've lost this battle." I pulled up my pants, buckled my belt, walked over to where I left the pictures, and picked them up. I needed to keep one set of originals.

Sasha sat with a stunned look on his face. He ran a tremulous hand through his hair and looked around the room as if he expected help from someone or something in the apartment. He groped for an answer. "I can have the computer guy put in a scar and then post them on the Internet or YouTube. Maybe even send them to your patients."

"You can shove them up your ass for all I care. The most important people in my life won't give a damn, and neither will I. In fact, we'll have a good laugh and be happy to point out your fumbling attempt to blackmail me with this first set, sans scar.

"My brother in particular will like that. What if whoever saw the pictures thought it was Dorian and not me? Did you consider that blackmailing me was like blackmailing him? Not a good idea to do that to the man who controls the money." Sasha opened his mouth to say something but then closed it again. I moved in for the kill.

"Besides, I doubt the authorities would appreciate your sending pornography over the Internet or via e-mail. That and attempted blackmail would likely lengthen your next trip to the United States by years in jail. Never mind a double murder charge. And don't forget how pissed my brother will be. All in all, not a well-played hand, Sasha. About as inept as how you've handled the RBC trial."

I walked to the window. On the street, the taxi was waiting. I went into my bedroom, wheeled my suitcase into the living room, and stopped in front of Sasha.

"I made some phone calls before you got here. I'm sure the bug picked them up, and you can listen to the tape after I leave. Now, if you'll excuse me, I have a plane to catch."

CHAPTER THIRTY-THREE

Jessie was waiting in the Indy airport. She ran into my arms as I walked into the terminal. I really hadn't been gone that long—in fact, I'd been away much longer on some medical trips in the past—but these five days seemed like forever. I was so thankful to be home and in one piece.

I folded her into my arms and whispered, "I love you." We both blinked back tears of relief.

I had called her from Moscow to say I was coming home early and why. Dorian laughed when I told him about the pictures. In fact, he wanted the copies to frame and pass off as himself. "The bunnies won't care," he said, "and might even like to pose for a new photo op. Maybe make it a theme for the next office party, or use it for the Christmas-card mailing. Besides, look at that muscular male body. More like me than you!"

Dorian promised he would fire Sasha, have the authorities arrest him for murder, and have John cancel the RBC study because it was too contaminated to save. He was unsure about Mikhail's role and held off a decision until he had a chance to talk with him.

I was not cut out for company work. I declined Dorian's offer to return. Insurance physicals were starting to look pretty good. At least those were not likely to get me in trouble.

Crystal still lurked in the bushes somewhere, but there was really very little I could do about her. I couldn't prove her attempt at "death in the time of cholera," as I could not prove her "zombification." I probably could get a restraining order to keep her away from me, but even if I did, I doubted it would do much good. She was too cunning to get caught. I planned to beef up our home security system.

Surprisingly, Dean Jim Hazelton came to my rescue—or I to his. He called and asked me to meet him in his office the next morning.

"Daniel, we need you back. The clinical program needs restructuring. You always lobbied for increased clinical teaching, and the curriculum committee finally agreed. We now find we're short teachers with clinical experience to implement the changes. I've already checked with Judge Dotter, and he has no problem with you teaching if you have no direct patient contact."

I started to protest, but he held up a restraining hand. "Now, hear me out. I know what you'd like to do, but quite frankly, you can't see patients unless you complete that stint under Lindorf, and I can't believe you want to do that."

"You got that right."

"Dotter said you can attend all the clinical conferences—in fact, I'll ask you to give some of them—so you'll have patient contact, albeit indirectly, at a distance. That'll have to do until all this works out."

"What do you mean, 'works out'?"

"I'm hoping if you do a good job at teaching—of course, that's a given—a letter from me to Judge Dotter might get him to reconsider his decision. All this will have blown over by then, and maybe, just maybe, he'll let you come back to the medical center and start where you left off."

That was a switch. When the dean needed me to fill a spot, I wasn't such a bad doctor after all.

I was irked by his attitude, but I had no choice. "When do I start?"

I returned to the medical center, to my old office and secretary, and full-time teaching. A month later, Hazelton asked me to run the entire teaching program. I gave about half the lectures and restarted my research. Life returned to normal—until another phone call.

My secretary took the call. "Dr. Sloane, a Mr. Anderson is on the phone. Says it's urgent."

I had last seen John a month or two after I implanted his defibrillator. His local doctor in New York City provided routine checks at three-month intervals and kept me apprised. He'd been doing fine for almost three years.

"Hi, John. What's up?"

"Daniel, this damn defibrillator keeps going off. I've had three shocks already today and two yesterday. The doc here says the defibrillator's malfunctioning, but he doesn't know why. I need to see you immediately. Dorian okayed me to fly out this afternoon on the company jet."

"Whoa. Not so fast. You know Judge Dotter said I couldn't see patients."

"I don't give a shit what he said. You put this damn thing in; you have to take care of it. I'm your patient for Christ's sake. You've got to do something. It's a mule kick in the chest when this goddamn defibrillator goes off."

"Okay, okay, I hear you. Fly out, and I'll get one of my colleagues to see you."

"Bullshit. Like Uncle Sam says, I want you. I'm leaving now, and I'll be there in two hours."

I called my lawyer, Dwight Walker, and asked what I should do. "Daniel, you can't disobey the court order. You could be held in contempt."

"What would that mean?"

"Up to Judge Dotter. He could give you a warning not to do it again, impose a fine, or put you in jail, depending on his mood."

"What do you recommend?"

"As a lawyer and an officer of the court, I have no choice but to tell you to comply with the court's order. Any other recommendation would be violating my ethical duty to the judicial system."

"What about as a personal friend?"

"Do what your own moral code dictates."

I hung up, propped my feet on my desk, and closed my eyes. My first thoughts were from so many years ago, when I took the final chemistry exam for Dorian. I could almost hear Professor High telling me life was a long race with emotional stress tests along the way that uncovered personal flaws. You needed to finish strong by not caving under pressure. I had the sudden urge to talk with him again.

"Angela, please get Professor Fletcher High at Dartmouth College in New Hampshire on the phone. If you can't find his number, my wife will have it."

A few minutes later, she walked into my office. "I'm sorry, Dr. Sloane, but I was informed Professor High died a month ago."

How sad, I thought. Fletch had been a good man who helped shape who I was. *What would he have done?* I wondered. Treating John defied the court and could get me in a lot of trouble. But he was a patient in need, and diagnosing and correcting the misfiring defibrillator was my specialty. It was something I could do better than anyone else in my group. I was caught between an ancient "rock" and a contemporary "hard place": the Hippocratic Oath and the US law.

CHAPTER THIRTY-FOUR

It didn't take me long to decide. "Angela, when John Anderson arrives, put him in my examining room and call me." *Fletch*, I thought, *this one's for you*. Dotter be damned.

John sat on the edge of the examining table. I stood in front of him, my hand resting lightly on his knee. I had finished my physical examination. It felt so good to be with a patient again. Somehow I had to find my way back to being a practicing physician again.

"John, when did the shocks start?"

John slipped on his shirt and tucked it in his pants. "Sunday, two days ago. I had been chopping some firewood, and about an hour later, toweling off after a shower, I felt a tingling sensation near the defibrillator."

"Show me where," I said.

He pointed to the area just below his left collarbone where I had implanted the device. "Then, *wham*! I got hit in the chest. The shock was so sudden, it threw me off balance, and I fell to the floor. Bumped my head on the corner of the sink." He fingered a yellowing bruise on his forehead.

"Did you lose consciousness?"

"No. I figured the defibrillator must've shocked a rapid heartbeat, so I didn't do anything because you warned me that could happen. But when I was dressing to go out—I had just put on my shirt—the damn thing shocked me again. This time I called my local doc, and he saw me in his office yesterday afternoon. But everything checked out fine, and he said he didn't know what was wrong."

"Did he check the defibrillator?" I asked.

"Yes. He said it showed the defibrillator shocked me for no apparent reason, but he couldn't figure out why."

"What did he tell you to do?"

"To take it easy, and if it went off again, call. After the third shock this morning, I called him, and he said to call you."

I studied the printout of the defibrillator's function. "I think I know what's going on." I placed the ICD programmer head on his chest over his defibrillator. "Move your left arm behind your back."

He was hesitant. "Am I going to get shocked again?"

"No, I've deactivated the shock. I want to see what happens to the defibrillator's built-in electrocardiogram."

I saw what I needed and studied the chest X-ray his doctor had taken. "Okay, here's what's wrong. Remember when I put in the defibrillator, I ran a long wire, called a lead, into your heart?"

"Yeah—well, sort of."

"That lead connects your heart to the defibrillator and has a break in it. Look at the X-ray," I pointed at the film in the X-ray view box. "It's very subtle, right next to your collarbone, and I can understand why your doctor missed it. You may have done it chopping wood."

John touched his shoulder gingerly. "Can you repair it?"

"Like wrapping it with electrician's tape?" I shook my head. "Not that easy. I'll have to remove the lead surgically and replace it with a new one. I'll put it in a slightly different position so, after you heal, you can chop all the wood you want."

"What about the defibrillator?"

"That'll remain. It's functioning fine. I'll connect it to the new lead."

"When?"

A lengthy jail sentence flashed through my head if Dotter found out. But I had already violated the court's orders by seeing John in the first place. I figured it couldn't get any worse.

"Right away, since you need the defibrillator 24/7. When did you last eat?"

"This morning. They forgot to stock the plane with food, so I'm starving."

I checked my watch. At least six hours since breakfast. "Then you're good to go."

"Will it be like the last time—you know, my dying and all?" His eyes got big, and I couldn't tell if he was looking forward to more war stories or was frightened.

"No, I'll sedate you with the propofol as before, take out the old lead, put in a new one, and connect it to the defibrillator. You'll be back on the plane by early evening with nothing more than a sore shoulder. No dying this time."

I booked my old electrophysiology procedure room under the name of a colleague and had John transported there. Ginger, who had been working for my colleague, assisted like old times, and the procedure went without a hitch. I replaced the fractured lead with a new one, checked the settings, and began to sew everything in place.

"Ginger, back off the propofol and let him wake up in a couple of minutes. I'm almost finished."

"Yes, Dr. Sloane."

I put in the last suture as the propofol wore off. I was standing near John's left shoulder, bandaging the implant site when he mumbled something that sounded like "Sasha."

Startled, I asked, "John, what did you say?"

"Um—Sasha—paid millions."

Not quite like pentothal, but the propofol had lowered his guard. "John, who paid Sasha millions?"

He was silent, and I repeated my question.

"Um—Sasha did."

"Sasha did what? You're not making sense. What did Sasha do?" I asked, my face close to his. "Did he pay millions or was paid millions?"

He stopped talking and yawned, opened his eyes, and asked, "Done?"

The propofol wears off quickly. "Yes, all done. Your new lead's working perfectly."

He sat up. "Thanks. That wasn't so bad, but I'm still sleepy." He stretched and yawned again. He flexed his left arm behind his back, testing the lead. When no shock came, he pumped his fist and said, "Yes!"

"John, what do you know about Sasha?"

His face paled, and his eyes grew wide. "Nothing more than you. Why?"

"You said something as the anesthesia was wearing off."

He grabbed my arm. "What did I say?"

"Something about Sasha being paid millions or paying millions. You weren't very clear."

"What else?"

"That's it."

Relief flooded his face.

"Is there more, John? What's going on?"

"All I know is what you told Dorian, that Sasha's sandbagged us by padding the study, being paid millions for recruiting phantom patients." I studied his face. I couldn't tell if he was lying.

"Was Mikhail involved?"

"I don't know. You'll have to ask your brother."

"I did, and he said he didn't know and was going to talk with Mikhail."

"Daniel, Dorian runs the company; you know that. He's bet heavily on Redex, and until this stuff in Russia happened, all was going well. We're the number-one NSAID in the US, thanks to our two published studies, and we've made a bundle of money."

"So?"

"So your brother got greedy and wanted worldwide dominance, hence the RBC trial in Russia. Bad choice, it turns out, and Sasha fucked us royally. I suppose we can repeat that study somewhere else, but I'd be content to call it a day and keep raking in the US cash. We've got Painex ready to fly for headaches soon."

"But that's not enough for Dorian?"

"No, it's not. He's obsessed with this. I think it's about outdoing your father."

"He's still got issues?" I asked.

John gingerly touched the bandages and sat up on the table. "Money can't be driving him. He's already got more bucks than he can spend on himself and his bunnies."

"You knew the old man. Hell, you worked for him long before my brother joined the firm. What's the problem?"

John's face creased. "Dorian needs to prove something to your father, even though he's dead. There was always competition between them. That's why your father kept Dorian in the basement, literally."

"Glad I never joined the company."

"You always did your own thing."

"After medical school, I never took another penny from him."

He nodded. "Your father once told me a story that explained his attitude toward you and your brother. He said if somebody was swimming and began to sink, he would help get his head above water. But if his head got too high, he would push it down again."

I gave a little snort.

"He was always pissed you didn't join the firm. He had no control of you otherwise." John glanced at his watch.

"Okay, enough. How're you feeling? Ready to fly back home?"

"You bet. Thanks for fixing me up."

CHAPTER THIRTY-FIVE

"What'll you do if Judge Dotter finds out?" Jessie and I were lingering in the dining room over coffee and an after-dinner cognac.

"I'll tell him the truth. As far as I'm concerned, patient care trumps the court order."

"And be prepared to take whatever the court throws at you, even jail time?"

I shrugged. "What else could I do? John needed me." Dotter's power scared me. The reach of a judge was immense, but in the end, it had been an easy decision. I was a healer, and medicine was my calling, not simply a profession I practiced fee for service. I had a covenant with the patient to relieve suffering, and that is what I did. Sounded corny, but it was simple, at least in my mind.

Those beautiful hazel eyes filled with tears. "I love you."

"And I love you too." I took a sip of coffee and stared at the grounds in the bottom of the cup.

"You have that spacey look. What're you thinking?" Jessie asked.

I pointed at the cup. "Can you read coffee grounds like you can read rocks?"

"I can't read either. What's bugging you?"

"Dorian," I said.

"And?"

"And that there may be more to it than Sasha stealing money from the RBC study."

"Like what?" she asked.

"Like other people involved, maybe politicos. There's too much money for one guy, even one who's director of the Chaznikov."

"Daniel, this isn't a chemistry class. You're not responsible for Dorian anymore."

"I know. Still, he's my brother and may need my help."

"What is it exactly you want to do?"

"I think I should go to New York City and find out what's going on at SP."

"Why not call Dorian and ask him?"

"I don't think he knows what these guys are doing to him. I need to talk to Mikhail. I think he's the ringleader."

It was two in the morning, and I couldn't sleep. I was at my desk in the converted extra bedroom, thinking about what John had said, swirling ice in a glass of Grey Goose vodka—I'd picked up some bad habits from my Russian buddies—when my computer dinged with a message.

Mickey Mouse! After Dorian notified the authorities about Sasha and stopped the RBC study, I never expected to hear from him again. He was now using online messaging.

> MM: Dear Dr. Sloane: I hope I am not to cause you more serious troubles, but we still have problems here. Nothing has changed like you said. Sasha still directs Chaznikov Institute, and the RBC trial still goes with false patients. I am sure you did your best, but powerful people are involved and many millions of dollars for them. Maybe this trick cannot be stopped, but I want you to know what goes on. By the way, Katerina is quite beautiful, no? There is good reason she is used often for such things.

I messaged back:

> DS: That was not my body in the pictures.

The messages flew as they had in Moscow.

> MM: Ha! So you say. Maybe you had a good

time and didn't tell anyone, especially your wife? ☺

DS: Not so.

MM: Why, because of a little appendix scar? If the computer expert was so good, maybe now he could draw a scar over this McBurney's Point, and Sasha will publish the pictures after all.

DS: How do you know all this?

I waited for the next message.

MM: We heard Sasha talk about it.

We? Christ! Everybody was listening to everybody. I looked around the room. Could there be bugs in *my* house? But why would Moscow want to reach that far? Still, it wouldn't hurt to check.

MM: You are still there?

I answered:

DS: Sasha won't publish the pictures.

MM: Why not?

DS: Because he's afraid of what my brother might do if people thought he was the one in the picture.

I didn't need to tell him Dorian's real response.

MM: Maybe true. But the big problem is why wasn't Sasha arrested?

DS: My brother said he reported Sasha to the police, and they were going to

arrest him. He also was going to stop
the study and reclaim as much money as
possible.

MM: Nothing has happened. In fact, Sasha
bought a new house in Rublyovka. I will
send a picture. He used his helicopter
this day to go to work. They put a
landing place on the Chaznikov research
building.

About ten seconds later, I opened an e-mail attachment that showed
a four-story brick house elbowed between two clones on a small piece of
snowy land with a silver Mercedes in the driveway and a helipad on the
roof. I recognized the car.

DS: Nice. I guess courtesy of my brother
and SP.

MM: Yes, and Sasha does not seem to be
in any danger from Russian police. Maybe
the pictures worked on you, yes?

DS: No, the pictures did not work. I
did what you asked me to do, and I know
my brother did what I asked him to do.
If anything got messed up, it's at your
end, not here.

MM: Maybe that could be true if Sasha
has some political protection, but also
maybe not. I think perhaps you could
give your brother another talk?

DS: I'm going to New York tomorrow, and
I'll talk with him.

MM: He needs to stop the money going to
Sasha and get the police to arrest him
for the murders of Igor and Leonid.

DS: Who are you and why are you doing this? Were you the guy I sat next to at the lecture?

MM: Maybe consider me like your Mark Felt.

I had to stop and think for a moment.

DS: Deep Throat?

MM: Yes, but for that to work, you must be like Woodward or Bernstein to expose this scam. I will contact you after you talk with your brother. If you want to talk before then, send a message "Tolstoy calling."

My screen went blank.

CHAPTER THIRTY-SIX

"Dorian, what in hell's going on in Moscow?"

We were sitting on a brown suede couch in my brother's office, facing the picture window overlooking Columbus Circle. The new sofa was covered in leather soft as cashmere. But something was different in the redecorated room. I just couldn't put my finger on it. Unnerved, I stood and walked around the office. Dorian watched, stroking the back of the couch, an amused look on his face.

I scanned the room. The chandelier was the same—then it hit me. "You murdered Father!"

That chuckle. "So you *did* notice. John and I had a fifty-dollar bet about that. I said you'd spot it in an instant, and he said no way."

"Where'd you bury him?"

"Storage space in the basement. Dorian Senior now looks out on a room not much bigger than Dorian Junior did for five years before Senior died and Junior became CEO. I couldn't burn a $35,000 painting, much as I wanted to."

"And the board?"

"Can go fuck themselves. They don't run the company; I do. I've made them a pot full of money since Redex was approved, and I don't think there's one among them who cares about the passing of Father's portrait. All they care about is the stock price. That's been awesome, by the way. Too bad you gave yours to the voodoo lady. You made her a very rich woman. Up from $37 a share last year to a $111, close of business yesterday. Nobody's going to bitch about substituting an original Chagall for the portrait of Dorian Senior."

I swirled the wine glass and sipped.

"Like it?" Dorian asked.

"I do. What is it?"

"A 1995 Chateau Margaux. A bargain at only $800 a bottle. I bought five cases. Hard to get."

"When did you become a wine connoisseur?"

"Beats drinking that coarse grain mash you've taken a liking to," Dorian said, sipping.

"You're to blame for sending me to Moscow in the first place. Are you ready to talk about what's going on there?"

"Sure. It's exactly like I told you. I fired Sasha and told the *militsiya* about him, about the murders, and so on. I gave them all the stuff you gave me. They said he'd be arrested and jailed, and they would try to get as much of my money back as possible. End of story. What's the problem?"

"What about Mikhail?"

"What about him?"

"Didn't he introduce you to Sasha to begin with?"

"Yes, but totally innocent. He knew Sasha, made the contacts, and helped set up the study. But that was it. He wasn't aware of any subsequent events. This is all Russian mafia."

"You believe him?"

"I do. He's got too much at stake to bullshit me. Mike, as he wants to be called now because he's exchanged his green card for an American citizenship—and he gets very pissed if I forget and call him Mikhail—receives a percentage of net sales for inventing Redex."

"So he would profit as much as anyone in the company—you included—if Redex became the world leader."

"True, Daniel, but not if we're all in jail. I'm pleased with the US sales, and if that's it, so be it. Six billion a year isn't half-bad. I can live with that." Dorian stood, stretched his arms over his head, and slowly bent to touch his toes. He remained in that position, counting aloud to thirty.

"Back still bothering you?"

He nodded. "Ever since the disc surgery. I only played twenty minutes of basketball this morning before I had to stop. Won't be long before I quit entirely."

Dorian flipped open a white porcelain Limoges pillbox sitting on the black marble coffee table in front of the couch, spilled two chocolate-colored pills into his palm, and popped them into his mouth. A swig of the Margaux washed them down.

"When did you change the color of Redex? Wasn't it red?"

Dorian looked flustered for a moment. "Good observation, doctor. This isn't Redex," he said, pointing to the pillbox. "It's Painex, our new baby."

"I didn't think it had entered clinical testing yet."

"Pre-market release, only for me," he said, picking up the pillbox and shaking it. "Prototype."

"Wasn't it for headaches?"

"That's how we'll market it, but it works great on any painful inflammation, like my back."

"Okay, back to Moscow. How do you know if Sasha's actually been arrested?" I debated sharing information from Mickey Mouse. I trusted my brother, but something held me back.

"I asked the same question," he said, walking over to his desk. He sat down and turned on his Apple. After the musical jingle, he gestured for me to look over his shoulder.

"This e-mail came from the Moscow police two days ago." He clicked on an entry in Outlook and double-clicked the attachment.

I stared at a mug shot of Sasha with numbers across his chest, another picture of him in a jail cell, and the front page of the *Moscow Times*. It was the only English newspaper in Moscow and highly reliable. The story on page one opened with a picture of Sasha and a lead paragraph describing his arrest for murder and grand larceny.

"I could challenge this stuff they sent and claim they staged it all. Then I could travel to Moscow and actually make sure Sasha was in jail. Even if I did, and saw him in a cell behind bars, they still could've rigged it. Just like *Mission Impossible*," Dorian said.

"When does it stop? When do you believe what anyone says?" I asked.

"I'll tell you when—when I get my money back. That's the bottom line on all this shit. I don't give a flying fuck whether Sasha's in jail, goes to trial, or whatever. I only want my $100 million, or whatever's left of it."

Dorian's phone rang. He picked it up, listened a moment, and said, "Bro, you'll have to excuse me. I'm having some bunny troubles that'll take awhile. Why don't you go talk with Mikhail—I mean Mike—and then come back here in an hour or so for a Macallan before we go to dinner? You remember the twenty-five-year-old scotch? I've got some left with your name on it."

"I hear my friend Sasha was not so nice to you," Mikhail said as we sat down in his office.

"We did have an interesting time together. But not nearly as interesting as the pictures made it out to be."

Mikhail laughed. "He's a slippery guy, but I guess the police finally caught up with him."

"Seems like it, Mikhail—I mean Mike. Do you know anything more than what Dorian knows?"

"Like what?"

"Has he really been arrested and put in jail?"

"Why would you doubt that? Dorian showed you the e-mail from the police, didn't he?"

"Yes, but all that could've been doctored. Sasha's good at doing that. Suppose he's living in Rublyovka with a nice new car?"

"Suppose. Suppose my grandmother had wheels, she'd be a pushcart."

"What are you talking about?"

Mikhail laughed. "You never heard that expression? I grew up with it. Suppose this, suppose that. My father always answered with that pushcart story. Suppose Sasha's living in your apartment building right here in New York City and riding to restaurants in a chauffeured Rolls-Royce with one of your brother's bunnies? You can suppose all you want."

"Don't you have other sources in Moscow who could check?"

"Perhaps I do, but why would I want to do that? I have no reason to think the police are lying."

"But what if they are?"

Mike studied my face. His eyes narrowed in concentration, the humor gone. "You must have some information to make you suspect he's not in jail like the picture showed. What is it?"

I stopped talking as I decided what to do. I tried to read his body language. I didn't know whom to trust anymore. If I was reluctant to share Mickey Mouse with my own brother, I sure as hell wasn't going to tell Mike. But his face was impassive, and he sat relaxed. This didn't seem like a guy worried about getting caught doing anything illegal. Maybe he really did have nothing to do with it.

"Nothing, really, only curiosity and suspicion of the Russian system. There's a lot of US dollars floating around that could buy a boatload of protection from powerful people, maybe powerful politicians."

I probably wasn't as pokerfaced as he was. He stared for a long time.

"I think you know more than you're telling," he said finally. "You need to tell me what you know."

"I already did. Why would I not tell you?" I asked.

He shrugged. "I don't know. But you're hiding something. I can tell." His face was getting red, and he started to breathe faster. "I can *feel* it."

I stood, stretched my legs, and looked around his office. He had mounted his diplomas on the blue-and-white-striped wallpaper, and they were impressive. In the center of the wall behind his desk hung a framed certificate from Sloane Pharmaceuticals displaying the "Distinguished Patent Award" for Redex Discovery, signed by my brother. A $10,000 check went along with the recognition. I pointed at the certificate. "Very nice, and well deserved."

He smiled. "Yes, thanks. It was a nice surprise."

"And now, Painex. Maybe another distinguished patent?"

"Yes, we're working on it. It should be ready soon."

"Dorian got an early supply?"

"What do you mean?"

My eyebrows rose. "He took two while I was in his office. He said he hurt his back playing basketball."

Mike sat silent for a moment, a quizzical look on his face.

"Some sort of miscommunication here?" I asked. "Right hand doesn't know what the left hand's doing?"

"True." He played with the earring. "I gave your brother samples from the first lot last week, but he wasn't supposed to tell anyone yet because we didn't want anything leaked outside the company. I guess he was pretty eager to try them."

"He'll be able to give you an early report if it's as good as Redex."

"Yes, I guess he will. But it's totally confidential. Please keep this quiet." I sensed some undercurrent. Mike wasn't any more open with me than I was with him.

I stood and held out my hand. "Mike, congratulations again on your patent award and also on becoming a US citizen. Both well deserved. And I hope Painex lives up to the success of its parent drug."

As I left Mikhail's office, I had no idea what—if anything—was wrong between my brother and his senior vice president, director of research. I asked Dorian about it at dinner that night, but he blew it off. I left him with an uneasy feeling in my gut.

CHAPTER THIRTY-SEVEN

I had an early flight to Indianapolis the next morning. Dorian offered to drive me to LaGuardia, but he had gone to his Hampton house after dinner, and I didn't want to have him drive back. I'd catch a cab after breakfast.

Casey, the doorman, was on duty as I exited the elevator.

"Good morning, Doctor."

"Good morning, Casey. Is there a café close by for breakfast, perhaps on Madison? I have an hour before I need to catch a cab."

"Yes, sir, a small French bistro near here on Madison." He held the door for me. "I'll walk you to the corner and point it out."

We turned left and strolled along Eighty-Sixth to Madison. After the light changed, Casey walked me a quarter of the way into the street. Traffic was nonexistent at 6:00 a.m. We stopped, and he pointed to the east side of Madison, a little north of where we were standing. "See that blue awning on the next block—"

The squeal of tires cut him off. We both spun toward the sound and saw a Lincoln Town Car peel off Eighty-Sixth Street traveling east, make a hard left onto Madison, and come barreling at us. I froze as the black missile hurtled with accelerating speed.

The driver's inexperience saved our lives. He raced the Lincoln too fast for a tight turn, and the big car's momentum swung it wide, tires skidding. Casey whirled and shoved me hard toward the curb. His heroics kept him planted an extra second as the rear end whipped by and smashed hard against his hip. The impact hurled him to the ground as the car flew past and crested the hill on Madison before I could see driver or license plate clearly.

I ran to Casey. His left leg was twisted at a grotesque angle, and the thighbone was poking through the skin. The perforation was bleeding but not pulsing, so the break likely missed the femoral artery. He probably would've bled to death otherwise. I dialed 911 on my cell phone for an ambulance, took off my jacket, and laid it over him to ward off shock.

"I'm so sorry, Casey. This is all my fault." I felt terrible.

He held on to my arms, trying to sit up. Tears of pain welled in his eyes. "How bad?" He turned his head away from the wound.

"Fracture at midthigh. You'll need surgery, but you should be okay." I heard sirens in the distance. Several bystanders gathered near us, a human shield waving off any cars.

He was writhing on the pavement. I put my arm around his shoulders and lowered him to the ground. "Rest, my friend. The ambulance will be here any second."

I wiped his forehead with my handkerchief. A police cruiser raced toward us, followed by an ambulance.

"In my twenty-two years—" he stopped, coughing and trying to catch his breath—"as doorman, that's as close—" *cough, cough*—"to road kill as I ever came." He quit talking again and took several deep breaths. "You think the guy was drunk or maybe on drugs?"

"Could be, Casey, could be."

What I really thought was that Crystal had escalated her battle plan. I had had another near miss.

CHAPTER THIRTY-EIGHT

Abandoning notions of breakfast, I caught a cab to LaGuardia. At the airport, I called the ER doctor at the Mount Sinai Medical Center and was reassured Casey was stable, already in surgery, and expected to make a full recovery, albeit with a pin in his leg.

My flight left on time. I breathed a sigh of relief as the wheels left the tarmac and I could look down at Manhattan from ten thousand feet and rising.

I sank back into my seat with my Bloody Mary and rubbed my bruised knee, glad I had been wearing jeans and not suit pants when I hit the ground. Crystal's vendetta had failed three times, but unchecked, she was eventually going to succeed. Mikhail also worried me. I had a hard time calling him Mike. He'd always be a Russian to me. His outright accusation that I knew more than I was telling him told me *he* knew more than he was telling *me*.

We landed two hours later, and I walked through the parking lot, eyes wide open. It was 10:30 in the morning, but attempted murder turned me into a pretty good people watcher. As I spun the key to start my car, I had a fleeting vision of it exploding, like in so many gangster movies. Surely that was too high-tech for Crystal.

Wednesdays were a second call day for Jessie, and she stayed home unless the OR staff became overloaded. I thought we might catch some alone time together, so I called from LaGuardia to let her know when I was arriving.

My timing could not have been better. When I walked into the bedroom, she was just stepping out of the shower, had her back to me, and was drying off. I stood there, watching as she ran the towel over her body. She was almost as beautiful from the back as from the front. There was something very arousing, voyeur-like, about watching a naked woman—even your wife—who doesn't know she's being watched. She took her time wrapping the towel around her head, turban-fashion, and ever so slowly turned around—and held her arms out to me.

So much for not knowing she was being watched.

"Welcome home, darling." She stood there, as gorgeous as when we first made love in Africa, breasts still firm, and waist slim. She walked toward me, hips sashaying and a smile on her face. "I've missed you."

I took her in my arms and held her tight. I unspun the turban towel and ran my fingers through her moist hair, down her back, and over her buttocks. I bent to kiss her gently on the lips. She took my hand and led me to our bed.

An hour later, Jessie reached for my hand again and lightly kissed each of the fingertips. "I love you."

"I love you too."

"I've been thinking," she said.

"About what?"

"Crystal."

"She's on my mind a lot too, trying to avoid getting killed," I said.

"Do you think she really tried to kill you? The hit-and-run doesn't seem her style."

"Then who?" I asked.

"I don't know. Maybe that Sasha guy?"

"Pretty long reach from Moscow."

"Maybe he has friends," she said. "I feel so badly for her."

"You got to be kidding!"

"No. Think about this for a minute. She's lost forever what we just shared."

I started to object. Jessie interrupted me with a finger on my lips. "I know what she's done, but think about her being a single mother with two small children to raise and no man to share it with, no matter how much money she has. Think how robbed she must feel about the life stolen from her as the wife of the world's greatest basketball player."

"You've certainly changed your tune since she zombied me."

"I have, because despite all you've been through, we still have each other, and she has nothing."

"Nothing except my money."

Jessie brushed my snide remark aside with the back of her hand. "When you came home from Moscow after what you'd been through, and when you walked into the bedroom an hour ago and I knew you'd almost been run over, my heart burst for you—and for me, *that I still have you.* You didn't think I only happened to step out of the shower, did you?"

Apparently my face said I did.

"Men! So easily fooled."

"Women! So crafty and calculating."

She smiled as I kissed her.

"But then I started thinking about Crystal and feeling sorry for her," Jessie said.

"I seem to remember—seems like a hundred years ago—saying that you were a good person. Remember where we were?" I asked.

"Of course—Africa, on the way back from the Maasai village and the curse. But I said *you* were a good person. And right after that, you proposed," Jessie said.

"Sort of."

"Crystal must've loved Randy like I love you. I'll bet that's why she didn't want to allow the autopsy initially. The thought of someone cutting up the man you love gives me chills." Her body shook as she said that, and I held her tight.

When she stopped shaking, I sat up in bed and propped my back against the headboard. Jessie did the same, pulling the sheet to her chin. I put my arm around her shoulders, and as she nestled into me, I asked, "Why do you think she changed her mind about the autopsy?"

Jessie was silent. Her eyes had a faraway look of concentration.

When she didn't answer, I said, "I'll tell you what I think."

"What?"

"Her adoptive father-in-law made her realize it was important to find the cause of death so she could sue," I said.

"That's it? That simple? I wonder."

"Wonder what?"

"You're too gullible. I've been thinking about this for quite a while," Jessie said.

"And?"

Jessie got out of bed. My eyes followed her nude back as she slipped into her robe, turning sideways to flash me a fleeting profile of her breasts before tying the robe closed. The smirk on her face told me she knew exactly what she was doing. She sat down at her vanity table and began brushing her hair. A beautiful woman naked beneath a robe while brushing her hair—man, I was getting aroused all over again.

Several moments later, she ended my fantasizing. "Let me ask you a question."

"Shoot."

"How well did you take a medical history from Randy when you examined him that first day in the hospital?" She stopped brushing her hair and looked at me in her mirror.

"What kind of a question is that? Come on, Jessie. You of all people know me. That's what I do for a living."

She nodded. "Exactly my point. I do know you. Don't you think you would've spotted Randy's body language if he were lying when he told you his father was alive and well, still playing basketball at age seventy? And so would the Rochester Clinic doctors? Besides, there was no reason for him to lie. What would he gain?"

"What're you getting at?"

"Maybe everything he told you was the truth, and the notion that his father died as a young alcoholic only surfaced *after* Randy died."

The thought hit me as if her words had weight. I jumped from the bed and went to her. "My God, you really think so?"

She turned and gave me a grin. "Nice bod, but you might want to put a robe on." I saw my nude reflection in her vanity mirror and turned around.

It's fascinating how the setting impacts acceptable dress or undress. Here we had just made passionate, uninhibited love, and now I was embarrassed standing nude in front of my wife. At another time, she could be walking on a beach wearing little more than a thong and bra top, but need a cover-up when she walked ten feet off the sand to sit down for lunch at the beachside bistro. And require another change for dinner at the same restaurant later that night.

I sashayed my bare butt at her as I walked away.

"Not bad buns," she said, laughing. "I'll keep you around for a while."

I went to my bureau, pulled a pair of shorts from a drawer, and slipped them on. "Geraldo had an affidavit from Randy's adoptive father as proof," I said, returning. "And the birth certificate, the autopsy report, and all that stuff."

"True, and your lawyer objected to their admissibility, but Dotter overruled. I bet it wouldn't be hard to forge such documents, and no one, as far as we know, checked on their authenticity."

"You think all that was staged to make me look incompetent and sway a jury?"

"Could be, and for revenge. She was mighty mad then—and still is, obviously," Jessie said.

"Then the man Crystal ID'd as Randy's adoptive father—what was his name, Herman?—could've been his real father. And if that's the case, what about William Jackson? Where does that leave the guy they said was the biologic father?"

"What I think," Jessie said, going to her closet, "is that William, the drunk who died young, could've been any kind of relation—uncle, cousin, or no relation at all. Just someone who died young of a heart attack. They took a chance using him as the real father and figured we wouldn't follow up. But without all those documents, it was simply her word against yours. That's probably what her father-in-law used to convince her to allow the autopsy."

"They also took a chance on what they'd find at Randy's autopsy," I said.

"True, but it worked pretty well."

"Well enough to give her a new life and screw up ours."

CHAPTER THIRTY-NINE

"In rare circumstances, when the party against whom a judgment is made—in this case, us—had no means by which to ascertain the truth or to know if fraud or perjury had been perpetrated, the court can set aside a previous judgment."

We were in the law offices of Caleb, Harris, and Walker talking with my attorney, Dwight Walker, about Jessie's idea. We sat around one end of a long polished walnut table in the firm's boardroom. The royal-purple carpet, leather club chairs, and oil paintings on the paneled walls of Super Bowl XLVI hosted by Indianapolis could've been used as props in an exposé on why lawyers' fees are so expensive.

"It's true we really didn't have a chance to explore the factual basis of those documents, Daniel," Dwight said, "and the judge seemed to have already made up his mind as to their authenticity and admissibility. In fact, the way he was acting, I think he knew the outcome of the trial at the very beginning." Dwight had removed his suit jacket. The gold cufflinks on his white shirt sparkled in the light. He wore his blue polka-dot bow tie. I was tempted to ask if he had any other.

"Isn't that grounds for an appeal or something?" I asked. The richness of the surroundings was stifling, and I got up to look out the window. It opened onto Monument Circle, the heart of downtown Indianapolis, dominated by the ornate soldiers and sailors shrine to Indiana's war dead.

Dwight swiveled his head to follow me. "No, because Crystal's lawyer, Jesus Geraldo, will argue we had our chance to research those documents during discovery depositions and to dispute them in cross-examination during the trial. We tried to do both without success. Plaintiff will say they gave them to us in plenty of time for us to do due diligence. Actually, if you remember, the documents were cleverly buried in a pile of about a hundred other documents and delivered by courier only a day before the trial started. We'd have to convince the judge we had no means to ascertain the truth in that short amount of time and that the documents were forged. Those will be two critical points he'll insist on."

I sat down again. "But if we can prove they lied about Randy's father, the judge might believe Crystal also lied about my saying Randy could return to basketball."

"True, but that's a big if."

"You don't seem too optimistic."

"I'm not."

"What do we do next?"

Dwight stood, went to the bookshelf, and retrieved a bound leather volume labeled *Indiana Law* from the floor-to-ceiling bookcase. He opened it to a page marked with a Post-it.

"We prepare a document called Motion to Set Aside the Judgment and file it with the court," he said, pointing to the page in the book. "The court would then schedule a hearing to listen to the motion. Before the hearing, Geraldo and I would each file briefs outlining our positions. At the hearing, we give oral arguments before Judge Dotter. Naturally, Geraldo will defend the documents he filed as being accurate and true, and we will contest them."

"What happens then?"

"The court decides which one of us it believes and whether to set aside the previous judgment or perhaps order a new trial."

"Do we testify and have witnesses, like at trial?" I asked.

"Depends. If there's a special witness who can provide evidence key to the decision, Dotter probably would allow him or her to testify."

"What're the chances of our success?"

"Less than 10 percent."

"Shit!" I slapped the table, stood again, and walked around the room. "How can that be if they're lying?"

"We have to prove that first." Dwight put his hand on the book lying open on the table. "Remember, you had a fair trial and were found to have committed malpractice. It all hangs on whether Geraldo can support the authenticity of the documents, and we can prove they lied and we had no way to uncover the truth. If witnesses are allowed, I'm sure he'll find more than one who'll swear Randy's real father died and Herman's the adoptive parent."

"Can't we get the real adoption documents?"

"The adoption agency they list is a place where, for a price, they'll come up with any 'legal' document you want. The court has considered them the 'real' adoption documents."

Jessie had been sitting quietly listening to us and spoke up for the first time. "The answer's in the DNA. It's like a plain old paternity suit, isn't it? Hollywood 101. Who's Randy's real father, Herman or William?"

I sat down next to her and gave her a kiss on the cheek. She always saw through the bullshit and nailed the issue.

"Yes, I suppose it is," Dwight said, closing *Indiana Law*. He crumpled the Post-it and threw it in the garbage.

"Can't we order Herman Jackson to give a sample for DNA testing?"

Dwight shook his head. "Jessie, we can request Judge Dotter to do that, but the odds are he'll refuse."

"Why?"

"Without some evidence of foul play, no judge would allow that. Despite all that's happened, we have no evidence of any wrongdoing. Dotter wouldn't reopen the case and order DNA testing based on a hunch or on the unsupported assertions of a biased party—us."

"Then we'll have to get it another way," Jessie said.

"How?" I asked.

Before she could answer, Dwight interrupted. He stood and held up a hand like a cop stopping traffic. "No, Jessie. It's probably better I don't know."

CHAPTER FORTY

Canterbury Hotel, Indianapolis

Herman Jackson sat at a secluded table in the back corner of the newly redecorated Turner's restaurant in the Canterbury Hotel. Built in the 1850s, the hotel was listed in the National Registry of Historic Places as a "luxury boutique hotel with European traditions." Reproductions by van Gogh, Cézanne, Manet, and Monet hung on the polished oak panels.

In 1992, the ninety-nine-room hotel became nationally famous when heavyweight champ Mike Tyson was found guilty of stripping and raping an eighteen-year-old Miss Black America beauty pageant contestant in room 606.

Herman Jackson finished the sixteen-ounce New York bone-in sirloin strip steak, rare, a loaded baked potato, and sautéed asparagus with a touch of garlic. He stole another look at the attractive blonde sitting alone at the bar, pushed back from the table, and groaned a full stomach rumble. He took the brief Jesus Geraldo had written from his attaché case and began to read.

Coffee and brandy arrived unbidden, and Herman adjusted a table lamp to read the brief as he sweetened and then tasted the hot liquid, alternating it with glances at the bar and sips of the Courvoisier.

Geraldo's brief countered Daniel Sloane's accusations that Herman was Randy's real father. After reading the brief twice, Herman had to admit Sloane and his lawyer had done an impressive amount of fieldwork to buttress their case, but Herman felt confident he had his defense in order. William was dead and had been a known drunk, with two DUI convictions. The fact that he was no relation to Randy Jackson was irrelevant. There was no chance for DNA samples, unless they could find them in his cremated ashes. Herman had an army ready to testify William was Randy's father. Hell, William had no relatives, or at least none that would come forth. The documents claiming Herman was the adoptive father were substantial and would withstand scrutiny.

Crystal, surprisingly, was the weak link. Though she wanted revenge for Randy's death, she had disliked Herman from the day they met. She hated that Randy financed his lifestyle, including his many women and their problems. Fortunately, Herman was able to convince her they'd collect millions suing Daniel Sloane for malpractice. Without that lure, she wouldn't have agreed to the autopsy, and without the autopsy findings, no cause of death could be established. But it had all worked even better than he plotted. Both he and Crystal were incredibly richer for it. And Crystal had her lust for revenge partially sated.

He finished reading the brief a third time and set it aside. He had no doubts Judge Dotter would deny the motion.

Satisfied, Herman sat back, savored the last drop of the double espresso, and finished his cognac. As soon as he did, the waiter returned with a Marie Brizard anisette, knowing he liked the sweet anise taste after the brandy.

He turned his full attention to the blonde still sitting alone at the bar. He figured she was in her midthirties, waiting for her date.

He called over the waiter. "Tom, who's the pretty lady?" He nodded in her direction.

"I don't know, Mr. Jackson. She's been there quite a while."

"I know. Find out what she's drinking and buy her another with my compliments."

"Yes, sir, right away."

The waiter walked to the bar and whispered in her ear. She turned, a head twist followed by a shoulder roll, and looked at Herman. He tipped his head at her, smiled, and held up his half-empty brandy glass. She smiled back. Herman pointed at the empty chair at his table and raised his eyebrows. The blonde studied him for a moment. He watched her eyes explore his entire body, the table, and the ostrich skin briefcase at his feet. Then, deliberately, she shrugged, picked up her glass, and sauntered over. She was even lovelier up close, with large blue eyes, a turned-up nose, Angelina Jolie lips, and a Dolly Parton chest.

Herman rose to his feet and pulled out the empty chair. "Care to join me?"

She hesitated, appraising him again before answering. "Okay. Only for a drink, though." He pulled out the chair for her, and she sat down.

He extended his hand. "Name's Herman, but my friends call me Champ."

"Well, Champ, I'm Glenda. My friends call me Glenda."

"I've been watching you at the bar for the last hour or so. Waiting for someone?"

"Stood up, Champ," she said, a wry look on her face. "I had a dinner date with a guy I've been meeting here a couple of times. Guess he got a better offer."

"Doubtful, but I'm sorry to hear that. Can I substitute?"

"Dunno. Maybe. I like champagne—the expensive kind."

"Me too." He called over the waiter. "Tom, please bring a bottle of Dom Perignon 2000." He looked at her. "Will that do?"

She nodded. "Good start. Let's see where you finish."

Two bottles later, the second a 1996 vintage, Champ and Glenda had become best friends. He signaled Tom for the check.

"Put it on your room tab as usual, Mr. Jackson?"

"Perfect, Tom. Thank you." He signed the tab, and Tom walked away.

"You have a room here?" Glenda asked, brow arched.

"I do. Actually, I live here. It's a great hotel, wonderful restaurant, and right in downtown Indy. Perfect for what I do."

"Which is?"

"Hedge funds. I need to meet with various businesspeople downtown during the day, so I work out of the apartment I own on the sixth floor."

"Mike Tyson—"

He put up both hands, palms toward her. "I know. Room 606, a few doors down the hall from my place."

She sat with a contemplative look as he made his play.

"I'd love to show you the apartment. It's quite attractive, and I'm sure you'd enjoy seeing it."

A smile played in the corners of her mouth, the Jolie lips pursed. "And what else? Your etchings?"

He laughed. "Maybe, but that'll be up to you."

They walked slowly to the elevator, arms linked and hips rubbing. Her head rested on his shoulder. The elevator arrived quickly at 1:00 a.m., and the ride to the sixth floor was brief. He guided her into the hall, and they walked to room 612. Champ pressed his thumb against the groove in the lock until he heard it click. He opened the door for her.

"Oh, nice," she said, standing in the entrance to the living room. "But I can't walk on that white rug with shoes on." Glenda kicked off her heels. Champ spun her around, hugged her close, and kissed her.

"Not bad for an older man," she said, smiling and pushing him away.

"Good genes. My father died at ninety-four, in bed with a woman half his age. And today is my birthday, February 27. I'm seventy-two."

Glenda laughed. "Happy birthday. And you want to prove you're your father's son, I know. But first, I want to see your apartment."

He waved a sweeping hand in front of her. "Living room, and through there," he pointed, "the bedroom. That's it."

"Slow down, Champ, slow down." She took him by the hand. "Remember, etchings and all that stuff—and I decide. Isn't that what you said downstairs? Mike Tyson's room was 606, not 612."

He laughed. "Okay, we'll do it your way." He stopped and pointed. "This is the living room. It was the main room of the suite when I bought this apartment six months ago. But it wasn't big enough, so I knocked out a wall and merged two suites into one. Now I have a six-room apartment, about three thousand square feet. Just right for an old bachelor and his occasional companion."

"Who's half his age—yeah, I know."

They walked into the living room, and she trailed a hand over the top of a white leather couch that matched the rug. Her fingers danced along the soft material, tracing a pattern.

"Does it work?" she asked, nodding at the fireplace along one wall. "I've always read about making love on a bearskin rug in front of a roaring fireplace." She looked around. "But no bearskin rug."

"No, but one out of two isn't bad," he said, flipping a wall switch. The fireplace sprang to life, and dancing flames suffused the room with a soft yellow glow. "If it was daytime, I'd have the concierge send up the rug, or go out and kill a bear."

"Hmm, lovely," she said, palms stretched toward the fire. He came up behind her and kissed her neck. She turned and, taking his elbow, steered him toward the kitchen at the end of the living room. "Do you cook?" she asked.

"No, but sometimes I like to eat alone or with a friend," he nodded at her, "away from the noise downstairs. The Turner chef comes up and cooks dinner. We could try that sometime, if you like."

She didn't answer and turned to the hall off the kitchen. "Where does that lead?" she asked, eyes glancing in that direction.

"Master bedroom, a guest bedroom, and my office. Which would you like to see?"

She took his hand. "Okay, Champ, you've been a very patient boy. Now you can show me your etchings."

He lifted her off her feet, and she let out a surprised squeal. He carried her down the hall. Their cheeks touched, and she lightly kissed him on the lips. "Eager are we, Champ?"

"Timing," he said, "it's all about timing, Glenda. You got to seize the moment." He squeezed her to make his point, and she squealed again.

He stopped at the first door and set her down. "Master bedroom, Madame. Pleased to have your company."

A large, round bed in the center dominated the room. Her face questioned him.

"Revolves 360 degrees so I can follow the sun, the moon, or whatever." He pushed a button, and the drapes parted, revealing a wraparound picture window facing north and west around the corner of the building. He toggled another switch, and the bed rotated clockwise. "It's a fun thing to do," he said.

She sat on the edge of the turning disk and dragged her feet on the celery-green rug. She laughed.

"What's so funny?"

"The rug tickles my feet." She patted the mattress beside her. "Okay, Champ. Let's see how young you are and whether you really are your father's son. Come over here."

He silenced the bed and stood in front of her. Smiling, she undid his belt, unzipped his pants, and let them fall. She looked up at him. "Can you handle your shirt without my help?" He nodded, unbuttoned his shirt, and shrugged it off.

Glenda stood, slid her dress over her head, unsnapped her bra, and stepped out of her panties. Gently she pushed Champ down on the bed.

"Wait a minute," he said, struggling to sit up.

"What's the matter?"

"I need to put on a condom."

"You want to make love to a rubber glove or a beautiful woman?" she asked, slowly sliding down on top of him.

An hour later, when he was snoring loudly, Glenda reached for her purse, took out a pair of underpants, and put them on. She slid out of bed and crept into the hall. She quickly dressed, tiptoed out of the apartment, and caught a cab to the UIMC Hospital, only four blocks away.

CHAPTER FORTY-ONE

My private phone line rang.

"Daniel, it's me, John."

I was immediately alarmed. "Are you okay? Are you getting shocked from the defibrillator?"

"I'm fine, Daniel. No, no shocks since you put in the new lead. This is about something else."

I heard hesitancy in his voice and waited for him to continue. When the silence stretched on, I prompted, "I'm listening."

"Remember when you asked me what I knew about Sasha as the anesthetic was wearing off?"

"Yes, so?"

"I told you all I knew—then."

The phone was silent again. "Go on."

"Something else has happened."

Again, silence. I didn't want to push, though all my senses were focused on his voice. After a moment, he continued.

"This morning I was on a Skype call to my brother in Paris."

I waited. I noticed I was breathing faster.

"Sometimes with Skype you get a message at the bottom of the screen that so-and-so is calling somebody. My computer showed Mike was talking."

I said nothing, but he didn't need any more prompting. "Mike's new office is right next to mine, in the executive suite. We share a common kitchen area. I went in and listened. I thought maybe he'd be talking to Sasha, but he wasn't."

His voice quivered, and he stopped again.

I squeezed the phone to wring the words out of him. Finally, I lost patience. "John, for Christ's sake, spill it—will you? Whatever you want to say, just say it!" I pictured him sitting in his office, hunched over the phone, cupping the receiver, white-faced, and scared.

"He was talking to Sergei Lopakhin—"

"Putin's scientific advisor and physician." My eyebrows rose in surprise. "You know him?"

"I don't, but my brother told me he met with Sergei at the start of the RBC trial, and they had dinner at the Café Pushkin."

"Lopakhin's the most powerful physician in Russia. Owns a bunch of hospitals, is president of the Russian Academy of Sciences, and received the Order of Lenin from the old Soviet Union three or four times. Putin just named him for the Demidov Prize, their equivalent of the Nobel. Some pretty heady stuff."

"I'll say. How's he connected to Sasha?"

I heard a chair scrape, footsteps, and a door close.

"Sorry. I was making sure the door to my office was locked." He let out a long sigh. "Turns out Lopakhin's the brains behind the scam. He planned the whole thing and set it up with Mike."

"How do you know? That's a pretty damning accusation."

"They were arguing on the phone, and Mike was shouting. I could hear every word, at least his side. From what they said, Sasha'd been taking too big a cut and stiffing Lopakhin, who called Mike to square it."

"What'd Mike say?"

"That he'd take care of it."

"Does Dorian know any of this?"

"Daniel, I honestly don't know. His name never came up."

"You think Mike's been doing all this behind my brother's back?"

"Seems that way."

"Hard to believe the CEO of Sloane Pharmaceuticals had no knowledge of any of this."

"Hell, I'm the senior VP chief financial officer reporting directly to the CEO, and I didn't know about it. The books balanced, the RBC summaries all added up, and the company's making money. It wasn't like this was in the States and you could count actual patients entering the study."

It was possible, but I couldn't believe Dorian would let them skim money if he knew about it. And if that were the case, I doubted he would've let me go to Moscow. Too chancy I'd find out something.

"What're you going to do?" I asked.

"Keep my head down until the bullets stop."

I Googled Mikhail Borovsky and learned only what my brother had said at the board meeting: top of his Moscow chemistry class, Harvard PhD, scientist at Valley Labs in Indianapolis, then recruited to SP. There had to be more, but how did I go about finding it? Mickey Mouse had hacked into Natalia Smirnova's computer. I wondered if I could do it.

I entered "computer hacking" in Google and was amazed to see a whole body of literature on how to become a hacker, legal and illegal. Hackers even had their own homepage. But I didn't have the time or patience to learn—or the skills. Mickey Mouse did.

I searched my last messages and found the one I wanted. I typed in "Tolstoy calling" and waited for Mickey Mouse to get back to me.

Ten minutes later, he answered me.

    MM: You want to talk?

    DS: What do you know about Mikhail
    Borovsky?

    MM: Not so much. He and Sasha were
    roommates in Moscow when Sasha was
    studying chemistry and Mikhail
    medicine.

    DS: That's it?

    MM: Brilliant, but bad temper. Once got
    into a fight with a guy a hundred pounds
    heavier and almost killed him with a
    knife. The university suspended him one
    term.

    DS: My brother said Mikhail had nothing
    to do with the scam, but I think he did.
    Can you find out?

    MM: What you want I should do?

DS: Hack into his computer. See who he's been e-mailing. Or maybe check out his bank account to see if there's been a large deposit recently.

MM: Slow up. Why you want this?

DS: I think he's the brains behind the scam and set it up with Sasha from the very beginning.

MM: His computer will be harder than Natalia's. I'm sure your brother's company has firewalls that stop hacking. Maybe he could help us get in.

DS: I don't want to involve him, at least not yet. He's got enough trouble maintaining credibility with the FDA here in the US after terminating the RBC study.

MM: You know, Sasha still lives a good life. Important people must protect him. In Russia, that is our system. And that makes more of the danger for all of us.

I debated telling him about Lopakhin but decided not to. I still didn't totally trust him.

DS: You have any better ideas?

MM: Give me some days to find it out. I will be back to touch you soon.

I was working on my next day's teaching assignment when my direct line rang.

"Daniel, it's me, John."

"Not your defibrillator going off again?"

"No, still working perfectly. Something else has come up."

"Okay, what?"

"I need to talk with you."

"What's up?"

"Mike stopped by to see me."

"And?"

"He knows I was listening when he talked to Lopakhin."

"How'd he find out?"

"I think my office is bugged. I'm calling you from my cell phone, and I'm outside, walking along Central Park South, away from the office. Mike asked me what I knew."

"You should have been more cautious."

"Thanks," John said. "Now you tell me."

"What did you say to Mike?"

"That I knew nothing, that I happened to be in the kitchen while he was calling. I don't think he believed me, and he certainly wouldn't if my call to you was taped."

"Did you tell Dorian?"

"Yes, but he shrugged it off. Said I was imagining things. I'm scared, Daniel. I don't know what to do." His voice shook.

"You want me to fly in?" I would, but I didn't know what good it would do.

"No, not yet. Just be there if I need help."

"Absolutely."

My phone rang at three the next morning. Jessie instinctively reached for it, probably thinking it was the OR.

"For you," she said in a sleepy voice and dropped the receiver on my chest.

"Daniel, it's me, John." *Oof.* I heard him grunt in the background.

"What's the matter?"

"This goddamn defibrillator. It's shocked me five times in the last hour! Just keeps going off. I barely catch my breath, and the next shock hits. I'm going crazy with it, Daniel. You've got to make it stop."

"Do you have a magnet at home?"

"A magnet? I don't know. What kind?"

"Anything pretty large that you can place over the defibrillator, like when I tested it in the office. That'll deactivate it."

"No, nothing like that." *Oof.* "Shit! Again! That one hurt like hell!"

"Call 911 and get to an emergency room. They'll know what to do." I heard a crash. "John, did you hear me?"

No answer. "John? John!"

A woman picked up the phone. "I'm John's wife. He just fell to the floor. He's not moving! My God, I think he's dead!"

"Quick, hang up and call 911. Then do CPR."

"I don't know how!"

"Okay, call 911 now! Then call me back." I got out of bed and went downstairs to the kitchen. I could do nothing but wait. Whatever was making the defibrillator fire could end up killing him. I brewed a cup of coffee and sat down, hoping for the best but prepared for the worst.

Close to 6:00 a.m., the phone rang.

"Is this the Sloane residence? Dr. Sloane, please."

"Speaking."

"Dr. Sloane, I'm Dr. Jerome Bradford, ER doc at Montefiore in the Bronx. I'm told that John Anderson was your patient."

"Was?"

"Yes, I'm sorry. He passed away ten minutes ago. His wife asked me to call you, said you implanted his defibrillator."

"Yes, I did. What happened?"

"The thing went crazy. I've never seen anything like it. Something messed up the electronics. It kept shocking his heart until it actually triggered his sudden death and then couldn't stop what it started."

"Did you try a magnet to deactivate it?"

"Of course, first thing. But it was like something else was controlling

215

it, some outside force. It wouldn't respond to the programmer at all, or anything else I did."

"You did CPR and all?"

"Did that and IV amiodarone, epinephrine, the whole nine yards. But since we couldn't control the defibrillator, nothing else worked."

"You could've cut the lead."

He gasped. "Oh my God, I didn't think of that. I'm so sorry. Shit, I might've saved him."

"Can you explant the defibrillator and send it to me?"

"I'll need permission from his wife."

"Naturally. But please do it quickly, and send it FedEx." I gave him my address and FedEx number.

Here I'd been thinking about hacking into computers, and someone had hacked into John's defibrillator, reset the software, and turned it into a murder weapon. Mikhail was high on my list. This was way out of Crystal's league.

CHAPTER FORTY-TWO

"Before you call your first witnesses, Mr. Geraldo and Mr. Walker," Judge Dotter said, "I want to know what's new that's not set forth in your brief."

We were in court hearings over the Motion to Set Aside the Judgment. Dwight told me Geraldo was about to parade a host of witnesses all testifying that the drunk, William Jackson, was Randy's biological father who died of a heart attack at age thirty-seven and that his older brother, Herman, was his adoptive father. Dorian had lent me $20,000 to cover my legal fees so I could afford this hearing. If it didn't go well, I was in deep trouble.

I looked across our defense table at Crystal seated at the plaintiff's table on the other side of the aisle and had to resist the urge to get up and strangle the woman. I didn't feel the pity Jessie had, just contempt. She had tried to kill me three times. But she just stared back with her evil look and didn't break eye contact until the judge spoke again.

Dotter continued. "It's not my intention to waste the court's time simply to rehash what we already know. And from what I read in both your briefs—yours, Mr. Geraldo, as well as yours, Mr. Walker—" he looked first at Jesus and then at Dwight—"neither of you have provided compelling information not revealed at trial."

"If it pleases the court, Your Honor," Dwight said, waving a sheet of paper in the air and walking toward the judge's bench. "I've just received lab data on a critical test, the results of which are not in my brief. I would like to lay foundation for its admissibility with my first witness."

"So, there *is* something new. That'll be refreshing. Proceed, Counselor," said Dotter.

"I call as my first witness Dr. James Falcone, director of the genetic testing company ExamineYourDNA." Dwight established his credentials as an expert geneticist, and Geraldo agreed.

"Did your laboratory test certain DNA material delivered to you by UIMC Hospital?"

"Yes, we did," Falcone answered confidently. I suspected he had testified many times before.

"And is the information in this report," he showed him the paper, "an accurate presentation of your results?"

"Yes, it is."

"Your Honor, may I offer this document to the court for its consideration?" Dotter gave permission, and Dwight handed Geraldo a copy and one to the bailiff for Dotter.

Dwight asked Falcone, "Are these the results of DNA analysis on tissue samples from Herman Jackson?"

"They are."

"In addition to this analysis, did you have two other genetic laboratories perform the same analyses and compare tissue obtained from Herman Jackson with tissue from Randy Jackson?"

"I did," said Falcone.

"Randy Jackson was cremated. Where did you get samples of his DNA?" Dwight asked.

"From pieces of his heart that were saved at autopsy because of the litigation."

"And what do all three labs prove to a reasonable degree of medical certainty?"

"That Herman Jackson is Randy Jackson's biological father, actually to a degree far greater than the phrase you lawyers use, 'to a reasonable degree of medical certainty.' The odds are far greater than 50 percent. More like ten million to one that Herman Jackson is Randy's biological father."

I heard Crystal gasp.

"Now, wait just a damn minute," Geraldo burst forth, jumping up and seeming to forget himself. "I'm sorry, Your Honor, but I object to this last-minute presentation of a new report. I haven't examined it to determine veracity."

"No, but you agreed that Dr. Falcone be recognized by the court as a medical expert, and this is his report. If I remember correctly, Counselor, you presented some last-minute documents yourself during trial, which I allowed. Defense filed this motion and established foundation, so let's hear what they have to say. Go ahead, Mr. Walker." Apparently, Dotter had forgiven Dwight's breach of court etiquette from the trial.

Crystal jumped to her feet and started to scold Herman Jackson. The five "relatives" Geraldo had brought to testify on behalf of the plaintiff began to buzz among themselves. A group of Randy Jackson fans started stamping their feet, yelling, "Randy, Randy!" Only reporters from the *Indianapolis Star* and *Sports Illustrated* were on hand. Both began dialing cell phones, and fingers flew, typing text messages into iPads.

"Order! Order! Order in my courtroom!" shouted Dotter, slamming the gavel on his desk. "You'll all be quiet, or I'll instruct the bailiff to clear the courtroom." Silence settled in like a low cloud. "Another outburst, and I'll hold you all in contempt." He glared at the spectators, at Crystal, and at Geraldo, ignoring Dwight and me.

"Now, Mr. Walker, proceed."

"Thank you, Your Honor. As I said, the labs made the appropriate DNA comparisons. We even used a genetic lab I know Mr. Geraldo trusts, since he's used them in past cases." Dwight smirked at Geraldo. "These tests established parentage without any doubt whatsoever."

"Assuming, as a hypothetical, you have done this and your results are accurate, what bearing does this have on the case?" Dotter asked.

"Thank you, Your Honor. It means that Randy Jackson's father could not have had premature coronary artery disease. He's sitting here in court, looking quite healthy." Dwight pointed at Herman. "Therefore, he could not have bestowed on Randy a genetic risk for an early heart attack. That means that the history my client, Dr. Daniel Sloane, took from Randy Jackson regarding his father being alive at seventy and well enough even to play basketball was accurate. That in turn means my client could not have known Randy was at risk for premature coronary disease, at least by family history. Further, Your Honor, it calls into question other statements made by plaintiff about what my client is accused of, what information plaintiff used to establish malpractice, and a whole host of things, Your Honor."

"Let's not get carried away with too many assertions on the basis of this one test, Counselor, before we hear from Mr. Geraldo."

"Yes, Your Honor, thank you. I'm happy to stop at this point and answer any questions the court or plaintiff has. Dr. Falcone can step down if Mr. Geraldo has no questions for him."

"None," Geraldo said, heaving himself to his feet as Falcone left the courtroom. He stared at Dwight seated at the defense table, and me alongside him. He shook his head, letting the drama unfold. Then he turned to the judge.

"Your Honor, it seems this proceeding," he swept a hand around the court, "boils down to the DNA and its accuracy to determine paternity."

He looked at the paper in his hand and jabbed it with his index finger. "I don't dispute the accuracy of the findings from these labs," he said. "They're reliable and honest labs, and as the learned counselor has stated, I've used at least one of them." He took another look at the sheet. "Actually, two of them. And certainly Dr. Falcone's credentials are impeccable.

"However, what I do challenge is the allegation that the DNA came from my client, Mr. Herman Jackson. We received no court order to provide a sample, and to the best of Mr. Jackson's knowledge, he hasn't provided a sample for analysis. Therefore, I question whether the DNA tested is actually Herman Jackson's. Until that can be established to a reasonable degree of medical certainty, plaintiff has no case, Your Honor, and I move for immediate dismissal of these proceedings."

"Now just hold on, Mr. Geraldo. You're moving a bit too fast, also. There'll be no dismissal, so your motion is denied. You both agreed to this hearing, and we'll continue in an orderly fashion." Dotter looked at our table. "Mr. Walker, I assume you're prepared to provide answers to Mr. Geraldo as to the origin of the DNA alleged to be Herman Jackson's?"

"Yes, sir, Your Honor. It was obtained by a courier who received it directly from Mr. Jackson himself."

"That's a lie!" shouted Herman from the gallery, jumping up and waving his fist. "No way in hell did I provide a *courier*," he spat the word, "with my DNA."

Dotter banged his gravel. "Mr. Jackson, perhaps you forgot my warning a few moments ago. You are hereby fined $500. Another outburst will land you in a detention cell for a week and a fine of $5,000. You can do the math for a third outburst. Am I clear on that?"

"Yes, Your Honor, I'm sorry. It's just that they're lying through their teeth—"

"Enough! You will speak through your lawyer only. Mr. Geraldo is quite capable of talking to this court in a civil fashion. Understood?"

"Yes, sir." He sat down.

"Mr. Walker, I assume you're prepared to provide the court with access to this courier?"

"Yes, sir, Your Honor. The courier is waiting to testify."

"Fine. Why don't we take a fifteen-minute recess so everyone can collect his or her thoughts. Then we'll talk to this courier."

Fifteen minutes later, we were back in court.

Dwight said, "I'd like to call Ms. Gloria Valdez to the stand."

A woman rose from the back of the gallery, her blonde hair gathered in a tight bun, and walked to the witness box. She wore a tailored black business suit with an off-white blouse that suggested a female executive attending a corporate luncheon.

After she was sworn in, Dwight said, "Please tell the court your full name and address."

"Gloria Valdez, 201 North Croton Boulevard, Yonkers, New York."

"Pretty far from home, aren't you, Ms. Valdez?"

"A bit."

"What do you do for a living?" Dwight asked.

"I'm a part-time hairdresser."

So much for the business executive.

"And the rest of your time, what do you do?"

"I provide escort services."

"I see. And where do you work?"

"Usually in New York City, but if it pays, I travel to other places as well."

"Such as Indianapolis?"

"Correct."

"And did you provide escort services to Mr. Herman Jackson at some time in the past?"

"Yes, I did."

"She's lying!" Herman muttered loudly to Geraldo. Dotter scrunched his eyes into a squint but said nothing.

"When did you do this?"

"About a month ago."

"And during that time, did you obtain a sample of Mr. Herman Jackson's DNA?"

"I did."

"To the best of your knowledge, do you know if DNA can be obtained from hair follicles?" Dwight asked.

"Objection, Your Honor! She's hardly an expert on this topic," Geraldo said.

"True, but she is a hairdresser, and I'm curious if she knows. Overruled. You may answer, Ms. Valdez," said the judge, looking at her.

"Yes, it can, Your Honor."

"All right then, you obtained the DNA from him. How did you carry it out?" Dwight asked.

"What do you mean, 'how did I carry it out'? How did I carry out getting the DNA from him, or how did I transport it?"

"Let's start with the transport. How did you transport the DNA from Mr. Jackson to the lab, or did you drop it off somewhere else?"

"I dropped it off at the UIMC lab."

"In what receptacle?"

"One of the oldest known to man or woman."

"And that was?"

A tiny smile played on her lips. She waited so long, Dotter prompted, "Please answer the question, Ms. Valdez."

"My vagina."

The courtroom erupted. Dotter banged his gavel, the reporters redialed their cell phones, and Crystal jumped up and shouted, "No! No!"

Only Herman sat quietly, a look of dawning recognition on his face. He gave a nod so miniscule I think I was the only one who saw it. But he knew. He knew what we had done to him and his bullshit lies.

"Order! Order!" Dotter shouted. The bailiff echoed his command, and gradually the spectators settled down.

Dwight resumed. "When did this take place?"

"February 27, this year."

"Where?"

"At Mr. Jackson's apartment in the Canterbury Hotel."

"How did you remember the date so precisely?"

"Herman told me it was his birthday and that he could still perform pretty well for a man who was now seventy-two years old." As she said that, she removed a hairpin and shook her blonde hair free. Herman's eyes got big. He mouthed, "Glenda." She glanced in his direction, smiled, and turned back to Dwight.

"I assume that—I am trying to ask this delicately. Herman Jackson placed his DNA in your—er—receptacle in the usual fashion?"

"If you're asking whether or not we had sexual intercourse, the answer is yes. And, yes, Herman ejaculated his sperm into my vagina. He wanted to use a condom, but—"

"Thank you, Ms. Valdez, we have enough information. After he— um—ejaculated, what happened?"

"We both fell asleep."

"And then?"

"I woke, slipped out of bed, and put on a pair of waterproof underpants—you know, the kind old people wear who are incontinent so they don't leak through. I had brought a pair with me. Then I left his apartment."

"You brought along these special underpants fully expecting you would have sex with him. Is that correct?"

"I haven't had a man say no yet."

"Doesn't that make you a prostitute rather than, what did you call it, an escort?"

Gloria had been carefully schooled. "Not at all. I get paid to be an escort. If I want to have sex with a client, that's on my own time, as a consenting adult. I definitely do not get paid to have sex with anyone. That would be illegal." She looked at Dotter for confirmation, but he sat stone-faced.

"But you were charged with getting a DNA sample from Herman Jackson, were you not?"

"Yes, so?"

"Isn't that getting paid to have sex with him so you could obtain a sample of his sperm?" Dwight was asking all the potentially damaging questions before Geraldo had a go. They had rehearsed this morning before the hearing.

"No, absolutely not. I could have gotten his DNA off the rim of the glass he drank from or, as was suggested earlier, hair samples. Or I could have raked his face with my nails to snag some skin." She flashed her nails catlike at Dwight and curled her upper lip into a comical tiger snarl. I could see Gloria was enjoying her moment in the sun. "I chose to do it my way because I thought it would be fun. And it was. He's a pretty sexy guy. Reminded me of OJ before the murders. We had a good time." She gave Herman a big grin and a wink.

And damn if he didn't smile back and sit up straight in his chair, preening, looking all pleased with himself. "I might even collect some more DNA in the future," she said with a snicker.

The courtroom erupted in laughter, and Dotter had to quiet it again. I caught the glimpse of a smile before he put his hand to his face to hide it.

"One last question. You personally transported the samples to a lab. How did you do that? What happened?"

"With my tighty-tights on, I took a cab from the Canterbury to the UIMC Hospital, went to the emergency room, and told them who I was. They were expecting me. The chief of gynecology was paged and did a pelvic examination. He suctioned out the sperm, and after that, he cleansed my—um—'receptacle' with a spermicidal solution. The whole thing took maybe thirty minutes. I caught another cab to the downtown

Marriott to sleep. I flew back to New York on Delta at 9:50 the following morning."

"I assume you had agreed to some sort of a financial arrangement for this escort service you provided?"

"Yes, I was paid $5,000 plus first-class travel expenses and hotel accommodations."

"No further questions, Your Honor. Your witness, Mr. Geraldo."

Dotter interrupted. "Let's break for thirty minutes, then resume."

When we returned, Geraldo was pacing around the plaintiff's table looking distraught. The judge asked Gloria to return to the witness stand and reminded her she was still under oath.

Then Geraldo attacked.

"Ms. Valdez, isn't it true you hire out for sex, as you did here? That you are nothing more than a prostitute hired by a pimp?" He pointed to me.

She kept her cool. "No, I hire out for escort services. The sex is optional and solely at my discretion, as I said before."

"Do your clients pay more if they have sex with you?"

She shook her head. "No, absolutely not. I charge $500 an hour, regardless of the activity."

"But you charged ten times that amount here."

"That's not true. Including travel time, I spent ten hours or more on this gig."

It appeared Geraldo knew he was losing. He had already conceded the veracity of the genetic testing, he had challenged how the samples were obtained and lost, and now he was failing to paint Gloria as a prostitute. I knew he had only one other thing to try.

"How quickly did you go to the UIMC Hospital after you left the Canterbury?"

"Immediately."

"How do we know you didn't stop for another—how did you phrase it—gig, before you went to the hospital?"

"Objection, Your Honor. There's no indication Ms. Valdez did that. If necessary, I'm sure we can establish a timeline to document when she and Mr. Jackson left the restaurant to go to his apartment, the time she left the Canterbury to take a cab to the hospital, and when she arrived in the hospital's ER. Further, I'm sure we can locate the cab driver who took her to the hospital and verify she had no other 'gigs' en route."

"Sustained."

As big as he was, Geraldo looked like a deflated balloon, or maybe "dirigible" would be more accurate. He sat at the plaintiff's table, thumbing through notes, stalling for time. Finally, Dotter asked, "Do you have any more questions for this witness, Mr. Geraldo, or can we dismiss her?"

He stood and addressed the judge. "I'm finished with her, Your Honor. Thank you." Gloria stepped down.

"Are we done then, Counselors?" asked Dotter.

Walker stood. "I'm finished, Your Honor."

"And you, Mr. Geraldo?" One of Geraldo's assistants was busy whispering in his ear, and he took a moment before answering.

Geraldo's eyes opened wide. His face lit up, suddenly reinflated—in fact, almost bursting. He nodded vigorously at his assistant and patted him on his back. I saw him mouth, "Well done, son," and turn to the bench.

"Your Honor, if it pleases the court, I would like to call Dr. Daniel Sloane as my next witness," he said, beaming.

I was stunned. Why on earth would Geraldo want to question me?

CHAPTER FORTY-THREE

"Do you swear the information you are about to give this court is the truth, the whole truth, and nothing but the truth, so help you God?" The court stenographer read the ritual, my left hand on the Bible, the right one upraised.

"I do."

"Please state your full name and address for the court," Geraldo requested, taking over. As I did, it dawned on me where he would be going. I started to sweat as my anxiety grew. From victory to defeat, even incarceration, during one hearing.

"Dr. Sloane, do you know a man named John Anderson?"

"Yes, he is—was my patient. He died a few days ago."

"Sorry to hear that," Geraldo mumbled without pausing. "Did you implant a defibrillator—I think it's called an ICD, short for an implantable cardioverter defibrillator—in him after he was resuscitated from sudden death at a baseball game?"

"Yes, I did."

"Please tell the court when you did this."

"I don't remember the exact date."

"Approximately then."

"About three years ago."

"And did John Anderson do well after that implant?"

"Yes, for a while."

"For a while. How long?"

"Until a couple of months ago."

"What happened then?"

My hands were damp. Beads of sweat accumulated on my forehead.

Though I had never discussed with Dwight what I had done, he anticipated what was happening.

"Objection, Your Honor. This line of inquiry has nothing to do with the hearing before us. I ask the court to intervene and instruct the defense counselor to cease this line of questions."

"Where are you going with this, Mr. Geraldo? Is it relevant?" Dotter asked.

Geraldo turned to the judge. "Your Honor, it's somewhat tangential to the specific focus of the hearing, but nevertheless, I think the court will find it extremely interesting and important."

"All right, you may continue, but come to the point quickly. I think I've heard all I need to make a ruling, and my patience is wearing thin."

"Thank you, Your Honor." He turned back to me. "Dr. Sloane, you were saying that your patient did well initially and then developed a problem with his ICD. Do I have that right?"

I nodded.

"I'm sorry, Doctor, have you so quickly forgotten the instructions the court gave you at your trial? My, how memory fades."

"Objection, Your Honor. Sarcasm is uncalled for," Dwight said.

Dotter raised his eyebrows, but before he could rule, Geraldo continued. "You have to say yes or no. The court stenographer cannot record a head nod." His tone dripped with condescension.

I wanted to choke the bastard. "Yes."

"And what was his problem?"

"The defibrillator lead had developed a premature fracture and was causing the ICD to shock him inappropriately."

"These shocks, are they painful?"

I started to nod again and caught myself. "Yes, and they can be dangerous as well."

"How so?"

"They can cause the same life-threatening heart rhythms they're supposed to stop."

Geraldo dismissed that response with a hand wave. "And did your patient call you and tell you about this problem?"

"He did."

"And what did you instruct him to do?"

"To come to our hospital, and I would have one of the electrophysiology doctors see him and evaluate the problem."

"One of the doctors, you say. And which one did you have in mind?"

"We have a fairly large group; it could've been anyone of them."

"I assume, then, you picked one of them to see your patient, because we all know you could not take care of him yourself, right? After all, Judge

Dotter's orders explicitly stated you could only see patients if overseen by a board-certified cardiologist. Then when you violated that proviso, he ordered that you couldn't see *any* patients until you completed a formal clerkship under Dr. Lindorf's tutelage. Isn't that correct, Doctor?"

I was silent.

"Did you not hear the question, Doctor? Would you like it repeated?"

"No, I heard it, *you son of a bitch*," the latter under my breath.

"Well, the court is waiting for your response."

"John begged me to see him. He said, 'You put the defibrillator in; it's your responsibility to take care of me.'"

"And so, in direct violation of this court's orders and risking a citation for contempt of court, you treated John Anderson as a patient, without any supervision and without taking the remedial course under Dr. Lindorf. Am I correct, Doctor?"

I didn't respond.

"Correct, Doctor?" Geraldo repeated. "You did this knowing that you could be fined, imprisoned, or both for such a flagrant, willful, and conscious violation of the court's orders, of *Judge Dotter's orders*. Correct, Doctor?" He glanced at Dotter with a smug look. Dotter remained a sphinx, but I thought I saw his eyes flare momentarily.

But I had had enough of Jesus Geraldo's bullying. He had pushed me to my limit –and beyond. "That's correct, Counselor. And I'd do it again in an instant because patient care is the most important thing I do. And I do it quite well, regardless of how you've tried to mischaracterize me."

"I'm not trying to characterize you any which way, Doctor. Your own actions do that."

"Well, call it whatever you like, but you've portrayed me as an incompetent physician who forgets to write things down or order appropriate tests or warn about certain risks."

"Thank you, Doctor, that's enough. Just answer—"

"Well, Mr. Geraldo, you're wrong, totally wrong. I've saved more lives than you'll ever—"

"*That's enough, Doctor!* There's no question pending."

I paused, but I couldn't turn it off. "Maybe not, but this whole malpractice case has been a trumped-up affair, a farce you've fabricated. I took excellent care of Randy Jackson. I explicitly warned him not to play basketball, I tried to find the cause of his blackouts, and I told him to come back for a cardiac catheterization—"

Geraldo cut me off. "Your Honor, will you instruct the witness to answer the questions posed and not digress?"

"Doctor Sloane, Mr. Geraldo's request is appropriate. Only answer the questions he asks you. Mr. Walker on redirect can ask anything further you wish to cover." Dotter's tone was flat, and I couldn't tell what he was thinking. Frankly, I didn't care.

Geraldo stationed his huge bulk in front of me, hands on hips. "Did you, or did you not, defy the orders of this court by treating Mr. Anderson? That's the only question pending, Doctor. Only answer yes or no. Did you defy Judge Dotter?"

"You're damned right I did," I exploded. Geraldo tried to cut me off, but I continued. I was risking the forbearance of the court, but I wasn't going to stop. I couldn't stop. "Saving my patient's life was then, and is now, more important than what a judge," I turned to Dotter, "I mean no disrespect, Judge Dotter—what *any* judge orders me to do or not do. If I have to pay the penalty for disobeying the court's orders while affirming the Hippocratic Oath, so be it. I'm prepared to do so because one code transcends the other. We're talking about saving a human life here, not some abstract legal issue."

When I finished, my face was flushed. My heart was pounding. I had clenched my fists so hard my knuckles were white, and my nails dug into my palms. I took a sip of water from the glass the bailiff had placed on the side arm and breathed deeply to slow my breathing and regain control.

The courtroom was deathly silent. Then it started. I heard clapping in the audience. First one pair of hands and then another. I looked up. Finally, people stood and were all applauding, raising their fists in the air. I looked at Dotter, expecting him to blow a stack, but he still wore that same sphinxlike expression.

He let the outburst continue a few moments and then banged his gavel. He stood and said, "I've heard enough. The witness is excused. Court's adjourned until ten tomorrow morning. I will give my decision at that time." He turned and left the courtroom, black robe fluttering in his wake.

We were all stunned. Geraldo, Walker, all of us, just looked from one face to the other, eyebrows raised, bewildered.

I stepped down from the witness box as Jessie bolted from the gallery and flew into my arms.

"I love you, you big jerk. And if you go to jail, I'll bake you a pie with wire cutters in it. You did the right thing, and I'm so proud." She hugged me around the neck, kissing my cheek and then my lips.

Dwight shook my hand. "Well done, Daniel. Better said than anything I could do." Geraldo scowled at me. The two reporters thrust recorders in my face and bombarded me with questions. I looked at Dwight. He shook his head.

"No comment. Nothing to add to my testimony a moment ago. The big story will be tomorrow at 10:00 a.m."

Crystal stood at the back of the courtroom whispering to the big muscled guy who had escorted us from Randy's funeral so many months ago. Though her face was close to his, her eyes were riveted on Herman, who was leaving the courtroom with his arm around Gloria's waist. The phrase "if looks could kill" must've started with someone like Crystal the Pistol. Her eyes revealed murder in her heart. She fingered the silver disk around her neck.

Gloria, a.k.a. Glenda, was leaving with a sweet smile on her face. I silently thanked Dorian for her contact information.

Jessie and I left the Noblesville courtroom and drove home. "What will he decide?" was all we could talk about. We sliced and diced the hearing all through the Thai takeout and well into the night, finally falling into an exhausted sleep.

CHAPTER FORTY-FOUR

"All rise. All rise. This court is now in session. The Honorable Horace J. Dotter presiding," the bailiff announced at precisely ten the following morning.

Dotter entered from the door behind his desk, holding some papers in one hand and his robe shut with his other. He glanced at the courtroom, muttered a brief, "Be seated," and sat down himself.

He took a few moments to arrange papers on his desk until the murmuring in the courtroom subsided. The room was filled to capacity. Reporters from all over the United States had flown in during the night, and TV crews were lurking outside, choking the hall with people. Gloria and Herman sat together in the packed audience, as did Jessie and Dorian, who had flown in this morning. I sat with Dwight at the defense table, a few feet across from Geraldo and Crystal at the plaintiff's table.

"I have given much thought to these proceedings," Dotter began, scanning the courtroom, "as well as to the court trial months ago. Our judicial system is imperfect, as we all know, but it's the best we have." Murmurings began again, and he held up a hand, silencing them. "We've all read about people wrongly imprisoned who were freed after many years of incarceration on the basis of new DNA evidence. While this hearing does not achieve the importance of such a severe state of affairs, nevertheless, DNA does figure prominently, and that information should be used appropriately.

"You may be interested to know that according to English Law practiced in many countries such as England, Australia, and Canada, a malpractice trial such as the defendant had months ago would be held before a single magistrate skilled in medical and scientific issues. The case can then be decided solely on its merits with none of the charades and grandstanding we commonly see in American courtrooms in front of juries. And which we definitely saw in this case." Dwight and Geraldo shifted uncomfortably under Dotter's hard gaze.

"But that's not our system, and we have to deal with our own unique reality. Given that, I have had to formulate a decision for this hearing.

"After rereading the transcripts from the malpractice trial of Doctor Daniel Sloane and listening to yesterday's proceedings, I'm of the mind we were too severe in our judgment against the doctor and there was validity to his arguments about how he cared for Randy Jackson. That said," his voice built to a crescendo, "the doctor nevertheless violated directives from this court," his voice softened, "albeit to render appropriate medical care, but nevertheless, breaking the law. That cannot go unpunished."

Oh, shit, I thought. *Here comes jail time.*

"But, first things first. The DNA evidence in this instance is irrefutable, agreed to by both parties, and calls into question much of the plaintiff's case, as the defense has opined. Therefore, I am vacating the judgment previously entered in favor of the plaintiff and, with it, the monetary award. Plaintiff is hereby ordered to return any and all monies paid by Dr. Sloane toward satisfaction of the judgment within thirty days."

Crystal inhaled sharply, made a fist, and bit down on the first knuckle. She slowly shook her head in disbelief. "No! No! No!" she sobbed, muting her outburst with her fist. I hoped Dotter didn't plan to be driving too soon. I had no doubt she'd be sticking pins into his look-alike doll, and I didn't want him running head on into a drunk driver.

Dotter stared down at the spectator gallery, giving them a hard look that squelched any eruption. There was none. He continued. "Second, Dr. Sloane is free to practice medicine without supervision in the manner he performed prior to the trial. I think he's a good and conscientious doctor."

It was my turn to make a fist, jerk an imaginary chain, and mouth, "Yes!"

"Finally, there's the matter of contempt of court." Dotter turned to me. "You cannot defy the court, Doctor, no matter how good your intentions. The law must be upheld. You have given me no choice but to find you in contempt of court. You will pay a fine of $10,000 and spend thirty days in jail for consciously and willfully disobeying the court's orders—"

I was shocked—until he continued.

"—which I am suspending with the certitude I will not see you in my courtroom ever again." He gave a brief head nod to punctuate the end of the admonition, struck his gavel, and said, "One last thing before court is adjourned."

He searched the courtroom until his eyes found Herman Jackson.

"Mr. Jackson, inadvertent false testimony happens in court frequently, for example, when a witness misspeaks, remembers events incorrectly, or maybe lies about his age. The operative word is *inadvertent*. Willfully giving false testimony under oath or providing false documentation on a point material to an investigation is perjury, which federal law defines as a felony punishable by a prison term up to five years. I am instructing the district attorney to investigate the documents you provided in the malpractice trial against Dr. Sloane. I am also interested in the DA searching for Dr. Sloane's missing discharge dictation."

His eyes flicked to the plaintiff's table. "And, Mr. Geraldo, you may have a problem here as well. Depending on what the DA's investigation uncovers, you may be facing disciplinary proceedings, potentially a suspension of your license, and perhaps even disbarment. You are both instructed to cooperate fully with the DA's office and not to leave Indianapolis until this is cleared up to my satisfaction."

With that, he rose abruptly as he had the day before. "Court is adjourned," he said, and left the courtroom.

The press converged on me as I left the courtroom, shoving microphones in my face with TV cameras rolling.

"How do you feel?"

"What does this mean to you and your family?"

"How will it change your life?"

"What will you do now?"

I gave crisp answers as we pushed our way through the crowd and jumped into Dorian's Escalade. I thought one particularly persistent reporter was going to get into the car with us, but I managed to close the door, and Dorian pulled away.

The crowd enveloped Dwight as he emerged from the courthouse. It reminded me of a flock of birds swooping like a single cloud from the sky. Geraldo stood alone, bewildered, still in a state of shock.

"Good job, bro," Dorian said as we drove off. "Let's do it again sometime."

"No more, thank you. I'm done with lawyers and lawsuits. You can do the next one."

"Hmm." Dorian gave me a funny sideways look. "Maybe I will."

CHAPTER FORTY-FIVE

We celebrated with dinner at Fleming's Steakhouse in Indianapolis, where Jessie and I ate once or twice a month when our carnivorous cravings overpowered our dietary discretion. Dorian said he needed to give the bunny circuit a rest and joined us for dinner and a sleepover in the guest bedroom.

As we sat down, I thought about being just an ordinary doctor who once again could practice medicine. Dotter's words that I was a "good and conscientious doctor" reverberated in my brain and almost made me feel lightheaded. Getting my money returned was great, but erasing the stigma of "bad doctor" was far more important. Dotter gave me back the life Crystal had stolen.

"What shall we drink?" Dorian asked, scanning the menu. "Maybe a bottle of Dom Perignon champagne with the ahi tuna appetizer, and then a Laville white Bordeaux for the Caesar salad. And finish with a Gallo Single Vineyard cabernet sauvignon for the steaks. How's that sound?"

"I thought Gallo only made jug wine."

"Wait till you taste this one, little brother. Gallo bottles an exquisite single vineyard cab in small amounts. Most people don't know about it. I'm surprised this restaurant even stocks it."

"None for me."

We both looked at Jessie.

"Designated driver?" Dorian asked. Jessie smiled and shook her head.

I looked at her, my eyes wide. "You mean—"

She nodded and grinned.

I stood and took her in my arms. "When did you find out?"

"Yesterday, but I didn't want to say anything until the hearing was over."

"I love you." I kissed her gently. "Do you know if it's a boy or girl?"

"Too early to tell, the doctor said, but I want it to be a surprise anyway."

"Life can be lovely. Congratulations, you two. I'm going to be the best uncle this kid ever had."

"I hope so. But remember, Uncle Dorian, bunnies have long ears, short tails, and fur," Jessie said. We all laughed.

My brother assumed the role of tamada. We toasted each other, Dotter, Randy, Gloria, and almost everyone we could think of, including Geraldo. All but Crystal. I saved my last toast for my unborn son—I knew it would be a boy. The Gallo barely lasted until the last bites of steak.

"They have the most fantastic chocolate dessert called a lava cake," Jessie said.

"Jessie, I'm so stuffed, I can't, really."

"You have to try it, Dorian, if nothing else then for your health. Dark chocolate's good for your heart. We'll order one with three forks."

Ten minutes later, the waiter, a tall, good-looking guy, set the round, dark brown, ten-thousand-calorie cake in the middle of the table. A snowcap of vanilla ice cream slowly melted on its peak, running creamy rivulets down the sides like volcanic streams of melting lava.

"Who's first?" Jessie asked, handing each of us a fork.

"Pregnancy cravings?" Dorian teased.

"Not yet. It's just so good," Jessie said as she scooped a hole in the side of the chocolate mountain. We all watched as it bled dark syrup. "It's orgasmic," she said, tasting the first mouthful. "You've got to try some."

Dorian and I each took a forkful and echoed Jessie's bliss.

"A fitting end to my brother's victory." Dorian licked his lips. "*Sweet* victory."

"Thanks for coming, Dorian, and for the loan, and for Gloria. I couldn't have done it without your help."

"My pleasure, little brother. Glad to be of assistance. Even though you were the one who got me into this, way back when Randy sprained his ankle."

"God, that seems almost like another lifetime. I can't believe it was more than three years ago."

"Redex has been an interesting journey for all of us," Dorian said, staring into the distance with a thoughtful look. It lasted only a moment as we demolished the rest of the dessert. After espressos, Dorian paid the tab, and we staggered to our feet.

"Keys," Jessie demanded, hand outstretched. "I'm the only sober one."

Dorian patted his pockets. "Can't find them."

"Maybe because we used valet parking," I reminded them.

"Good thinking. Ask the valet to drive us home."

"Never mind," Jessie said. "You twins pour your butts into the backseat and leave the driving to me."

Jessie drove, and I was starting to sober up by the time we reached our house. "Anyone for a nightcap before turning in?"

"Are you nuts?" Dorian said. "You must have a hollow leg. Not me. I'm for bed right now."

"Me too," Jessie said.

"Okay, you both go to bed like good little children. I'm still too high to sleep." I kissed Jessie good night, gave a shoulder pat to Dorian, and sent them off. I went into my den.

A message from Mickey Mouse was waiting on my computer.

MM: Hacking is hard work. Contact me.

I sat down in front of the computer and messaged him.

DS: I'm here. What's happening?

MM: Did you look closely at the lovely
    pictures of you and Katerina?

DS: Of course. How do you think I found
    out there was no appendectomy scar?

MM: Maybe it would be good to look again.

DS: I gave my set to my brother.

MM: Too bad.

DS: Why?

MM: You need to study them again. I will
    send an attachment. Look carefully.

In twenty seconds, my computer chimed, and I opened the e-mail attachment: a close-up supposedly of my butt while I was taking Katerina from behind. My hands gripped her hips as I pulled her toward me. Her head, at the edge of the picture, was turned over her right shoulder, looking at me with dreamy, half-closed eyes. She seemed to be enjoying herself.

I messaged Mickey Mouse.

> DS: So? I have it open and see nothing I didn't see before. This was part of the original series.
>
> MM: Yes it was, and you studied it before. It is quite amazing how we see only what we look for. You looked for McBurney's Point and found it. Now you don't see what is so obvious.
>
> DS: Stop playing games. What are you talking about?
>
> MM: How is your brother's back?
>
> DS: What do you mean?

I zoomed the picture. What I saw stunned me.

> DS: How'd you find this?
>
> MM: We have here people paid to look for such things. But this was unexpected.
>
> DS: Who took the pictures?
>
> MM: Your brother met with Lopakhin the same time you met with Sasha. After you returned to your apartment, he spent the night with your friend, Katerina. A photographer took the pictures, and Sasha used them to try to blackmail you.
>
> DS: No computer manipulation?

MM: Not necessary. Sasha did not know your appendectomy scar, and your brother must have forgot about it, as you forgot his scar from back surgery.

DS: What else did your people find out?

MM: Nothing yet. We have troubles hacking Mikhail's computer. SP's firewall is quite solid. But we will have success eventually and get what we need. You were right. I am sure Mikhail is part of this whole scheme.

DS: And my brother? Did he know he was being photographed with Katerina, or was Sasha planning to blackmail us both?

MM: Perhaps either. Once we open Mikhail's computer, we will find out.

DS: But the difference is enormous. I can't believe my brother didn't tell me.

MM: We are aware very well of the implications.

DS: Is there anything I should do from this end?

MM: Maybe have another talk with your brother.

DS: Talk with him? I'm going to tear his damn head off!

CHAPTER FORTY-SIX

But I didn't tear his head off. I guess I wanted to believe he had nothing to do with the pictures. I fell into bed and snuggled next to Jessie, my hand resting on her abdomen. The booze anesthetized my brain, and I didn't budge until the seven o'clock alarm. My head was a little cloudy as I staggered to the bathroom. Coffee was first on my agenda.

It's interesting how jobs get allocated in a marriage. For some reason, making coffee was mine while Jessie enjoyed an extra ten minutes of sack time, and I always grumbled about having to clean the coffee pot. Our unwritten rule was that whoever poured the last cup cleaned the damn thing, but she always left a tiny bit, so I got stuck.

"I'm ready for my coffee," she announced, flouncing into the kitchen and pecking my cheek good morning. She timed her entrance to when the percolator shut off, brewing done. But I loved seeing her then, makeup-free, freshly scrubbed, and bubbly about the day ahead. I poured her cup. "You are so good," she cooed, flashing that light-up-the-room smile. "The perfect husband, who always makes the great morning cup of coffee and never complains about cleaning the pot. Hmm, good."

"Harrumph," I replied.

I poured my second cup and sat down next to her. I told her about the picture. A serious look replaced her coquettish demeanor.

"Sasha must've hidden cameras in the Night Flight," I said.

"You don't think your brother posed?"

"And let Sasha blackmail me? No way. Jesus, Jessie, he *is* my brother."

She sipped her coffee and was silent for a few moments, staring out into space. "So?"

"So you've seen how he's helped us through all this bullshit."

"Yes, but those pictures are giving me bad vibes."

"What's the matter with you? He's been there with us all the way. You know he has."

"I have what?" Dorian asked, entering the kitchen yawning.

"You've been there helping. In fact, it was you who warned me about getting involved with VIPs in the first place."

"Indeed I did. What's the issue?"

"Wait a minute." I went into my den, unplugged the computer, and brought it into the kitchen. I set it on the counter. "This is the issue," I said, clicking on the attachment.

Dorian's eyes got big as he studied the screen, and then he smiled. "Ah, yes, it was a wonderful night. She's really a great fuck. Sorry you didn't get a taste," he said, looking first at me and then smiling at Jessie.

"But I got blamed."

"So you did. Kind of like our apple fight when we were kids."

"Dorian, this is serious," Jessie said.

"So was that, at the time."

"I want to know how Sasha got those pictures. Did you know he was shooting them?" I asked.

"Don't be stupid, little brother. I'm pretty good at screwing a bunny, but I'm no porn star. Even I couldn't keep it hard if I knew someone was taking my picture. So no, I had no idea. He was doing it on his own, protecting his interests, I guess. Probably figured he could use the pictures against either one of us, depending on who was messing with his rip-off. Pretty clever, now that I think about it." Dorian sat at the table and poured his coffee.

"But why did you let me think Sasha dubbed my picture when it was you all the time? And why didn't you say something earlier?"

"What was the harm?" he shrugged, palms up. "You trashed Sasha's blackmail scheme quick enough. Since it stopped there, I saw no reason to tell you. I thought it was just a big joke and forgot about it."

"No, Dorian," said Jessie, pushing away from the sink where she was rinsing the coffee cups. "You've got to do better than that. You coincidentally have dinner at the same place as Daniel, end up getting photographed making love to a woman he was having dinner with, and let him get blamed for it. What kind of game are you playing? Whose side are you on?" She stood, staring at him, hands at her sides, dripping water on the floor, her face stern. "He's your brother, for Christ's sake."

Dorian turned to me. "Haven't I been helping? I gave you a job, lent you money, got you an escort service. Shit, I even played basketball with your patient."

Jessie had a stubborn look, with narrowed eyes and set mouth. She was tiny next to him but held her ground. The image ran through my mind of the guy more than twenty years ago standing up to the line of tanks in China's Tiananmen Square.

"Dorian, you loved every minute of it. And you loved being big brother to my husband."

"So?"

"So he may trust you, but I'm starting not to."

"C'mon, Jessie," I said, walking over to her with a towel to dry her hands. "Be fair. Dorian's had to launch Redex while all this was happening and still helped."

She shook her head slowly, staring at Dorian. Finally, she snapped the towel from my hands, threw it in the sink with a disgusted look, and stalked off.

"What's with her?" Dorian asked. "You two have a fight?"

My eyes followed her retreating figure. "No, nothing like that." I turned back to Dorian. "But she makes some good points. Can I trust you? Put it all together for me. What's going on in Moscow?"

"Of course you can trust me. I'm your brother, for Christ's sake." He pushed back from the table and crossed his legs, relaxed. "It's now clear Lopakhin and Sasha planned the whole operation to swindle money from the RBC trial by billing for fictitious patients at ten K each."

"But you met with Lopakhin a few weeks ago."

"I was beginning to doubt the numbers and wanted to confirm my suspicions, so I flew over, and we met at the Night Flight. I didn't know you were there. The stuff with Katerina was serendipity. I found out from Lopakhin he and Sasha squabbled over money from day one but kept the operation going anyway. The two guys who were killed—I've forgotten their names—were a part of the operation in the beginning, felt they weren't getting enough money and ratted to the authorities. Trouble was, Lopakhin *was* the authorities, so that got them drowned.

"Now I've got the real authorities involved, and Sasha's in jail, as I told you. Lopakhin will follow. The police e-mailed me they were going to arrest him tomorrow. I've recouped about $50 million of the $100 million so far," he said, downing the last of his coffee. "And I've got to get back to the city, even though the dinner and sleepover were fun, and I'd love to stay and do another night." He stood, stretched, and slowly bent to touch his toes.

"I don't know," I said, wanting to believe him. "Why didn't you even say hello when we were in the same restaurant?"

"I was there to do business, just as you were. When I finished with Lopakhin, I bumped into Sasha. He told me you were there, but by then you had already left. I spent some bunny time and flew home the next day."

"And Mikhail?"

"Mike? Just happens to be a Russian who made the original contact with the other two, since they were friends. He wasn't part of the scam."

"You sure about that? I think he's the guy who arranged the hit-and-run and John's death."

Dorian swept the idea away with the back of his hand. "No way. The guy wouldn't kill a fly. I'd check your friend Crystal, if I were you. Far more likely a killer, and has a reason to do it. Mike doesn't."

"Maybe so, but I think that was too violent for her—out of character. And hacking into a defibrillator, way out of her league," I said.

He sat back down, and I poured more coffee for both of us.

"Trust me on this one. It's her. Did the cops trace the car?"

"They tried but came up dry," I said. "It was a look-alike Lincoln rental and not owned by any city agency. None of them had a car with a dented left rear fender."

"Or they had one and fixed it real quick."

"Could be. In any case, they were no help. Did you follow up on the doorman?"

"I did," Dorian said, taking a bite of toast. "In fact, I visited Casey in the hospital after his surgery. He did fine."

"John's wife doing any better? She was pretty broken up at the funeral."

He shook his head. "She's taking John's death very hard. Blaming you for putting in the defibrillator. 'If Daniel hadn't put it in, John would be alive today.' What'd you find when you analyzed it?"

"Nothing helpful. Some outside source reprogrammed the software to deliver lots of shocks to his heart, but I knew that before I interrogated it. FBI's taken over."

"Really?"

"Something about violating interstate trade made it their jurisdiction. They confiscated the defibrillator and are using some pretty sophisticated equipment to try and find the hacker."

"Think they'll find anything?" Dorian asked.

"I have no idea."

He sipped his coffee. "Good coffee. When I make it, the stuff comes out weak as dishwater or potent as Drano."

"Secret's using bottled water and premium hazelnut ground coffee."

"I'll have to remember that." Dorian wiped his mouth and stood. He looked around the kitchen. His eyes caught the computer screen, still showing the porno picture.

"By the way, how'd you get this picture? I thought you gave me your only copies. You keep one?"

"No, you have my copies. A friend sent this one."

"What do you mean, a friend?" His look changed, and he became quite alert. "How could anyone but Sasha have copies? And he's in jail. What're you not telling me, Daniel?" He put his hand on my arm.

I couldn't reveal my source. Mickey Mouse was the key to finding out about Mikhail.

"Only a friend in Moscow. Leave it at that. He's on our side."

He squeezed my forearm with his fist. "No, I can't, bro. There's too much going on to only 'leave it at that.' I want to get my money back—all of it—and I need to know all the players. Who's your friend? Does he work at the Chaznikov? How did he get the picture?"

"Dorian, I'd like to tell you, but I can't. It wouldn't be fair to my—friend."

"That's bullshit, bro. Bullshit. Who're you loyal to? Me or your 'friend'?" He stood and walked over to my computer.

"What're you doing?" I stood also.

He closed the top. "I'm taking this with me to find out who your friend is."

"The hell you are," I said, stepping in his way. "Put that back down on the counter." He looked at me, not moving. "Now, Dorian, I mean it."

Computer under one arm, he pushed me in the chest with his other hand. "Out of my way."

I didn't budge. "No. Put the damn computer back on the counter, Dorian. It doesn't belong to you."

With his back to me, he slowly set the computer down on the kitchen counter. Then he whirled and swung his fist at my head. His reach was short, and his punch landed on my shoulder, spinning me around.

I crashed into the kitchen table, knocking plates, cups, and the coffee maker to the floor with a loud clatter. Dorian followed through and grabbed me in a face-to-face bear hug, my arms trapped at my sides. We were pretty evenly matched, although he was in better shape, and I knew I couldn't last long.

He was squeezing the air out of me, and I was getting lightheaded. I brought my right knee up as hard as I could into his groin. He grunted, released his grip, and went down clutching his crotch.

I heard a scream and looked up. Jessie, white-faced, ran into the kitchen. "What are you two doing?" she yelled. "Stop it this instant!"

Dorian was writhing on the kitchen floor. I was leaning back against the refrigerator, trying to catch my breath. "We had a disagreement over the computer." I nodded in its direction, sitting on the counter. "Dorian wanted to take it, and we had a tussle."

"Why did he want to take it?"

Dorian sat up with his back against the wall. I was still panting, but his breathing had returned to normal.

"Because your husband is hiding something important, and I tried to get his computer to find out." As he said that, Dorian lunged at me and grabbed my legs.

I went down, hitting my head on the edge of the kitchen table. The pain was excruciating. I was momentarily stunned. Dorian was on top of me in a flash, his hands around my neck. I couldn't breathe. The room started to fade.

Suddenly, he released me. I gasped for air. I pushed him off, and he lay on the floor dazed, blood trickling from a head wound. Jessie stood over him, holding the neck of a wine bottle.

"Thanks," I said, rubbing my neck. "This thing got a little out of hand."

"A little? My God, he was going to choke you to death. That's hardly a little out of hand." She put the bottle down, scooped up the computer, and left the room. She returned in a minute or so, as Dorian was regaining consciousness.

He sat up, gingerly touching his head. "What'd you use, a sledgehammer?" he asked Jessie.

"No, but I will next time."

"No next times." He stood, extended his hand to me, and stretched his back. "Sorry, my fault. I'm too hyper about Russia. I see spies everywhere who're trying to prevent me from getting all my money back. If I can't trust you, I guess I can't trust anybody."

I shook his hand, but when he went to hug me, I tensed up. Jessie reached for the wine bottle. But it was only a hug.

"Okay, folks, it's been fun, but I've got to get back to running a drug company."

"Want me to drive you to the airport?" I asked.

"Thanks, but no. I called my pilot earlier. He should be here any minute."

On cue we heard a car horn. A silver Lexus had pulled into the driveway. "That's him now. I'm out of here."

Dorian gave me another hug and walked over to Jessie. He put his arms around her and bent down to kiss her cheek. She stood stiff as a doll.

"Don't be mad." He held her at arm's length and smiled into her face. "I'm sorry I lost my temper. I love you and your husband very much."

She yielded, not entirely smiling, but close. "You always could get away with murder, couldn't you?"

He grinned. "Part of my charm." He gave the kitchen one last glance and left.

CHAPTER FORTY-SEVEN

"I don't trust him anymore, not one bit."

I rose and held her, kissing her gently. "That was a helluva whack, especially for a pregnant lady. Thanks."

"That'll teach him to mess with my man." She stood on her toes and kissed my neck. "You still have his finger marks."

"Where?"

"Here," she brushed her lips along my neck, "and here, and here."

"Careful, we won't make it through breakfast, and we both have to go to work." I touched my neck where she had kissed. It was sore. "He's lucky you didn't give him a concussion."

"I would have, but I didn't want to ruin a good bottle of cabernet. Next time I'll grab a cheap one." She sat, poured cereal into a bowl, added skim milk, and took a spoonful. "You believe him, all that stuff about Mikhail and him not knowing anything?"

I sat down next to her. Milk dripped from the corner of her mouth. I dabbed at it with the tip of a napkin.

"I want to, but I guess I don't either. The reality is it doesn't matter to us anymore, and that's wonderful. I'm free to practice again. That's the most important thing. What happens to SP is irrelevant."

"True, but aren't you curious? Something's going on. Stop and think." She put the spoon down and pushed back from the table, crossing her legs. "Dorian's behavior makes no sense, with him going to Moscow and not telling you when you were already there."

"I guess you're right," I said. "But if he knew what they were doing, why would he let them steal all that money from his company? That he did nothing may be the biggest thing supporting his innocence because he didn't know what was happening."

She shook her head. "I don't buy that. If he didn't know, why isn't he more upset and jumping all over this now that he's found out?"

"He *is* upset, Jessie, and he *is* on top of it. He's got the cops arresting Lopakhin tomorrow, and they've already arrested Sasha. I think."

"What do you mean, *you think?*"

I told her what Mickey Mouse said about Sasha.

"You've been interacting with this guy and haven't told me?"

"I'm sorry. I didn't want to worry you, so I've been trying to work this out myself."

"Retreated into your man cave? Let me in. Maybe I can help."

"What time's your first surgery?"

She looked at the kitchen clock. It was eight o'clock. "I have time. Tell me what's going on."

I told her all I knew. "I don't know who to believe."

"There's got to be a motive for your brother here."

"Like what?"

"Like maybe a cut of all that money Sasha and Lopakhin were stealing. Probably easier to swindle in Russia than here in the U.S., and maybe hide it in a Swiss bank? Now that I think of it, that may be why he did nothing and pleaded ignorance," Jessie said.

"Steal from his own company? Why take the chance when he's already got more money than he can spend?"

"C'mon, Daniel, look at Bernie Madoff. You can never have enough money." She held out her coffee cup. I filled it. "Why did he go ballistic over your computer, trying to find out about Mickey Mouse—your *Deep Throat* guy? He almost strangled you for it! And you still believe he's not involved?"

"He's my brother, and I love him. Simple. Maybe I'm blind to some of his mistakes. The sins of the son are the faults of the father. So yes, I cut him slack. I always have."

"Daniel, you're too trusting. I think you *are* blind to what he's doing. He wanted your computer to find Deep Throat because DT could screw up their whole deal. When they find him, I bet he ends up swimming like those poor brothers."

"What do you think I should do?"

Jessie was silent and then shrugged. "First, probably warn your Russian friend. Then I don't know, but I don't trust Dorian."

"I guess I could go to Moscow. But even if I did, the authorities would show me only what they wanted me to see. A hundred million bucks, you can be sure it's spread around, keeping a lot of people quiet, buying a lot of loyalty. But the real thing is I no longer have a dog in the fight, so why should I care? If he wants to steal, let him steal."

"Because he's your brother, that's why."

I rubbed my neck. "You're sounding like me. I said that an hour ago." Our marriage has always worked that way. One of us veered off the path we knew we should take, and the other pulled him or her back.

"Your first patient's ready, Doctor," Ginger said, poking her head into my office.

I was back at work seeing patients again and was starting a long day with eighteen scheduled. They had filled my calendar in hours when the hospital sent notice of my return. I had cared for many of them for years, and we were growing old together. Originally presenting with heart problems, as they aged, they developed the usual troubles of the elderly, such as chronic lung disease, cancers, and arthritis. I had treated a number of them with Redex. Uniformly, they improved. Despite my doubts about Mikhail, I silently thanked him for his invention.

This morning, two of them, a middle-aged man with bad knees from football injuries in college and a twenty-six-year-old woman with juvenile rheumatoid arthritis, complained of recent onset angina.

"What did it feel like?"

"A grabbing pain, right here over my heart," the woman said. "I was bowling with the girls when it happened right after lunch. If I sat down and rested between games, it would gradually disappear." The man gave a similar story of chest pain, his while having sex. Neither had any risk factors. Both had normal cholesterol levels. Their calcium scores were very low and heart echoes were normal.

At the end of the day, I pored over their records at my desk. I tried to make sense of new onset angina in low-risk individuals. I had at least ten of them under the age of forty in my clinic. And it hit me.

I did have a dog in this fight.

CHAPTER FORTY-EIGHT

Sloane Pharmaceuticals was working three shifts a day to keep up with the demand for Redex and to start Painex production. Even at 11:00 p.m., the building was lit, and workers moved in and out like midday in the city. I had debated wearing a suit and acting natural, or dressing in dark clothes like the thief I was about to be. I chose a jacket and tie with the idea I would bluff my way through as Dorian. I had a better chance being the CEO than a perp breaking and entering.

I needed to search Mikhail's office and go through his files. MM had not been able to bypass the computer firewalls, and his usefulness as Deep Throat was waning.

New York was unseasonably warm for late March, and I was hot in my three-piece suit. A gentle breeze blew in off the Hudson, promising that spring would soon melt February's snow. Clouds skittered across the night sky, momentarily blocking out the moonlight. I hoped my employee card still opened the gate to the underground parking garage. When it did, I parked in my brother's space.

A computer tracked card use, but I had no choice. I slipped my executive pass into the parking garage elevator slot. I was betting all my chips tonight, and when I was found out in the morning, I'd either be a hero or a thief. Card activity would be irrelevant.

I took the elevator to the executive offices on the fortieth floor. Most of the bustle at this hour was confined to the labs on the thirty-third, thirty-fourth, and thirty-fifth floors, and I figured the executive suites would be deserted. At least, that's what I hoped. I also chose the time carefully. It might be late enough to avoid security, but not too late for the CEO to be working if I bumped into a guard.

I strode purposefully to my brother's office, eyes straight ahead, the CEO on a mission.

Footsteps sounded behind me, keeping pace with mine. I hurried. So did they.

"Dr. Sloane, working late tonight, are you?"

I ignored the voice and kept walking. The footsteps quickened.

"Dr. Sloane, excuse me." I felt a hand on my arm and whirled around.

I was face-to-face with a security guard, my worst fear. He was a muscular guy, a shade shorter than me, with rust-colored hair and a thick neck. He wore a silver metal badge on his right chest and a nameplate on his left. Hector Quintero. He looked vaguely familiar.

"Yes, Hector, I am. I appreciate your checking up on things."

"Not a problem, sir. Can I be of any help?"

"No thanks. I'm fine. I only need to do a few things in my office, and then I'm leaving."

"Fine, sir. Have a good night." He accelerated his pace and turned the corner.

I stopped and leaned a hand on the wall, quieting my nerves and slowing my breathing.

That was too close.

After a moment, I came to the waiting lounge in front of my brother's office. Dimmed overheads lit the reception area, casting flickering outsized shadows on the dark wood walls.

I stood in front of my brother's office door staring at the identity camera. We *were* identical, after all. It should work, even in the subdued light. The distant memory of another substitution—the analytical chemistry final exam at Dartmouth more than twenty years ago—flickered briefly through my mind. I held my breath until the *click* of the opening office door triggered normal breathing again.

I went straight to the central drawer of his desk. Locked, as I expected. I jammed the blade of the Swiss Army knife I'd bought on the way over into the top of the drawer and pried it open. Sitting in the middle was the white office pass card I needed.

I left the office, the door closing behind me, and walked to Mikhail's office. I slid the plastic in and out of the door slot and pushed. The door swung open soundlessly.

I went straight to Mikhail's desk and pried open the center drawer, as I had Dorian's. I really didn't expect to find much. I wasn't disappointed. It held the usual assortment of pencils, a couple of cheap rollerball pens and—hold it. I pulled the drawer all the way out. A wooden partition created a false back and hid a space behind it. *War and Peace!* I riffed the pages and turned to 165, but this was an English translation with no missing pages.

The office door opened behind me. Mikhail walked in.

"You know, Daniel, you should stick to your hearts and leave the detective work to the professionals, especially at this hour." He looked at his watch, and the corners of his mouth turned down. He saw the book I was holding. "I expected you and left that as a present. I thought you might like to read *War and Peace* with all its pages intact as Tolstoy wrote them."

Before I could move, he called in a loud voice, "Hector, you can let yourself in." Hector walked in, Taser gun drawn with the red laser dot bouncing on my chest.

"Hello, Doc." Now it registered. Crystal's bodyguard at Randy's funeral. The guy who'd escorted Jessie and me out. "Nice to see you again."

I looked from Hector to Mikhail, trying to make the connection.

"I arranged for him to be your escort, Daniel. Silly for us to be alone tonight, isn't it?"

"How did you—"

"Daniel, I've watched every move since you returned from Moscow. Your phone's bugged, your house, your computer, everything's been under surveillance—even lovely Jessie, the mother-to-be."

"Sonofabitch." I half collapsed into a chair and shook my head to clear the butterflies. I had to think. Whom had I implicated? "Mickey Mouse—?"

"Swimming with the two brothers, I'm told. He was quite clever. It took a bit to find him."

"You bastard."

"Got to be tidy. Can't have loose ends messing things up."

I started to get out of the chair.

"Stay there, Doc," Hector said.

I looked at him. "It was you who ran over Casey, wasn't it?" Hector smiled and turned to Mikhail but kept the Taser dot bouncing on my chest.

Mikhail sat down in the chair facing me. "An unfortunate accident obviously meant for you. I'm glad he made it okay."

"And John?"

"Yes, poor John. When we redesigned these offices, I was worried about sharing kitchen space with him. Turned out I was right. But to reprogram his ICD? That was sheer brilliance. It did take a bit of engineering, but one of my friends in the lab was dazzling and very creative."

"The FBI—"

He dismissed them with a sneer. "They can take the defibrillator apart, wire by wire, and won't find a thing. It's all software programming, completely untraceable."

"Why, Mikhail, why all of this?" I waved my hand around the office. "You made a pile of money, got accolades worldwide. Why do all of this?"

"Do not call me Mikhail. I'm a US citizen, just like you, and my name is Mike. To answer your question, I think you finally suspected the truth. The entire thing's a farce. A charade."

I sat there, shaking my head. "Redex?"

"Yes, Redex. The whole idea of a pure BD inhibitor was flawed. It does relieve inflammation and pain—that much is true—but at the price of heart attacks and strokes."

His chin sagged, and his eyes grew sad. "I really thought I had made a major contribution for mankind. I really did."

He stood, walked over, and pointed at the patent award framed on his wall. "I hoped I would be acclaimed in the same breath as Pasteur, Fleming, and other past giants. And, yes, maybe even become a Nobel laureate. But now it's all turned to crap." He welled up for a second and turned his head away from me. Then he grabbed the patent award, yanked it off its hook, and hurled it against the wall. The glass shattered, and the frame splintered, pieces falling on the blue rug.

"What about the two arthritis studies you published? No heart attacks or strokes in those patients."

He laughed and sat back down. "'Edited for clarity,' shall we say? Since all of the information from the investigators came back to me to compile, it was easy to change. I eliminated the strokes and heart attacks, which made Redex look great. Arthritis improved without GI symptoms. But patients died because of the unintended consequences of BD inhibition."

"And the RBC trial?"

"Same thing. I had Natalia do there what I did here. But I had to buy off Sasha and Lopakhin by letting them recruit fake patients. Those stupid Platzov brothers eventually wouldn't be bought, so they went swimming instead. And your Mickey Mouse! Deep Throat, indeed. Just another doctor whose buyout price became too steep. How dumb do you take me for? Sasha told me you sat next to the man at the lecture, and he gave you a copy of *War and Peace*. We haven't found his girlfriend yet, but we will. You were so sure of yourself, the smug MD so superior to a PhD."

"Mikhail, I never felt that."

Mikhail flipped me the back of his hand. "Doesn't matter, does it? What matters is that we keep this sham going as long as possible. Soak up the billions in sales now because, sure as hell, all will come crashing down if the real evidence leaks out. Lawsuits will pile up like 747s waiting to take off. But we've hidden the files very well, so unless someone takes the trouble to contact each investigator, retrieve old records, and recalculate the complication rates, we're home free."

"Somebody could repeat the studies."

"Not likely. Who'd pay for them? Certainly not us, and no other drug company's going to put up the hundreds of millions to test their drug against Redex, now the acknowledged king of the NSAIDs. No, in several months, all will be forgotten."

"Why?"

"Research records must be kept three years, like IRS tax records. Then we notify each investigator to delete all patient records. We say it's for patient confidentiality. The three years are up, so we're starting that now. When it's finished, all proof of complications will have been destroyed, and Redex will reign supreme. After that, we'll introduce Painex. Another example of MD stupidity, to think they're different drugs."

He was so sure of himself.

"You made no mistakes?"

"Only that I sent you to Moscow in the first place. But I liked the power of my new job and control over a 'real doc,' especially one who was the brother of our CEO, also a 'real doc.' When I realized my error—this was before you found out anything, but I worried you *might* uncover our scam—I sent dear Crystal along to be sure you didn't return. She almost succeeded. Stupidly, Sasha saved your life."

"He was concerned what my brother would say."

"Yes, he was. But I'm not. Sadly, Daniel, you know too much, and I have to tidy that loose end. But we can't do it in the company's headquarters, can we?"

His eyes found Hector, leaning against the wall. "Duct tape's in a kitchen drawer. Bind his hands. Then take him to the car."

Christ. He was planning to kill me. My heart raced.

I had maybe twenty seconds when Hector went into the kitchen. I charged Mikhail, knocking him out of the chair and into the wall with a thud. He scurried along the floor like a crab, but before I could catch him, I heard a sound like static and felt searing pain rip through my back and neck. My muscles locked up, and I was falling.

Then nothing but blackness.

CHAPTER FORTY-NINE

I opened my eyes to blackness.

I shook my head, but all remained dark. Something was pulled down over my eyes. My muscles were sore as hell, especially my back and neck. I remembered the agonizing pain and paralysis. Taser! I had been tased.

My hands were secured behind me, and my ankles taped together. I tried to straighten my legs, but they hit a wall. I was doubled up, almost chewing on my knees. I panicked and tried to yell, but my mouth was taped shut. I squirmed and twisted but couldn't move. When I tried to sit up, I bumped my head on a low ceiling.

Taking slow, deep breaths, I forced myself to get control. As I relaxed, it felt like I was moving. I heard rumbling, a motor running. I was in the trunk of a car. Mikhail talked about taking me someplace. I had to get loose before—

The car's momentum slowed, and the car turned right, throwing me against the left side of the trunk. In a few seconds, I heard tires crunch on gravel, and the car stopped. Two car doors clicked opened, slammed shut, and I heard the scratch of a key in the trunk. The lid popped, and I took a deep breath of fresh night air.

Mikhail grabbed me under one arm, and Hector the other. Together they lifted me out of the trunk. I stood on wobbly legs.

"Mmmm," was the only sound I could make. Mikhail lifted a corner of the hood over my head, grabbed one end of the tape across my mouth, and yanked, setting my lips on fire. "Bastard!"

"Make all the noise you want, Daniel," Mikhail said. "We're in the middle of lots of trees and no neighbors."

"Where?" The word echoed within the hood. Was this where they planned to kill me?

"You'll find out in a minute. First, I need to undo your ankles so you can walk." He cut the tape, and I stretched my legs.

"No funny stuff, Doc," Hector said, pressing the gun in my ribs. "Just walk. We'll guide you."

They each took an arm. Looking straight down, I could see my shoes on a flagstone path set in a lawn. I planted my toe on an edge, fell, and tried to roll away. Hector was on me in an instant, a knee in my back and a hand tightening the hood. He pushed my face down. I could smell wet grass.

"That was dumb, Doc. For a smart man, you're being stupid." He tapped something metal on my head. It must've been the Taser gun butt. "You like electricity? Try that again." They scooped me up once more and this time held my arms tight as we walked.

"Four steps," Hector warned, squeezing my arm. I used my feet like a blind man's cane and shuffled up the steps. Hector pulled me to a stop, and I heard a doorbell. After several moments, the door opened, and I was pushed inside. No one said anything, and I just stood there. Finally I said, "What the hell's going on?"

Mikhail pulled off my hood.

"Good evening, Daniel. Welcome to my home."

My brother stood in the entrance wearing a ruby-red silk dressing robe.

Like Lot's wife, I became a pillar of salt, unable to move. "I don't believe what I'm seeing."

"Believe it, bro. It's real. I'm real. Come in, and I'll explain."

"Tell them to untie me."

"Sadly, I can't do that. You've forced me to make some hard choices, and this is one of them. These guys," he tipped his head at Mikhail and Hector, "have just followed my orders."

"You're behind this whole damn thing!"

He took me by the arm. "Come in first, and let's sit down. We'll have a Macallan and relax. I'll explain everything."

Dorian led me out of the oversized white-and-black marble entry into a library that was larger than the entire first floor of my house. The wood was dark, maybe cherry, with carved Baroque bookcases filling two walls, volumes of books spilling out. A balcony circled the room. Tiffany stained-glass windows faced east, and I imagined a dramatic sunrise. Or maybe it was west and a pretty sunset. Didn't matter much.

"I liked Pushkin's house so much, I replicated it. Before you ask, no, I haven't read them, but the books were here when I bought the place. They give it a nice homey, intellectual feel, don't you think? Especially with a fire roaring." Dorian picked up a remote from a table nearby and pushed a button. Flames leaped in the fireplace.

"I read somewhere that Hugh Hefner has the same thing in the Playboy mansion." He chuckled and I shivered, hearing that sound. "Keeps him warm when wearing this robe."

Hector shoved me into an oversized stuffed chair. I sank into the pillows. He remained planted in front, but with my hands bound behind me, I doubted I could get up without help.

Dorian and Mikhail walked off, whispering in the far corner of the library near an aircraft-carrier-sized desk. I could see that Mikhail was agitated, his hands flying all over, eyes darting around the room. His face was flushed. Dorian patted the air in front of him, apparently trying to calm him, and kept mouthing, "No, no."

I couldn't believe what was happening. This was my brother, for Christ's sake, my twin brother, *identical twin brother*, whom I loved and who loved me, I thought. I had no doubt he was arguing my fate with a killer. The scene was as surreal as a Dali painting.

Mikhail said something to him and pointed a finger at me. Dorian shook his head even more vigorously.

Finally, Dorian exploded. "It's your own fucking fault. I told you not to send him to Moscow in the first place, but you wouldn't listen. Mike, you'll obey my orders, you hear?"

Mikhail strode toward me, stopped, and narrowed his eyes. He knifed his hand flat and slid it across his jugular. Then he sneered, mouthed, "Stupid MD," and stomped out of the room.

Dorian walked to a bar behind my chair. I turned my head, but he was outside my peripheral vision. Ice jingled into glasses, liquid bubbled, and ice crackled.

Dorian came to the front of my chair and held out an amber drink in each hand. His hands shook slightly. "Macallan. You pick." He smiled. "No poison in either glass."

"Go to hell, Dorian. This is no goddamned cocktail party. I'm your brother! And how the hell could I take a glass anyway? Untie me now before that lunatic comes back."

Sadness lined his face. Finally, he shook his head no and held the drinks out again, swirling the peace offering. "We can settle this like brothers."

I turned my head away. A scotch would taste good but—no way. "Go to hell. Go to *fucking* hell."

Dorian shrugged and handed a glass to Hector, who grinned as he raised it in a mock toast and took a sip.

"Daniel, Mike told me he explained the research studies to you, and that's fine. I'll only add that I would've lost it all if Redex had tanked. This whole way of life"—he swept a hand around the room—"would've vanished. Plus, I couldn't hold my head up in front of you, or even stand in front of that picture of the old man looking down at me. I really had no choice."

"That's crap, and you know it. You had choices, but you took the easy way out, like you've done your whole life. Because of you, thousands of patients have suffered heart attacks and strokes. Many will die, and many others will be left incapacitated." I shook my head at his impassive look. "The enormity of what you've committed is overwhelming. Doesn't this have any impact on you at all? All the people you've hurt?"

He bunched his eyebrows. "I'm sorry for that."

"You're sorry for that. Unfortunately, your sentiments—which I don't believe, by the way—are too late to help them." My hands were beginning to get numb. I shifted in the seat. Hector took a step closer, but Dorian waved him back. "Plus, you've committed scientific fraud."

He raised both arms, palms up. "Oh my, now that's a big fucking deal. What's that going to get me, a cell on death row?"

"Maybe not, but it's still illegal. You've also defrauded the US government because they'll have to pay many of these medical bills, and you've swindled investors who bought company stock high. They'll sue if this information becomes public because the stock price will fall like a rock."

"Again, not likely to be death-row punishment or even as bad as Madoff. But the operative word is 'if.'"

He was right. *If* no one found out, nothing would change, except for more patients having heart attacks and strokes. "You were taking Redex yourself. I saw you do it. Weren't you afraid of the risk?"

"You mean the time I told you it was Painex?"

I nodded. "Then, but before that, you said you were taking it for your back. You told me it helped you play basketball, to beat the ex-pros."

"I lied, Daniel." He went to the aircraft carrier and brought back a Limoges pillbox. It looked the same as the one in his office. He opened it and took out a chocolate-colored pill. "Only simple ibuprofen. Painex would have the same side effects as Redex. I wasn't about to take it either."

He held the pill close so I could read the imprint. "I quit Redex as soon as early reports of complications trickled in."

"Before or after I treated Randy Jackson?"

He pressed his lips together and shook his head. "Before."

"You sonofabitch. You knew. You knew it caused heart attacks, and you let me give it to Randy Jackson. *You killed him, not me!*"

A piercing, chilling scream erupted from the next room. Crystal bolted out in a red bathrobe identical to Dorian's. It fluttered over her bare feet as she ran. She grabbed a long pair of scissors from the desk and charged Dorian, hand raised.

Hector fired.

Crystal stopped in her tracks, electrocuted. She stiffened, her back arched, and rigor contorted her face. She dropped the scissors, fell headlong onto a couch, and rolled off onto the rug.

"Goddamnit, Hector. Why'd you tase her? I could've handled it."

"She was going to stab you, boss."

"No, that was only her hot-ass temper, which she loses at least once a day. You sure ruined my morning fuck, though. It was the best. Thanks a lot." He walked over and stood over the prostrate form, prodding her side with the toe of his slipper.

"Now that she knows, you'd better tie her up and take her out of here." He finger-combed his hair and looked around, almost bewildered. "Christ, for a mansion, this place is getting pretty crowded."

My eyes traveled from Crystal, starting to move her arms and legs, to Hector taping her hands, and then to Dorian, who had returned to stand in front of me. I still had trouble believing what I was seeing.

"What the hell's going on, Dorian? Are you nuts? Have you totally lost your mind?"

"No, maybe a little goofy, but not nuts, at least not yet." He jerked his head in Crystal's direction. "The Pistol came on to me after your hearing, when her money evaporated, and she saw her father-in-law walk out with the bimbo. Left me a note with her phone number. We met, had some fun for a while, and she moved in here about a month ago. One bunny's as good as another. You have a problem with that?"

"Doesn't she have kids?"

"I don't have the vaguest idea and don't really care. If she does, she must've dropped them off somewhere. They're not here." He paused, and then that chuckle. "At least, if they are, I haven't seen them. But it's a big house."

Hector rolled Crystal onto her stomach and finished taping her hands behind her back. He grabbed her by the upper arm and pulled her upright. She was unsteady, and her eyes were vacant as he led her off. I knew exactly how she felt.

"The sixty-four-thousand-dollar question now, little brother, is what do I do with you?"

CHAPTER FIFTY

"Why'd you start messing with my brother?"

Crystal and I were sitting in the kitchen of the third-floor guest wing, following Dorian's orders for Hector to treat us like family. I couldn't believe I was at the same table with her. Hector had removed our bindings, and we were drinking coffee, almost civilized in the midst of all this madness. I had tested the doors, all locked and very thick, and the windows, the same. Even if I broke one of them, three floors straight down was a jump I'd attempt only if we got really desperate.

"Because I wanted to get you, and after failing twice, figured I could track you through Dorian."

"You didn't exactly fail. You made me pretty sick each time."

"But you didn't die. Frankly, I don't know how I would have reacted if you had. I was angry, but I'm not a murderer."

"Oh, really? Could've fooled me."

She snorted, "Ha," and sipped her coffee. "I'm still furious as hell, though now at your brother."

"You're furious? Big deal. What about me? You took my money, ruined my reputation, and damn near killed me twice. If we weren't both sitting in this same pile of crap, I'd strangle you right now!"

"But you got it all back. I lost my man forever."

"I'm sorry about that. I did everything—"

"I know you did, but I still wanted to hurt you bad. I had to lash out at somebody. I'll make it up to you."

"Yeah, right, if we get out of here alive."

"We will." She fingered the silver disk around her neck, brought it to her lips, and kissed it. "We will."

"What is that?" I asked, nodding at the disk.

"My good-luck charm. Wards off evil." After a moment, she said, "I hate him."

"My brother? That makes two of us, and a whole lot more if news of all this gets out."

"Will it?"

"Eventually, but the sooner the better. All those lives are at risk with every dose of Redex they take."

"Don't doctors report complications?"

"Less than 1 percent do. Not enough to build a case."

She fell silent, stirring her coffee. "What do you guess they plan to do with us?"

"Mikhail's crazy. He'll stop at nothing to protect his drug. I'm more afraid of him than my brother."

"And Hector?"

"You know him. A thug who takes orders."

"Would they let us go if we promised not to tell anyone?"

"Doubtful, and besides, how could you keep quiet? Think of all the wives like you whose husbands—"

Her eyes moistened. "More coffee?" The long, red fingernails reminded me of that hand around my neck. But she seemed a different person now, even though she was still angry, perhaps less vindictive. Maybe some of her venom had leaked away.

Crystal started sobbing and had to set the coffeepot down. She searched out my eyes. "Goddammit, how a storybook life can turn on a dime. We had everything. The whole world was ours. And then Randy sprained his ankle—" She shrugged, helpless. She brushed teardrops away angrily as they slid down her cheeks.

The door flew open. "Up, both of you." Hector stood there, pointing the Taser at us. "Mike called to get you ready for a ride."

Crystal's back was to the door. Hector startled her. She jumped from the table and knocked over her coffee cup, spilling hot liquid in her lap. She danced in pain and grabbed for a napkin as the coffee burned her thighs. Hector, distracted, watched.

I seized the coffeepot handle and winged it at him. He fought off the glass but the coffee sloshed out, burning his face. He was momentarily blinded, and I jumped for him. I wrestled with his Taser hand. We both crashed to the floor as the gun went flying across the room. Hector was stronger than me, and I felt him begin to slip from my grip.

"Stop!" Crystal pointed the gun at Hector. "You want to feel what you did to me? Just keep on fighting." He quit abruptly, and we slowly untangled. "Move off to the side," she motioned with the gun, "and sit on the floor. Now! Do it!"

Hector shuffled over, sat down on the rug, and leaned back against the wall, knees to his chest. "Don't you move a muscle," she said, handing me the gun.

"Hector," I held out my hand, "the duct tape you were going to use on us." He reached into his jacket. "Slowly. Only your thumb and finger!" He pulled out the roll. "Flip it here and move onto your stomach, hands behind your back."

I handed the gun back to Crystal and moved toward Hector. As I reached out to take the tape from his hand, he grabbed my wrist and yanked me toward him. Off balance, I tripped over his legs, and he sprang at Crystal, hands out to grab the Taser.

She shrieked—and pulled the trigger! One dart hit Hector in the belly, and the other in the right thigh.

"Aiyee!" he screamed and collapsed, his muscles in tetanic contraction from the electricity ripping through him. I grabbed the duct tape, rolled him onto his belly, and taped his wrists behind him before the shock wore off. Then I taped his ankles and bound wrists and ankles together.

Crystal collapsed onto a kitchen chair, breathing rapidly and looking dazed. The Taser gun dangled from one finger, the wires still connected to the darts in Hector.

I turned Hector onto his side and removed the keys from his pocket. His eyes took a moment to focus. "What were you planning to do?" I asked.

"Nothing, only obeying orders."

"Whose?"

"Mike's."

"Which was?"

"When he called, I told him what happened, and he said to bring you two downstairs. He was on his way over. Then we were going for a ride," Hector said.

"Where's my brother?"

"I don't know. He wasn't in the room when the call came. It was on my cell phone."

I tried to disconnect him from the Taser wires. "Gun won't do you any good without a replacement cartridge," Hector said.

"Have you got one?"

He shook his head.

I took a napkin from the table, stuffed it in his mouth, and taped it in place. Crystal handed me the gun. "Just leave it. You ready for downstairs?" I asked.

"What about him?" She tipped her head at Hector.

"Leave him for now. We'll come back to get him. Or if not us, Mikhail will." I didn't want to think about that.

"You got a plan?" she asked.

Her question triggered my memory of the SEALs' "Two is one; one is none" motto. Always have a backup. I didn't even have plan one, never mind a backup. I shook my head. "Just to get the hell out of here before Mikhail gets back."

"But he's on his way?"

I nodded. "We need to move fast."

"Wait a minute," Crystal said. "I have an idea." She disappeared into an adjacent room and returned a minute later. "Here," she said. "Now we're ready."

"Smart lady." We had a plan.

She smiled. "Told you I'd make it up to you."

I locked the door, and we exited to Hector's muffled cries.

The carpeted stairs from the third floor to the second were in the back of the house, and we charged down. A sweeping, wide staircase connected the entry foyer to the second floor. I motioned Crystal to stop and got down on my belly. I slid along the floor until I could peer around the corner and look down the stairway to the marble lobby below. Empty. But through the front windows I could make out car lights coming up the drive.

I stood. "Hurry." I pointed at the approaching lights. "We'll wait for him in the library."

We raced into the big room a minute or two before Mikhail walked in. He saw us and came to an abrupt halt. "You two patch things up?"

We were sitting in the big easy chair Hector had pushed me into earlier, Crystal on my lap, kissing my neck. Her blouse was unbuttoned, and my hand cupped her breast.

"Don't you get tired of wearing that ridiculous Hefner robe?" he asked.

I smoothed the red silk. "Good enough for *his* bunnies, good enough for mine."

Mikhail nodded at Crystal. "Hector told me he tased her, and you got pissed."

I removed my hand from her blouse—slooooowly—and Crystal buttoned up.

"Mike, you could fucking knock before you come bursting in here. We might've been a little further along." I smiled at Crystal and ran a hand along her thigh up her skirt. She batted her eyes at me and patted my cheek. "And, yes, we did make up, if it's any of your business."

"Where's Daniel?"

"Upstairs with Hector." That seemed to set him thinking. He walked off a little ways toward the stairs, looking up at the landing. He scratched his head and turned back to me.

"You're okay with me taking him? I was prepared to take them both."

"I'm not, but I don't really have a choice if we're going to see this through to the end. Crystal promised she'll keep quiet, so she stays." Crystal smiled at Mikhail, and he nodded agreement.

Mikhail stood in front of the chair and let his jacket fall open. I could see a handgun in his belt. "Just to be clear. It'll be a one-way ride. I don't want to have a fight with you over this, but it has to be done my way."

I gently nudged Crystal off my lap and pushed out of the chair. Mikhail backed off, keeping a safe distance between us. "You made your point, Mike. But remember, Daniel's still my brother."

"It'll be quick and painless. One shot to the back of his head. I promise to—"

Dorian walked in from a door in the back of the library. He stared at me standing close to Crystal, then Mikhail. "What the fuck's going on?"

Mikhail's mouth dropped. "Daniel, what're you—"

"I'm not Daniel, you dumb shit. I'm Dorian!" He was wearing the identical red robe.

"Bullshit. This is Dorian," he said, pointing to me.

"Goddamnit, you little asshole," Dorian said, rushing toward Mikhail.

"Stop!" Mikhail drew the gun from his waistband. "Hold it right there, whichever one you are." He glanced from Dorian to me.

Dorian stopped and turned to me. "What in hell you doing, bro? What's going on?"

"You tell me, *Daniel*. How'd you get free? And what'd you do to Hector?" I asked.

Dorian started to walk toward Mikhail and held out his hand. "Give me the fucking gun, Mike. This is all bullshit. I'm Dorian, your boss, and I'm going to fire your ass if you don't stop the games."

Mikhail backed away. "Keep back, Daniel, keep away. I swear I'll shoot you right here if I have to." He cocked the gun, but Dorian kept walking toward him.

The explosion made us all jump as the bullet pierced the large, ornate mirror on the wall over Dorian's desk. It collapsed in a cacophony of sound, shattering into slivers that rained down on the walnut surface. Dorian ducked and fell to his knees after the bullet whizzed over his head. His face was white.

"Jesus Christ, you fucking madman. You damn near killed me."

"I will next time, if you don't stop where you are."

"Mike, it's me! Don't you see? Dorian!"

Mikhail looked from Dorian to me and back again, eyes wide and confused. His face was getting red, and he was breathing hard. He pointed his gun first at me and then at Dorian. He shifted to me again.

"Where'd we have dinner last night?" he asked me.

Clever.

"If you're Dorian, where'd we eat last night?"

I started to sweat and breathe fast. The silence grew.

"Well?" Mikhail asked, waving the gun at me.

"Le Bernardin," Crystal answered.

"Not you!" he screamed. "Him!" He aimed the gun at my head. "Smart-ass MD. Not so smart anymore, eh, Daniel?" He cocked the gun.

"Stop it, Mikhail!" Dorian yelled. "Stop this bullshit!"

"You're Daniel!" he screamed and fired.

CHAPTER FIFTY-ONE

I just lost it. I tore at Mikhail, heedless of the gun, and bowled him over. He pulled the trigger again, but the bullet went wild. We fell in a tangle, me on top, and I ripped the gun from his hand.

I beat him. I beat him in a rage. I beat him with my fists for my murdered Russian friends, for John, and for all the patients he harmed. I pummeled him until his face was a bloodied mess and he stopped moving.

I stood, panting, and saw Dorian lying on the ground, holding his belly. Crystal crouched at his side. I ran to him.

"Get some towels and call 911!" I screamed. I got down on the floor next to Dorian and cradled his head in my lap. His abdomen was a pulsating red river. I tried to dam the flow, but it was no use. My twin was dying.

"Why'd you do that?" I asked him, tears filling my eyes. I shook my head and blinked to clear my vision.

Sweat poured off Dorian's face, and he panted to breathe. He tried to smile but could barely move his lips. "Opperman's Pond, Danny. Opperman's—" He stopped, gasped, fighting to catch his breath.

I tried to quiet him. "Dorian, rest. The ambulance'll be here in a couple of minutes." But I knew it would be too late.

He shook his head. "The coin toss … you won … I should have been … the one through the ice … felt guilty … all these years—so sorry—"

His eyes rolled back into his head as he died in my arms. A cold chill swept through my body as half of me died. I just sat there, numb, rocking my brother in my arms … slowly back and forth.

CHAPTER FIFTY-TWO

"Tell me again why Mikhail thought Dorian was you?"

The funeral was over, and we finally had a chance be alone. The last two days had been filled with police questions and funeral arrangements. The house was quiet as we sat on the couch in the living room. I sipped a Chalk Hill Chardonnay. Jessie drank tonic water. We had buried Dorian in Crown Point Cemetery in Indianapolis.

"Because Dorian called Mikhail by his real name. He had promised to always call him Mike, and when he yelled out, *Mikhail*, Mikhail thought it had to be me. He shot him."

She snuggled against me on the sofa, the corner of her terrycloth robe tickling my nose. "You think Dorian did it on purpose?"

I pushed the robe off my face. "Of course he did, Jessie. Dorian was saving my life."

We both fell silent. I replayed in my head the whirl of events over the last week. Mikhail and Hector were both in jail, Sloane Pharmaceuticals' money was frozen pending an investigation, and the Russians finally had arrested Sasha and Lopakhin. Mickey Mouse somehow had survived and was the major witness against the scam. The FDA had announced an immediate recall of Redex and barred production of Painex. Crystal was back with her kids, and Herman and Geraldo were under investigation.

But I had lost my twin and older brother—by twelve minutes. We were identical, Dorian and I, but not at all alike. I didn't believe for a minute he was evil or that he would have let Mikhail kill me. He was just so caught up with Father's ghost he lost sight of everything else.

Jessie took my hand, placed it on her belly, and looked up at me.

"What?" I asked.

"You know why Jews never name a child after someone still living? Why this little guy," she pressed my hand down against my unborn son, "could never be Daniel Junior?"

I shook my head. "No idea."

"Because they feared the Angel of Death might make a mistake and take the wrong person."

I had to think for a moment to make the connection. Then it hit me. "The Maasai curse?"

She nodded.

"So Enkai got his people mixed up and confused Dorian for me?"

Jessie gave a tiny smile and held me close, tears streaming down her face.

The name of the institutions, drug company, drugs, and characters are all fictitious. The book contains no intended representation of, or references to, actual persons living or dead, companies, drugs, or events that may have transpired. Any such resemblance is a coincidence without intent on the author's part. The names of NBA teams, companies, universities, and clinical care groups/hospitals are used to create an aura of authenticity, but they played no actual part in the story.